VICIOUS ICON

RUINED ROCKSTARS BOOK FOUR

HEATHER ASHLEY

Vicious Icon
Copyright © 2020 by HeatherAshley

ISBN: 9798766938217

Published by DCT Publishing
Cover Design: Black Widow Designs

Contact the author at:
www.heatherashleywrites.com

The characters and events portrayed in this book are fictional. Any similarity to real persons, living or dead, is coincidental and not intended by the author.

Welcome to my dark side. It's gonna be a long night.

BISHOP BRIGGS

BOOKS BY HEATHER ASHLEY

RUINED ROCKSTARS:

STEAMY ROCKSTAR ROMANCE

DEVIANT ROCKERS
FALLEN STAR
DIRTY LEGEND
BROKEN PLAYER
VICIOUS ICON
TAINTED IDOL
WICKED GOD

HOLLYWOOD GUARDIANS:

DARK BODYGUARD ROMANCE

CAPTIVE
CHASED
HOSTILE
DECEIT

TWISTED SOUL MAGIC:

MAGICAL REVERSE HAREM ROMANCE

CROSSED SOULS
BOUND SOULS

EMERALD HILLS ELITE:

ACADEMY REVERSE HAREM ROMANCE

TWISTED LITTLE GAMES

NO ONE SUSPECTS THE SHY ONE IS THE REAL THREAT...

ONE
JERICHO

"Is he dead?" one of the voices in my ear wondered.

"He's on mute, but he's still there," I answered, adjusting my headset. My eyes were locked onto the screen, and I gripped my controller tightly in my hands. My team and I had spent more hours than was healthy over the last week trying to get past this mission, and it looked like this would be the time if no one fucked it up.

"We have to wait for him to respawn," the slightly husky and sexy as hell voice belonging to the only girl on our team responded. I tried not to notice how my already rapid heartbeat kicked up to a new level. That was nothing new where LunaGirl was concerned.

"Alright, he's here. Let's rollout," DeathMinion, the fourth member of our team commanded, and I tried not to bristle. Taking directions from others wasn't something I easily did. Ever.

We crept along deserted streets, focused in on our target. Just as we reached the objective, all hell broke loose. We'd come prepared, but the other team was better, and we quickly got our asses handed to us. Again.

I repressed the urge to smash my controller against the wall and squeezed my eyes shut, taking a deep breath. "Fuck, I'm out. Maybe we'll have better luck tomorrow," DeathMinion said before signing off of the game. Once he was gone, FatUncle followed him, and that just left LunaGirl and me. A devilish grin crossed my face.

"Hey, Luna," I breathed into the mic, lowering my voice to almost a growl.

She laughed that throaty laugh of hers that always turned me the fuck on. "Hey, Wicked. Nice campaign, even if we did get our asses kicked."

Flirting with Luna over this game was what I looked forward to most these days. It wasn't playing sold-out shows with Shadow Phoenix, the band I was the drummer for. It wasn't accepting awards, doing interviews, or any of the other boring-ass shit that came along with being someone famous. Nope. It was this right here—LunaGirl and her sultry voice and no clue who I was in the real world. Her and this game were the only places I let myself really be who I was deep down inside, the only safe places I had to let the darkness out to play because LunaGirl got off on my need for control.

"Speaking of asses," I started, leaning back into the soft pillows on my couch and getting comfortable. "I bet you've got some hot as fuck silky or lacy panties covering yours, don't you?"

Luna laughed again, softer this time and more mischievous. "Wrong."

I licked my lips, leaning forward and resting my elbow on my knees. If anyone knew the version of me that I let LunaGirl see, they'd be shocked. To the rest of the world, right down to my closest friends and bandmates, parents, even my best friend, Kennedy, I was either an asshole or a shy, quiet guy. But Luna knew the real me, even if she didn't know who I really was.

And the real me was one twisted motherfucker.

I lowered my voice even further, adding a hardness to let her know I wasn't to be fucked with. "You know better than to lie to me, Luna."

"Oh, I'm not lying, Wicked. It's just... I knew we'd be playing tonight, and I decided not to wear panties at all."

The irritation at her disobedience faded, and my desire spiked in its place, but I wouldn't let her know. "Did I tell you you could play without panties?"

"No, but-"

"But nothing. That's not how this works; you know the rules. When it comes to your body and your pleasure, who's in charge?"

Her soft intake of breath was music to my ears. "You are."

Luna's compliance made my dick harden, and I slid my hand down my body until my palm rested on my firm length. I squeezed to give myself some of the friction I craved and held back the groan wanting to escape my lips. Instead, I refocused my attention on the girl in my headset, the one giving herself over to me so freely.

"Yes. I am. Which means next time you don't go without panties unless I say you can. Understood?"

"Yes," she agreed, her voice breathless. That one word out of her lips turned my cock to fucking granite, her whispered agreement everything I needed, and she was the only one who I allowed to give it to me.

"Good girl. Now, are you wearing a skirt like I told you to?"

"Mmhmm."

"Put your hand on your chest and slowly slide it down every curve of your body," I ordered, wishing like hell I could watch her do it. "And stop just before you touch your sweet little pussy."

I leaned back into the cushion behind me again, undoing the button on my jeans and sliding the zipper down. Listening to every hitch in her breathing, every shift of clothing and skin, I reveled in the small whimpers and sounds of pleasure Luna made on the other end of the headset.

"I'm there," she practically moaned, and I knew if I were in the same room as her, she'd be begging for me to touch her. To glide my tongue along her hot core until she quivered and screamed and came undone under my touch.

Instead, we had this. And I wasn't complaining, but sometimes I wanted more. "Now, take those soft fingers and slip them down over your clit."

Her breathing sped up as she obeyed, but I was only getting started. "Does that feel good?"

Her affirmation came as a moan that washed over my body. The sounds she made had heat crackling through every single vein until I was burning with a hunger so intense I might fucking explode. But still, I wouldn't let her hear the effect she had on me.

Based on the sounds she was making and the fact we'd done this countless times over the last six months, I could tell she was getting close to coming. "Stop," I demanded, stroking my cock another couple of times while I listened to her let out a shuddering breath.

She whimpered. "What?"

"I said fucking *stop*." I left no room for her to question me in my tone, but she did it anyway.

"Why?"

"Not that I have to explain myself, but you knew the rules, and you went against them anyway. Next time you think about doing something without asking me first, remember how this feels." Yes, I was aware I could be a cold bastard. Cruel even. It was part of why I hid my true self from the world. Because I fucking *liked* how I was and that scared me sometimes.

She huffed but didn't argue. I'd trained her well. "Now, you don't touch yourself until we talk tomorrow, Luna, or next time your punishment will be a lot fucking worse. Do you understand?"

"Fine, Wicked." The irritation in her tone made me smile. It pissed her off that I wasn't letting her come, but she liked this game we played just as much as I did. And I imagined that in her normal, real life she didn't let anyone else boss her around or tell her what to do. We existed in this tiny bubble where we gave each other what we needed.

"Same time, then?" I asked casually, aware that neither one of us were getting off tonight and tucking my still-hard shaft back into my jeans.

"Yes," she snapped. Her frustration oozed through the headset, and I grinned like I'd won a fucking prize. Why the fuck was I like that?

"Have a good night, LunaGirl. And remember what I said. No touching."

"Go fuck yourself," she grumbled so quietly I almost couldn't hear her, and I fought back a laugh. The girl had a toughness to her that I admired even if I craved her submission.

"What was that?"

"Nothing. Talk to you tomorrow, Wicked."

"Not quite, Luna. I heard what you said, and I won't stand for that shit. And as you suggested, I think I *will* fuck myself. And you're going to listen to me do it without touching your soaking wet pussy." I pulled my dick back out and wrapped my fingers around it, moving my fist up and down as I imagined burying myself inside Luna.

Gripping my cock harder, I flexed my hips upward, pushing my dick further into my grasp and stroking the tip, finding a rhythm that brought me closer and closer to relief. I was distantly aware of Luna's irritated silence, but that only served to stoke my arousal.

My cock got impossibly harder, and I finally found my release, letting out a low groan of pleasure and coming all over my hand. My body shuddered as satisfaction carried all the way down to my toes curled into the carpet under my feet. I made a fucking mess, but it was worth it. "Luna?"

"Yes?" she grit out, her annoyance palpable through the speaker.

"I'll talk to you tomorrow, beautiful girl. And I hope you don't deprive yourself by misbehaving."

She sighed. "Goodnight, Wicked."

She signed off, and then I was alone, how I usually liked to be. I pulled off the headset and dropped it beside me. It was blissfully quiet in my house and I relished it. The silence was a rare commodity in my life, and when the band wasn't touring or promoting a new album, I tried to spend as much time in it as I could.

But now I had energy to work off. Pent up sexual energy. Despite my climax a few minutes ago, I barely felt any relief. This thing I had going with LunaGirl wasn't going to be enough for much longer. I briefly wondered whether she'd be interested in a more up close and personal relationship before dismissing the idea.

Standing up, my jeans fell to the floor, and I stepped out of them before bending down to pick them up and folding them neatly. Crossing the house, I went into my bathroom to clean up, then pulled my boxer briefs down and stepped out of them. I went into the bedroom, digging through a drawer to find my favorite pair of swim shorts and pulled them on.

Grabbing a towel on my way to my backyard and the inviting pool there, my mind drifted back to thoughts of Luna. If my face weren't so fucking recognizable, meeting her in person wouldn't be a problem. But all it would take was one picture, one recording, one video, or even just one well-timed story to any media outlet anywhere to fuck up my whole world.

I snorted, imagining what my parents would say if they found out the kind of man I really was. The kind filled with darkness I was afraid to let out.

They already regretted adopting me. Despite my success, they never let me forget what a disappointment I was to them. They'd told me the story of how I'd come to be theirs a thousand times, bringing me to the US from Japan as a baby, but the weight of their expectations had nearly crushed me. The only child they'd ever have, brought into their life to fill a void they couldn't fill on their own.

But I had to live my life on my terms, even if that meant a shitty relationship with my parents. Still, I didn't want to embarrass them. In their minds, it was bad enough that I was a musician. They hated my fame more than I did. So, I kept my desires and my true nature well-hidden, locked deep down in a box wrapped in titanium chains. The only person who had the key was LunaGirl, and even then, I kept her at arm's length.

Tossing the towel onto the plush lounge chair, I dove into the lukewarm water, gliding through the liquid until my lungs burned and I was forced to come up for air. The weight of the water pressed against my body on all sides, and I found it comforting like I always did. This was where I found my peace, slicing through the water with the world muffled. Nothing could touch me here, not even the air.

Lap after lap, I pushed myself, kicking off the wall again and again until every muscle burned, and I was gasping for air. I finally surfaced, pushing my hair back off of my forehead and wiping the water droplets away. I blinked up at the setting sun, wondering if it was still light wherever Luna was, or if, like her name, she was looking up at the bright moonlight.

I also wondered if a day would come where she wasn't the first thing I thought about when I woke up or the last thing I thought about before falling asleep.

After wearing myself out in the pool last night, I fell into a fitful sleep. Visions of a faceless girl haunted me all night long, and I woke up unsettled. But I had shit to do, so I couldn't afford to linger on whatever the fuck my subconscious was doing.

Instead, I got up, swam my morning laps in the pool, and headed to the studio to meet the guys. We were recording our eighth album, and I still couldn't quite believe that shit. It blew my mind that anyone wanted to listen to the music we made, let alone millions of people around the world.

Maybe if we weren't so hugely popular, I wouldn't have to hide my true self. But our following showed no signs of slowing down. If anything, we picked up more and more fans with every album we released. I was almost numb to it now.

Sometimes I wondered what my life would look like if I walked away. If I'd be free.

But there was a deep-seated need inside me to create. To express parts of myself that had no other outlet. And if I lost that, I wasn't sure what I would become.

Walking through the nondescript front door of Mixed, the studio the label picked to record this album, the neon blue lighting tinted everything, including the five guys who were standing around waiting for me. I fucking hated being late and gritted my teeth, holding back the swell of annoyance and my desire to lash out. Instead, I pulled the drumsticks I always carried around out of my back pocket and started twirling them as I sat on the white leather sofa next to Maddox.

"Nice of you to join us," his clipped words chafed at my need to cause pain, but I swallowed it down and adopted my usual mask of indifference instead. I never let my emotions control me. It was too dangerous.

"*I* think so," I retorted, ignoring his glare and instead focusing on spinning the wooden stick between my fingers in a calming rhythm.

We were all feeling on edge, but I was the only one who kept that shit locked inside. Everyone wore their stress in the form of creased brows, scowls, and flattened lips. I could practically cut the frustration in the room with a knife. And it all centered on one man and one man only: Richard Bennett.

"If you guys are ready, I'd like to get started this century," the engineer slash producer snapped, and I watched as the temperature in the room dropped a solid ten degrees, and the tension skyrocketed. Maddox's jaw ticked, Zen's nostrils flared, and the arms folded across True's chest flexed as if he were holding himself back from launching his fists at Richard's face.

Even Griffin, Maddox's brother who'd been hanging around the band for the past couple of months, had his eyes narrowed in the direction of the asshole who refused to do his fucking job. All of our band meetings before we ever stepped into a studio, all the writing sessions Zen had done, this fucking guy was ignoring all of it. Everything we knew we wanted, he didn't give one single fuck.

If he got his way, this album would be whatever cheesy-ass washed-out version of overproduced music he and the record label decided they wanted from us. But we had no plans of letting that shit slide.

No, we'd put up one hell of a fight if we had to. I almost hoped he wouldn't do what we asked because the part of me that craved violence and darkness would throw a goddamn party if I let it out to play with this asshole.

I wasn't sure he was worth it.

"Maybe if you'd listen to our fucking ideas, we'd already be done," Maddox grumbled next to me before lifting off the couch and stalking into the booth.

Zen stared down Richard with a glare that could have melted steel, while True and I followed Maddox into the booth. Griffin settled himself into the couch while Zen was the last to move behind the glass, slamming the door behind him so hard the walls shook.

It was a *really* great environment to be creative in. Internally, I rolled my eyes at my own sarcasm. I stepped behind my drum set, lowering down onto the stool. True and Maddox picked up their instruments, and Zen pulled on his headphones and moved in front of the microphone.

On the other side of the glass, Richard sat in the white office chair behind the mixing board. He leaned forward, pressing the button that let him talk to us in the soundproofed room. "Start whenever you're ready."

Zen glanced back at me, and I nodded before smacking my sticks together a couple of times and then hitting them against the snare in front of me in a punishing rhythm. We had a vision for this album, and we all felt as a band that we'd earned the right to some creative freedom. We'd done whatever the fuck the studio wanted us to for the last seven. This one was ours.

I was lost in the beat, every other thought muted while I let the rhythm consume me, at least until Richard interrupted.

Stopping us halfway through the song, I gritted my teeth to keep from snapping. Working with Richard over the past month was always like this. I was completely fucking over it.

"What now, *Dick*?" Maddox taunted, his voice laced with the contempt we were all feeling.

"Your bass line's off from the drums. And why is there no chord change in the middle eight?" he demanded, and I wanted to climb over my drum set and shove my stick through his goddamn eye. No fucking way was the tempo of my bass line off. I was a fucking legend when it came to rhythm, and this douche expected us to believe *I* was the problem here?

"Yeah, I'm out," I declared, standing up and tucking my sticks into my back pocket. The guys didn't even hesitate, putting their instruments into their cases and filing out of the studio behind me. Griffin rose off the couch and joined our parade past Richard and toward the door.

I held up my middle finger as I passed by the producer on my way out.

"Where the hell are you going? We've got the studio reserved all day!" Richard yelled, his face turning a fucked up shade of reddish-purple.

"We're done compromising our music for what you or the label thinks is right. Let us know when you're ready to let us fucking *play,* and we'll be back." Zen pushed through the front door, and we all followed. I gave Dick another one-fingered salute before I followed Griffin outside.

"What now?" True asked, hefting his guitar case into the back of his Jeep.

"My house," I said, sliding into my car. "We'll record it the way we want, and I'll play around with the composition and see if I can get the sound we're looking for."

Zen nodded, and Maddox and Griffin got into Mad's Maclaren, pulling the doors down to close them. Fuck the label and fuck Dick. My adrenaline spiked as a spark of excitement took root inside me. I was itching to test out everything I'd been messing around with in my home studio, and thanks to an incompetent exec at the label, it looked like I'd get my chance.

TWO
MOON

My nose twitched as I held back a sneeze, cursing the dust particles flying through the air. Pulling open the blinds and flipping on the open sign were Terra's job, but she was late. Again. Dusting was her job, and my ticklish nose was evidence she was slacking in that department, too. I took a deep breath, closing my eyes and trying to center myself. I pressed my palms together in front of my chest and pushed my arms up overhead, releasing the breath and planting my feet until I was almost in a tree pose.

Despite practicing and teaching yoga for years, and even owning my own studio, I still couldn't bring my foot up to my inner thigh and complete the pose with my eyes closed without falling over. Doing it a half dozen times in front of classes was always good for a laugh. I tried to keep it real. Even an old seasoned yoga pro like me could still fuck things up just like everyone else. The point was I never let my limits hold me back.

Slowly opening my eyes, I heaved out a sigh and walked into the back to change for class. My studio had a small changing room, and I needed to slip into my stretchy clothes before the first clients of the day stepped through the door.

My first class of the day was hot yoga, and there was just something about starting the day pouring out buckets of sweat and toxins that invigorated me for the rest of the day. My mom used to say my name fit me—I was a hurricane of chaos and mayhem, too full of energy to even sit still. That was my favorite thing about yoga. It fed my soul in a way nothing else could. I could still move but also quiet my mind.

The door chimed as a couple of my favorite early morning students filtered through the door, travel mugs of tea in hand, and already dressed for class. The pair of women carried towels, to mop up the aforementioned buckets of sweat, and warm smiles. They had calming energy that I was drawn to, and I greeted them as they passed by me on their way into the studio.

The class filled up quickly, and I found myself walking around and adjusting forms, giving people praise, and dropping down next to them to do the stretches, too. This yoga studio was my baby. My pride and joy. The longest thing I'd ever stuck with, and I'd opened it on a total whim three years ago. Over the last three years, I poured myself into this place and made it everything I wanted it to be.

The most appealing part? No limitations whatsoever.

And somehow my studio had found its way into the lives of some celebrity wives in the past couple of months. I didn't know how it happened, but surprisingly they were some of my favorite people. They were down to earth and, dare I say, even normal.

Today I didn't have to worry about them, though. Today was just for the normal folks who wanted to find a little bit of peace in their day. "And now shift back into Downward Dog," I guided, making sure to keep my voice soft and slow as I kept my eyes on everyone's form. I slowly walked through the rows of bodies with their hips back and heads pointing at the mat.

"Don't arch your back," I corrected Mrs. Lyons before placing my palm gently along her spine to fix her posture. She straightened underneath me and groaned, and a grin tugged at my lips. The stretches felt so much better with good form.

Finally, class ended, and before I knew it, another one began. With Terra being a no-show this morning, I was stuck teaching the class and manning the phones and front desk. Somehow I managed to juggle it all and by the time closing rolled around, I was starving and exhausted.

Wearily, I glanced up at the door, plastering on a smile even though I basically wanted to die at that point. It dropped off my face immediately at the sight of my best friend, Bexley. I didn't need to hide my suffering from her for the sake of selling classes. A little wrinkle formed between her eyebrows. "I knew today was going to be shit for you, but you look even worse than my instincts told me you'd be."

Rolling my eyes, I pushed myself up off the counter where I was currently leaning my entire body weight and wondering if I could make it my permanent home. "Terra no-showed on me again."

"I told you she wouldn't be a good employee," she unhelpfully pointed out. Bexley was a self-proclaimed psychic, and I had to begrudgingly admit that her "instincts" were spookily accurate. She wasn't the kind of psychic who saw dead people. She was the kind who got hunches about the future or about people when she met them.

"Are you here to point out obvious shit or take me to dinner?" I whined, feeling extra cranky about the fact my stomach was disappointingly empty. All I wanted to do was have dinner with Bex and then go home and unwind with my favorite game, and maybe even my favorite asshole gamer. No one knew I played, not even Bexley. It was my own little escape.

"Take you to dinner, obvs." She stepped around the counter and shut the lid on the laptop open in front of me, bending down to grab my purse out of the cabinet I kept it in. She threaded her arm through mine and pulled me toward the door, pulling the string on the *open* sign on our way out the door. I turned to lock it, and she handed me my purse.

We started walking down the sidewalk in front of my shop. I'd picked this location because it was in a cute little neighborhood with tons of old buildings and little shops, but it was close to the beach, too, so I got some decent tourist business. We were close enough that I'd been toying with the idea of adding yoga on the beach classes at sunrise and sunset.

"I hope you don't fight me on this, but we're going to Pinkie's." Bexley gave me a look that dared me to disagree with her, but she'd find no argument from me. Pinkie's made the best tacos I'd ever had, and after this day, I was more than ready to shove a taco or six down my gullet and wash them down with copious amounts of tequila in the form of blended blackberry margaritas.

"Fuck, yes," I agreed, and she grinned at me before tossing her purple waves over her shoulder and striding forward down the sidewalk with even more purpose. Her arm was still linked with mine, but she was about six inches shorter than I was, so her dragging felt more like a casual walk to me.

"So, tell me about this idea you had," she prompted, and if this had been my first day with Bex, my jaw would have dropped open at how she somehow always knew what was on my mind without me having to say anything.

"I had to do a project for my business development class where we created our dream business. We got to plan it out and develop it in a hypothetical setting."

"Mmhmm," she said, encouraging me to continue as we weaved through people out for an early evening walk along the boardwalk we'd just stepped out on.

"And I created a full-on wellness retreat. Yoga classes, but also nutrition, spiritual healing, getting in touch with your intuition. Really a place to relax your mind and body at the same time."

"Like rehab?"

I bit my cheek to keep from snapping. I was hangry after all. "No, not like rehab. Not really. More like a place you go for general wellness. I won't be equipped to deal with detoxing people from drugs or anything like that. I don't want to touch any part of that shit. No, this would be a place for people who are overworked and stressed to the max, people who are overweight and don't know where to start to get healthy. Stuff like that."

"Hmm." I had absolutely no idea what Bexley meant by that sound.

"What?" I stepped in line for the tiny taco stand that's popularity meant a long wait for their delicious food.

Bexley shrugged her shoulder. "I don't think that's the path you're supposed to be on."

I folded my arms and tapped my foot against the hot concrete. "And what path do you think I'm supposed to be on?"

That little wrinkle between her eyebrows was back. "It hasn't revealed itself yet. But I do know it's not that retreat thing."

"How about we see where life takes me?"

She made that infuriating humming noise again but thankfully dropped the topic. We ordered more tacos than we could possibly eat before claiming one of the few open tables to wait for our meal. "How's teaching life?" I asked her, wanting to shift the conversation away from me.

Bex decided when we were in kindergarten that she wanted to be a teacher and had never once changed her mind. When we were teenagers, and she really started to realize she had a gift for knowing what would happen to someone, she doubled down on the teaching gig. She always said spending her time around kids was the best thing she could do for her energy because they were mostly innocents who hadn't been tainted by the world yet.

That and she wanted to be able to help the ones who really needed her. My girl was a saint.

She sipped the frozen margarita that sat in front of her before huffing out a breath. "The kids are great. The problem is the adults. The administration wants to cut the time we spend on art and creativity to fit more test prep into the day. And the parents are pissed off because their kids are overworked and not enjoying school like they should be. They're third graders for fuck's sake. They already took away one of their two recesses, and now they want to take art?"

I was content to sit back and let Bexley rant about the injustice of the public school system all night if she wanted to, as long as the conversation didn't swing back around to me and my future plans. I'd never been the type of girl who had my shit together or really knew where my life was going. I stumbled onto yoga once when I stepped into a class to escape a sudden downpour on my way home and decided after that one class I wanted to open a studio.

Winging it, I learned as I went, devouring as much info as I could. I was trying my best to be a responsible adult with plans for my future, but I still didn't know what the hell a 401k was, and someday I'd have to pay back the student loans for the MBA program I was putting myself through, but I tried not to think about that.

A loud slurping sound came from my drink as I sucked the last few icy drops up, finishing it off with a contented sigh. I wasn't sure I'd ever been so full, and I definitely needed a walk. But the stress had mostly melted away during my dinner with Bex.

"Do you need a ride?" she offered, digging her keys out of her purse.

Shaking my head, I slid off the bench and stood up. "I think I'll walk. It's only a couple of blocks."

"Suit yourself. Text me when you get home." She'd always been watchful over me, and I made sure never to ask if she'd had one of her feelings something was going to happen or if that was just how she was.

With a quick hug, I watched her walk to her car and turned to start toward home. I moved slowly, enjoying the evening sun on my skin and the gentle breeze that always blew in off the water. There were a lot of people out right now, and the area around the boardwalk near my shop was alive with color and energy.

The faint notes of a band playing inside a bar up ahead floated through the air, and my lips curved into a smile. I loved music; it sunk into my bones and spoke to my soul. I drifted closer, closing my eyes and swaying to the music. The bar door was open, and I went inside, heading straight for the little open spot in front of the makeshift stage.

I twirled around, hopping on the balls of my feet and shaking my hips to the upbeat rhythm. No one else was dancing, and I could feel people staring, but I didn't care. My colorful hair swished around my face as I let loose to the rhythm and the smoky voice from the woman belting out a song. I threw my hands into the air and did a shimmy as the music came to an end.

"If you guys are enjoying our music, please check out our YouTube channel. Just search Tuesday Told a Secret to unlock the magic," the tiny girl flashed a devious smile at the crowd, and her eyes settled on me for just a second before the band bowed. Scattered applause sounded as they started packing up, and I walked up to her.

"Thank you for sharing your music with me. I didn't know I needed that, but I feel so much better!" I gushed at the petite woman who smiled, and the guy on keyboard behind her winked at me.

"Anytime, beautiful. We play here most Fridays," he said and I could tell he wanted to keep me talking, but I wasn't really interested. I'd been on a journey of discovering myself for a few years now and while that did involve a quick no-strings-attached hookup every now and then, I was content with what I had going on right now.

Plus, he was cute enough, but no sparks were flying, no butterflies erupting—just a big fat nothing going on in the lower half of my body.

"I'll keep that in mind," I promised before turning to leave, finishing the short trip to my condo.

As I turned the key in the lock and swung the door open, my phone rang. "Perfect timing," I murmured, pulling my phone out of my purse and kicking the door shut with my foot.

"Hello?" I pressed my phone to my ear as I bent over to sniff the bunch of wildflowers I bought at the tiny florist shop on the corner yesterday.

"Moon? It's Terra," she girl breathed into the phone, sounding like she either had a cold or had been crying.

"Nice of you to call this morning," I chastised.

"I know. I've just got a lot going on. Listen, I'm not going to be able to make it in tomorrow."

I let out a heavy sigh as I spun around, testing how dry the soil was on my favorite fern that grew in my living room window. "Don't bother, Terra. I need someone who calls when they're having an issue and who doesn't take every other day off. I wish you luck in figuring out whatever it is that's going on, but I can't have you work for me anymore."

I didn't even bother saying I was sorry because I wasn't. Terra had been a weight I'd been carrying around for longer than I should have, and I was done with that now. I made a mental note to put out the help wanted sign tomorrow morning when I opened the studio.

She huffed into the phone. "You don't have to be rash-"

"It's not rash. It's been coming for a while. And like I said, I'm done. Your last paycheck will be down at the desk tomorrow if you want to pick it up. Otherwise, I don't think we have anything left to say to each other."

I took her silence as my cue to hang up. I plugged my phone into the charger and then grabbed my cute vintage watering can, filling it up with water. I moved around my apartment, making sure all of my plants were taken care of. There was something about having a small space filled with life that made me happy, so I kept green plants everywhere I could fit them. Some had colorful blooms, and others were leafy, but it didn't matter.

Inhaling deeply, oxygen seeped into my lungs. The air in here smelled clean and fresh, like when you stepped into a forest or a greenhouse. Finally done, I plopped down onto my cushy sofa, sinking back into the colorful throw pillows. My laptop sat on the table in front of me where I'd left it this morning, and I pulled it into my lap, looking over the schedule for tomorrow. With Terra no longer an option, that meant another day of teaching classes and handling the front desk.

Tomorrow was the mommy and me class. That was the class the celebrity wives came to, and I loved seeing them and their adorable offspring. But teaching it? That was a little too close. I was still raw from the loss of my own mom. Seeing that mother-child relationship gutted me. My mom and I had always been close, up until she'd disappeared fifteen years ago without a word to anyone. For a long time, Bexley was convinced she was alive, but I'd given up hope of that.

If she was still alive, wouldn't she have tried to find me? My two best friends growing up had been Bex and my mom. There was no way she would've just left without saying goodbye. I didn't care what Bexley's intuition told her, my mom was gone for good, and the thought of seeing all the moms tomorrow made my stomach turn.

Blowing out a breath, I closed my laptop and instead picked up my controller. I pushed the center button and waited for the soft chime of the console turning on. All the good vibes from dinner with Bex and dancing with the local band were gone, and in their place was a deep-rooted sadness I didn't want to feel.

Instead, I'd escape into a game where I could be someone else for a while. And maybe, if I was good, I'd even be allowed the release I'd been needing for days.

THREE
JERICHO

My front door slammed open, and I jolted out of bed, not bothering to pull pants on over my boxers. If someone were breaking into my house at six in the morning, I'd kill them before they had the chance to worry about my outfit choices. I quietly pulled my bedside drawer open, sliding the knife I kept there into my hand before creeping into the hall.

Moving stealthily down the cold concrete floor, I pressed my back against the dark walls. I held my breath as I listened for movement, and I noted the footsteps quietly moving my way. Tightening my grip on the hilt of my knife, my muscles tensed as I waited to spring at whoever had the balls to enter my home without my permission.

Poised to stab first and ask questions never, I brought the knife back so I could thrust it forward and barely stopped myself in time as my best friend, Kennedy, stepped into view. She shrieked and clasped her hand to her heart, or where her heart would be if her newborn son, Nico, didn't currently block it. Instead, her hand flew to the back of his head, where he was strapped to her chest in some sort of cloth wrap thing.

"Jesus, Jericho. Were you going to *attack* me?" she asked, still looking a little wild-eyed and breathless.

"Fuck, yes. You didn't think you should text before you walk into my house at six a.m.? You weren't even quiet about it." I walked back into my bedroom to put the knife away, not bothering to wait for her to follow. I knew she would.

"I did text. You just didn't check your phone. Again." She sat down at the foot of my bed, making herself comfortable among the rumpled blankets.

I picked my phone up and scrolled through all the messages I'd received since last night. My assistant could deal with most of the bullshit that came in, but Kennedy and the guys I always handled myself. Sure enough, there was a message right on top. I squinted my eyes to make sure I read it right. "No. No fucking way."

"Come on," she pleaded, flashing me the pout that she knew would get me to do whatever she wanted. Damn her.

"I am not going to mommy and me yoga with you." I would hold firm this time. I had one weak spot in my life, and it was this blonde-haired woman who somehow climbed her way into my heart and became the friend I never wanted or knew I needed. She just *got* me, and because of it, I let her get away with shit no one else would. That still didn't mean I was going to a class full of moms and their drooling, crying babies.

Not in a million fucking years.

"Please," she begged. "Do it for your nephew. Amara was supposed to come, and she bailed on me. I hate going to this stuff by myself."

"Already using Nico to get what you want? Nice." I applauded her slowly, in a sarcastic sort of way that had her narrowing her eyes at me.

"How about you come to yoga with me, and I don't tell the guys about your love of anime porn?" A smirk crossed her face because she knew she fucking had me.

And how the fuck had she found out about that?

"Damn you." I flopped down on my bed and pulled the blanket up over my head, resigned to my fate, but not liking it one bit.

Kennedy crawled up the bed and ripped back the blanket. I glared up at her before my eyes dropped to Nico's tiny arms waving around. Sighing, I held my arms up in the air. "The least you could do is give me my nephew since you're fucking up my whole morning."

She scowled at me. "Language, Jericho."

"What, morning?" I asked, slapping a confused look on my face. We stared at each other before she broke first, giggling as she unwrapped her son and handed him over. I'd never admit it if anyone asked, but the little guy fit in my arms like he was meant to be there. I never pictured myself as a dad because I liked shit orderly. Quiet. Clean. But the first time I held Nico? I started to question what I wanted for my future, and that scared the shit out of me.

Not even Kennedy knew, and I wanted it to stay that way. I was in no position to settle down, and I didn't know if I ever would be. Brushing those thoughts away, I smiled down at the little bundle in my arms and watched as his eyelids grew heavy and finally closed. I laid him against my chest, and his back lifted up and down with his even breaths.

"I swear you're the fucking baby whisperer or something," Kennedy whispered as she stretched out next to me, staring at the ceiling.

"It's not my fault he likes me more than you."

"How dare you. I gave him li… you know what? You're right; he does like you better," she admitted with a quiet laugh.

"How about you leave him here with me and just go do whatever you want to today? Spa day or whatever the fuck you girls do."

"No way are you getting out of going to this class with me, including using offers to babysit to bait me. I've been looking forward to getting my body back in shape for two whole months, and now that I'm finally in the clear, I'm doing this. And your lazy ass is coming with me." She sat upright, scooting off the edge of the bed. "Where do you keep your workout clothes?"

I nodded toward the door on my left. "In the back, middle drawer."

She disappeared into my closet, and I closed my eyes, relaxing into the moment and trying not to think about whatever the fuck I just agreed to. That was how my relationship with Kennedy was. Her getting me to do shit no one else could. I still wasn't sure how that had happened.

When she popped back out a few minutes later, I didn't bother opening my eyes until something soft hit me in the face. I took one hand off Nico's back and grabbed whatever it was, pulling it off my eyes. I twisted my neck so I was looking at her upside down. "You could've hit your son."

"It's not like a shirt is a deadly weapon, Jericho." She looked down at her watch. "We've gotta go in fifteen minutes. Hurry up and change." She walked around the bed and bent down to gently lift Nico off of my chest. I sat up and grabbed the black joggers she left at the end of the bed as she walked out of the room.

She tossed one last serious look over her shoulder and pointed her finger, whisper-yelling in my direction. "I mean it. Fifteen minutes and I'm dragging you out of here whether you're ready to go or not."

After she closed the door, I pulled the shirt she picked out over my head, glancing down at it. My lips twisted up into an almost-smile. A fucking Shadow Phoenix tee. Of course she'd do that to me. She probably hoped I'd have to fend off all sorts of unwanted attention because she just liked to fuck with me like that. If it happened, I'd get her back, though.

Next, I yanked up my joggers until they settled low on my hips and headed into the bathroom to get ready. When I was done, I pulled open the door and walked into the living room where Kennedy was sitting on the couch with Nico strapped back to her chest.

"Do I need to bring a baby to this bullshit?" I wondered, moving into the open-concept kitchen to grab a banana.

She snorted. "Where the hell would you get a baby?"

"I could borrow True's," I shrugged.

Kennedy's eyes flicked up to the ceiling as she thought about it. "Probably wouldn't be the worst idea. You don't want to come off as some weird perv."

"Okay, I'm out. I'm not doing this." I tossed the banana peel into the trash and opened the fridge, looking for a bottle of water.

"I'm just fucking with you. You'll be with me, you're fine. But let's pick up Phoenix on the way just in case. And you *are* doing this." She stood up from the couch and crossed the room, pulling a bottle of water out of my fridge. That's how things were between us, though. Comfortable. She treated my house like her own, and I did the same with her and Zen.

Nico started to stir in his wrap thing, and she rubbed his back and bounced him a little. She and Zen really were great parents, and a little pang of something I had no fucking interest in touching bounced around in my chest. "Are we going or what?"

"Yeah, we're going. Text True and tell him we're going to stop by and pick up Phoenix if we can get him to let us have her for an hour or so." I chuckled because the odds of that weren't great. True was the most overprotective and hands-on dad I'd ever met. He was completely in love with his little girl and hardly ever let her out of his sight.

She rolled her eyes but wore a grin. "If he says no or ignores you, I'll call Amara, and she'll force him."

"Devious. I'm into it." I tucked my phone into my pocket. "Do I need anything else?"

She shook her head. "I have an extra mat in the car. Just bring your moody self and try to accept that you're *going* to relax even if I have to force you into it." Little did she know I regularly did yoga shit to keep myself in check. The fluid movements and breathing helped me in the same way swimming did. My mind and body were singularly focused and in control, just the way I liked them.

I pulled my phone out as I walked to the front door to lock it, shooting a text off to True.

Jericho: Mind if I borrow your kid for an hour?

True: WTF

Jericho: Your wife bailed on Kennedy, and I'm being dragged to mommy & me yoga. Least you could do is lend me your daughter.

True: …

I pocketed my phone and grabbed my keys out of the bowl I kept on a table by the garage. "He's not going for your idea of picking up Phoenix."

Kennedy grinned at me, a wicked grin that was just a little too wide. "Oh, that's not going to work for me. Give me two minutes. Can you get him in the car?"

Sometimes being an uncle was fucking weird, like how I had a car seat in one of my cars for times just like this. But the rate we were going? I'd need more than one soon, between Zen, True, and Maddox all settling down.

I pulled Nico out of the wrap around Kennedy's body and cradled him in my arms as he blinked his bright green eyes up at me, the exact same shade as his dad's. He was a quiet kid and stared up at me as I crossed the garage and opened the car door. "Can you believe your mom's making us do this shit, Nic?"

Leaning carefully over the rear-facing seat, I strapped him in, making extra sure the straps were tight, and the harness was in the right place. I sure as fuck wasn't going to be responsible for anything happening to my niece or nephew when they were with me. Not only did I love those kids like they were mine, but I didn't have a fucking death wish. If something happened to Nico on my watch, Zen would kill me and make it slow and painful. I had no doubt that someday if I had a kid, I'd do the same thing.

Kennedy climbed in the passenger seat as I closed the door on Nico and slid behind the wheel. "We good?"

"Oh, we're good. Head to True's first," she ordered with a satisfied smile. She twisted in her seat and looked back at her son before turning back toward the front and watching the garage door lift.

I let her pick the music on the short drive to what was quickly becoming the Shadow Phoenix neighborhood. True and Zen were neighbors, and Maddox lived a couple of blocks over. I was the outsider, but my house was only about ten minutes away. I preferred it that way, to keep my distance. But Kennedy never let me forget that I was part of the family.

After the short drive and adding a second car seat into the mix, Kennedy directed me to her favorite yoga studio. I had no clue what to expect. I imagined incense, a bunch of women in overpriced athleisure competing for who'd lost the most baby weight or some shit—all in all, not my scene.

Why the fuck I let her talk me into shit like this was a fucking mystery I needed to solve and quick. The last thing I needed was some stray paparazzi snapping a picture of me in a mommy and me class complete with baby accessory.

No fucking thank you.

If that happened, they'd be on my ass for a goddamn month trying to find out what was going on. As I parked, I decided to bring it up. "If I see one cell phone camera pointed in my direction, I'm getting the fuck out of there."

"You're not allowed to bring phones into class, but agreed. If anyone has a phone, we'll leave." She unhooked her seatbelt and pushed the door open, hopping out of my Range Rover and stepping up to the back seat to grab Nico.

Kennedy would understand my absolute fucking disdain for the vulturous paparazzi who hounded the four of us. Unlike my bandmates, I liked to stay in the shadows where I could revel in my darkness. It wasn't something I wanted the outside world to witness or judge.

Because make no mistake about it, my soul was inky black deep down inside. My demons, they lived just underneath the surface. It was why I always had to stay in control. I lost control once upon a time, and I couldn't let it happen again.

Pulling open the door to the backseat, I leaned inside and unbuckled Phoenix. She stared up at me with her bright blue eyes and then grinned, flashing me the few teeth she had. She wasn't quite walking yet, and thank fuck for that because trying to do yoga and wrangle her at the same time was going to be an exercise in futility.

Kennedy grabbed the bag full of diapers and bottles and shit she carried everywhere with her, and I pulled it out of her hand, slinging it over my shoulder while I held securely Phoenix in the crook my other arm. She squirmed and babbled incoherently at me as I followed Kennedy into the studio.

The front door opened silently as we made our way inside, but the air didn't smell like I thought it would. I imagined sandalwood and patchouli, but it was fresher than that. More like clean laundry and strawberries but not overwhelmingly so. It was oddly refreshing and made me want to take a big fucking lungful of the air.

We were running a little late, so everyone was already in the studio. When I looked through the glass walls, I could see women settling on their mats, babies and toddlers in their arms scattered across the hardwood floor.

"Fuck. Can you hold him while I set this down?" Kennedy thrust Nico in my direction while she pulled the bag off my shoulder, and I grabbed him with my other arm, balancing both of my best friends' kids against my chest. She stepped over to a little cubby area and tossed the bag in haphazardly, brushing a piece of her blonde hair out of her eyes.

"We should just skip," I suggested, bouncing myself up and down like a goddamn carnival ride or some shit when Nico started to whimper. Phoenix eyed him as if she were waiting to see what he'd do to decide if she was going to join in or not, and I held my fucking breath because I had no idea what to do with a crying baby.

This was already a complete fucking shit show, and a quiet morning doing laps in my pool was sounding better and better.

Kennedy lifted Nico back out of my arms, and his whole face lit up like she hung the goddamn moon. I looked away at the unconditional love on both of their faces because I couldn't stomach it, focusing instead on the yoga mats at her feet. I tightened my grip on Phoenix and leaned down to pick up the mats. "Ready to get this over with?"

She rolled her eyes but took her mat from me, and I bent down to pick up the other one. "You could at least pretend you're happy to do this with me, your best friend." She batted her eyelashes up and me, poking me in the chest with her finger.

Inside, her words chipped away at my cold, dead heart. But on the outside, I kept up my usual stoic mask of indifference. "Zen, True, and Maddox are my best friends."

She punched me in the arm, and Phoenix's eyes went wide as she was jostled just a little. Kennedy was a lot smaller than I was, and her punch hardly moved me. "That's bullshit, and you know it. We're besties. You need to accept it."

Rather than wait for me to deny it, she pushed past me toward the studio, flinging the door open and walking inside with purpose. I followed behind her, gripping the yoga mat in one hand and Phoenix in the other. Every eye in the room turned to us as we walked in, and my eyes narrowed as I scanned as many faces in there as I could. It was mostly what I thought it would be—a bunch of moms in high-end yoga gear with layers of makeup caked on their faces and perfectly styled hair.

Who the fuck were these chicks trying to impress? I was the only guy here, and I sure as fuck had zero interest in any of them.

I followed Kennedy to the back and laid my mat out with one hand. It was awkward as hell, but I managed before I helped her get hers down. We both sank to the floor, and I propped Phoenix in my lap. She looked back up at me, her wide blue eyes watching me as if she were asking *what the fuck do we do now?*

A voice from the front caught my attention, and I searched for who it belonged to. It was just a little raspy, sultry even, and the sound of it had my blood thrumming in my veins. It was also familiar, but I couldn't place where I'd heard it. I leaned to the side, trying to look through all the people in front of me, but it was fucking useless.

That voice led us through some simple warm-up stretches, but most of the women here were bullshitting and gossiping with each other and not even attempting the workout. I paid attention to every goddamn syllable and tried to picture the woman who that voice belonged to.

I imagined she had long legs, luscious curves, and a smile that held the promise of secrets and a little bit of magic. Lying on my back, I lifted Phoenix above my head, and she squirmed in my hands, kicking her feet and swinging her tiny fists through the air. Kennedy giggled beside me as Nico drooled on her face.

"Fuck," she laughed. "I should've brought a towel."

I chuckled and refocused my attention on getting through the poses. The instructor had us in something called *bridge pose,* and I was trying to balance on my ass while not falling over on top of Phoenix. I was sure I looked like a complete fucking idiot. I glared around the room, making sure no one had a phone on me.

That seductive laugh sounded from nearby, and I perked up a little. "You're going to hurt yourself if you keep your back curved like that." A hand slid across my lower back, and I swear to Christ every place her palm touched me lit up like a thousand fireworks exploding all at the same time. I almost jumped out of my fucking skin, but instead, I whipped my head around to where she was kneeling next to me in all of her technicolor glory.

Her green-blue eyes were the color of the water in the Maldives, and I sank into their depths. They danced with amusement as she watched Phoenix repeatedly smack me in the face with her tiny fist as I gawked like a fucking asshole. When my gaze met hers, her lips parted, and she inhaled sharply. I wondered if she felt the magnetic energy between us. Where I was gray tones and blacks, she was an explosion of color, fucking luminous and saturated in a rainbow. Her hair was wavy and sat at her shoulders, dyed a kaleidoscope of colors, from magenta at the top, and shifting into teal at the tips.

She lifted one shapely eyebrow as I watched her, not giving a flying fuck that I looked like an idiot or that I hadn't said one word to her. I finally pulled my head out of my ass but swallowed hard when she adjusted her position, and I got a look at her tight curves wrapped in Spandex. "Thanks."

She tilted her head to the side with a wide smile. "So, mommy and me class, huh?"

I gave up trying to hold the pose and sat up, repositioning Phoenix so she was facing out and could see what was going on around us. She liked it when I did that. "Yeah, and?" I snapped because I never said I wasn't an asshole, and it was pretty much my default setting at this point. "Is that a problem?"

She shook her head, those colorful waves taunting me and making me want to wrap them around my fist. "Nope. I was just wondering whose baby you stole."

Admittedly, I didn't look like the parent type with my dark hair, shadowy eyes, and almost every inch of skin covered in tattoos that twisted down my arms and up my neck. I was about to snap at her again when Kennedy laughed beside me. "Jericho didn't steal her, just borrowed."

The instructor laughed and pushed off the floor, standing to her full height. My gaze zeroed in on the exposed skin of her flat stomach, and I couldn't look away. Her body called to me like she was meant to be mine, and my new singular focus was seeing her writhe and thrash underneath my body as I commanded her pleasure and made it my own. I turned and quickly handed Phoenix off to Kennedy, who looked at me like I'd lost my goddamn mind.

But there was no way in hell I was holding onto a baby while I fought off a hard-on. No. Fucking. Way.

She winked at me, fucking *winked*, and moved to help Kennedy with her form. I closed my eyes and tried to focus on my breathing. Even if the instructor was hot as fuck and my body was drawn to her like a fucking addict to their next hit of heroin, the odds that she would be into the same type of shit I was when we fucked were low.

But when Kennedy asked her name? My eyes snapped the fuck open because suddenly, I had to know. "I'm Moon."

Moon. An unusual name for the most alluring woman I'd ever seen, and I thought I'd seen every type of woman there was. Her name rolled around in my mind, like a soft caress in the furthest reaches of my thoughts.

I tried to tune out the girls laughing together, but I lost the battle with myself to not watch her stand up and walk away. She walked with confidence, her back straight, her ass tight and curvy. I wanted to bite it, to sink my teeth in until she was marked as mine.

I'd let myself want her, but acting on it was a whole other beast, one I wouldn't let get the better of me.

FOUR
MOON

"Tell me about how he jumped out of his skin again," Bexley snorted, sloshing her Manhattan over the rim of her glass.

"I barely touched him, and I thought he was going to fling the baby right out of his lap." I chuckled as I sipped my own Old Fashioned. Tonight I wanted to be fancy, so we dressed up like flappers from the 1920s in sparkly dresses with fringe and hit up a whiskey bar. Who said you needed to wait for Halloween to dress up? So what if people stared at us as we walked into the bar?

She tossed her head back and practically cackled. "What was a huge tattooed guy doing in a mommy and me yoga class anyway?"

I crossed my legs and took a sip of my drink, the sweetness dancing across my tongue. "He came with a friend. When she cornered me after class, she called herself his bestie and told me she dragged him to class with her." I laughed, remembering how excited she was to slip me his number.

Bex traced her finger around the rim of her glass, her expression thoughtful. "Do you think he'll come back?"

Shaking my head, I uncrossed my legs and took another sip. "I doubt it. But she did force his number on me."

Her eyes widened. "What are you going to do with it?"

I shrugged and grabbed an olive from the charcuterie on the table, popping it into my mouth. "I haven't decided yet."

"But you thought he was hot." She wasn't asking, and a wide grin spread across her lips.

Brushing my hair over my shoulder, I tapped my glittery fingernails on the surface of the table. "He was not at all my usual type, but *better*. He had that whole bad-boy vibe that I usually avoid, but there was something so magnetic about him. His eyes pulled me in and made me want to dig into every dark corner of his blackened soul. And that was after only a couple of seconds." I threw my hands up before burying my face in my palms. "I sound crazy," I mumbled.

Bexley patted my arm gently. "Moon. Look at me." I lifted my eyes warily, grabbing for my glass, and taking a healthy gulp. "I know you've been fully focused on living as much life as you can for you and your mom both, but it's okay for you to have something a little more permanent. Something just for you."

I blinked back the sudden stinging in my eyes and lifted my glass to take another sip with a shaky hand. My mom disappearing when I was twelve was something that still haunted me even fifteen years later. Dad and I knew she'd never take off on us, and I'd given up on her still being alive years ago because of it. Now, I tried to experience everything life had to offer for both of us, hoping that if she was looking down on me, that she was proud of who I was.

Sighing, I pushed at the base of my now empty glass. "Eventually, I will. But with the studio and school, my plate's full. I don't have time to add anything else and still be able to enjoy random nights out like this with you."

"Fine, but promise me you won't close yourself off?"

"Bex..."

She leveled me with a hard look and pursed lips. "You realize not giving this guy a chance is doing exactly the thing you said you'd never do—turn down an opportunity that comes your way."

Damn, she had me and the promise I'd made myself years ago. "I'll think about it." It was the best I could give her.

She slammed her hand down on the table, making our empty glasses rattle and drawing the attention of a bunch of the tables around us. "We need to dance," she declared before jumping out of her seat and teetering unsteadily on her sky-high heels.

Throwing her hand out and steadying herself on the table, she laughed before shimmying her shoulders, which made all the sparkly fringe on her dress catch the light. "C'mon."

Her hand gripped mine as she yanked me up and the heat from the drinks we'd been tossing back loosened me up. I giggled as I followed the path she was weaving through the crowded bar toward the front where a piano sat. As she clutched my hand and pulled me forward, my gaze drifted around the room. I noticed no one else was dancing, but that never stopped me, and part of the reason I loved Bexley was that it never stopped her, either.

The music wasn't exactly the dancing type, a slower and more sultry type of jazz. But, holding hands with Bex, I closed my eyes and swayed to the gentle notes pouring out of the piano. Eyes burned into me from all sides, but I ignored them all. I was used to the attention. You didn't fade into the background when you did whatever you wanted no matter if it was appropriate or not.

Still, the tiny hairs on the back of my neck stood up and not in a good way. My eyes snapped open as Bex leaned closer and whispered in my ear, "Don't look, but there's a burly tattooed guy in leather staring you down hard, and not in a nice *I want to fuck your brains out* sort of way."

I shivered, suddenly feeling completely sober. For a while now, I'd been feeling like someone was following me or watching me, but I didn't have any proof. I'd never caught anyone, and Bex's description of a tattooed man in leather didn't exactly give me a comforting feeling.

"Want to go?" she offered, flicking her gaze over my shoulder for a fraction of a second before looking back at me with concern.

And all at once, the only thing I wanted was to get the hell out of here and get home. The sequins on my dress were itchy, my head was starting to pound from my sudden sobriety, and the dude in the shadows creeping on me pushed me over the edge. I nodded at Bex, and we walked quickly to our table and grabbed our purses.

A large hand wrapped around my wrist and spun me so my back was pressed into the table, and my heart rate skyrocketed. I looked up into bloodshot brown eyes and a face that wore a crooked smile. "Hey, gorgeous. How 'bout you let me buy you a drink?"

"Why?" I asked sweetly, ripping my arm out of his loose grip.

He narrowed his eyes before repeating my question. "Why?"

"Mmhmm. Why should I let you buy me a drink? What are you hoping to get out of it?"

He reached up and scratched at the more than day-old scruff on his jaw as his eyes went even more glazed over than they'd already been. Finally, he let his gaze travel down the length of my body, and I took that as answer enough. Rolling my eyes, I tightened my grip on my purse. "I think I've got it. Look, you're not exactly my type." I'd just discovered my type is tall, chiseled, and has a blackness inside that my light itches to fix.

He scoffed and ran his hand across the obviously toned abs underneath his button-down. "Sweetheart, I'm everyone's type."

"Not mine." I narrowed my eyes, daring him to keep pushing.

Bex moved up beside me and glared up at the guy who couldn't seem to take a hint. "We're leaving."

Spinning on my heels, I followed her out, threading through the crowd. When we were outside, I took a deep breath, and my heart rate finally slowed. As we waited on the sidewalk for our Lyft, I exhaled loudly and looked over my shoulder.

"He didn't follow us. There were too many people," Bexley assured me, weaving her arm through mine and resting her head on my shoulder.

"I wonder what the hell that was all about anyway? Why was he lurking like a creeper in the shadows watching us?"

"Not watching us, Moon. Watching you."

Her words sunk in as we stood in silence on the sidewalk. The night had lost its excitement and appeal, the glitter of my dress dulled under the yellow street light. Who was that man, and why had he been watching? I wasn't the kind of girl who lived my life stepping on other people's toes. I didn't leave a path of enemies in my wake. So, what was his deal?

The sedan pulled up to the curb, and Bex and I slipped inside. I rested my forehead against the cool glass as I watched the city go by. "Want me to stay over?" my best friend offered.

"No, I think I'll change into something comfy, grab a glass of wine, and lose myself in a video game until I'm too tired to think." I didn't tell her I was secretly hoping WickedExecutioner would be online, and I wanted to get lost in more than one game with him.

"You and your video games," she chuckled before rolling her eyes. "I don't get it."

"And you don't have to." I booped her on the nose, sort of regretting filling her in on my gaming habits earlier tonight. "There's just something… freeing about being able to lose myself in a game." I shrugged.

"If you say so." She untangled a couple of long fringe pieces from each other on the front of her dress as the car pulled up in front of my tiny house.

I gave her a quick side hug and promised to call her tomorrow before I shut the door and made my way inside. I locked the door and turned on all the lights, kicking off my heels and peeling off my dress as I walked through the house. I was still shaken up about what happened at the club, that unsettling feeling of being followed, being watched.

Stepping into my room in nothing but my underwear, I pulled on a comfy pair of lounge pants and a tank top before stopping in the kitchen to pour a glass of wine. My hand shook a little as I poured, and I took another deep breath.

Finally, I flopped down on my comfy couch and grabbed my headset, pulling it over my ears and turning on the console. My stomach fluttered as I waited for the system to boot up. I didn't have the energy to lie to myself about why my nerves were suddenly firing on all cylinders. It was Wicked. He had this hold over me. Talking to him let me stop having to think for just a little while. I didn't have to be the business owner or the daughter left behind to pick up the pieces of her shattered heart when her mom disappeared mysteriously.

I could just let him take control and enjoy the pleasure he brought me. And that kind of release was what I needed tonight. My mind flashed to the dark eyes from yesterday, and I wondered if Jericho was anything like Wicked. If they both had the same sort of mystery lurking underneath, one that I found myself drawn to.

A giddy feeling bubbled up inside when I logged in and found him there as if he were waiting for me. I slipped my headset on. "Hey, Wicked," I greeted, feeling the tension melt out of my body at just the thought of hearing his deep, gravelly voice.

"Luna, I didn't expect to see you on tonight." He said my username like a caress, and I sank lower into the couch cushion, sighing at the shiver his voice elicited in me.

"Yeah, I was out with a friend, but the night didn't end great, so I thought I'd get on and try to put it behind me." I sipped my wine, resting my controller in my lap. I wasn't all that interested in playing the actual game or blowing shit up; mostly, I wanted to talk to Wicked. I didn't know what that said about me.

"A friend?" Any softness that had been in his voice was gone, and for some ridiculous reason, that sent a thrill through my body. Was Wicked *jealous*?

"Yeah, my best girlfriend, Bex. We dressed up and got whiskey drunk. Or whiskey buzzed, I guess."

"Hmm."

"I don't know what that means."

"It means I'm fucking relieved you were out with a girlfriend, and some other guy didn't have his hands on you." He practically growled the words, and the small smile I had on my face got bigger.

"Why, Wicked. Are you jealous?" I teased.

"You're goddamn right I'm jealous. No one but me gets to put their hands on you. You're *mine*." The words were possessive, but they were also sensual and filled with a dirty vow I knew he'd find a way to fulfill someday.

"And how are you going to make me *yours* if you don't even know where I am or what I look like? Or my real name? What if I'm hideous? And what's to keep me from going on a date tomorrow night?"

He growled into the headset, and it was honestly hot as fuck. "You do *not* want to test me, Luna. I swear to fucking god I will get my IT buddy to hack the shit out of this game and track you down, and then I'll show up on your doorstep and bend you over my knee for doubting me."

Why was his possessiveness such a turn on? That was not something I'd ever let slide from anyone in the past. If a man tried to tell me what to do, I was done. Immediately. I was not the kind of girl that put up with anyone telling me what I could or couldn't do. But Wicked? He did funny things to me. He soaked my panties, made my heart race, and left me panting and wanting more. Always.

I bit my lip, wanting to push him a little. "Well, I met this guy the other day.

He took me by surprise, and his friend gave me his number. I've been thinking about calling him and asking him out."

"Do. Not. Fucking. Test. Me," he grit out, and I grinned like an idiot.

"So, I shouldn't call him?"

"Luna." His voice was laced with malice and warning, dangerous and cruel as it burrowed into my body and wrapped itself around my heart.

I blew out a breath. I was too shaken from tonight to really play this game right now, but something about Wicked's claiming me as his made me feel safe, even though he wasn't physically here. "Don't worry, Wicked. I like that you think of me as yours. I think of you the same way, as mine. And only mine," I emphasized because I wasn't into sharing.

"There's no one but you, Luna." He sighed, sounding marginally calmer. "Now tell me what happened tonight. You sound weird."

I set my wine glass down on the coffee table and pulled the throw blanket draped over the back of the couch around me, trying to chase away the sudden chill. My eyes flicked up to the big, bay window in the living room but the curtains were pulled shut. "It wasn't a big deal. Bex and I were dancing, and this wasn't exactly a dancing sort of place, so we were the only ones up there. But I had that feeling, you know? Like you're being watched?"

"Someone was fucking watching you?" Danger dripped from his voice and the hair on my arms lifted, both in arousal and, if I was honest, a little bit of fear. "Who?"

"I don't know. I didn't see him. Bex said he was covered in tattoos and wearing leather."

"Why would someone be watching you?"

"I wracked my brain the entire way home trying to figure out why anyone would be keeping tabs on me, and I've got nothing."

"Have you noticed anyone watching before?"

I shook my head before realizing he couldn't see me. "No."

He exhaled, but still sounded more than a little pissed off when he demanded, "If you see him or anyone else following you again, you get on here and tell me. Immediately, Luna. Don't fucking wait. And I *will* come to you, wherever you are, and take care of the problem."

I shivered as if his hot breath had just skittered down my neck. "Okay, Wicked."

"Make me a fucking promise," he commanded.

"I promise." And I really did mean it. I was fine standing up for myself, but I had no idea how to handle some weird stalker I might've randomly picked up somewhere, and I didn't want to face that alone. My dad wasn't exactly the overprotective type. He was more of the live and let live type of parent, so I'd be mostly on my own.

But that promise? It meant maybe for once I didn't have to be, even if it was a false sense of security.

FIVE
JERICHO

The tremble in Luna's voice last night had me on edge today. I hadn't let her sign off the game until her soft breathing brushed across the mic, and I knew she fell asleep. Her vulnerability called to something inside me, some need to protect and tell the world she belonged to me and nobody would fucking touch her as long as I was breathing.

I already texted Sebastian this morning and put him on the case of tracking Luna down. I was sure as fuck not waiting for something to happen to her. I might not act on the information yet, but I wanted to have it just in case.

It wouldn't take him long, but as much as I wanted to, I couldn't focus on her right now. Our album was a fucking train wreck. *Richard,* the shitty producer the label forced on us, sucked at his job and couldn't get the music to sound right.

The notes played in my head, the chords and rhythms and the melodies. I could see it just as much as I could hear it, but it wasn't my job to compose the tracks. My frustration level was boiling over today, though. Especially after last night with Luna and how pissed off I was that she was out there in the world somehow possibly in danger and my goddamn hands were tied.

My knuckles ached as I clenched my fingers into a fist again, and I itched to punch someone. A loud banging on my front door had me pushing off my couch and stalking across the concrete floor. I ripped the door open so hard, I was surprised it didn't pull off the hinges.

"Jesus, who's about to die?" Maddox wondered, looking me up and down as True and Zen pushed past me and into my house.

"I don't know, keep staring at me like that, and I'll have an answer for you." Rage boiled inside me, and keeping it under wraps was harder than usual. I needed to put a heavy bag in my gym before I killed one of my best friends.

Maddox eyed me up and down again before ignoring me and pulling out his phone. He brushed past me as if I hadn't just threatened his life and started texting. I slammed the door closed behind him and stalked back into the living room where my friends made themselves at home. Zen was sprawled out on my couch, True was perched on the arm of my leather chair, and Maddox leaned against the wall while he texted.

He finally slipped his phone back into his pocket and looked up at me. "Connor's outside, but I asked him to grab his boxing shit. You want to hit someone? He'll be back in fifteen minutes, and you can go toe to toe with him."

Leave it to Maddox to know exactly what I needed. I gave him one sharp nod before I folded my arms across my chest and paced back and forth across my living room. I was too amped up to sit down; I needed to move.

"What the fuck is going on with you?" Zen wondered as his sharp gaze followed me around the room. "I haven't seen you this pissed off and out of control since…" He didn't have to say it. We all knew. *Since Kayla*. I'd stayed far away from hookups or relationships since that epic fuck up all those years ago. A quick, meaningless fuck wasn't worth the risk of losing control. My hand worked just fucking fine.

But today I was in chaos, and the guys could see it. I didn't know what had me more fucked up—Luna or this album. "I'm dealing with some shit, but more than anything, this fucking album is making me want to murder someone. I can't handle Richard and his tired beats and compositions. It sounds like he's trying to make us into some ripoff K-pop shitshow."

"A-fucking-men to that," Maddox agreed. "So, what did you have in mind?"

"I spent the off year working on audio engineering and song composition, and I want to see if I can get the sound we're after on my own."

True nodded. "Yeah, okay. I trust you more than someone the label saddled us with."

"Same." Zen still watched me pace. "What do you need from us?"

My fingers twitched as I raked my hand through my hair because I still needed to fucking hit something. "Since we're not recording today, let's just do one song here. Let me mix it and play with it and see what we think. If we agree and like the direction, we'll confront Dick."

Maddox snickered, and Zen shot him a look. "What, dude? You don't name your kid Richard unless you want him to be called a dick. Those are just fucking facts."

My lip twitched, but that was as close to a smile as I was going to get. The door opened, and I twisted around, on high alert again. My fucking nerves were on edge. Connor stepped into the room carrying a duffel bag and locked eyes with me before jerking his head at my backyard. I turned back to the guys. "Give me an hour, and we'll start."

I started to walk toward the back of the house when something occurred to me. I turned back to Maddox. "Can you have Griffin come over?"

His eyebrow lifted. "I can, but why?"

What the fuck was it with everyone questioning me? "I can't operate the recording and mixing equipment and play the fucking drums now, can I? I want him to sit in for me for this song."

"He's going to freak the fuck out," Zen laughed.

"Can I tell him?" True wondered, holding out his hand to snatch Maddox's phone, but Mad held it out of his reach.

"Not this time, T." His fingers flew over the screen, and I turned to follow Connor outside.

Every muscle in my body ached, but the darkness inside me was settled for now. I stepped out of the shower and dried off fast, dressing in jeans and a t-shirt. I wasn't trying to impress anyone. I stopped in the kitchen on my way down to the basement studio to grab a bottle of water.

The guys were nowhere to be found, so they must've already gone downstairs. The small bit of relaxation I'd managed by beating the shit out of Connor vanished when I stepped into the studio and saw the guys in the soundproof glass box where I'd normally be with them. Except in my place was Maddox's little brother Griffin sitting behind my drum kit. I swallowed back the urge to tell him to get the fuck out. We needed him even if I didn't like the look of him behind my drums.

I pushed into the small room, and everyone's attention snapped to me. I was sure as fuck not a fan of attention, which I realized was ironic, but instead of slinking back into the shadows, I needed to give the guys some direction if I wanted to make this happen.

"Play *Vicious* from the beginning. Don't stop. I want a recording all the way through." I turned to Griffin as he twirled a stick between his fingers. "You know it?"

"Dude, he's been at every session for months," Maddox stepped in, and I glared at him.

"Last I checked, I wasn't asking you. Butt the fuck out." I turned back to Griffin. "Well?"

Instead of answering, he played the rhythm perfectly. After about thirty seconds, I stopped him. I would never admit it, but the kid was good. As good as me. And he had the song down.

I spun without another word. I didn't need words to fill empty space like most people. I was perfectly content to live in the silence. In fact, I preferred it that way, unless I was making music. Stepping out of the room, I let the door close behind me and sat in front of the audio mixer.

My finger pressed against the button that would let me talk into the booth. "Ready?"

Four heads nodded, and I pressed the button again. "Count them off, Griff, and then start." I let the button go and made sure everything was turned on and working to record. For the next two hours, they played the song over and over. I adjusted and recorded enough that I thought I could put together a workable song. I had each of them spend some time playing their pieces alone in the booth, and then I kicked them the fuck out of my house.

There was a reason as a group we didn't hang out here. I fucking hated people in my space. They got it and never took offense, but even if they did, I wouldn't care. Quiet solitude was something I craved. Except right now there was nothing to keep my mind from drifting to Luna. The fear in her voice last night had me restless. Was she okay? I wanted to kick my own ass for not giving her my name or phone number last night in case she needed me. I hadn't been on the Xbox all day today. What if she had a problem and tried to let me know?

I clamped right down on that shit. When the fuck had I turned into this person? I didn't get upset or worried about women. Never had. And I sure as fuck didn't hand out my name and phone number. As much as I hated it, my name was recognizable. For all I knew, Luna could plaster my number all over the fucking internet, and I'd never get left alone.

I was driven by a need to know who she was, to learn everything about her before I let her in. An image of purple and blue hair and turquoise eyes pushed its way to the forefront of my thoughts; the hot yoga instructor from class with Kennedy the other day threw me off. She tempted me in a way no other woman ever had, except Luna, and I didn't really know her. Luna represented a fantasy for me, something I wished could be my reality. But she was safe. She wasn't here and so I couldn't hurt her. I couldn't lose control even if I wanted to.

That itch to fucking punch something was starting to claw its way through my body again.

Until Sebastian got back to me, I needed to leave my goddamn Xbox on but keep my distance. I need to bury myself in fucking music until I got something usable because between Luna's issues, the yoga instructor I couldn't get out of my mind, and the shitty way Dick twisted our music into something unrecognizable, I felt like I was losing my fucking mind.

Minutes melted into hours as I sat in my studio, tweaking and layering the pieces of our music together. I set up an app on my phone so if Luna messaged, I'd get it down here, but otherwise, I was lost to the outside world. Heels clicking on the concrete floor finally pulled me out of my mind, and I scrubbed my hands down my significantly more stubbled than usual face before standing up and stretching.

"Jesus, Jericho. How about some sunlight? Maybe a shower?" Kennedy wrinkled her nose before setting a bag from my favorite sushi place down in front of me.

"It's been like eight hours max. There's no way I smell." I sat back down and narrowed my eyes at her wrinkled nose.

Her face broke out into a grin. "I know, I'm just fucking with you. Zen said you were probably going to lock yourself down here, so I wanted to make sure you remembered to eat."

"He's lucky he treats you right because I'd have to fucking kill him if he didn't, and I don't really want to have to murder one of my best friends." I popped the top off of the container of perfectly crafted rolls and rooted through the bag for the chopsticks.

She giggled, and I glanced up at her. "Trust me, there is *nothing* he wouldn't do for me." Her eyes had taken on an unsettling dreamy quality that made me uncomfortable.

"Are you thinking about fucking right now?" Plucking the wooden sticks apart, I pinched a roll between them and took a bite.

"Maybe. That's beside the point." She waved her hand in the air. "Talk to me about Moon."

"Who?"

She huffed. "The girl who teaches my yoga classes? Super hot, you couldn't take your eyes off of her?"

"What about her?" On the outside, I was indifferent, but inside, a storm was raging. One look from that girl and I was sucked in, pulled into her orbit, and not sure how to deal with what that meant. I also promised Luna I was hers. So I was choosing to ignore it, to bury my feelings so deep down they'd disappear.

"That's how you want to play this?" She crossed her arms and stared at me with her wide blue eyes. She didn't blink, but she also couldn't intimidate me.

"I'm not playing anything. You know I don't date." I dipped my second roll in soy sauce before biting it in half.

"So if she called and asked you out, what would you do?" Her tone was a little *too* interested, and I froze, turning to her.

"What did you do?"

She bit her lip. "I didn't do anything."

I narrowed my eyes and dropped my chopsticks, standing up out of my chair. "Kennedy. What the fuck did you do?"

She sighed, but she didn't back down. It was part of why I liked her. She wasn't afraid of me and called me on my bullshit. "Nothing. But I was hoping you'd want to go to class with me again."

Exhaling, I dropped back into my chair and picked the chopsticks back up. "Mommy and me?"

She nodded.

"No fucking way."

"Fine." She pinched the bridge of her nose and sighed loudly. "I'm going to let you get back to it, but the guys are coming by tomorrow morning. I'll send breakfast with Zen."

"Thanks for this," I mumbled around the bite I was chewing.

"You owe Nico some Uncle Jericho time," she tossed out over her shoulder as she walked back upstairs and out of the house. Somehow Kennedy always knew what I needed, and there was a tiny space inside my otherwise cold, black soul where she and the guys from the band had dug their way in and taken up permanent residence despite my best efforts to keep them away.

The hours continued to merge together one after another until my eyes were gritty and half-open, and heavy footsteps stomped down my stairs. I rubbed my eyes and stood up, my tight muscles screaming at me for not moving for who knew how many hours. But I had a song. I had a fucking song that was *perfect* and everything our music should be. Fuck Dick and fuck the label for forcing him on us. I knew I could make my vision a reality.

"Okay, dickhead. It's the crack of fucking dawn, and you dragged me out of bed with Ryan. You better have something miraculous to show us," Maddox grumbled as he plopped down on the leather sofa I kept down here.

"When everyone's here, I'll show you, and until then, you can just fucking wait. You want coffee?" I offered because I sure as fuck needed some. He grunted, and I took that to mean yes, so I went upstairs and brewed some. As I lifted the two mugs to take them back downstairs, the front door opened, and Zen and True came inside laughing about who the fuck knew what.

"Hey, mommy!" True teased, and I shot him a death glare as I pictured every single way I could destroy him. That mommy shit could *not* stick.

Zen snickered next to him, and I moved my glare to him next. "I dare you to call me that again." I made my voice low and menacing because even though they were my friends, I had no issues beating the shit out of them or worse.

"Someone's sensitive. I hear those hormones can be a real bitch," Zen joked, his eyes sparkling with challenge. I set the mugs back onto the counter and calmly strode across the room before punching him right in his face. He laughed as he stepped back from the force of the impact, ignoring the blood dripping from his nose, and True gripped my shoulder.

"Enough." He looked at Zen and then back at me. "Got something good to show us?"

Zen still laughed as he moved past us into my kitchen and poured himself a mug of coffee and grabbed a paper towel to soak up the blood as if I hadn't just punched him in the face. I shook my head and followed him. This wasn't even close to the first time any of us had hit each other, and it wouldn't be the last. I grabbed the two cups I'd set down and followed my bandmates downstairs.

Shoving Maddox's coffee into his hands, I sat down in front of the board I'd called home for the past eighteen-plus hours. "Now shut the fuck up and listen."

I pressed play and let the notes and tempo of our newest song fill the space in the room. All three guys had their eyes closed listening. When it was finally over, Zen was the one who weighed in first.

"Damn. The way that modulates between keys is impressive."

True opened his eyes and nodded in agreement. "Yeah, and the meter changes on the chorus are perfect. I never would've thought of that."

"You fucking nailed it, Jericho." Maddox jumped up and clapped me on the shoulder. My lips tilted upward just a little, which was about as close to a smile as I usually got. My chest swelled with pride.

"So, we agree?" Zen questioned, turning to all of us. "We take this to Richard and tell him it's what we want?"

"We've got an hour. Upload that to the Cloud, would you?" True pulled out his phone. We kept a Cloud account that we all shared for music ideas. It was the easiest way to keep track of everything. With a couple of clicks, I had it done.

"Done. I'm going to shower, and then we can take off." I pushed out of my seat and headed up to my room. I just hoped Dick wouldn't live up to his name and could be reasonable.

The song cut off midway through and Dick's—sorry, *Richard's*—face wore an expression of boredom that made me want to punch him. Repeatedly. Until all that was left was a bloody heap. "If you want to waste your limited time off on shit like this, go right ahead. But the label put me on this assignment because I know what sells. Do you know what doesn't sell? This kind of depressing indie garage-band style shit. No one wants to hear that, and more importantly, no one will buy it."

My fingers curled into fists, and I cut my glance over to Maddox whose jaw was clenched so hard the muscle was ticking. Zen had his arms folded across his chest, and True stared at Dick incredulously. "When was the last time you produced a hit song?" he asked calmly.

Dick spluttered, and his chubby face turned red. "I- None of your goddamn business. The label assigned me to produce your album, and that's what I'm going to do. Now, if you're done wasting my time, we're behind. *I'm* the one running the show, and it would do the four of you good to remember it."

Griffin chose that moment to stroll into the studio but quickly read the room. "Fuck. What happened?"

I pushed off the wall I'd been leaning against. "Dick here decided he's going to make our music his way without giving one single fuck about how we want it to sound."

"Shit." He glared at the moron producer for us, and I warmed up to the kid just a little bit more. He played on *Vicious*; it was his beat the guys played to, so he had a vested interest in the outcome.

"Band meeting outside. Now." Zen moved past Dick, shoulder checking him hard on his way out.

"We don't have time for this," Dick argued, trying to step in True's path.

True stood even taller, and I was reminded how imposing he could be when he wanted to. "Get the fuck out of my way or I'll make you."

Dick hesitated for a second, and True took a step forward. Finally, the asshole producer figured out that this was a fight he had no hope in winning and moved aside.

"Smart move, Dick." Maddox glared at him as he passed. I followed the three of them out and turned at the last second back toward Griffin. "Are you coming?"

A look of surprise crossed his face quickly before he schooled it into a more stoic *I don't give a fuck* expression and followed me outside.

Once we were all standing on the sidewalk outside, we huddled together in a loose circle. I noticed Connor, Ryan, and Indy forming a sort of perimeter around us. Maddox's eyes locked on his girlfriend, and I had to shove him in the shoulder to get him to look away. He glared at me but didn't say anything.

"What the hell are we going to do about that asshole? It shreds my soul a little more every time we have to step into the booth with him and hear the amateur bullshit he turns our music into." Zen had a storm raging in his green eyes, and I bet mine didn't look much different.

True, the peacekeeper, held his hands up. "Let's go in there and do what he says today and then meet tonight to figure out something more permanent because I sure as hell am not putting my name on the garbage he's been creating."

"Fine," I agreed. "But, I'm getting copies of the raw files of everything we record today to take home with me."

After we all agreed, we filed inside to spend the day wasting our time with Dick. He'd be giving me today's files even if I had to take them from him violently.

SIX

JERICHO

"I talked to Marcus, and he refused to take Richard off as producer." I ran my hands through my hair in frustration at the sound of our manager-slash-agent Montana's voice through the speakerphone. "He said he has a contract and that he was picked because they thought his style complemented yours. He's refusing and says if you don't show up to record at every scheduled session, he'll sue you guys for breach of contract."

Last night our emergency meeting resulted in a whole lot of venting after another spectacularly awful day in the studio with Dick. Zen put Montana on the case and asked her to share my composition with the label and get Dick taken off as our producer.

Now we sat around Zen's living room with his phone on speaker between us, listening to our manager tell us how fucked we were. "Can they do that?" Zen held Nico against his chest as his son slept in his arms.

True watched wistfully, and I knew that motherfucker wished he had Phoenix with him. My phone vibrated in my pocket, and I looked at the screen. Sebastian was calling, and that meant only one thing—he'd figured out who LunaGirl was.

When I looked up, Maddox was watching me. He lifted an eyebrow, but I tilted my head toward the kitchen and hopped up, leaving the rest of the guys to deal with the shitshow from the label.

"Tell me you found her." I didn't bother answering with any pleasantries. I wanted to get to the fucking point.

"Do you seriously doubt my talent that much?" I pissed him off, but I couldn't care less.

"Just tell me," I ground out, quickly losing what little patience I had after the clusterfuck of this morning.

"I'd tell you to fuck off no matter what you're paying me, but I'm a professional." He took a deep breath. "Lucky you. Your mystery girl lives right here in LA. Just down the I-five."

I glanced back at the guys as tingles ran down my spine, but none of them were paying attention. Luna lived locally? "What's her name?"

He laughed. "Apparently she's a real-life comic book hero or something because her name is unbelievable. *Moon Mayhem*. Who names their kid something like that?" Sebastian was cracking up, but ice had started running through my veins.

Moon?

It couldn't be a coincidence I'd met two girls with the same weird as fuck name in the past week. Right? "What else?" I demanded.

"Looks like you scored because she owns her own yoga studio. She lives in a one-bedroom house in Manhattan Beach. I've got a whole file. I'll email it to you now." Clicking sounds from what I assumed was his keyboard traveled through the phone as I leaned back against the counter and ran a hand through my hair.

"Okay, sent. Let me know if you need anything else." I ended the call but didn't pocket my phone. Instead, I pulled up the email and scanned through it. Moon owned her house and her studio, was an only child, and her mom had disappeared under suspicious circumstances years ago.

Interesting.

There wasn't much else of interest except the picture Sebastian attached. I knew I was in trouble based on my body's visceral reaction to the colorful beauty staring back up at me from the screen. First, the crushing weight that had been sitting on my chest for the last two days lifted in relief because LunaGirl— Moon—lived an hour away. If something happened, I could be there fast and take her away to someplace safe.

Like my bed.

My heart raced in a staccato rhythm, fast and sharp, as excitement tore through my body at the idea of Moon writhing on my black sheets, her mouth parted in ecstasy. My lips quirked up in an almost-smile as I wondered what I should do with this information now that I had it. My dick had never reacted to a woman as it had to both Moon and Luna, and now any internal war I'd been waging about what to do about the sexy as sin yoga teacher vanished with one phone call.

I didn't have to choose between the girl of my fantasies and the reality that was a dangerous temptation. My thoughts spiraled into depravity and perversion in the best way, and only True's calling my name snapped me out of it. I turned in the kitchen and leaned against the island to hide how hard my dick was.

"What the hell are you doing over there? True called you like six times," Maddox chastised me, but I was in a much better mood than I had been a few minutes ago, so I just flipped him off and adjusted myself before I walked back into the living room and sat down.

"What's the damage?" I asked no one in particular.

Zen sighed and absently rubbed Nico's back. "Unless we want to take on the label in court, we're stuck with Dick."

Maddox was leaning back against the couch with a scowl on his face, and True had his knees balanced on his elbows while he looked down at the floor. Finally, he lifted his head. "We've been doing this a long-ass time. Don't you guys think our music is worth fighting for? I say we call their bluff and fire Dick."

Maddox sat up. "I'm down for that, but then who's going to engineer the album?"

All three of their eyes turned to me, and I sighed. "Look, I love composing and producing. It's fucking fun, and I lose myself in it. It quiets the demons down, you know?" Maddox nodded along as if he knew what I mean. "And you all know I hate the fucking spotlight."

Zen chuckled. "I'm surprised you stuck with us this long, to be honest."

"But where does that leave the band? I'm not a fucking magician. I can't be in two places at once," I pointed out one of the many flaws in this plan.

It was silent in the room outside of the sound of Nico's gurgling baby noises. "What about Griff?" True finally said.

Maddox perked up. "I didn't even think about that. He'd lose his shit if we asked him to step in. He's been practicing and learning for months. He knows our stuff inside and out."

Zen's unnaturally green eyes turned on me with all the fiery intensity he usually kept locked inside except for with his wife. He was excited by this idea. I could tell. "What do you think?"

I rubbed my palm across my cheek and against the smooth skin at my jawline. "As much as I don't want to admit it, Griffin's good. Maybe better than me, and I'll ruin any of you who repeat that outside of this room." I glared at all of them to make sure they understood my threat before stopping at Maddox. "I think you better call your brother and get him the fuck over here."

"We're really doing this? Because once I make this call, that's it. I'm not going to dangle his dream in front of his face and then snatch it away." Maddox twirled his phone between his fingers.

"Okay, so we vote. Raise your hand if you want Jericho to produce and Griffin to take over on drums." True raised his hand, and so did Zen and Maddox.

"Fuck you all since my vote doesn't count, but I'm in, too." I raised my hand.

"Dude, your vote counts most of all. We wouldn't kick you out for anything. You have to go voluntarily," Zen admitted, passing Nico off to Kennedy, who just walked in the room. She didn't say anything, just leaned down for a kiss and left with the baby, but not before giving me a knowing look. I was sure Zen filled her in on everything that was happening.

"Good to know. I need a smoke," I announced, pushing myself up off the couch and digging in my pocket for the joint I stuffed in there earlier. I fucking hated change, and me not being the drummer for Shadow Phoenix anymore? Huge. Fucking. Change.

I walked across the open living room into the game room at the front of the house and plopped myself on the sectional in front of the TV that took up almost an entire wall. I needed space to process. The fame part of making music had never been something I enjoyed. If I could've made music professionally but stayed out of the public's interest, I'd have figured out a way to do that shit years ago. But that wasn't how stardom worked.

For years I tried to stick to the shadows. I hardly said two words in interviews, letting the guys who handled that shit better than I ever could deal with it. I lurked in the back, hoping to be left the fuck alone. And mostly it worked. I didn't get the same media attention as the other three guys. I rarely had to worry about paparazzi following me around. And even if they did, I was private as hell. They never got anything interesting out of me and always gave up quickly.

By now, Zen, Maddox, and True knew to leave me alone when unexpected changes popped up. I flicked my lighter and held it to the end of the joint, breathing in the cloying smoke, letting it burn my lungs until my body screamed at me to purge it out on a long exhale.

My muscles started to relax almost immediately as the weed did its job, numbing me to my churning stomach and the edgy feeling of needing to hit something. Most people's anxiety manifested itself as the need to run away, but not mine. I was a fucking fighter through and through, and when I got anxious? It turned to rage and the need to destroy.

The weed helped take the edge off.

It was the only thing I'd ever found that helped besides giving into the violence and sex. And sex was too risky. I couldn't chance losing control again because next time, I might actually kill someone. I sunk into the cushion of the couch and kicked my feet up on the ottoman in front of me, letting the high take over my body. I didn't even turn on the TV, just lost myself in the feeling and the random thoughts skittering through my brain.

Time lost all meaning, and what must've been at least half an hour later, the door swung open and Griffin sauntered in. I turned to nod my head in greeting as he passed by the game room, and despite the cocky swagger he walked with, his eyes didn't lie. He was fucking ecstatic to get this chance. And he should be. I'd kick his ass if he weren't.

Reluctantly, I peeled my heavy as fuck body up off the sofa and walked back into the living room. I didn't know what the guys had done to pass the time, but I didn't really care, either. Griffin sat next to his brother, and I couldn't help but notice how alike they looked. Dark eyes, dark hair, and similar height, but Griff was thinner like he didn't spend every waking hour in the gym like the rest of us, and he was on his way to having as many tats as Z and me. If he were going to keep up with the guys, he'd have to start working out more, and that was a conversation I trusted Maddox to deal with.

I looked around, but none of the guys were jumping into the conversation, so I took the reins and stared Griffin down. "We voted, and we want you to take my spot." There, I laid that shit out there like no big deal even if this was fucking insane, and I sort of felt like I was floating outside of my body. We still had legal logistics and shit to figure out, but I'd been drowning in my own unrest for a long time now. Maybe this time change would be a good thing.

"You're fucking with me." Griffin turned to his brother. "Are you fucking with me?"

Maddox shook his head. "That Dick asshole's got to go, and Jericho's burnt out on all the celebrity bullshit that comes with the gig. You know the music, and you've impressed us for a while. The spot's yours if you want it."

Griffin studied each of us individually, and I stared him down. *Hard.* I wasn't about to sit by and let this kid fuck up everything we built. "As long as you don't fuck it up," I added.

"I won't."

We spent the next couple of hours going over all the logistics of the switch, and Zen called to let Montana and Harrison know what we were up to. They were on our side, and we sure as hell were going to need them to make this work.

Finally, we sorted everything out, and I got the hell out of there. Spending too much time with people, including my boys, was fucking exhausting. I could only pretend to be mostly normal for so long before I wanted to rip my skin off and crawl out of it like the monster I was.

And despite everything that happened today, I was strangely at peace with my new role in the band. My thoughts had shifted at some point today away from Shadow Phoenix and my future to the girl with kaleidoscope hair and ocean eyes who haunted my thoughts.

I tried to tell myself I wasn't racing home to see if she was online, but it was a big fat fucking lie. I pulled into my garage and then jumped out of my car.

"Calm the fuck down," I snapped at myself like a psycho.

But my heart was racing, and a surge of adrenaline crushed all the caution out of my body and replaced it with excitement. I was fucking *excited*. To talk to a girl.

What the hell was I doing?

My rigid cock and I were in agreement: We wanted Moon. This primal need to make her *mine* surged up from the darkest depths of my soul, and I didn't know what to do with it. I wasn't the caveman type, but if another man so much as looked at Moon, I'd kill him. And what did that say about me?

Maybe I didn't know myself as well as I thought I did.

I pushed the button to turn on my gaming console and waited for it to load, considering what to do with the information now that I knew LunaGirl was Moon and that she lived close by. My lips twisted in a half-smile as an idea formed.

My heart leaped, fucking *leaped* in my chest when I saw Moon was online. I slipped my headset on and opened a new message to her inviting her to chat. She accepted right away, and something foreign and warm settled in my chest.

"Hey, Luna." I kept my voice low and even. I didn't want to give away the game yet. "Any sign of the guy who was watching you?" If there were, I'd drive there tonight and take her home before driving back and hunting him like a fucking animal, but I wouldn't tell her that.

"Wicked." She purred my username in a husky voice, and my dick got even harder. I could practically feel it pulsing, and she'd only said one word. "I haven't noticed anything, but I've still got that feeling that I'm being watched. I just don't have any proof."

Now that I knew LunaGirl was Moon, the flexible and intriguing girl who'd managed to become the sole focus of every fucking fantasy I'd had since I met her, talking to her like this was different. It was almost more intimate. And it was time for the games to begin. "Remember when I said you were mine? And no one else was allowed to touch you?"

"I remember." Her voice was throaty as if my possessiveness turned her the fuck on. Huh.

"I want to test a theory. I want you to ask that guy out."

"What guy?"

"The one you met, the one you said took you by surprise." I let a rare smile take over my face for a split second before burying it. I didn't want to risk her hearing it in my voice.

"Why?" All traces of arousal disappeared from her voice, and now she just sounded confused, but that was how I wanted her. I had a sick need to discover how she felt about me if she didn't know I was Wicked. This was the only opportunity I'd ever get.

"Because I want to prove to you that you're mine, that you'll always be mine, and that it doesn't matter who you go out with because no one can ever measure up to me."

She laughed. "Wow. You're really full of yourself."

"You're goddamn right I am, and for good reason. Now, are you going to do it?"

"Fine, but only because he was sexy, and I was thinking about it anyway. Not because you demanded it." Was it possible to be jealous of yourself? The clenching of my jaw told me it was. I had to take a deep breath and remind myself she was talking about *me* even if she didn't know it.

"Doesn't matter how sexy you think he is if he's not me." Moon and I, we had a connection. That first moment our eyes met in the yoga studio, something I never expected snapped into place for me, and I knew she felt it, too. Her fighting the inevitable was fucking useless, and I wouldn't waste time on it. It was why I wanted her to pursue her mystery stranger. I wanted to prove to her that it didn't matter whether or not she knew who I was, our souls had called to each other— her light to my dark—and now we were intertwined.

Her soft sigh carried through my headphones and made me want to pull her into my arms and give her what I knew she needed. But not yet. "This would be so much easier if he was you."

My teeth cut through my cheek as I bit down to keep from giving myself away. I hummed a non-committal response instead. I'd save the big reveal for when she followed through. "When are you going to do it?"

"I don't know. Maybe this weekend." I made a mental note to clear everything off my schedule.

"Luna?"

"Hmm?"

"I'm holding you to that. If you don't ask him, I won't let you come for a week." Realistically I wasn't stupid. I knew she could get herself off if she wanted, but there was something about our relationship, some trust we'd built that my instincts told me she wouldn't. She was just as invested in our little game as I was.

"Yes, sir." Her not-so-innocent grin was obvious in her voice, and I growled into the microphone as my dick hardened again in my jeans. Moon Mayhem was going to kill me.

The five of us met on the sidewalk outside the studio the next day. Maddox, Zen, True, and I all wore matching pissed the fuck off looks on our faces. Griffin, he looked a little lost. "Get your fucking head in the game. I know you're new, but we go in there as one solid unit. Don't let that motherfucker sense even one weakness he can exploit later," I snapped at him.

"Ease up, Jericho," Maddox warned as he took a step closer to his little brother.

I shifted my eyes over to meet his. "No, I don't think I will. We've all been doing this too fucking long, and you know exactly how people like Dick are. The second we tell him he's out, he'll start looking for ways to claw his way back in."

Zen sighed and ran a hand through his hair. "Jericho's right. No one loses their temper and hits him, and we say as little as possible."

"And I've already got my phone ready to record the whole thing," True adds, waving his phone at us.

"Let's get this bullshit over with," I finally ordered, and I led the guys inside.

Dick—I refused to call him Richard anymore because to me, he was just a huge fucking dick—was sitting in his chair and scrolling through his phone. He looked up when he heard us come in and plastered his fake-ass smile on his face, the one that didn't reach his calculating eyes. "I hope you all came ready to work after the other day. You didn't leave me with anything usable."

I wanted to scoff, but I held back. I took those same files home and turned them into a song that I thought could be our first single off the new album. Dick didn't know shit about our music, or maybe music in general. "We did come ready to work as a matter of fact," Zen started, but I cut him off.

"You're fired. Get the fuck out." Maddox stepped up beside me so our shoulders were almost touching, and he glared down at where Dick still sat in his chair. He hadn't moved, had barely even reacted when the words left my mouth.

"Did Jericho stutter?" Maddox asked him, narrowing his eyes into one hell of a glare.

Dick sat up straighter and started scrolling through his phone again. "You can't fire me. Marcus personally hired me for this project. He's the only one who can fire me."

I leaned down so I was towering over him, and he existed only in my shadow. "Let me make this perfectly fucking clear. You. Are. Fired. Whether you leave or not is unimportant. We don't have to record here, so either you get the fuck out, or we do. Either way, you're done." The muscles in my back and arms tensed with the need to hit something, but I swallowed the feeling down. I would not lose control. No matter the hurricane raging inside of me, I never let that shit out. I was a master of hiding the depths of my emotions.

He made no move to leave, so I spun on my heel and trusted the guys would follow me. Their footsteps sounded behind me as I made my way to the front door. Just as I pushed it open, Dick made his move. "Get back here! You can't walk out. The label-"

Zen was closest to Dick and turned back to handle him. I watched with a blank expression on my face. Zen got in his face but didn't lay a single finger on him. "Didn't you hear us? We don't give a single fuck what the label wants. We're done with you."

"I'll sue! The label will take you to court. All you're doing is wasting everyone's time," he sputtered annoyingly, his face turning that unhealthy red-purple shade again.

"Then fucking sue. We're out." Griffin held the door for Zen but let it slam in Dick's face. He rammed his palm against the glass, but all of us ignored him as a unit. We were done being held hostage by the goddamn label. There was only one thing I truly cared about in this entire world, and that was my music. A set of turquoise eyes flashed across my mind, but I pushed the dangerous thoughts away. My music was my life, and no one would threaten it without paying the price. If the label tried to fight us on this, I'd make sure they burned to the ground, and we rose from the ashes like the motherfucking phoenixes we were.

SEVEN
MOON

Damn WickedExecutioner and his demands.

How did I let myself get tangled up with someone like him? I wasn't the kind of girl who liked being told what to do. I was a free spirit. I let my mood take me wherever it wanted. Outside of my business, I didn't make plans. I lived spontaneously, trying to experience as much as I could. Having limitations put on me? That was the opposite of how I wanted to live.

And yet Wicked drew me in. At first, it was because he was safe, a fantasy come to life in an intangible way. I could spend a few hours a week with him online and not lose myself. I could let him make decisions. Turned out, sometimes being spontaneous was stressful because I never felt like I was doing enough, *experiencing enough.*

Life had so much to offer, and if I wanted to spend the night watching Netflix, guilt weighed on me. Was I wasting my precious time? I'd been going hard at life for years now, and sometimes it felt like I was moving in quicksand. The faster and harder I moved, the deeper I sank. It might be fucked up, but Wicked offered me a break from the unending expectations of myself, even if only for a minute.

The weight of having to live for my mom was heavy.

I pulled the crumpled piece of paper out of my pocket and studied it. Just ten digits, but they meant so much more. I hadn't dated anyone in months because my impulsiveness threatened every man I'd ever given a shot. A five-year plan? No, thanks. Did I want to settle down someday? Sure, if I met the right person. But did I want to plan out every single detail? Not a chance in hell.

I didn't know what was holding me back. It was just one phone call. He might not even remember me or want to go out. It wasn't like he gave me his number himself or tried to get mine. His friend slipped it to me. *Ugh.*

Before I could overthink it any more, I pulled out my phone and entered the number, but then I changed my mind. I jumped off my couch and grabbed my laptop, pulling up the program I used to keep track of the students taking my yoga classes. I clicked on the search bar and typed in *Kennedy Taylor.* Deleting out Jericho's number, I plugged hers in instead and hit the *call* button.

"Hello?"

"Kennedy?"

"That's me. Who's this?"

"It's Moon. From yoga?" I twirled a lock of my blue and purple hair around my finger.

I could hear the smile in her voice when she responded, "Ohmygod, Moon! What's going on?"

I bit my lip because this was embarrassing. "I hope I'm not overstepping, but when you passed me Jericho's number, I've been trying to figure out what I wanted to do with it. But I usually don't just call or text a guy to ask them out. It's boring, and there's a chance they could say no."

She laughed. "Truth. So what did you have in mind?"

Time to bite the bullet and fill her in on my crazy idea, one I'd been thinking about all day. "Does your friend Jericho have anything that he's really attached to? Like a picture or a shirt or anything?"

She was quiet for a second, and then it sounded like she snapped her fingers. "I'd say his drums, but they're huge, and I don't know what you have in mind, but he'd probably kill us both if I messed with those. So the next best thing would be his Xbox."

I grinned like an idiot before her words really sunk in. "Wait, drums?"

"You didn't recognize him? Even with the t-shirt?"

T-shirt? "No? Should I have?"

"Well, going into this, you should know that he's in a band with my husband." She sounded hesitant, but I had no idea why. I distantly remembered her husband being some sort of celebrity.

"...Okay? So they get together and play in the garage or something on weekends?" I wasn't following and didn't understand why she was telling me this. If I convinced him to go out with me, we could talk about our interests on the date.

"No, sweetie. That's their job. How do I put this..." She took a deep breath. "Two years ago, the band—Shadow Phoenix—put out an album, and it sold more copies across the world than any other album. Ever. And that was after they were already massive."

The smile slid off my face. "Wait. What?"

"If you go out with Jericho, you're going to be bringing a lot of unwanted attention to yourself and any possible relationship you might have. Lucky for you, Jericho isn't popular in the media because he always keeps to himself... or tells them to go fuck themselves." She giggled. "Either way, I didn't really know what I was in for when I met Zen. I wanted you to be able to go into this informed."

"So, is he like a celebrity or something?" My brain was not processing what she was telling me.

"One of the most popular in the world," Kennedy confirmed.

My heart raced, but it wasn't from nerves. I wasn't freaking out. I was itching for the experience, to see what it'd be like to date someone famous. It wasn't that I wanted the attention. I definitely didn't. It was that I imagined his life was exciting and glamorous, and I wanted to peek in on it and see what all the fuss was about.

Did I actually care about money or fame? Not even a little bit. But the excitement? The adventure? Sign me up.

"Are you okay?" Kennedy wondered when I didn't say anything right away. "Maybe it was a stupid idea to give you his number."

I couldn't let her think that. I wasn't upset, just thinking it all over. I usually didn't take long to make a decision and jump in with both feet. "I'm great. Curious and a little bit excited, honestly."

"Excited?" She sounded weary, as if she was afraid I was a groupie or something. "About which part? I was horrified when I had to deal with a swarm of photographers for the first time."

"Not about that part," I assured her. "About the part where he's had all these experiences I'd never get a chance to hear about otherwise, or about how he's probably traveled the world and seen so much. Getting a glimpse of that excites me."

She exhaled loudly, and I imagined it was in relief. She seemed really protective over Jericho. "I'm glad to hear that." Her voice perked up. "Now, tell me about your plan."

I'd spent the last day buried in Google search after Google search, trying to plan the perfect date for Jericho and me. I didn't know him at all except for the seconds I'd spent with him and what Kennedy told me. Oh, and all the questionably accurate shit on the internet, but I took all of that with a grain of salt. I didn't learn anything useful other than he'd never once been spotted with a girl or a guy as a date.

I clicked out of my search window and opened a map instead. From what I could tell, Jericho was a serious guy. He didn't really let loose, which checked out with how he acted in my class, too. He was stiff and seemed uncomfortable. I smiled to myself when I thought about shoving him outside his rigid life and having some fun tomorrow.

Knuckles rapped on my door, and I jumped up, checking the peephole before I opened the door. I still had that creepy feeling I was being watched, but I hadn't seen anyone, so I started to think I might be going a little bit crazy.

"Perfect timing," I declared while swinging the door open to reveal a grinning Kennedy with a tote bag slung over her shoulder. I gestured for her to come in, and she stepped inside. "Where's the little man?"

She rolled her eyes and laughed. "With his daddy. I couldn't pry him away."

I chuckled and closed the door. I hadn't met Kennedy's husband but based on what she told me on the phone yesterday, I could only imagine what her husband might be like. I never pictured rockers as parents. It didn't really fit the image.

She whirled back around to face me. "Look, I can't stay, but I wanted to make sure you had this for tomorrow. Text me and let me know how it goes." She handed me the tote bag, and I glanced inside as a slow smile crossed my face.

"Thanks for this. Hopefully, he doesn't kill me." She squeezed my arm gently on her way past me and out the door. At this point, there was no turning back. Hopefully, my plan worked out.

Blinking the grit out of my eyes, I stumbled to the kitchen to make coffee. I'd barely slept last night as my mind ran over every possible scenario that could go down today. Best case, Jericho would think what I'd done was cute and go along with my plan. Worst case, he'd think I was nuts, cuss me out, and I'd never see him again. My stomach clenched at the thought of that last one.

I poured my coffee and sipped it as the fog slowly cleared. Glancing at the clock on the stove, I realized I didn't have much time to get ready before I needed to send the text. Kennedy assured me she'd make sure Jericho didn't have anything on his schedule today, and she said she'd enlist her husband and the other guys in the band if she had to.

Dumping the rest of the bitter liquid into the sink, I rinsed the mug and headed for the shower. The next hour passed in a blur as I washed, dried, and curled my colorful hair into beachy waves. I kept the eye makeup neutral except for the black lining my eyes and the mascara, both of which I thought made my blue-green eyes stand out.

Finally, I pulled my outfit on, opting for distressed cutoff denim shorts and a black crop tank top. I hoped we'd be doing a lot of walking today, so I slid into my Birks. The tote bag Kennedy dropped off yesterday was sitting by the front door, and I hefted it onto my shoulder as I stepped out my front door, making sure to lock it behind me.

Almost instantly, all the tiny hairs on the back of my neck lifted with that stupid awareness of someone watching me. Trying to be nonchalant, I glanced over my shoulder, scanning the street, but nothing seemed out of the ordinary. I shook off the feeling, kicking myself for being so paranoid. Maybe I needed to meditate more, and the stress of the shop and not knowing what I was doing with my life was starting to get to me.

Instead of thinking about it, I got into the car, turned up the music on my drive and sang along as loud as I could. The drive to the bakery didn't take long, and as soon as I stepped out of the car, I reached over to the passenger seat and grabbed the tote bag. My phone was gripped in one hand, and I held the Xbox in the other and snapped a picture of just my hand holding onto the machine. Then I typed out a text.

Moon: If you ever want to see your Xbox again, meet me at *Buttercream Bakery* in one hour.

I set the pilfered Xbox back in the tote bag and stuck it in my trunk, not wanting it to be stolen while I went inside for breakfast. It didn't take long for my phone to vibrate with a response, and my lips curled up into a smile as I read the message.

Jericho: Who the fuck is this? And how did you get that?

Moon: Less questioning, more driving. You wouldn't want to lose out on all the save data.

Jericho: I'm going to kill you.

Moon: Can't kill me unless you show up, now can you?

My heart was beating like a hummingbird lived in my chest, and my adrenaline was pumping. Somehow when Jericho said he'd kill me, I thought he sort of meant it. He had that look in his eye, that darkness like he was capable of anything, and if he ever let the monster out, he wouldn't have boundaries.

Why the hell did that excite me when it should scare me away?

I thought about it while I ate a cupcake for breakfast, lost in thought as the sweet vanilla sponge melted on my tongue. Forty-five minutes later, I'd long since finished my cupcake and stared out of the window people watching. I rarely ever sat still and just watched the world around me. I liked interacting with the world, engaging with it in case I missed out on anything. There was something peaceful about sitting here being an observer. It was a good distraction from the anticipation humming through my body. I was terrified Jericho would reject me and think this whole idea was stupid. And if he didn't like it, he'd never like me because this kind of date was who I was.

Spontaneous and a little bit crazy.

A breeze caught my hair as the door opened. Jericho walked in wearing a black baseball hat pulled down low over his eyes, but I knew it was him. He had this confidence about him that drew me in. The black t-shirt he wore hugged his muscles and showed off the ink running down his arms and creeping up his neck. My fingers ached to trace the black lines engraved in his skin, but I locked my hands together around my empty coffee cup instead.

His jaw was locked tight and he looked pissed off, but I expected that. He had no idea what he was walking into, and I was surprised he hadn't brought anyone with him. For all he knew, I could have been a stalker or a crazed fan. He stalked deeper into the little bakery, every step getting closer and closer to where I sat.

He finally stopped in front of my booth and looked down. As soon as my eyes locked with his, it was like all the people around us disappeared. The noise, the colors, everything faded into the background as I fell into his darkening eyes. Eyes that drilled me with a look filled with wicked promises.

"Moon." His clipped tone let me know that despite his gaze being full of promise, he was pissed off at me for luring him here this way. At least he wasn't yelling.

"Jericho." I could play this game. "Want to sit?"

He eyed me before surprising me by sliding in next to me instead of across. Our thighs touched, and I was suddenly surrounded by his scent and the heat coming off his skin. He smelled like fresh air and danger, and I wanted to breathe him in. He leaned close to me and ran his fingers across my jaw, gripping my chin between his thumb and index finger, but his touch was gentle. He turned my head so I was forced to look into his eyes.

"Why did you steal my Xbox from me?" His eyes probed deep into mine, and I knew I couldn't hide anything from him when he looked at me like that.

"I didn't steal it. I borrowed it."

"But why my Xbox specifically?"

I lifted one shoulder before dropping it back down. "Kennedy said outside of your drums, it's your favorite thing. I had to make it something you'd want to get back, or you wouldn't have shown up."

"Hm." The noise sounded almost like a growl from deep in his throat as his thumb stroked the skin at my jawline, making it hard to concentrate. "And why did you want me to show up?"

"I thought we could go on a date." He dropped his hand from my skin as if I were on fire and broke the hypnotizing eye contact when he looked away, clenching his jaw.

"I don't date."

"Then I guess you'll never get your Xbox back since I'm going to keep it if you turn me down." I tried to ignore how much I missed his hands on my skin and shoved away the disappointment that he didn't seem like he would go for the idea.

He looked back at me but I couldn't read the expression in his eyes. The shadow from the hat he wore made his already dark eyes into black pools that were impossible to interpret. Finally, he sighed and surprised me when he reached for one of my hands still gripping the coffee cup. He wove his fingers through mine as if he wanted to touch me just as badly as I wanted to touch him, even if he hated it. He couldn't seem to help himself, and something about that made me light up inside.

"One date?"

I nodded. "But I get to choose what we do and for how long."

"Fuck. Fine." His words seemed less than excited, but his body leaned closer to mine, and he gripped my hand in his like he was afraid I'd take it away.

"Great. Let's go. The gates are about to open." I used my other hand to push against his bulk, but he didn't even budge.

"Gates?"

"Yep. So move, or we're going to get trampled trying to get to the best rides." He finally slid out of the booth but didn't let go of my hand. Even though he didn't know where we were going, he led the way out of the bakery but stopped when we were outside.

"Do you want to take my Jetta or-"

"We'll take my car. Leave yours here, and we'll come back for it later." A shiver ran through my body at his commanding tone. There was something about him that reminded me of Wicked, the same authority in his voice that left me wanting to do nothing but obey.

I nodded as he led me to his Range Rover and opened the door. He waited for me to get in and reached up to grab the seat belt and pull it across my body. His fingers brushed my hip as he locked it in place, and goosebumps erupted across my skin. Just one touch from him through my clothes and every nerve ending in my body was at attention, begging for him to touch me again. How did he do that?

Jericho held his hand just over the exposed sliver of skin where my tank top didn't quite meet the top of my shorts like he was in a trance, mesmerized by that tiny bit of flesh, but he shook his head quickly, and the spell was broken. He didn't look at me once as he moved away and shut the door.

As he walked around to the driver's seat, I let out a shaky breath. I'd never been so affected by someone before in my life. I had a feeling I was in way over my head, in danger of drowning, and with no clue how to get myself out.

Or if I even wanted to.

He slid his powerful body behind the wheel, and I watched the muscles flex and shift under his clothes as he settled in and pushed the button to start the engine. He finally looked my way, and it was as if he were swallowing me whole with just his gaze. With Jericho, somehow the world didn't matter when he looked my way. It happened the first time I saw him, but I chalked it up to the fact I had low blood sugar from skipping breakfast and hadn't ever had a man take my mommy and me class.

But my body's reaction to him wasn't a one-time thing and it wasn't going away. If anything, with every look and every touch, he was feeding my habit, making me crave him more and more. Getting close to him would be dangerous, but at this point, I didn't know if I could stop. I wanted to crawl under his skin and make him itch for me like I did for him.

It was a good thing I didn't plan out my future because I found myself suddenly willing to break all the rules for the stranger beside me with the tarnished soul.

"Where are we going?" he finally asked, and I had no idea how long I'd been lost in his eyes this time.

My lips curved up into a smile. "The happiest place on earth."

EIGHT
JERICHO

Fucking *Disneyland*.

I couldn't imagine anywhere worse for a date. Kids screaming, long lines in the heat, crowds. It was like my version of the ninth circle of hell. But Moon's eyes lit up as we got our tickets and went inside, and she smiled so wide, I felt it in my chest.

How could I deny her something that made her happy?

She grabbed my hand and tugged me forward through Main Street's bright colors and nostalgic vibe toward the giant castle straight ahead. The guys and I had come here a few times, gotten drunk, and rode the rides, but I'd never come sober or with a girl. I had no idea what she planned or expected of me.

She stopped in front of Cinderella's castle and reached into her purse before she pulled out something I couldn't quite make out and then shoved it on my head. "What the fuck?"

She laughed and pulled a hat with mouse ears and a bow onto her head. "You've gotta do the full experience, Jericho."

I reached up and felt my own hat and ears. Fuck.

"I got you classic black to match your eyes," she joked, poking me in the ribs with her finger.

"My eyes are brown."

"Sometimes," she agreed. "But even then, they look almost black. Anyway, come take a selfie with me."

She lifted my arm around her shoulders and burrowed into my side. "Smile," she ordered, grinning up at me, and I looked down at her face so full of happiness and her eyes so full of light I never wanted to forget how she looked at this moment.

"There. That wasn't so hard now, was it?" I looked down at her phone screen, and even I had to admit we looked good together—her bright smile at the camera and me looking at her like my world revolved around her, even with those stupid fucking ears on my head.

"Hey, text me that," I demanded, and she eyed me like she was trying to decide if I was serious. Soon she'd find out just how serious I was when it came to her. She didn't know it yet, but she was mine. I had no idea when I'd become this version of myself, the possessive asshole who was jealous of things like phones and friends because it meant sharing the girl I was into.

It was more than that, though. I wasn't just *into* her. I wanted her to want me, to need me, to be as possessive of me as I was of her. Moon texted the picture of us to me and then slid her phone into her back pocket. She adjusted her purse, but I didn't move my arm from around her shoulders. I also didn't take off the stupid fucking hat. If it made her happy, I could endure it for one day.

"Where to?" I plucked the map she'd grabbed on our way in out of the top of her bag and unfolded it with one hand.

"How about I pick a ride, and then you pick a ride, and we see where the day takes us?" I resisted the desire to put my foot down and demand we make a full itinerary. Spontaneity gave me fucking hives, and the thought of having no idea where we were going next or how long we'd be here today or where we were going to eat lunch was almost too much. A familiar urge to press for control started to claw its way through my veins, and I clenched my jaw to keep from lashing out and forcing her to bend to my will.

But then Moon started walking without waiting for my answer, and if I didn't want to stop touching her, I had no choice but to follow along beside her. "Alice in Wonderland is one of my favorite rides. When the flowers sing, it makes me happy."

"Does everything make you happy?" I lifted my hand off her shoulder and ran it through the colorful strands of her hair, playing with her waves.

A dark shadow crept across her expression, but it was gone almost as quickly as it came. She shook her head. "I'm human, Jericho. Things bother me and make me upset or uncomfortable or scare me just like anyone else. The difference is I try not to let those feelings grab ahold of me. I want to live as much life as I can, and if I let myself get bogged down in all the negativity the world has to offer, I'd find myself depressed and unable to get up off the couch. That's not a great place to participate in the world."

We walked in silence, or as silent as a theme park can be, for a few minutes while I thought about her words. "Isn't it fucking exhausting being happy all the time?"

She tensed up against me before she relaxed again as we got into line for the ride. A forty-five-minute wait for some singing flowers? Now I remembered another reason why I hated this place.

She reached up and took my hand that was playing with her hair and laced her fingers with mine instead, leaning her head against my shoulder. Her stupid plastic mouse ears tickled my jaw, but I barely noticed as the rest of my body was sparking to life with her close proximity. "Sometimes," she finally admitted. "Sometimes I wish I could just spend the weekend lounging on the couch eating junk food and binging shows. But that's not my life."

"Why?" The line moved forward a couple of inches, and we shuffled forward.

"This is heavy first date talk. Are you sure you want to go there?"

I nodded. I wanted to know everything about her, but most of all, I wanted to know what made her tick. I wanted to dismantle her piece by piece and figure out her every like and dislike, what made her sad or cheered her up, what made her feel safe, and what she was scared of. I wanted to know every single detail that made up Moon Mayhem down to the very last thought in her head. I wanted to own every cell in her body, every thought in her mind, every hope, dream, wish, and fear. Everything of hers was going to become mine to safeguard, to worship, and to satisfy.

Like I said, she was already mine; she just didn't know it yet.

"Okay, well, growing up, my family was perfect. My mom and dad were in love, and they loved me. I adored them, and we were close. I'm not one of those people who came out of early childhood with scars. My wounds came later." Moon moved even closer, and it was my turn to tense up because someone hurt my girl. It may have been a long time ago, but they would fucking pay for causing her pain.

I forced myself to relax and focused back on Moon as she kept going. "A little after I turned twelve, my mom started acting weird. She withdrew into herself, and dad and I couldn't figure out what was wrong. I thought I did something to push her away."

Her face was so expressive, and the depth of her sadness took me by surprise. So much time had passed, I wouldn't have thought her wounds would still be this fresh. She looked anguished, her eyes shining with unshed tears, and I leaned down and brushed my lips against her forehead. It wasn't a kiss of passion, but one of support and comfort. I wanted her to know she could tell me anything.

We slowly continued moving through the line as she talked. "She stopped spending time with me, and basically shut us completely out until finally she just disappeared."

My eyes narrowed as I studied her. "What do you mean 'disappeared'?"

"I went to bed one night, and when I woke up the next morning, the front door was wide open, and she was gone. I've never seen or heard from her again. The cops thought with the front door open it might have been kidnapping or something, but there wasn't any proof one way or the other, so she just remains a missing person case. I have no idea if she's alive or dead, but I like to think that if she were alive, she'd have come back to us. The mom I knew up until those last few months would've done anything in her power to make it back to me, and she never has. So I figure she's probably dead."

I squeezed her hand as we moved forward some more. "She might not be." Based on what Moon told me, and considering I wasn't an optimistic guy, she was probably right, and her mom was dead. But there was a slight possibility she wasn't. I made a mental note to talk to Connor about it.

Moon shrugged. "If she isn't, that means she purposefully walked away from my dad and me. That hurts almost as bad as if she died, the fact she didn't want me enough to stay."

I let her go and stepped in front of her until she stood only an inch away.

I gripped her chin between my fingers, relishing in the feel of her smooth skin against mine. Her eyes slowly lifted. "No one who knew you could ever not want you. You're magic and light and all that's good in the world. You attract even the darkest and most depraved people like me because we want to get close enough to have you shine a little bit of your goodness on us. So don't you ever fucking tell me that she walked away from you because you weren't wanted. It's not possible, and I won't have you talk about yourself like that."

The strength of my feelings for this woman already was shaking my stable foundation, and the intensity of emotion coiled inside of me where she was concerned was unprecedented. I never expected to feel this way about anyone, yet here I was ready to defend Moon from even her own harsh words about herself.

The look in her eyes slowly transformed from agony to wonder as she took in what I said. She reached her hand up to run along my jawline and caress my cheek, lifting up on her toes until her mouth was a breath away. "Is that really how you see me?" Her eyes hadn't left mine, and I struggled to contain the wild joy running through me at the look in her eyes when she looked at me.

I nodded once because I didn't want to speak, and she closed the distance between us, brushing her lips against mine. But with that first press of her soft, pillowy lips, I took over and devoured her with my kiss like a man starved. And maybe I was, starved for love and affection and something deeper than the life I'd been living until now.

My hand drifted down her back, my fingertips gently running along the slivers of bare skin at her back and her neck where her shirt dipped. She shivered under my touch as she matched the intensity of my kiss with her own. Her lips fit to mine like they'd always been meant to be there, and her taste fulfilled a craving I never knew I had. With this kiss, it was like everything came into focus, like the world around me had been blurry until Moon swept in, and suddenly I could see clearly.

Someone behind us cleared their throat, and I pulled back, hugging her close to me while I glared at the middle-aged man behind me. Were we at the most family place that existed? Sure. But did I give a fuck when it came to getting lost in my girl?

Not a single one.

She sighed as she leaned her cheek against my chest, and I wasn't sure there had ever been anything more perfect than this moment. My instinct was to tuck her into my side and protect her from the world, to wrap her up in me until I was all she could see and carry her off to my house where no one could ever hurt her again. I wanted to tie her to my bed and fully make her mine like I'd done over the game we played together so many times. But she didn't know I was WickedExecutioner. She didn't know that I knew who she really was—not just LunaGirl but Moon Mayhem. She didn't know that I knew how she liked my controlling tendencies, that she got off on them just like I did.

After a fucking eternity waiting in the hot sun, we climbed into the ride, and Moon gripped my hand in hers. It wasn't a thrill ride, more of a slow wandering through a psychedelic drug trip. At least that's how Alice in Wonderland always seemed to me, and this was no different. I stopped watching my surroundings and instead watched Moon light up and gasp and laugh as she watched as we passed through the different scenes.

When we finally got off the ride, she climbed out but never let my hand go. I had never been a touchy-feely guy, and affection usually made me uncomfortable, but Moon was the exception. I had a feeling she'd always be the exception to every one of my rules.

Once we were free and clear of the ride, she spun around and threw her arms around my waist, leaning back to look me in the eye. "Your turn. What are we going on next?"

I grinned wickedly at her. "I hope you like being wet."

Her lips parted, and her pupils dilated, and I immediately regretted my choice of words because now I'd be walking around Disneyland with a hard-on. Moon's face was so expressive I could practically see every lust-filled thought working its way through her imagination, and I wanted to act them all out.

Every. Single. One.

"It just so happens I do," she finally answered after shaking her head adorably as if I couldn't see what she was thinking about.

I ran my hand over her side, pushing the fabric of her shirt up a little with the movement and tracing my thumb across her ribs until I was brushing the underside of her perfect, soft tit. "Why don't we see how wet I can make you?" I murmured near her ear.

Her eyes widened, and she looked around. "Here?"

I laughed and leaned over, dropping a kiss on her sweet lips. "No, in Critter Country."

Her eyebrows furrowed. "What?"

I let out a low chuckle and pulled her closer to me. "We're going on Splash Mountain." I let her go, and she gaped at me before whacking me in the arm.

"That wasn't funny! You got me all," she gestured wildly with her hands seemingly at a loss for words.

"All what?"

She pushed me again, and I laughed. "You don't play fair."

"Never said I did." I wrapped my arm around her waist and stuck my hand in the back pocket of her shorts. Leaning over, I whispered in her ear, "Now be a good girl, and maybe later, I'll show you how wet I can make you in a different way."

She sucked in a breath but didn't say anything, which was exactly the reaction I hoped she'd have. Moon may be chaotic and impulsive, but she was also submissive where it counted—in my bedroom. A perfect fit for me and my need for control.

After we did a couple more rides, Moon declared it was time for lunch. We walked into New Orleans Square and found a restaurant. She excused herself to the bathroom, and I made a phone call to Montana because if Moon wanted to do the Disney experience, I'd show her how good I could make it. I shoved my phone back into my pocket as she made her way back toward me.

I couldn't tear my eyes off of her as she got closer and a shy smile I didn't know she had crossed her face. The girl didn't seem like she had a shy bone in her body.

We took our time eating, and Moon filled me in on her best friend and their weird antics and adventures and her dad and how their relationship was close, but she could see that he struggled because she reminded him of her mom. Moon's dad had never given up hope she was still alive and would come back to him someday.

I was starting to understand how he felt. Now that Moon was in my life,

I couldn't handle going back to the monotone existence I'd been living up until now. I didn't do a lot of talking, but I was fine with that. Outside of my career, there wasn't a whole lot interesting about me. I wasn't close to my family, my friends were all in the band or worked for the band, and my hobbies were all mostly solitary activities. I was happy to indulge in Moon's need to share all of her vibrant stories with me.

Moon tried to pay for the check, and I gave her my coldest glare. True, she asked me on this date, but there wasn't a chance in hell I'd let her pay for anything while we were on it. When we stood to leave, my hand slipped to her lower back as naturally as if it'd always been meant to be there. Her skin was hot underneath my palm, and electricity rushed through my body at the contact.

When we stepped outside, there was a man in a Disney polo shirt waiting for us. "Mr. Cole?"

"That's me." I stepped forward and shook his hand briefly because he held it out for me, and I figured if I smacked it away that'd be rude.

"If you'll follow me," he started, turning and walking off, continuing to talk, but I tuned him out. Instead, I turned my attention to my girl, whose forehead was wrinkled as she watched him.

"Who's he?" she finally asked.

I shrugged my shoulders. "Someone who works for the park. I called my manager and had her request a private escort. We can get on any ride without a line, and then later, I've got another surprise for you."

She huffed. "This was supposed to be *my* date. I planned it."

"And now I'm using the benefits I get for being a *celebrity*," I rolled my eyes, "to let us experience more than we would have been able to otherwise. Isn't that what you're all about? Experiencing as much as you can?"

She opened her mouth to protest and then slammed it shut again. I had her there, and she fucking knew it. Moon finally leaned into me as we followed our escort through the park. "You're lucky Kennedy told me about what you do before I asked you out because I would be freaking out right now if I hadn't had time to process it."

I chuckled darkly. "It wouldn't have made a difference in the end, though, and we both know it."

"What's that supposed to mean?" She looked up at me and narrowed her eyes.

"Don't act like you don't fucking want me, like you don't feel the connection between us. You might be able to lie to yourself, but you can't lie to me."

Moon lifted her chin. "I never said I don't feel it. I just wanted you to explain."

"So, you admit you feel drawn to me?"

She stopped walking, and we faced each other. I had no idea where the escort was going, and I didn't give a shit. Her turquoise eyes lifted to meet mine. "When I look at you like this, it's like the entire world disappears. Nothing else matters or exists but you and me. I don't care about anything else. I don't *want* anything or anyone else." She tore her eyes away and shook her head. "I've never felt like this before, and when I say it out loud, it sounds really unhealthy."

I tucked my fingers under her chin and tilted her face up to mine again. "And what would you do if I wanted to see other people or let another woman touch me?"

Her eyes narrowed, and her lips pressed into a line. "No one gets to touch you but me." The sick, twisted bits inside me rejoiced at her proclamation because I felt the exact same fucking way.

"Same goes for you, beautiful girl. If another man so much as touches you, I'll make sure he'll never use that hand again." I hoped she didn't underestimate how serious I was about her or what I'd do to someone who touched what was mine.

Our guide made his way back over to us and waited nearby. A few people were starting to take notice and pull out their phones. I was going to end up all over the fucking internet with the stupidest fucking hat known to man, and I couldn't even be upset about it because if it happened, publicly Moon would be the first girl I'd ever been photographed with, and I was fine with that.

Considering this was our first official date, it seemed fast to proclaim anything publicly, but I'd been talking to LunaGirl online for months. We were more than compatible; we fit each other like a lock and key.

Moon studied me but finally turned back to the guide and gave him an apologetic smile. "Sorry. Lead on."

The sun was starting to set as we stumbled off the last ride of the day. We managed to go on at least half the rides in the park, and it turned out Corey, our guide, was actually a decent guy. He didn't hit on Moon once, but I caught him watching me a few times throughout the day, which I was perfectly happy with. If he'd done the same to my girl, we would've had problems, so his interest in me meant I could enjoy the day in peace.

Corey led us back to Main Street and told us to wait on the sidewalk until it got dark. As soon as the sun was fully set, he pulled us into the middle of the street. I moved Moon in front of me so her back rested against my chest, and I wrapped my arms around her while she leaned against me. I nuzzled my face into her neck and hair, inhaling her sweet strawberry scent. "Did you have fun today?" I murmured.

She sighed contentedly. "I don't know if I've ever had more fun. Thanks for agreeing to come with me."

"Anything for you, beautiful. And next time, you don't even have to kidnap my Xbox. You can send me a text anytime, anywhere, and I'll be there."

She spun in my arms just as the fireworks began to burst overhead, lighting her beautiful features up in vibrant flashes of color. "Same goes for you."

I ran my thumb along the velvety skin of her cheek. "I need to tell you something." Maybe this wasn't the right time, but I'd learned from past mistakes, and I wouldn't start a relationship with Moon off on a lie. I couldn't let things with her go further until she knew the truth about me.

She leaned into my touch and stared up at me, waiting for me to speak. I brushed her wild hair away from her face, delaying for just a minute longer telling her the truth. "We already know each other. Well, sort of."

That adorable wrinkle between her eyebrows popped up, and I smoothed it out with my finger. "How is that possible? I would've remembered meeting you before."

"Not if it wasn't face to face."

"I don't know what that means."

"It means I'm WickedExecutioner."

NINE
MOON

My forehead wrinkled in confusion. "What?"

"I'm WickedExecutioner; you're LunaGirl." Jericho brushed the hair back from my face and stared into my eyes, but I needed some distance to process. I pushed lightly on his chest to get him to step back, and I closed my eyes to think.

Could that be possible? What were the odds that not only was my occasional online hookup and gaming buddy an internationally famous musician but also that he lived nearby *and* had attended one of my yoga classes?

Bexley would say it was fate or divine intervention. Maybe she'd be right. I didn't believe in coincidences. I opened my eyes and watched him as he watched me. His gaze was filled with something like concern, though I wasn't sure that was quite it. Maybe he was afraid I'd yell and scream and run. But in reality, I almost wanted to laugh.

The situation was ridiculous, and a giggle bubbled up and I couldn't hold it back.

Fireworks continued to explode overhead, lighting Jericho's face up in color and then casting his already dark features in shadow. Our private conversations in our game over the past few months ran through my head, and I bit my lip. Jericho knew every deep, dark desire I'd never admitted to anyone else.

And he knew exactly how to fulfill every single one of my fantasies.

His eyes darkened even more as he watched me as if he was reading my mind, and they dropped to where I still held my lip between my teeth. The pad of his thumb tugged my lip out from between my teeth, and he rubbed it gently. Every cell in my body screamed to lean in closer, to press up onto my toes, and steal the kiss I wanted so badly.

"Fuck, Moon. Stop looking at me like that." Jericho's voice was low and husky as he dragged his eyes back up to mine. "Tell me what you're thinking."

My fingers snaked up the side of his neck, tracing his ink, and I tugged him closer until our lips were only a breath apart. "I'm thinking," I dragged the words out slowly, and he groaned as I ran my fingernails through the short hairs at the back of his head. "I couldn't be happier that you're Wicked." I brushed my lips across his before he pulled back in surprise, his eyes searching mine.

"You're *happy*? That sure as fuck isn't what I was expecting you to say."

I tugged him back down to me. "You should probably know now I don't like doing what's expected of me."

His dark chuckle sent tingles throughout my body and made my lower belly clench in anticipation. "You're going to test every single bit of my patience, aren't you?" He brushed his nose back and forth against mine but never closed the tiny space between our lips. My senses were in overdrive, begging him to lean in, but he never did.

"Probably," I admitted, a smile tugging at my lips. "But, I'll be worth it."

"Oh, baby. I do not doubt that." And then he leaned in, and I was lost in his kiss. This was a kiss staking ownership, claiming me as his for the world to see if they dared look our way. My knees went weak with the bruising force of his lips on mine, the way he demanded entrance as if nothing could keep him away. I was sinking in his taste, drowning in the feel of his body against mine.

I wanted more.

So much more.

A soft moan worked its way up my throat as my fingers drifted down the hard planes of his body to fist in the soft cotton of his shirt, gripping it and pulling him closer. No matter how much closer we moved to each other, I had a feeling it would never be close enough.

We finally broke apart as the crowd shuffled around us, the fireworks show now over as they dispersed into the dark night. We both panted, but neither of us moved further away from each other. There was virtually no space between us. We'd eliminated nearly every molecule that stood in the way of our bodies pressing together. I wanted to sink in Jericho's warmth, press my soft curves to his hardened muscles, and as I looked up into his eyes, I gasped at the dark promise held there.

Oh, we weren't done. Not by a long shot.

"Park's closing. Please exit in an orderly fashion," a bored-sounding park employee announced, and it broke the spell. I shook my head lightly and stepped back, dropping his now rumpled t-shirt from my grip, but he grabbed my wrist, lifting it to his lips and pressing a kiss to the underside that made me shiver and left tingles in its wake like fucking magic.

His eyes had darkened to the point that I couldn't tell where his pupils ended, and the deep brown of his irises began. Jericho's blackened gaze ran down my body leaving a trail of goosebumps on my skin. "Fuck. How far away do you live from here?"

I had the same immediate need for somewhere private as he did. "About forty minutes."

He cursed under his breath but laced our fingers together and led me out of the park and back to his car. Once we were inside, I started to give him directions back to the bakery to pick up my car, but he just flashed me a smirk and turned the other way. "I don't know how you celebrities do things, but I need my car. I don't have extras just lying around."

His chuckle wrapped around me, and I had to make a conscious effort to hold on to my irritation. All I wanted to do was melt into everything Jericho, and that was a dangerous place to be. There was a reason I hadn't had a boyfriend in forever. Men tended to want to tie me down and control what I did, and when they didn't get enough of my attention, they bailed.

Resisting Jericho felt impossible, though. It was like he'd already peeled back my skin and burrowed somewhere deep underneath where I'd never dig him out. For months the sound of his voice had been my safe place, the person I ran to when I was scared or stressed, and he took it all away and made me feel protected. And in person? He was hotter than I could have ever hoped.

"Don't worry about your car, beautiful girl. I had someone take it back to your house."

I turned to stare at him, my mouth dropping open. "You *what*? How the hell did you do that?"

"I made a call and had it towed to the address my computer guy had for you." He said the words like that was the easiest thing in the world.

"Why would you do that? I could have driven myself home."

Jericho took his eyes off the road long enough to glance my way before he interlaced our fingers and rested our hands on his thigh. "I wanted to drive you."

I wasn't sure whether to swoon or scream. He hadn't given me the option, just taken over. It was sweet and infuriating at the same time. Mostly, it was nice that he'd been thoughtful enough to think about what came after our date.

Finally, I sighed heavily and leaned over the console to rest my head against his shoulder. I didn't want to ruin the perfect date we just had. "Thank you for taking care of my car and driving me home."

His shoulders relaxed, and he turned to drop a kiss on top of my head. "There's nothing I wouldn't do for you, Moon. Not one single goddamn thing."

If I could only pick one word to describe Jericho, it'd be *intense*. Funnily enough, I didn't hate his intensity. I actually found myself reveling in it. I peeked up at him through my lashes before settling in and closing my eyes with a contented sigh. Being able to lean on Jericho was something I never knew I was missing from my life, and now that he was here, I wasn't sure I wanted to let him go.

I must've fallen asleep because my eyelids fluttered open as the car came to a stop. "Good nap?" Jericho teased as I lifted my head off of his shoulder. I rolled my head from side to side to try and work out the kink in my neck from the awkward position I'd been in for the past half hour.

I yawned and nodded before I hopped out of the car in front of my house. It was dark, and the street was mostly deserted except for a couple of cars parked around us, and my car was in the driveway as promised. As soon as I stepped around to Jericho's side of the car, he slung his arm over my shoulder. It was like he couldn't stop touching me, not that I was complaining.

It'd been a long time since I had any non-platonic affection, and I was soaking it up like a sponge. I pulled out my keys and shoved them in the lock, letting us into my tiny space. I shrugged out from under his arm so I could walk inside. The door frame wasn't exactly meant for two people to cross the threshold at once, at least not like we'd been standing. I spun around and tossed Jericho my keys, giggling as he bobbled them before finally catching them in his palm. "If you want your Xbox back, it's in the trunk of my car."

He laughed, a rich, warm sound I suspected not very many people got to hear. "I'm going to make you pay for that." My thighs clenched together at his dirty vow, and I watched him walk back out the front door, the muscles in his back straining under his black t-shirt.

A few minutes later, he came back in carrying the machine and set it by the front door before he closed and locked it. He tossed my keys on the little table I kept next to the door for exactly that reason, and then he stalked toward me, his eyes hidden under the dark locks of hair that fell over his forehead.

He looked dangerous, like a black hole ready to absorb me and leave nothing behind. I'd never be able to escape the force that was Jericho, reeling me into his orbit. He crashed into me, not stopping to ask permission or move us somewhere more comfortable. His hands roamed my body, almost frantically as we tore at each other between brutal kisses.

My shirt disappeared over my head, and I clawed at his, trying to pull it off. He stepped back and let me, and I dropped it to the floor as his rough fingers ran across my lower back and pulled me into his body.

Heat rushed through me at the feel of his skin on mine, and I let out a soft moan as his erection pushed into my stomach. He never stopped kissing me as his hand slid slowly up my back before unclasping my bra. His lips ripped away from mine as I panted, and he pulled the straps of my bra down my arms. I felt exposed under his heavy stare as he stood back and took his time studying my newly exposed breasts.

I bit my lip and turned to look out the window, uncomfortable under the weight of his stare. It wasn't that I disliked my body, but I could imagine every imperfection that he was seeing, and I couldn't help but compare myself to the perfect modelesque women he must be exposed to every day of his normal life.

His clean scent swirled around me as he stepped closer and the heat of his body seeped into mine. I gasped and covered myself with my arms as someone stepped in front of my window. Jericho's head whipped around as he stepped in front of me. "What's wrong?"

My body trembled as I watched the hooded figure move away as if they knew they'd been caught. I lifted a shaky finger toward the window. "There was just someone there watching."

"Fuck," he bit out and grabbed his shirt off the floor before stalking toward the front door and yanking it open. "Stay here." His tone left no room for argument, and I bent down to gather my clothes. My heart was pounding so hard, I thought it might jump right out of my chest. That window didn't face the street, and I didn't have any neighbors on that side, which meant whoever was looking in on us had meant to do it.

After I pulled my clothes back on, I huddled on the couch, pulling my knees into my chest. I didn't know what had me more freaked out—the person peeping through my window, or Jericho being out there with some mystery creep who could be dangerous. What if he got hurt? Or worse?

I swallowed the lump in my throat and blinked away the stinging tears in my eyes. Jericho was the one that would do the hurting, not be the one to get hurt. Logically, I knew that. But emotionally? He was only human, and I cared about him more than I'd even admitted to myself.

I jumped a little when the front door swung open, and Jericho walked inside, all his muscles coiled and tight, ready for a fight. He raked his hand through his hair and then moved to sit next to me, pulling me into his side and wrapping his arms around me. "Are you okay?"

I nodded and burrowed my face into his neck. "Who was that?" My words were mumbled into his skin.

He hugged me tighter as if he were clinging to me just as much as I was to him. "I couldn't tell, but it was definitely a man. He ran and jumped into a car parked a block down. An old clunker sedan that had nothing defining about it, and from that far away, I couldn't get any details like a plate number or anything. You have any enemies, baby?"

I lifted my head and stared at him incredulously. "Enemies? I run a yoga studio, Jericho. I keep to myself. Who would be my enemy?"

He shrugged. "I didn't want to assume anything. So, maybe you have a stalker situation." He smirked.

"What about this strikes you as funny?" I snapped.

He kissed my nose, and his grin widened. "It's not that someone could be stalking you that's funny. It's that I have a bit of a history with stalkers. The band has a whole team ready to deal with them if that's what this is, so you don't have to worry."

I groaned. "Why does that not make me feel better? What the hell have I gotten myself into with you?"

He held up his hands in surrender. "Hey, you were being watched before you even knew who I really was. That's not on me."

My eyes started to sting again. What the hell was going on? Who was watching me, and what did they want?

Jericho moved even closer, sensing I needed the closeness to deal with how creeped out I felt. "You're going to stay tonight, right?" I whispered, worried he was going to leave me alone here tonight. I'd never once been afraid to stay the night in my own house. I'd lived alone since I was eighteen years old and had never worried about it until right now.

He pressed a kiss to the top of my head and hugged me into his body. "Don't worry, beautiful girl. I'm not going anywhere."

TEN

JERICHO

I'd never been harder than these past three days. Fuck. Spending every night in Moon's bed and not burying myself inside her had both my dick and me on edge. I was fairly certain I had a permanent case of blue balls.

Maybe I was being melodramatic, but my cock was about to stage a revolt, and I couldn't blame him. Her soft curves and sweet scent were driving me insane. I groaned as she ground her tight curves against me in her sleep. Moon was just the right amount of curvy, but she was toned as fuck and flexible, too. I guess yoga really did do a body good.

Despite the torture, there was no fucking way I'd leave her alone while some pervert watched her.

If I didn't have a meeting for the band in an hour, I'd say fuck it and have her screaming my name before she was even fully awake. As it was, I was already cutting it too fucking close.

Sadly, my morning was going to look a lot different than I wanted.

I moved to get out of bed as quietly as I could. Moon was so peaceful as she slept in my arms every night; I was secretly glad to have a reason to stay with her even if I hated that it was because some asshole out there was following her.

Every night I watched her sleep, not wanting the morning to come because it meant having to let her go.

I wanted to kick my own ass for being such a bitch about how I felt about her, but Moon and me? We felt inevitable.

I slipped my clothes on and bent to kiss her on the forehead before I left. I lifted my phone and snapped a picture of her sleeping, knowing I'd probably spend more than half the meeting tuned out and staring at the photo on my phone. I couldn't get enough of her.

Obsessed might be the best word to describe how I felt about Moon. Not in a harmful way, more in a she-consumes-all-my-thoughts-and-I-always-want-to-be-with-her sort of way. And I hadn't even fucked her yet. I shivered when I thought about what her tight pussy would feel like clamped around my cock.

I sucked in a deep breath of cool morning air as I stepped out the front door, trying to convince my dick to stand down. My Range Rover was parked in what had become my usual spot at the curb in front of Moon's house, and I swiveled my head from side to side, looking up and down the street. It'd become a habit to look for the sketchy sedan from a few nights ago. Nothing looked out of place, and I couldn't stand out here all day, so I reluctantly slid behind the wheel and took off.

Every morning I hated leaving just a little bit more than the day before. My life wasn't something I could just ignore, though. People depended on me now more than ever, and I had shit to do. But Moon being on the other side of LA with a fuck ton of traffic between us didn't sit right with me, either. As I merged onto the freeway, I pressed the button on the touchscreen console for Connor.

"Jericho. I've gotta admit I'm surprised to hear from you." His deep voice boomed over my speakers, and I winced and turned the volume down. "I thought you were too badass to ever need a lowly bodyguard like me."

I rolled my eyes. "Yeah, well, I'm also human and can't be in two places at once."

"Ah, so this isn't about you at all," he figured out.

"No, don't say a fucking thing, but I need someone to shadow my girlfriend." A smile tugged at the corner of my mouth. I hadn't talked to Moon about labels yet, but in my mind, that's what she was to me. Actually, she was much, much more.

"Holy shit. I must've woken up in an alternate reality this morning," he started, completely ignoring my threat and laughing his ass off instead. My fingers tightened around the steering wheel. "Jericho Cole calling me for help *and* having a girlfriend? Guess I owe Sebastian fifty bucks."

"I'm going to punch you in the face the next time I see you," I promised.

"Oh, I'd like to see you try."

"Remember what happened the other day in my backyard?"

"That was a lucky fucking hit," he grumbled, suddenly all traces of humor gone out of his voice.

"Sure it was," I mocked. "Who are you going to send? I want someone there in the next hour."

"Hold on." The sound of typing worked its way through the phone. "You want Indy or Ryan?"

"Isn't Ryan with True and Amara?"

"She is, but they don't have anything going on. If you want her with your girl, I can have Indy take over for a couple of days." His serious bodyguard mode was on, and it reassured me. When I couldn't be there with Moon, I needed him or one of his team to be.

"Send Indy. I'll text Moon and let her know." It wasn't that I didn't trust Ryan or think she was capable; it was more that I didn't know who was watching my girl and Indy had been doing the job longer. He'd also be able to destroy anyone who tried to hurt Moon. Ryan hadn't earned that trust with me yet.

"Fine. Anything else?"

"Not sure yet. Have Indy watch out for anything suspicious, and I'll fill him in when I get home this afternoon." I clenched my jaw, realizing too late my slip up.

"Home?" Connor sounded almost gleeful at my accidental admission. The truth was, I had started to think of Moon's house as home. The tiny, disorganized hole-in-the-wall she called home was quickly worming its way into my heart, similar to the girl who lived there.

I'd never been materialistic, so I didn't mind that her place was tiny. Sure, I enjoyed being comfortable and never wanting for anything. I especially loved being able to have everything in my space exactly how I wanted it with no questions asked. When I was a kid, and my parents ignored me in favor of their own miserable lives, I promised myself I'd always live for myself.

If I didn't, who would?

That meant always putting myself first above anything else. At least until I met Zen, Maddox, and True. Even Griffin was weaseling his way underneath my armor, damn him. Exceptions were made for my bandmates a long time ago, but I hadn't let anyone else in since then.

If you let people in, believed the sparkly dream of unconditional love and other fairytale bullshit that doesn't actually exist, you set yourself up for getting your heart ripped out and torn to shreds on a scale words couldn't actually describe.

That'd already happened to me once, and I sure as fuck wasn't going to let it happen again. I was in real danger of letting Moon into the place that I kept locked away, the part of myself I never let anyone into because it'd already been damaged beyond repair. If that piece of me took another hit, I wouldn't be able to recover.

There were no guarantees in life, but if I weren't careful, she'd hold my very existence in the palm of her hand. Hell, maybe she already did.

"I said what I said. Have Indy there in," I glanced at the clock. "Fifty-three minutes." Pressing the *end* button, I stepped on the accelerator a little bit harder, wanting to get this meeting over with and get back to my girl.

Fuck, I was in so much trouble.

"And we'll be headlining? As in on the main stage?" Maddox clarified, leaning forward and resting his forearms on his thighs. I didn't miss the excited gleam in his eye.

Montana nodded, flicking her fiery red hair over her shoulder. "They're setting the lineup now, but they know it's last-minute, so they're willing to make whatever accommodations we have work. This looks like it's going to be the next Coachella. There's no way we're turning it down."

Griffin had his phone out and was tapping at the screen. "What's the festival called again?" He looked up, waiting for Montana's response.

"Fury Fest."

"How very *rock* of them," I drawled, rolling my eyes.

Zen chuckled next to me. "Let's hope the show and venue are more original than the name."

"Forget the name," Montana snapped. "It's easy to remember, and that's all that matters. That and you guys will be headlining. It'll be the perfect place to showcase some of the music from the new album. Test the waters with a live audience."

Sitting up straighter, my pulse quickened. Getting to see how people reacted to the music I was putting together would be a first for me—and I didn't have very many of those anymore, especially when it came to music.

Montana turned to me. "They want you on drums for this one, Jericho, because it's short notice. Griffin will take over after the *Pulse* interview announcing the change in the band."

Griffin smirked at me. "Don't worry, buddy. I can keep your girlfriend company while you play."

"Oh, shit. Jericho has a girlfriend?" True spun his head in my direction so fast I was surprised he didn't hurt himself.

"Who the fuck told you that?" I cut a cold glare Griffin's way and ignored True completely.

He laughed, the fucker. I wondered if I was losing my touch if even the kid wasn't afraid of me. I might need to punch him in the face to rectify that. Maybe mess up his pretty boy look a little, so he'd know I was serious. "Connor."

"That gossipy asshole," I grumbled, folding my arms across my chest.

"So it's true? Kennedy said something, but I figured she was just being hopeful." Zen pulled out his phone and looked down at the screen. "If she isn't your girlfriend, you should probably talk to her about that before the show because Kennedy already invited her and her friend to go with us."

"Can you ladies finish your chitchat later? We have band shit to discuss," Montana scolded, tapping her foot impatiently as she glowered at us all.

"Go for it." Maddox moved his hand in a circle gesturing for her to continue as we all sat quietly. I continued my glare at Griffin, and he made sure to avoid looking at me. If he so much as looked at Moon in anything other than a friendly way, I'd break his fingers. I tried to convey that through my glower.

"The festival is this weekend," Montana started, and both Zen and True immediately protested.

"What the hell, Montana? That's not short notice, that's practically no notice! We need time to rehearse," Zen argued.

"I already talked to the label and Harrison. Everything's been rescheduled for next week, so this week is free for rehearsals." Montana was always on top of band business. She kept us in line like no other and always knew what we needed before we needed it. It was why we hired her to replace Elijah and had kept her around this long. He'd left huge shoes to fill when he moved overseas.

"I'll email you all the details, but the concert is Saturday evening. You go on at sunset on the main stage. Let me know if you ladies are going to need any special accommodations by Wednesday so I can give them enough time to get set up." She pulled a stylus pen from behind her ear and started moving it across her tablet screen.

We all murmured our agreement, and she turned on us. "Okay, get out. I have shit to do."

I pushed up out of the chair and made sure to shoulder check Griffin into the wall on my way out the door. I didn't want to stick around and get grilled by the guys about Moon. I wanted to get back to her house and make sure Indy showed up like he was supposed to and was doing his job how I thought he should do it.

Maddox followed behind me and laughed at his brother. "Dude, you should know better than to provoke Jericho by now. If the day comes when he picks a girlfriend, you better stay the fuck away unless you want to die an early and painful death."

At least Maddox knew me well enough to warn Griffin off. I didn't say anything to either of them as we rode the elevator down, and I got in my car. True jogged over and stopped me from closing my door. "Wait a second. We need to practice this week since you haven't been the one playing with us for a few weeks. Zen has the biggest space, so the guys want to do it there."

"Fine with me, but I can't work all night." I was about to set hard limits

I'd never put in place before because Moon needed me and if someone really *was* watching her, and it seemed like they were, no fucking way was I leaving her alone overnight even if Indy was there. The only way I could ensure she was safe was if she was with me.

"Dude, none of us wants to work all night, either. Amara will kill me if I leave her on Phoenix duty by herself all night. Let's just get through it as fast as we can. Be at Zen's in the morning, and we'll get started." I admired my friend's dedication to his wife and daughter. They hadn't wanted to hire a nanny, and that meant they were constantly exhausted, but I didn't know if I'd ever seen True happier.

"Yeah, sounds good. See you in the morning." He stepped back, and I closed the door. I backed out and drove out of the parking garage, clenching the wheel harder as I caught Griffin's smirk in my rearview mirror. He didn't know me that well yet, but if he kept that shit up, he was going to learn real quick why none of the other guys fucked with me and what's mine.

Indy nodded at me as I passed by him when I stepped in the front door of Moon's studio. "Give me five minutes, and then we're going to have a talk."

He lifted an eyebrow but didn't say anything as I turned the corner and watched my girl contort her body into a bend that didn't seem like it should be possible. My dick strained against my jeans at the pictures running through my mind of what positions I could get her in while I fucked her.

Indy stepped up beside me and watched Moon, and I wanted to tear his eyes out of his head. "Take your fucking eyes off of her," I growled out through clenched teeth.

He chuckled but turned away. "So what Connor told me is true then? You fucking her?"

I turned and slammed him against the wall with my forearm across his neck, but he was infuriatingly calm like this shit happened to him every day. I leaned in close to his face. "You don't fucking talk about her like that. Unless you're watching her back, don't look at her. Don't even think about her. Just do your goddamn job."

I let him go, and he chuckled at me again. I wanted to smash his face in, but I didn't think Moon would appreciate me doing that in her nice, calm studio.

"She's not really my type, bro. I just wanted to fuck with you." He slapped me on the back, and I relaxed just a little.

The glass counter stood just beside us, so I moved toward it and leaned my hip against it. "I asked for you to watch Moon because a couple of weeks ago she swore a guy was watching her when she was out with one of her girlfriends. Then, a couple of nights ago, we were in her house, and she saw someone looking in her window. When I ran outside to confront the asshole, he'd run too far for me to catch him."

Indy was listening intently, professional mode apparently switched on. I'd called Connor's team in on this for exactly this reason—they took their shit seriously, and they were the best at what they did. I expected no less and would trust Moon's safety with no one but them.

"Did you get a description or anything identifying about him when you pursued him?" Indy pulled out his phone as if he was going to take notes.

I shook my head. "It was dark, and he was wearing black clothes and a hoodie. He jumped in a beat-up old sedan and drove off. I didn't get the plate number or make or model."

"You want me here twenty-four-seven, or what are you thinking?"

"Originally, I planned to send you home at night when I'm there with her, but now I'm thinking having you or one of your team observing overnight might help us get this guy faster." I wouldn't fuck with Moon's safety, so if that was what it took, I'd do it even if I hated it. I could take care of her on my own, but I was only human and had to sleep eventually.

"I'll bring in Julian and rotate with him for a week, and we'll see how it goes." He typed out a text and then slid his phone into his pocket. "Does she have any enemies or anyone who'd be after her?"

"I asked her the same thing, and she said no. I haven't done any digging beyond that."

"Alright." He scrubbed his hand across his stubbled jaw. "We'll just observe for a week and see what shakes out. If I have to, I'll call Sebastian in to do some digging. Hopefully, it was just a one-time thing, and nothing will happen."

"Yeah, for his sake, let's hope he gave up because the story isn't going to end well for him if he's after my girl." Adrenaline coursed through my veins, and I started to feel edgy. My mind wandered to images of what I'd do to anyone who tried to hurt Moon. My violent fantasies played in front of my vision, and only Moon's hand sliding across my folded arms pulled me back.

I blinked down at her, and she watched me with concern. Indy had disappeared back to the front door where he watched the room. She lifted on her toes and pressed her soft lips against my cheek, but I turned and kissed her thoroughly.

She pulled back, breathless, and giggled. "Well, hello to you, too." Her eyes sparkled, and her cheeks were flushed from her class. Her skin glistened with sweat from the workout she'd just done, and I licked my lips, wishing they were her skin instead.

My hands moved across her hips and wrapped around her waist, pulling her into my body. I kissed her again, but she wrinkled her nose and pushed her palms against my chest. I reluctantly let her go, but not far. "I'm all sweaty."

I leaned down and ran my nose against her neck, breathing her in. "I like it when you're sweaty."

Moon moved her gaze to the side. "Now, you get to tell me about him and what he's here for."

I assumed she was talking about Indy and sighed before pulling back. "Thank you for letting him come with you today even though I didn't get a chance to explain. I couldn't stand the thought of you being vulnerable while some unknown threat could be out there lurking. Fuck that."

"Well, he told me you sent him, and I trust you." She ran her fingers down my arm, and my nerves sparked to life under her touch. My chest expanded at her words. She *trusted* me. A lump formed in my throat, and I tried to swallow it down. I didn't know if a girl had ever trusted me before. I didn't know if I deserved her trust.

She wrapped her arms around my waist, and I folded her in my arms, pressing a kiss to the top of her head. "I'll never let anyone hurt you."

ELEVEN
MOON

"I don't think I can pull this off." I eyed myself in the mirror, my gaze roaming over my outfit.

"Are you kidding?" Bexley jumped off my bed and came up beside me. "Your body is incredible. Show it off, girl."

"How much time do we have until Kennedy gets here?"

Bexley checked her phone as I took one last look in the mirror at the floor-length see-through dress. It had bell sleeves and shimmery gold stars all over it. It would be hot in the desert where the festival was being held tonight, and Bexley had somehow convinced me to wear this barely-there outfit. I wore a skin-tight black bodysuit that looked more like a one-piece swimsuit with a low cut back underneath. I didn't normally dress so sexy, but I wanted to look good for Jericho.

"A couple of minutes." She inspected my outfit again, tapping her finger to her lips and tilting her head to the side. "What shoes are you going to wear?"

I moved past her into my closet. "Wedges?"

She stepped up beside me. "No. Cowboy boots for sure. This is a *festival*." She reached down and plucked the pair of brown boots I hadn't worn in at least two years up off the floor and handed them to me.

A knock sounded on the front door as I pulled the boots on my feet. Bexley squealed and ran out of the room, ignoring Indy's glare as she flung open the door without looking through the peephole to see who it was.

I followed her out of the room and right into Kennedy's waiting arms. She was standing with Amara, Montana, and another woman I hadn't met before. She was gorgeous with brown wavy hair and tons of freckles. "Moon, this is Ryan, Maddox's girlfriend, and all-around badass bodyguard."

My fingers wiggled in a wave in her direction. "Hey. Badass bodyguard, huh?"

She laughed. "Yep. I work with Indy." She patted him on the shoulder, and he shrugged her off.

"No touching, Ry. I'd like to keep my arms attached to my body." Indy moved about a foot away from her and stood close to the door. He turned to look out the window, scanning the area.

"So, Jericho isn't the only possessive one of the bunch, huh?" I wondered with a grin. I'd spent very little time with these girls and only in my studio, but I'd always liked them.

"Oh, honey. No. These boys are insane when it comes to their wives and girlfriends, but you'll see." Amara shot me a wink. "Now, I don't know about you, ladies, but the baby is with her grandparents, and I'm ready to dance." She shook her hips and I laughed.

"There's champagne in the limo, and we've got a long drive ahead of us, so move it!" Montana ordered while slapping Kennedy on the ass as she passed by. Indy went out first, and we followed in a single file line to the limo waiting at the curb.

"By the way, that outfit is insane. Jericho is going to die when he sees you," Kennedy whispered into my ear as she linked her arm in mine.

"And he's going to want to kill every single guy there just for looking at you," Amara added, threading her arm through mine on the other side. "This is going to be so much fun."

We stumbled out of the limo two hours later under the late afternoon sun. There wasn't a lot of time before sunset when the guys would be hitting the stage. The long ride was spent gossiping, giggling, and sipping plenty of bubbly.

The girls of Shadow Phoenix were more than welcoming; they acted like they'd known Bex and me forever. Being in their company wasn't awkward at all, and I could see myself easily fitting into their group.

"Aren't you supposed to be working? I didn't know day drinking was in your job description," Kennedy snorted, and Montana threw her head back and laughed.

"Bitch, I earned this day. Those boys have put me through the fucking ringer lately, I swear to god." She stumbled a little in her strappy sandals and reached into the tote bag she had slung over her shoulder. "I almost forgot. Passes for access to the band." She handed them out to all of us, and I slipped mine into the leather fanny pack I'd strapped around my waist like a belt.

Ryan stood beside me, and I turned toward her. "Are you here to work or play?"

"A little bit of both," she grinned. "I'm not technically working, but it's hard to drop the instinct to watch our surroundings. I had some champagne, so I'll leave official guard duties to Indy and the other guys."

I assumed she meant her boss and the team she worked with who must already be here with the band. Bexley sidled up next to me and bumped her hip into mine. The festival organizers had done a great job of giving this place almost a carnival-like atmosphere with a Ferris wheel standing tall above everything, bright lights whirling around it.

The smell of fried food added to the atmosphere. "What stage are we looking for?" Bexley practically had to yell to be heard over the distant sounds of bands playing on the three huge stages set up and chatter of people around us.

Montana lifted onto her toes and shielded her eyes from the sun to see better. "There." She pointed toward the stage in the middle, the biggest one. As a group, we pushed our way through the crowds. There was no band on the stage now, and the crowd in front of it was sparse but starting to fill in in anticipation of seeing the guys perform.

We pushed toward the front of the stage, staking claim to the area right in front. I'd never seen Jericho play before, at least not outside of some YouTube I'd watched on the down-low, so I was beyond excited to see my man in action.

We hadn't talked about what we were to each other yet, but we were together in my mind. He'd spent every night for the past week in my bed, even if he'd been a frustratingly perfect gentleman about the whole thing.

That meant we hadn't had sex yet, even if I was basically desperate for him.

The sky turned that dusky pink-purple color, and I turned away from where I'd been talking to Kennedy and Bex to see that the crowd had filled in. Indy stood behind us with another guy that I was guessing worked with him and Ryan. They kept people who might bump into us at bay, and I was grateful for that.

A tall, gorgeous guy with lots of tattoos moved up beside me, and I glanced at Indy, who gave him a smirk. "Your funeral," Indy mumbled before turning back to watch the crowd.

I relaxed at Indy's reaction. It seemed like he knew the guy and was comfortable enough with him to let him around me knowing how protective Jericho was. Stretching out my hand, I introduced myself. "Hi, I'm Moon."

He flashed me a straight, white smile and clasped my hand in his. "Griffin."

Bex leaned around me, a wide smile on her face as her eyes trailed up Griffin's admittedly well-built body. "I'm Bexley."

"Hey." He nodded politely at her. Before we could do much more than introductions, the guys took the stage to deafening applause. I listened to a lot of indie artists, but even I'd heard of Shadow Phoenix before I met Jericho. I wasn't familiar with their music and didn't know them well, but I'd read their names in the tabloid magazines while waiting in line at the grocery store or washing trash TV on cable.

I barely took my eyes off Jericho as he flawlessly played one song after another. The lead singer, Zen's, voice was gravelly and soulful as he belted out the songs. My body swayed to the music, and Bexley and I jumped around and danced to every beat. Just before the last song of the set, my moves had me bumping into a hard body behind me. I whipped my head around to find Griffin smiling down at me. He leaned down to yell, "Sorry, people pressed in, and there was nowhere else to stand."

His hands found my hips, and I stiffened and moved as far forward as I could to put distance between us, and he laughed. "You won't even give me one dance?" he yelled close to my ear.

I shook my head and gave him an apologetic shrug. He was way too flirty for me, especially because I was feeling really wound up from watching Jericho play. A couple of times, he found me in the crowd, locking eyes with me while never missing a beat. It was hot as hell, and I felt his stare like electricity, live and arcing through my body down to my toes.

Sweat dripped down Jericho's body as he played, and the slick skin was like a beacon for my libido. What was it about a sweaty guy that made me want to lick him? Maybe it was just Jericho who had my core clenching and my nipples tightening under my bodysuit.

When they finished their set, Jericho didn't wait for the thunderous applause to die down. He stood up and moved off the stage like a man possessed, and when he appeared at the side of the stage and jumped down into the crowd, our eyes locked as people parted for him with gasps and cheers.

But he never looked away from me. His muscles were tight and bunched as he stalked toward me, the danger radiating off him was so damn sexy I thought I might combust.

As he got closer, I could see his hands curled into fists at his sides and how dark his eyes had turned. Had he seen Griffin trying to dance with me even as he played in front of thousands of people?

He stepped in front of me, and without missing a beat, grabbed the back of my neck and kissed me so hard the force tilted me backward. Jericho caught me, and as he devoured me for the world to see, I sunk into his kiss, and the clapping, whistles, and catcalls around us faded into nothing.

When he finally stood me up and let me go, I was breathless and unsteady. My lips were swollen from his assault, and my mind was dazed and focused solely on the way he was looking at me with wickedness gleaming in his eyes.

He dropped his hands from my waist where he'd been holding me steady and moved faster than I expected to where Griffin stood somewhere behind me, landing a punch right in his face. Griffin stumbled backward as his lip erupted with blood, but he was smiling. The effect was disturbing as blood coated his white teeth while he laughed.

Indy stepped in front of Griffin and held Jericho back with a lot of effort. The other guy who'd been working beside him had to step in and help. "Calm down, Jericho. There are cameras everywhere," Indy warned quietly, but Jericho was shooting a glare over Indy's shoulder at Griffin, who was still laughing like he thought getting punched in the face was the funniest thing ever.

"We're going to continue this later," Jericho promised, his voice quiet, but the low, menacing quality of it made me shiver. I'd hate to be Griffin right now. I glanced at him, and he didn't look worried, still wearing his mischievous smirk as blood dripped off his chin.

The guy with Indy tentatively stepped away from Jericho and turned to lead Griffin away from us and back through the crowd. "If I let you go, you going to go after him?" Indy questioned, eyeing Jericho.

"Not right now."

Indy nodded and stepped aside, clearing the last few people with phones raised in our direction. Jericho moved over to me and ran his fingers down the side of my face. I couldn't help but lean into his touch. "Was that really necessary?"

"No one touches what's mine." He said it so matter of fact, a surge of heat rolled through my body. The way he owned his feelings for me, his possessive nature was refreshing. It wasn't something I ever thought I'd want in a guy, but here I was eating it up and getting turned on by the powerful and violent nature of the man standing beside me.

I felt Jericho tense, and before I could register what caused it, he was stepping in front of me as a man in an expensive suit with what I could only describe as a blonde Jessica Rabbit on his arm casually strolled up to us. There was something about the appraising glint in his eye that was anything but casual, though, and Jericho's body language had me on guard.

Indy was still nearby, and he noticed the man approaching and started to move toward us.

"Hughes," Jericho spit out, the word laced with venom.

"Ah, Mr. Cole. Great show," the guy in the suit complimented, but his words sounded as fake as the boobs of the girl draped on his arm.

"Yep." Hostility rolled off Jericho, but the man just brushed it off and turned his attention to me.

"Aren't you going to introduce me to your friend?"

"No." Jericho moved a little bit more in front of me, so I had to look around him to see the man, who laughed and stepped closer, extending his hand toward me.

"I'm Marcus Hughes, president of Pacific Records. Nice to meet you…?"

Squeezing Jericho's tense bicep, I stepped around him and shook Marcus's hand. "Moon. It's nice to meet you, too."

"Great. It was fucking *nice* of you to show up, Hughes. See you." Jericho grabbed my hand and started to pull me away. He was being rude, but in the short time I'd known Jericho, he didn't seem to exude this level of hostility toward people unless he had a reason.

"Wait." Jericho's already rigid stance got even tenser with the word, but he stopped, and I almost ran into him. He turned, and I had no choice but to turn, too, just in time to see Marcus's smiling face. His smile was too wide, his eyes too bright. The girl on his arm looked bored as she twirled a lock of her hair around her finger.

"After playing tonight, don't you want to reconsider the changes you're forcing the band to make? You don't belong behind the board, Jericho. You belong behind the drums. Let a professional handle the mixing and composing." Marcus's words were probably meant to be sincere, but he said them with a haughty tone like he knew what was best and didn't care what the band wanted. I bristled, taking him in with narrowed eyes.

"I belong where me and the guys decide. You keep trying to force Dick, the world's shittiest producer, on us, and it's never going to fucking happen." Jericho took a step toward Marcus. "What more do you need me to say to get it through your thick fucking skull? Back. The. Fuck. Off. Marcus."

Marcus chuckled, obviously not giving a crap that Jericho was a coiled ball of violence on the verge of unleashing on him. I gripped his bicep tighter, trying to calm him down. "You don't know what you're starting here, Mr. Cole. But you're going to learn quickly that you're nothing more than an interchangeable cog in the machine I've built. You think you're special? Important? Unique? There are a million people with just as much talent who could make me money. I don't need you, and by the time my lawyers are finished, you'll be a long-forgotten memory."

Jericho smirked. "If that were the case, *Marcus*, why bother coming all the way down here and putting on this display?" He gestured toward the blonde girl, now scrolling through her phone. "We both know she's not your type. Now run along, Satan. I'm sure there's some poor soul that needs torturing."

He slung his arm across my shoulder, and we turned away from Marcus, not waiting for his response. I wasn't sure what to make of that whole exchange. I wasn't really familiar with how the band worked or what changes were going on with it. Kennedy and the other girls hadn't mentioned anything on the way here.

I leaned against Jericho's hard body as we walked slowly through the crowd, his clean scent swirled around me. He leaned down to whisper near my ear, "You in this outfit is my new favorite fantasy. I want to tear it off of you, tie your hands behind your back, and make you scream my name."

His dirty words sent tendrils of burning desire cascading through my body, and I shivered, remembering how, as WickedExecutioner, he liked to be in control. I also remembered how much I enjoyed surrendering to him.

I wanted him like I'd never wanted anyone else, but there was so much I didn't know. I felt like if I gave Jericho my body completely, I'd be lost to him for good. There would be no coming back from that, no pulling away and recovering myself. Once I let him climb inside me, he'd own my heart and soul, too. And before I let him in, I needed to be sure he was worthy, that he'd protect me from himself and never hurt me.

So for now, I grinned up at him, licked my lips, and suggested, "How about we start with the Ferris wheel?"

TWELVE
JERICHO

Moon and I were going to have to have a conversation about sex and soon. It was taking all the self-control I had, and maybe some inhuman level that existed deep inside that I'd managed to tap into, to keep my fucking dick on my side of the bed every night.

But every night, the situation got harder in more ways than one.

I groaned and pulled myself up out of bed for yet another cold shower. Moon didn't seem like she was in a hurry to physically take our relationship to the next level, and I couldn't go there with her until she understood everything about what happened with Kayla all those years ago.

I wouldn't risk hurting her for anything, and for me, sex was a point of weakness. It was a place where I could easily lose the tightly wound control I worked so hard to maintain and hurt her. She already had an idea of what I liked based on our conversations as WickedExecutioner and LunaGirl, but I wanted her to understand the risks of being with me.

I stared down at her sleeping peacefully in the bed and resisted the pull to crawl back in and get her flexible body underneath me. Instead, I leaned down and pressed a kiss to her temple before trudging to the bathroom for a shower.

An hour and a half later, I stepped into the recording studio the label had reserved for us. Dick was nowhere to be found, and I settled in the chair behind the mixing board, familiarizing myself with the equipment and waiting for the rest of the guys to show up. It was surreal that I was in this position and wouldn't be inside the booth today. I was running the show, giving direction, and bringing my creative vision to life.

The weight of that sat heavily on my shoulders, but I welcomed the challenge. A soft *woosh* carried through the room as the door opened, and my four bandmates made their way inside.

Maddox slapped me on the back as Griffin dropped down onto the leather couch in the corner. True perched on the arm of the couch, and Zen leaned against the wall, sipping the to-go cup of coffee he had cradled between his hands.

"Look at you, man. I hadn't imagined you taking over like this, but it fits. Now that you've got our back like this, I don't want anyone else touching our songs," Maddox admitted, slapping me one more time for good measure.

"Agreed," True and Zen echoed.

Griffin held up his hands. "I'm just the new guy. I'm happy to do whatever you guys think is best."

"On that note, how about you guys get in the booth and make some fucking music?" I swung the chair around so I faced the glass window to look inside, and they got themselves settled.

The next few hours flew by. Everything was in sync and working just as I imagined it would. The guys were clicking, and we were all on the same page with the sound we wanted. It was fucking harmonious, and I wished making music was always like this. We were professionals, and by the time we got to the studio, the music should be written and ready to be put into something that would not only sell but would fulfill all of our creative desires.

Long story short—Dick had no fucking idea what he was doing. He was toxic for us and our music, and today's progress made me even more ecstatic he was gone. I was willing to bet we'd have a fight on our hands over it if Marcus Hughes's little display at Fury Fest last weekend was any indication, but fuck the label, fuck Marcus, and most of all fuck Dick.

I must've been listening to Moon's best friend Bexley too much lately because Montana appeared as if I'd manifested her with my thoughts or some shit. She stepped up beside me as I watched the guys move through a tempo change. My finger moved toward the button to tell them to stop, but she stopped me. "Let them finish. You guys aren't going to like what I have to say, so let's not ruin what they've got going on."

I stayed on edge the whole rest of the song, and when they finished, I called the guys to come out. They took up the same places they'd been in this morning, but instead of on me, all their eyes were on Montana. Fuck, my eyes were on her, too, as the hair on the back of my neck stood up. One thing was for sure—I was going to hate whatever the fuck came out of Montana's mouth next.

"Marcus Hughes called me this afternoon and let me know that if you don't let Richard Bennett back in to work on the album and get Jericho back behind the drums, he's going to let his army of lawyers loose on you and tie you up in court from, and I quote," she made air quotes and rolled her eyes, "*now until eternity.*"

Everyone started talking at once. "Fuck Dick and fuck Marcus," Maddox gritted out at the same time True jumped up and said, "I'd like to see them try to stop us from making this album."

"Why is Marcus so hung up on this particular producer?" Zen wondered. "We've switched producers before, and it's never been an issue."

I spoke up. "Because *Dick* is Marcus's boyfriend, and we hurt his feelings."

Zen choked on the water he'd grabbed and was sipping. "His *what?* How the fuck do you know that?"

My lips tilted up in an almost-smirk. "I caught Dick blowing him in the bathroom at that stuffy as fuck party Marcus made us go to a couple of months ago. They forgot to lock the door."

"Holy shit." True started to pace. "How can we use that?"

Maddox chuckled. "Settle down there, Hamlet. I think the first thing we do is call in our own lawyers to go over our contract and figure out what we can negotiate with legally."

Zen already had his phone out, tapping away but then stopped and looked up to Montana. She'd been quiet so far. "Would it be too much for us to ask you to handle finding us independent lawyers and getting them on this? If not, it's cool, but we're in the middle of recording, and that's a whole other beast."

She pulled a tablet out of somewhere and started tapping. "Yeah, I've got this. Marcus has been on my shit list for years. I'm fucking giddy at the chance to make him suffer." She looked around at all of us. "I'll get out of here and start on this. Who wants my updates when I get the ball rolling?"

Zen and I exchanged a glance, and he sighed. "I do. I'll fill the guys in on everything."

"Good." Montana stuffed the tablet back in her giant purse after tapping a few more times. She looked up and flashed us all a devious smile. "I won't let Marcus get away with this. Have a good afternoon, boys. Make some music I can sell."

She strode out of the studio on a mission, and I almost laughed at the shitstorm in the form of a feisty redhead we'd just unleashed on Marcus and Pacific Records. But if they wanted to fuck with our music, they were going to get a goddamn war.

"Honey, I'm home," I quipped as I walked in the door to Moon's place. Indy raised his eyebrow at me as I passed by, and I glared at him in return. He chuckled but smartly didn't say a word.

"I'm out here," Moon called out, and just the sound of her voice had the muscles in my shoulders relaxing for the first time all day. I kicked off my shoes and walked through the tiny house to the even tinier backyard.

The sight in front of me made my heart stutter before kicking up to the next level. Moon in yoga pants and a tiny shirt bent into a position that, if I could just slide underneath her, would be perfect for riding my dick. As my cock swelled, I realized she'd been talking to me, and I hadn't heard a word she'd said.

"Has Indy seen you like this?" That tension that'd just dissipated was back full force at the thought of anyone but me seeing her body contorted like that in those clothes. Then I had to give myself a mental smackdown because Moon was a yoga teacher, and I'd never stand in the way of her doing whatever she wanted, even if it made me want to go on a murder spree.

She laughed as if I were ridiculous. "I don't know, but I don't think so. He mostly stays by the front door. He says he can see the front and back entrances plus the street out front best from there." Moon untwisted her body and nimbly got to her feet, throwing herself against my body.

Her sweet strawberry scent surrounded me, and I breathed her in, feeling like it'd been way too long since I'd felt her body against mine, even though it was only his morning. "We need to talk," I spoke gruffly into her hair.

She looked up at me and studied my face before nodding. "Okay, here. Let's sit." Moon tugged me over to her yoga mat in the tiny sliver of grass she tried to pass off as a yard and dropped onto it, sitting cross-legged. Once I was settled beside her, she yanked me down so my head rested in her lap, and she ran her fingers through my hair. I closed my eyes and hummed contentedly.

"What'd you want to talk about?"

"Us," I mumbled. She tensed up, and her fingers slowed before she picked her pace back up.

"What about us?" Her voice was a little tense and shaky.

"There are a few things we need to talk about. I've been telling people you're my girlfriend, but I never actually asked you how you feel about that," I confessed.

"Well…" she dragged the word out. "I know you've been sort of possessive over me, and I love it, I really do. But…"

Her fingers stopped moving like she was searching for the right word. "But what?" I prompted.

"But I have this thing about wanting to experience everything in life. I want to make sure that there's a line between you being possessive over me and you limiting the things you feel comfortable with me doing. Because if I'm going to be in a committed relationship with you, I need you to know that I'm also going to take every opportunity to participate in life that comes my way. Whether it's dancing in the rain, eating meat on the streets of Tijuana, or going down into the Paris Catacombs, if I get the opportunity to do something I've never done before, I'm going to take it. Ideally, with you by my side."

She rushed the words out as if she'd been bottling them up and then wanted to make sure she got them all out before she forgot some. My eyes were still closed, but my lips tilted up in a smile, a rare smile that I saved only for her.

"I'd never stop you from doing something you want to do unless that something is having sex with another guy. If you agree to be my girlfriend, your pleasure belongs to me and only me."

"You mean-"

I opened my eyes and stared up at her so she'd know how serious I was. "I mean you don't touch yourself unless I say so. I mean I haven't fucked anyone in a long fucking time because I have to be careful who knows what I like, and now my pleasure belongs to only you, too. And I mean that only I get to make you come from now on."

She was nodding her head before I even finished talking, and I sat up, pulling her to my lips so I could taste her like I'd waited for all day. A soft whimper worked up her throat as I nipped at her lower lip, sucking it into my mouth before releasing it and claiming her mouth again. She tasted sweet, like the smoothie I'd learned she always drank in the afternoons, and I drank her in a little more with every swipe of my tongue against hers.

Finally, I forced myself to pull back just as she fisted my shirt in an effort to tug it off. "There's something else we need to talk about, beautiful girl."

Her pupils were dilated, her hair was messy, and she looked like she wanted to crawl in my lap right out here. My gaze dropped, and her nipples were so hard I could make them out through the material of her tiny cropped tank top.

"Fuck." I took a deep breath. "You remember all the times we talked as Wicked and Luna?"

She nodded, shifting herself so her thighs pressed together, and my fingers itched to rip off her clothes and relieve the tension between her legs, but not yet.

"The way we talked? The things I liked?"

"Yeah, you were bossy." She shot me a tentative smile, and I gave her one back.

"Bossy's a good way to put it. I like having control over your pleasure. I get off on it, I need it," I explained as I watched her chest rise and fall with her quick breaths. "How do you feel about that?"

She bit her lip, and I couldn't have torn my eyes off of her mouth if my life depended on it. All the things I wanted her to bite and suck of mine danced through my mind like an erotic parade. Her voice brought my attention back to the present. "I like it," she whispered, and then her eyes lifted to mine. "I think it's hot."

I needed to be sure. "You do? Even if that means I don't let you come right away, or I want to tie your hands or legs or both up? Or blindfold you?"

She nodded as a flush painted her cheeks a pretty pink color. "Yes. When we talked as Wicked and Luna, I'd never been more turned on, and you weren't even in the same room. Can I tell you a secret?"

My heart slammed against my chest as an intense craving to sink into Moon raged through my entire body at her words. All I could do was swallow hard and nod.

"I have a fantasy…" Her voice was a caress of the words as they slid out of her mouth smoothly like she'd wrapped each one in silk. I'd expected her to be shy about admitting her fantasies, but I should've known better. Moon was a fucking goddess who owned every bit of who she was.

"Tell me," I demanded, and curled my fingers into a fist to keep from reaching for her. I'd never begged for anything in my life, yet here I was hanging on her every word, ready to beg if she didn't speak her dream into reality.

"I've always wanted to be tied up, maybe blindfolded. There's something so intense about the idea of being at someone else's mercy, not having to make a move, or think about what comes next. Just getting to exist in the pleasure. I've never told anyone, but that's what I want."

My need to touch her won out, and I hauled her into my lap and brushed her hair away from her face so I could look clearly into her eyes. "And do you want to do those things with me? Because I have to warn you, back when I was fresh out of high school, I was hooking up with a girl and I…" I looked away, not wanting her to see the guilt burning behind my eyes. The guilt that still haunted me to this day so badly that I'd never fucked another girl since that day. I'd tried, but I was too messed up over what happened to go through with it.

Her soft palm glided along my cheek, and she gently turned me back to face her. "It's okay. You can tell me. I'm not here to judge you."

I exhaled, wrapping my arms around her and digging my fingertips into her skin to ground myself. "I lost control, Moon. I won't go into detail, but I could've killed her. She was fine, but it was a close call. And I've been terrified of it happening again, so there's never been anyone since." There. My worst fucking fear had been voiced aloud, and now my traitorous body was trembling as I waited for her reaction.

"Hey," she said softly, and I shifted my gaze back to her. "It's okay. That was so long ago. And now that you know what can happen, you'll see the signs if you start to go there again."

"That's the fucked up thing—I don't know how it happened the first time. I said I'd never be with another girl until I figured it out so I could keep it from happening again, and I've thought about that night ten thousand times, and I still don't fucking know." I dropped my head and tried to take deep breaths as my heart battered my ribcage.

"I trust you." Her words broke me apart and put me back together all at the same time. "I trust you, Jericho. You'd never hurt me."

Of course, she was right. She wasn't Kayla, someone I didn't care about at all. This was *Moon*. The woman who seemed to be the opposite of me in almost every way, and yet somehow she got me. She knew what I needed, she pulled me out of the dark places I existed in, and she brightened my life in a way I could never have expected.

She also captivated me and made me want to shield her from the world while simultaneously giving her everything. And for the record, everything included my dick every damn day.

Finally coming to my senses, I tangled my fingers in her colorful hair and pulled her head toward me until our foreheads pressed together. "You're right, beautiful. I'd never hurt you. I'd rather die first. But I *am* going to make every single one of your fantasies come true, even the ones you never knew you had."

I stood up then with her still on my lap as she squealed and wrapped her legs around my waist. She dropped hot kisses on my neck as I walked, and my cock was hard and pressed right against her core. I could feel her heat through the layers of our clothes and an intense need to rip everything off of her and disappear inside her until the end of time tore at my resolve.

Walking with my dick hard wasn't easy, so I stumbled into the bedroom and kicked the door shut behind me. Her bed stood in the middle of the room, and I stalked over to it, dropping her down onto the soft mattress as she giggled and stared up at me with a mixture of wonder and lust. I stripped my shirt off and crawled on top of her, lowering my lips to hers for a heated kiss.

If all of our other kisses had been hot, this one was scorching. It wasn't just a kiss—it was a claiming, but not just me of her. No, she was giving just as good as she got, matching every stroke of my tongue, every bite. Moon was demanding I surrender just as I did the same to her.

I'd never be the same after this kiss, and I knew it, but I just didn't fucking care. I couldn't go back to the old Jericho, not now that I knew how good being with Moon felt. I was destroyed, the bricks in my psyche demolished into a pile of rubble that Moon was clearing away with every whispered word, caressing touch, and brush of her lips.

Nothing had ever been so sweet.

I forced myself back just far enough to pull off the scrap of cotton she considered a tank top, and I stared down at the perfect set of tits displayed in front of me. Moon scraped her fingers through my hair, scratching my scalp as I watched her, entranced by the perfect pink nipples pointed straight up at me and the just-more-than-a-handful size of her breasts. I wanted them in my hands and my mouth, and I couldn't decide what to do first.

Moon arched her back, trying to force me into action, and I chuckled darkly. "You're such a bad girl. Don't you remember how this goes? Hold still."

I felt my control snap into place, something I hadn't exercised in years, this sexual force that broke free inside me in these moments. I'd forgotten how fucking amazing it felt to be in this position, holding someone else's pleasure in the palm of my hand, getting to decide how best to unleash it on them. I was the circus master, and this was my arena.

A wild need to please Moon thrashed around inside me, demanding I take action, but on the outside, I stayed controlled and calm. She'd never know the intense rush of adrenaline spiking inside me at the thought of tying her up and bringing her to the brink of coming only to back off again and again until she felt like her body couldn't take anymore. Then, I'd do it again until I finally let her crash, to reach the peak, and it would be so much sweeter, so much *higher* when I did.

There was a giddiness in me at the prospect of seeing Moon come apart underneath me, on my fingers, tongue, or wrapped around my cock. Her eyes followed my movement as I stood up beside the bed and flicked the button on my jeans open, sliding my hand down into my boxers and fisting my cock. I gave it a long, slow stroke and threw my head back with a groan.

"Shit, that's so hot." Moon's voice was husky, and when I looked back at her, she was watching me from underneath dark lashes and heavy eyelids.

"Move into the middle of the bed," I ordered, softening my voice a little from the way I used to talk to Kayla. It'd been a long time, but Moon wasn't just some girl. She was *the* girl. I cared how she felt when this was all over.

She obeyed without question, and I watched her tits bounce as she settled into her spot. I stroked my cock again before reluctantly pulling my hand out of my pants. She watched me as I moved across the room to her dresser and opened the top drawer where I knew she kept her panties. "What are you doing?" she asked.

"Good girls don't ask questions." She was quiet then as I rummaged through the drawer, plucking out a few lacy thongs and sliding the drawer closed.

It only took me a few steps to move back beside the bed, and the mattress dipped under my weight as I climbed on. "Put your hands together in front of you like this." I crossed one wrist over the other to show her what I meant, and she followed my instructions.

I tied her wrists together securely using her panties before leaning down and dropping a heated kiss on her lips. I moved her bound wrists above her head so her back was arched up toward me, her tits in the perfect position for sucking, licking, biting… my imagination ran wild. I couldn't resist and lowered my mouth to one perfect pink bud and danced my fingers up her stomach until my hand found the other.

My tongue swirled around her nipple, and I sucked it into my mouth before letting my mouth pop off of it. Moon whimpered softly, and my dick somehow got even harder. Every sound I coaxed out of her made goosebumps break out across my body, and my balls tighten. If we kept going like this, I had no doubt I would come before I ever got inside her, and wouldn't that be a fucking shame.

Just as I was pulling her other nipple into my mouth, a knock sounded on the door. I tried to ignore it, but it happened again. I reluctantly moved my mouth off of Moon's body and stood up, stalking across to the door and ripping it open just enough to see what the hell was important enough to interrupt us. "There better be apocalypse-level shit going down," I growled at Indy, who looked apologetic, or at least that's what I was convincing myself so I didn't punch him in the face.

"Marcus Hughes called an emergency meeting downtown for the entire band. Something about focus groups and marketability. Said it couldn't wait until tomorrow, and the guys are here to pick you up."

"I'll be out in two minutes." I slammed the door in his face and leaned my forehead against it for a few seconds, breathing hard as I struggled to get my anger under control. That motherfucker Marcus knew exactly what he was doing. Focus groups and marketing shit? That wasn't an emergency. That shit could wait until normal business hours. He was pissed that we were undermining him and was going to torture us in retaliation.

Moon's soft body pressed against my back, the feel of her body against mine like a bucket of water to put out the fire inside me. "I'd hug you, but, well…" she laughed and held her bound hands up to one side.

I chuckled and turned around, quickly untying her and then wrapping her in my arms. I buried my face in her hair and breathed her in, trying to regain my composure. I sure as fuck was going to need it for the battle Marcus had in mind tonight. If he thought I was going to let this shit go, his summoning us to his office at all hours of the day or night for petty-ass reasons, he was in for a rude awakening.

"I have to go," I finally admitted, squeezing my eyes shut and soaking in the last seconds I'd have with Moon for the next few hours.

"I know, but I'll be here when you come back." The mood was somehow broken now, though, and we both knew it. By the time I got back tonight, she'd be asleep for her early morning classes, and I'd be too fucking exhausted by Marcus's bullshit.

But make no mistake about it, I'd make him fucking pay for stealing tonight with my girl.

THIRTEEN
MOON

It hadn't been twenty minutes since Jericho left with the guys, looking like he was preparing for battle. My body had mostly calmed down, and I knew tomorrow was an early morning at the studio since I still hadn't found someone to replace Terra, but no matter how hard I tried, I couldn't fall asleep.

Being crazy turned on and not getting relief would do that to a girl.

I had a feeling I wouldn't be able to sleep until Jericho came home. I sucked in a sharp breath when I realized he made my house feel like home. The place felt emptier without him in it. Sighing, I shoved the blankets off of me and walked out to the kitchen.

My stomach grumbled in protest at the fact I hadn't eaten dinner. It wasn't that late, so I pulled the fridge open and started rummaging around. Three sharp knocks rang out through the house, and I turned and looked at Indy, who was already looking through the peephole in my front door. He shook his head but had a smile on his face, so I wondered if Bexley had decided to pop in.

Indy swung the door open, and I glanced down at the yoga pants and crop top I was still wearing from earlier since I just threw my top back on when Jericho had to leave. Kennedy stepped through the door and grinned at Indy before she skipped across the house to me.

"I don't know about you, but none of us wanted to just go to bed with the guys getting called into that stupid meeting, so we thought we'd blow off some steam—dinner and drinks, but not too wild since we have the kids. We had to stop by and grab you since you're one of us now," Kennedy expl.

I laughed. "Okay, let me get changed." My room was only a few feet away, so it didn't take me long to toss on some respectable clothes before joining her back in the kitchen.

She wore a mischievous smile. "I was just talking to Indy, and since we have the kids, there's not enough room in my car for everyone, so you guys are going to be taking yours."

I snorted and looked at Indy. "Can you even fit in my car?"

He rolled his eyes. "I guess we're about to find out."

Kennedy was practically cackling. "He's going to have to fold himself in half. I'm definitely taking pictures."

Slipping my feet into my comfiest flats, I grabbed my keys off the counter and tossed them to Indy. "You're driving."

The three of us walked out to my bright red Jetta, and Kennedy pulled her phone out as Indy shot her a withering glare. She pretended she didn't see it, though, and I giggled as he unlocked the door and yanked it open. "Hey! Don't rip the door off the hinges!"

He climbed in, which took him a couple of attempts to slide the seat back and try and fold his long legs inside before he finally slammed the door. "Your chariot awaits," Kennedy exclaimed between giggles. I watched her try to catch her breath, holding her side as she walked back to her car and climbed in the passenger side. Ryan waved to me from where she sat behind the wheel. It was easy to forget sometimes that she worked with Indy.

The passenger door opened next to me, and I looked down to see Indy glaring up at me. "Get in. It's not safe to stand around out there like that. You're vulnerable."

I almost laughed at how cranky he was, but instead, I got in my car and shut the door. "Did you hear the plan?"

Indy was busy checking all the mirrors and adjusting everything to his gigantic size. He grunted a response. "We're just supposed to follow them, right?"

"That's what Kennedy said."

At least he wasn't going to ignore me. I didn't like it when people were mad at me. Ryan pulled away from the curb, and Indy followed, alternating his attention between the front windshield and all of the mirrors. I had to give the guy credit—he was hypervigilant and never let his guard down. I doubted he missed anything that happened around him, and that made me feel safe.

I pulled my phone out, connected it to the stereo, clicked on my favorite music app, and started a playlist. Indy shot me a look out of the side of his eye, but I ignored him. It didn't take long for us to pull up in front of a little Mexican restaurant, and my stomach growled.

Everyone climbed out of Kennedy's SUV, so I followed suit, not bothering to wait for Indy to give me the all-clear. I wasn't used to having a bodyguard, so I didn't really think about it, but in the blink of an eye, he was standing next to me, scowling. "Next time, you wait for me to check the area before just jumping out of the car."

My eyes wanted to roll so bad, but I held back. "Okay." There hadn't been any sign of trouble since the peeping Tom, and I wasn't sure that hadn't just been some random creep passing by my house. Still, Jericho insisted Indy stay with me.

I reminded myself that I was lucky they were taking the threat seriously.

Kennedy strapped her son into the wrap she'd woven around her body, and Amara looked to be doing the same thing with her daughter. We stood in a half-circle while we waited for them to get situated. When they were done, we made our way inside and snagged a huge table in the back. Dinner was delicious, and with the girls all keeping me company, the time passed quickly. My worries about Jericho and the meeting were pushed to the back of my mind as I laughed at some of the stories the ladies had.

I turned to Montana. "How come you didn't have to go to this meeting?"

She ran her finger along the rim of her half-drunk margarita. "I already told the guys I'd take on their war with Marcus Hughes over this album, but I sure as fuck am not going to sit through some ridiculous petty attempt by him to get them to bend to his will. And make no mistake about it—that's what this is."

Amara patted her stomach. "I don't know about you guys, but I'm stuffed. How about a walk to work off some of this food?"

I was *so* down for a walk. Stretching my legs was one of my favorite things to do after a big meal, and I also loved to see what kinds of new things I could experience in a neighborhood I'd never been in before. I looked to Indy, who was off to the side, talking with Ryan.

We paid the bill and stood up, and headed for the door. I waited for Indy to tell me I could go outside, and finally, after stepping out himself and scanning the area, he came back in and told me I could follow.

The night air was refreshing, and Kennedy linked her arm through mine. I looked down at her son, Nico, who was sleeping against her chest. "He's adorable."

She sighed. "He really is. He looks just like Zen, and he's the best baby. He almost never cries. Well, unless Maddox tries to hold him." She laughed quietly, I imagined so she didn't wake the baby.

A neon sign caught my eye as we strolled down the street as a group. "Okay, we are *definitely* going in here."

"Hell, yes!" Montana agreed, lifting her hands into the air. I had a feeling she and I were like minded in our adventurous spirits.

"I don't know..." Amara hesitated, and I nudged her.

"Come on. You don't have to get anything huge. Just a little something. Pleaaase?" For some reason, it was important to me we all do this together.

"Fine, but if True hates it, I'm telling him it was your fault." She grinned at me.

"Deal."

Ryan opened the door, and we all stepped inside, and she took up a place by the door, but I shook my head. "Oh, no, you don't. You're doing this with us."

"But-"

"Nope. C'mon."

She bit her lip, and then a grin stretched across her mouth. "What are you going to get?"

We walked over to the counter, and I let the guy know there were five of us getting tattoos so he could start preparing while we figured out what we wanted. I'd never gotten a tattoo before, but I'd always wanted one.

I turned back to Ryan, and all the girls were looking through the designs displayed. I bit my lip and smiled, hoping they didn't judge me for the snap decision I'd just made. "I'm getting a set of drumsticks right here." I patted my hip.

"Ohmygod, I love that. Okay, it's decided. I'm getting a microphone, same place," Kennedy declared, lowering herself by bending her knees to keep from moving Nico too much.

"We're really doing this, huh?" Amara's eyes flicked up to the ceiling and back to us. "Fine. I'll do a guitar in the same place."

We all turned to Ryan, and she rolled her eyes. "A bass guitar, obviously."

Montana clapped her hands. "Okay, bitches! I don't have a man in the band, so what am I getting?"

I grabbed her hand and pulled her over to the wall. "You're the one who keeps everything going for them, and they couldn't do this without you. So you're getting this." I pointed to the crown design that caught my eye when we first walked in. "You're the boss, the queen. Own that shit."

She threw her arms around me and jumped up and down. "Yes, girl!" She pulled back and blinked a couple of times. "Thank you for seeing me."

My heart crashed around inside my chest, and my stomach flipped. I always dove right into things without giving it tons of thought. Spontaneity was fun, and I lived for the rush I got whenever I did something new or unexpected. I hoped Jericho didn't freak out that it was so soon into our relationship, and I was marking my skin with a permanent reminder of him.

Montana walked off to tell the heavily inked guy at the front of the shop that we'd all decided what we wanted. Kennedy sauntered over to me and bumped her hip into mine. "So... you and Jericho. It's serious enough to get a tattoo dedicated to him?" The Cheshire-cat looking grin she shot me had me laughing.

"I like him a lot. Like a fucking *lot*. Everything feels so different with him than it ever has in relationships for me before. There's something about Jericho that just..." I didn't want to talk details with her because my relationship with Jericho wasn't something I wanted to share with anyone.

She laughed. "I get it. He probably hasn't told you, but we're best friends. At least, that's what I tell myself. When I saw how he reacted to you in your class, I had to act. I've never seen him with a girl before. Ever."

"He has that whole dark and brooding, intensely sexy vibe going for him that *really* does it for me," I giggled.

Kennedy sighed dreamily. "I know exactly what you mean. Zen has the same thing, except maybe less on the dark and broody these days. He's still sexy as hell, though."

The burly guy doing our tattoos called for a couple of us and led us to the stations that had been set up. Three of us went first, and the sting of the tattoo gun as the black drumsticks were carved into my skin was surprisingly welcome. I enjoyed the feeling of etching Jericho permanently onto my body. I only hoped he'd feel the same.

An hour later, we were all done with fresh bandages on our hips and the fading rush of adrenaline as we stepped outside. I gave everyone hugs, feeling like we'd bonded even more after this experience. They made me feel welcome in their group, not like an outsider Jericho had forced them to include.

They all climbed into Kennedy's SUV with Ryan at the wheel, giving me one last wave as they pulled out of the parking spot. I climbed into my car with Indy folding himself behind the wheel, and I tried hard to stifle my laughter at his attempt to get in. His shoulders were more tense than usual as he checked all the mirrors and started driving.

"Don't freak out," he started, which, of course, put me on high alert. "But a car's been following us since we left your house."

I spun around, searching out the back window. "Turn back around," his voice was commanding, and I listened immediately.

"Why are you just telling me this now?" My heart raced, and my palms were starting to sweat.

"I wasn't sure it was you they were following or if it was the other girls when we left your house. Ryan and I decided she'd go one way, and I'd go another when we left to see for sure, and the car followed us, not them." His fingers flexed around the wheel, and his jaw was tight.

"Oh, god. What should I do? Who are they?" My thoughts were frantic as I searched my brain for whoever could possibly be following me, but as usual, I came up empty.

"You should try to stay calm, text Jericho and tell him what's going on, and hold on. I'm going to lose him." My body pressed back into the seat with the force of my car accelerating. Indy deftly wove through traffic and dodged other cars as he wound through the city streets. He pulled one of his hands off the wheel and handed me his phone.

"Find Connor in there and dial him for me." I didn't hesitate to do what he said, and I handed him back the phone. He pressed it to his ear and began recounting in clipped sentences what happened and our current situation.

I pulled out my own phone and sent Jericho a text with shaky fingers.

Moon: I went out with the SP girls for dinner, and we were followed. We're in the car, and Indy's trying to lose them now.

My body shifted around as Indy took corners at high speeds and dove through cars and trucks to lose whoever was following us. That adrenaline that had been fading from my system was back in full force as I tried to breathe.

What felt like two seconds later, my phone vibrated in my hand lit up with Jericho's name. Indy had slowed the car down, and I frantically looked in his direction before answering. "Did we lose them?"

He pulled over and turned off the lights, staring out of the rearview mirror before nodding. "We lost them."

I exhaled a long, shaky breath before answering the phone. "Jericho?"

"Moon? Jesus fucking Christ. What the hell is happening?" His words came out gruff and fast like he was scared for me, and my heart warmed as tears pricked my eyes. This whole situation was so confusing. Why would anyone want to follow me?

"Indy noticed someone followed us when we left my house," I started.

"Hold on one second, beautiful." His voice was muffled as if he'd pressed his phone against his clothing while talking to someone else. I bit my lip as my eyes welled again. Indy watched me but didn't say anything and instead held out his hand for my phone. I passed it over to him, knowing that if I opened my mouth to explain everything, I'd lose it and not be able to stop crying. I needed to hold myself together, at least until I got home or could curl up in Jericho's arms.

He always made me feel so safe, and right now, I felt anything but. Indy spoke quietly into the phone, answering Jericho's questions, but I tuned him out, instead darting my eyes between the mirror and out the side window. It was so dark outside, and every single one of my senses was on high alert. My breaths were shallow, and I could hardly hear anything over the sound of blood pumping in my ears.

I didn't even register that Indy had ended the call and was holding my phone out to me until he gently said, "Here's your phone back." I jumped a little when he spoke and reached out to grab my phone, clutching it against my chest.

"Are we going home now? Is Jericho going to meet us?" I hated how my voice trembled.

Indy shook his head and turned the car back on. The headlights lit up the alley we were parked in, and I studied the graffiti on the wall closest to me. "We're going to a club downtown. Jericho was with my boss, Connor, and they're sending Julian to your house to set up surveillance equipment. While he does that, we're going to get lost in a crowd for a while. Have a drink or two. Jericho's going to meet us there."

I took a deep breath, trying to calm myself down. We were on our way to meet Jericho, and I trusted between him, Indy, and Connor, they wouldn't let anyone hurt me. My phone vibrated again in my hand, and I looked down at the text that just came in.

Kennedy: OMG, Ryan just told us what happened. We're dropping the kids at True's parent's and meeting you guys at the club.

Moon: You don't have to

Kennedy: Bullshit. You're one of us now. This is what we do.

Moon: Thanks

I passed the message on to Indy, who nodded once as if he'd expected that. "You guys really are like a family," I noted, breaking the silence as we drove. Both of us still watched out the windows and the mirrors, even though I had no idea what I was looking for.

"We've been through a lot of shit together, some of it pretty intense, and the only way we've made it through is when we all stick together. You should know that once this group accepts you as one of them, they're going to do anything to protect you."

Chewing my lip, I sat back and thought about everything he'd just said. I wasn't used to being so welcomed into a new group or having anyone look out for me or want to protect me. I had my dad, and we were close, but he'd always given me my freedom without a lot of care for consequences. He wanted me to be a free spirit, just like my mother, so he gave me the room to do that.

I never realized how rare it was to be raised that way until just now. Now all I wanted was to get that sense of safety and security back, and the only way I knew how was to wrap myself in Jericho's arms and try to forget about the outside world for a little while.

FOURTEEN
JERICHO

That text message fucked me up. Something inside me roared to life when I saw those words on the screen, and all I could think about was burning down the world to make sure my girl was safe. And who the fuck was following her? And why?

I was going to do whatever I had to to find out.

Connor got a call from Indy shortly before I got that text and his whole demeanor changed when it came in. Gone was the casual posture and disinterested expression. He'd become the protector I knew him to be and snapped into action. I only half paid attention to him, thinking it probably had something to do with Zen or True.

But when that text came in, everything came to a screeching halt, and I realized he was dealing with Indy and Moon. Marcus was droning on about some bullshit none of us were paying attention to, so I watched intently as Connor stalked across the room and jerked his head toward the door. I got up and followed him out, ignoring Marcus's weak-ass protests.

When we got outside, I folded my arms across my chest, and he started speaking. "I assume you know what's going on?"

I nodded. "Moon texted. I was just about to call her."

"Do it." I pulled my phone out and dialed her number. When she answered, her shaky voice almost undid me as my chest was ripped open, and my heart became a bloody puddle on the floor. My girl was scared, and I wasn't there.

Fuck, I couldn't handle this, but I had no choice. I had to keep my shit together for Moon. I asked her to hold on and pressed my phone against my chest. "Someone was following them," I filled Connor in.

"Indy called me while they were having dinner and let me know he suspected someone was tailing them when they left the house."

I lifted the phone back to my ear. "Moon?"

"It's Indy. She's a little out of it right now."

"Indy, tell us everything you know," Connor demanded, stepping closer.

"When we left Moon's house, I noticed an older model SUV following us a few car lengths back. I knew they were following, but I didn't know if they were following Moon or one of the other girls. When we were at the restaurant, I filled Ryan in. We decided when we left to go two separate ways to see who the car followed. They followed Moon and me. While we were at the restaurant, Ryan snuck out and got the vehicle description and plate number, so I forwarded that on to Sebastian already."

Connor rubbed his hand along his jaw. "Okay, and where are they now?"

"Lost them about two miles back. I put distance between where I lost them and where we're parked now just to be safe."

"Alright. I'm going to send Julian over to Moon's to set up surveillance. He'll keep rotating with you on watch. And while he does it, meet us downtown at Polarize."

My eyebrows lifted in surprise, and Indy echoed me. "Polarize? You want us to meet at a club?"

"Can you think of a better place to get lost than in a sea of drunk people?" Connor countered, and I had to admit, it made a weird sort of sense.

"No," I admitted. "Let's go. I'm not staying here for any more of Marcus's bullshit when my girl's scared and in danger. Fuck him." I reached into my pocket and pulled out my keys. "Indy? Thanks for taking care of Moon when I couldn't." I appreciated him, but the words were bitter coming out of my mouth. That was my job, and I hated that I hadn't been there because of Marcus fucking Hughes. He was already on my shit list, and now I understood I'd have to do something drastic to break away from him.

The label had been good to us, but now it just felt toxic as fuck.

I gave Connor thirty seconds to tell the guys what was going on, and then I was leaving whether they were coming or not. That club was ten minutes away, and I had no idea where Moon was in the city. I didn't want her to get there before I did.

It only took him half that before he, Griffin, and I were making our way down the elevator. The rest of the guys told him they needed to talk to their wives and girlfriends and would meet us there. Just like when I was a teenager, the guys never ran when shit got tough. When Zen dealt with his stalker or True with the mess that was Lexi, or even Maddox with the whole Yates thing, we'd all been there to do whatever needed to be done.

Now it looked like it was my turn to lean on my friends, and even Griffin stood beside me now. Connor snatched my keys out of my hand as the elevator doors opened into the parking garage. "Give me my fucking keys." I wasn't in the mood to be fucked with.

"I'm driving. You're not thinking straight." I practically jogged to my Range Rover and jumped in the passenger seat. Griffin got in the back, and Connor slid behind the wheel. I tried to calm my racing heart as the tires squealed, and we flew toward the club.

It was supposed to take ten minutes, but it only took a little over five before we were piling out, and Connor tossed the keys to the valet. We didn't have to wait in the long-ass line; the bouncer took one look at me and let the three of us in.

We were met inside by a girl who led us to a VIP table, and we settled in, waiting for everyone else to show up. When the girl took our orders, I wanted to have a drink for Moon when she got here, but I didn't know what kind of alcohol she preferred. How could I not know that? It felt like something I should know about the woman who had quickly become everything to me.

I vowed to learn everything I could about her. I wanted to spend hours asking her questions and getting to know her. I wanted her for so much more than her body, even though her body was incredible.

I shook my knee and played with my phone while I waited impatiently for Moon to show up. The other guys got there a few minutes after I did and ordered drinks.

Once Maddox, Zen, and True settled onto the VIP lounge couches, they started in on me.

"What the hell was that back there?" Maddox wondered. "Not that I'm complaining about being rescued from Marcus's vortex of misery."

"Jericho's girl's in trouble," True summed up, and I snorted.

"Yeah, if you call being watched and followed by someone and have no idea who it is or why trouble, then sure." My jaw clenched.

"Damn, well, I know a little something about what that's like. The girls will be here soon, and we're just going to drink and dance a little and blow off some steam until you can go home, but we're all here if you need us." Zen took his beer from the waitress.

"I'm not going to drink in case you need help," Griffin vowed from where he sat next to me, and I nodded at him in thanks, and he grinned. "But that doesn't mean I'm not going find someone to have a little fun with tonight, just in case you don't end up needing me."

I shook my head at the kid. I was still pissed at him for the shit he pulled with Moon at Fury, but the non-caveman part of me knew he was just fucking with me. He was getting a taste of what it meant being a celebrity, too; he was about ten years behind the rest of us. We weren't in the same place he was anymore, but he was Maddox's brother and now a part of our band, which meant we watched out for him. If he started down a path that would destroy him or the band, we'd all step in.

That didn't mean I had to just accept him as a friend, but I had to admit he was worming his way into my life.

I stood up and walked over to the railing at the edge of the VIP section, where it looked down on the dance floor. I scanned the crowd of people through the flashing lights, and Moon's colored hair caught my attention as she came from the hall where the bathrooms were. I pushed off the rail and practically ran down the stairs, meeting her halfway across the dance floor. When she saw me, her eyes lit up before shining with tears as I scooped her up into my arms, clutching her close to my chest and breathing her in.

Relief surged through my body, and every one of my muscles relaxed as I held her in my arms, pressing her body as close to mine as she could get. "Dance with me," she whispered against my ear, her warm breath making goosebumps break out across my neck.

I gripped her hip, and she winced. I raised my eyebrow. "Did that hurt you? What happened?"

She smiled up at me, but it was shy and uncertain. She leaned in to yell over the music. "I did something…"

My eyes traced the movement of her hand as she pulled down the side of her skirt and revealed a bandage. I frowned. Had she gotten hurt when Indy was driving? I'd kill him. She pulled the bandage back, and instead of an injury, what I saw had my heart thundering in my chest and possessiveness thrumming through my body.

The little drumsticks tattooed on her skin were for me. She was mine, and she'd carved a place for me permanently on her body. "You did this for me?" My voice was gravelly, and I almost couldn't get the words out. No one had ever done anything so incredible for me in my life.

She nodded and bit her lip, and I pulled it out from between her teeth with my thumb. I replaced my thumb with my lips, kissing the shit out of her and showing her with my body how much what she'd done meant to me. Finally, I pulled back and smirked at the flush on her skin and how swollen her lips were from my kiss. "I fucking love it."

Her full grin swept across her face as relief trickled into her eyes. She'd been nervous to show me what she'd done, that was obvious. But why? Had I not made it clear to her what she was to me?

Instead of more words, I decided to let my body do the talking for me. I pulled her further onto the dance floor, and we started to move. The way Moon could move her body, undulating her hips fluidly against me, had me harder than granite.

After three songs of basically fucking her on the dance floor, my dick was ready to stage a fucking mutiny, and I told Moon I'd grab drinks (turned out she liked whiskey) and be right back. She grinned at me and tossed her hair over her shoulder. "Hurry," she mouthed before rolling her hips and making me groan and adjust myself.

It didn't take me long to get our drinks, but when I turned back toward Moon, some guy was standing way too close and moved his hands to her hips. She stiffened and turned around, shoving the guy off of her. I stepped up beside her and passed her the drink, narrowing my eyes at the guy.

Over the years, I'd perfected my *don't fuck with me* look, and I gave it to this guy now. "I suggest you get the fuck away from my girlfriend and keep your hands to yourself."

The guy had the audacity to laugh, and I noticed Griffin step up beside me. The guy's eyes darted back and forth between us, but the cocky grin on his face never dropped. "She was into it, man. Maybe you need to do a better job of satisfying her or let someone else step in who can do the job."

I threw my head back and laughed. I was long past the years of getting into fistfights in clubs. I found you could do a lot of damage with your fists, but even more if you stayed calm and dug into people's psyche or their past, or their loved ones. Physical injuries could heal, but some things you could never get over. If he kept pushing me, he was going to get a whole lot more than my fists in his face.

He was going to find out what it was like to be crushed under my size twelve boot.

"Dude, I suggest you walk the fuck away before this gets a whole lot worse for you," Griffin yelled over the music from where he stood beside me.

"And what are you going to do if I don't?" This guy was a fucking idiot. I lifted my phone and snapped a picture of him. He blinked as the flash went off. Griffin stepped forward, and the guy tried to swing for him, but he ducked and caught the guy's arm, pinning them both behind him. I stalked forward and dug my hand through his pockets until I found his wallet. I plucked out his driver's license and held it up, snapping a picture.

"Now I know exactly who you are, Jack O'Neal. In twenty-four hours, I'll know everything about you, which means how best to ruin your life. Now, if you don't apologize to my girlfriend and get the fuck out of here, my friend is going to drag you outside, and I'm going to beat you within an inch of your miserable fucking life. And then the real fun's going to start because tomorrow I'm going to dismantle your life piece by piece until there's nothing left."

Jack had paled considerably as I talked, and he looked like he might throw up or pass out, but he'd fucked with the wrong guy. My girl had been fucked with enough today, and this guy I could do something about, and if he didn't listen, I'd make good on my threat.

"Yeah, sorry, man. Sorry," he nodded in Moon's direction, and she reached out and clung to my arm.

Griffin eyed me, and I nodded at him to let Jack go. Griffin pushed him a little as he released his arms, and Jack stumbled away from us, glancing back before getting lost in the crowd. Griffin turned to give us our privacy, but I grabbed his arm as he was passing by. "I could've handled him myself, but thanks for having my back anyway."

He grinned at me and then turned away, and I pulled Moon into my arms, swaying but not really to the music. It just felt fucking perfect to hold her. She sipped her Old Fashioned and passed off the empty glass to the waitress who passed us by. I'd lost mine somewhere in the confrontation with Jack, but she looked like she was starting to relax between the music and the alcohol.

"Can we find a dark corner somewhere and just get lost in the music?" she asked, shimmying her hips against me and making me instantly hard again.

The short skirt she had on taunted me, and when she turned her back to me and ground her ass against my dick, I almost lost it. I wrapped my arm around her waist and dragged her into the darkest corner of the dance floor where bodies writhed around us, but no one paid attention.

We kept dancing, the music pulsing around us as we moved to every beat. My arm stayed wrapped around her, keeping her pressed tightly against my body. Her hands snaked up around my neck into my hair, and she pulled my mouth down to hers. We collided in a frenzy of lips and tongues and teeth, the kiss more animalistic than anything I'd ever experienced, but after what happened earlier tonight, we were both desperate to feel each other.

I pulled my mouth off of hers and gripped her hand in mine, bringing it around and together with the other. I held both of her hands behind her back with one of mine in a tight grip and moved my mouth beside her ear. "I want you so fucking bad."

She closed her eyes and tossed her head back against my shoulder. The edges of my control were frayed, but this time when I lost it, I'd hurt myself before I hurt her. "Let me feel you," she pleaded, arching her back against me.

Her tits pushed out, and my other hand drifted up her body to brush across her hardened nipple before shifting down and sliding up Moon's skirt. I walked my fingers up her soft, smooth thigh until I brushed against her bare pussy. "You're not wearing panties?" I growled in her ear.

She shook her head and opened her eyes, shooting me a devilish smile. "I took them off in the bathroom just before you got here."

"Fuck," I muttered, stroking my finger across her slick entrance. She was so fucking wet she was practically dripping, and I slipped a finger inside her. The walls of her pussy squeezed my finger so tight I groaned, feeling myself get harder than I'd ever thought possible.

Reluctantly, I pulled my finger out, but I slid it up to her clit and circled it before moving back down and pushing two fingers inside her this time. Her whole body shuddered when my fingers moved inside her, and her hands strained against where I had them held behind her back. "You want more?"

"Please," she whimpered, and that was all the permission I needed.

I pulled my fingers out of her tight pussy and sucked them into my mouth, wanting to taste her. It wasn't as good as burying my tongue in her pussy, but I'd take it. And she tasted like heaven and every fantasy I'd ever had wrapped up in one.

Flicking the button on my jeans, I pulled my zipper down, making sure to keep my body pressed against hers. She kept grinding her ass against me to the loud bass as I pulled my cock free of my boxer briefs. If anyone looked at us, they'd just see us pressed together because I wasn't leaving enough space between us for anyone to get a look at my dick, and I sure as fuck wasn't giving anyone a chance to see what Moon had underneath her skirt. That was just for me.

Lifting the back of her skirt, I tilted her forward just a little, and I was balls deep inside her before I even realized what I'd done, but by then, it was too late. Her body felt too good wrapped around mine as I sunk into her heat. My hips shifted, and I claimed her, one thrust of my hips at a time. She moaned as I filled her, desperately rotating her hips as she cried out for me to move faster, harder, deeper. Who was I to deny what her body was begging me for?

The need to mark her, to make her mine in every sense of the word overwhelmed me, and I gritted my teeth against the pull to fill her with my seed, to watch it drip out of her knowing she'd be walking around with a part of me inside her the rest of the night.

And maybe hoping the seed took root.

The thought of filling her with my cum had me gripping her hip and slamming into her, forgetting where we were and that anyone who bothered to look our way could probably easily see what we were doing. But I hadn't been able to wait, to hold myself back until we got home. I needed to make Moon mine in every sense of the word, and I needed to do it *now.*

Our bodies slammed together, and her head stayed resting on my shoulder, her back arched as I let her hip go and moved my fingers up underneath her skirt to play with her clit.

I flicked and pinched it, alternating with rubbing circles and her pussy clenched around me. I picked up my speed as sweat dripped down my back, but I barely felt it as a different heat started to build inside me. I wouldn't be able to stop it. I needed to make Moon come now because my balls were already tightening, and I couldn't hold out much longer.

"Come for me," I demanded in her ear. "Come all over my cock." She cried out as her whole body tensed up and her pussy squeezed me so tight, I fell over the edge with her, spilling myself deep inside her.

We were both breathing heavily as our surroundings came back into focus, and I looked around, but no one was paying attention to us. I let out a breath, wanting to punch myself in the face for putting Moon at risk like I'd just done. What the fuck was wrong with me?

When it came to sex with Moon, it was like I lost complete fucking control of myself. I couldn't stop myself from fucking her, even if I knew it was risky. Even if I knew anyone could snap a picture of us together and post it all over the internet.

And as I withdrew from her body, I was reminded of the fact I didn't bother wearing a condom. Another place I'd failed to protect her. The idea of that had made me fucking crazy, knowing she had me deep inside her. It made my chest swell, and my dick start to harden again.

I let go of Moon's wrists and wrapped my arm around her waist, pressing a kiss to the curve of her neck before stepping back to tuck myself back in my jeans. I spun her in my arms and looked at the small smile on her lips and the sated look in her eyes. I leaned over and brushed her hair off of her neck before asking her, "Are you okay?" My lips brushed her ear, and she shivered.

"I'm great, but I want to do that again, and soon."

Fuck, so did I. I reached into my pocket and pulled out my phone, sending Connor a text.

Jericho: Are we clear to go home?

Connor: You're all good. I'll have Indy meet you at the parking lot.

Now that I'd been inside Moon, I wanted to feel her again and again, starting with getting her home now and taking my time showing her the level of devotion I had for her and her body one lick at a time.

"Let's get the fuck out of here." I gripped her hand in mine and led her off the dance floor, already anticipating losing myself in her all over again.

FIFTEEN
MOON

Jericho made me not care if I was careful, if *we* were careful because somehow I knew he'd never let anything hurt me. He'd never abandon me or leave me to deal with things on my own. Every time he turned them on me, the possession and love glinting in his dark eyes showed me everything I needed to know without him ever saying a word.

And that part of me that lived up to my name, that loved chaos and mayhem, hoped Jericho would tie himself to me forever because as much as I was his, he was *mine*.

Maybe I was sick in the head, but last night on the dance floor was the hottest experience of my entire fucking life. And there'd been nothing between us, no barriers, and for some reason that made it so much better.

When we got home, we spent hours enjoying each other and talking before doing it all over again until I was too exhausted to keep going, and after our last round, I passed out as soon as we finished in a sweaty, satisfied mess. I stretched and realized I was still naked as the sheet slipped down my body. Jericho was wrapped around me protectively even in his sleep, and I almost laughed out loud at all the things I was sure Julian had heard overnight.

Shifting slightly, I moved to reach for my phone on the nightstand. I had plans to meet my dad for breakfast today and didn't want to be late. I had no idea what time it was, but I definitely needed a shower even if it was only thirty seconds long. When I shifted again to try and climb out of bed, Jericho tightened his grip on me and pulled me back into his body.

I couldn't resist snuggling back into him, breathing him in, and turning to tuck my head up under his chin. Life was so much better with him in it. I decided to ignore my phone and let myself enjoy the moment, drifting back off to sleep with Jericho's arms tight around me.

My phone vibrating across my nightstand woke me up, and I swatted at it, trying to get it to stop without fully opening my eyes. I managed to grab it just as it stopped vibrating and started up again. "Shit," I cursed when I looked at the screen, swiping to answer.

"Hey, dad." I tried to keep my voice down, but Jericho was a light sleeper and stirred next to me.

"Hey, kiddo. I'm at the diner. Were you planning on joining me this morning?" There was humor in my dad's voice, and I jolted upright.

"Shit, sorry. Give me fifteen minutes." Jericho's arm snaked around me, and my whole body shuddered when he started pressing lazy kisses up my spine.

Just as quickly, his arm disappeared, and I turned around to see him pulling on his jeans. "Okay, Moon Pie. See you soon." My chest warmed at my dad's familiar nickname, and I tossed my phone down next to me.

"What are you doing?"

Jericho wore an expression that said, *what the fuck do you think I'm doing?* "Going with you, unless you'd rather take Indy along."

I tried to ignore the cold expression on his face at the suggestion and blew out a breath, running a hand through my tangled hair. "So, we're doing the whole meet the parents thing?"

His lips twitched as he moved around the end of the bed to my side and tugged me up to standing. His eyes raked down my still-naked body as the sheet fell away. Jericho's fingers trailed up my stomach and brushed across my tightened nipple. He leaned forward and pressed a kiss to my neck that had me trembling, and he smiled against my skin. "Do you not think we're serious enough for that yet?"

His words snapped me out of the lust-fueled haze he'd managed to put me into in the last thirty seconds, and he pulled back and met my eyes, watching me carefully. His expression was guarded like my answer had the ability to define what we were moving forward and also wound him. "I guess I hadn't thought about it, but yeah. I want you to meet my dad," I decided, and I meant it.

Relief flashed across his eyes before they settled into something cockier as a crooked grin spread across his face. I didn't realize how rare his smiles were until I saw him with his friends and realized he only smiles when he's around me. Jericho bent down and pressed a kiss to my lips before stepping away and leaving me cold. A whimper of protest worked its way out of my throat before I could shove it back down, and he chuckled darkly.

"Your dad's already waiting, beautiful girl. We can pick this back up after breakfast." He bent down and picked up his shirt, and I watched as his muscles rippled. After he pulled his shirt on, his voice broke me out of my trance. "Moon."

I broke my stare off of him. He really was so very gorgeous in a dark and dangerous sort of way; I could stare at him all day. I sighed and pouted a little because my fun was being interrupted, but I was excited to see my dad. It'd been a couple of weeks since I last saw him, and that was a long time for us. Since my mom disappeared, we'd been close, and that hadn't changed when I moved out.

I stepped into my closet and pulled on one of my favorite outfits. Jericho moved into the bathroom while I closed my closet door and studied myself in the mirror hanging on the back. My graphic t-shirt was knotted at my waist, showing a sliver of my toned abdomen, and the gauzy skirt I wore hit at my knees but hung lower in back. I scanned my shoes for my favorite lace-up peep-toe heeled boots, and finally, I pulled a lightweight patterned kimono over the top. My style was as eclectic as I was, and I loved it. One look at my outfit and you knew exactly what you were getting with me.

My hair was messy from a whole night of sex with Jericho, so I combed my fingers through it and pulled the top up into a messy bun, letting the rest of my colorful messy waves hang down to my shoulders. Once I heard the bathroom door open, I stepped into my room, and Jericho's eyes again raked down my body, stopped at the strip of skin on my stomach, and he ran his thumb along his lower lip as his gaze darkened.

Damn, that was hot.

He barely stepped aside enough for me to move past him into the bathroom to brush my teeth, and I had to press myself against his hard body to get inside. I'd never reacted to anyone like I did to Jericho, and every place my skin brushed against his set off a reaction in me, pulsing through my veins and settling between my thighs.

And he smirked at me like he knew exactly what he was doing to me, the bastard.

I shut the door and leaned against it, taking a couple of deep breaths and trying to get my raging libido under control. I'd had sex before, but it'd always been mediocre and nothing I really cared much about. But sex with Jericho was a whole other beast. I had a delicious ache from last night and could still feel him inside me with every step I took, and still I craved more.

I brushed my teeth in record time, and in just a couple of minutes, we were practically running the three blocks down to the diner where my dad was waiting for us. I wasn't that much shorter than Jericho, but somehow his legs ate up a ton more sidewalk than mine.

He held open the door for me, and I sucked in air as I walked inside. I really needed to do more cardio. Jericho followed me inside and slid his hand onto the small of my back where my t-shirt didn't quite hit the hem of my skirt. His skin touched mine, and that spark he seemed to always ignite in me made me twitch. Out of the corner of my eye, I saw him smirk.

My dad spotted us and waved, so we pushed through the other tables toward the back where he'd claimed a booth by the window. He stood up when we approached, a warm smile on his face but curiosity in his eyes when he noticed Jericho beside me. "About time, Moon Pie. I was going to eat without you." He laughed that same warm laugh he'd always had that made me feel comforted and happy before pulling me into a tight hug. He eyed Jericho but not suspiciously, just with curiosity. "Who's your friend?"

I stepped out of his embrace and back to Jericho's side, where he draped his arm over my shoulders and pulled me into his side. He extended his other hand toward my dad. "I'm Jericho, Moon's boyfriend."

Well, okay then.

My dad's eyebrows lifted as his smile widened. He shook Jericho's hand enthusiastically. "Boyfriend? Moon's never let me meet one of her boyfriends before. Sit, sit." He moved back into the booth and gestured for us to sit across from him.

My dad passed us a couple of menus before starting in. "I'm August."

Jericho handed me his menu. "Nice to meet you, August."

My dad leaned against the back of the booth and stretched his arm across the back, that wide smile still on his face. "You, too." He turned to me. "Now, Moon Pie, why have I heard nothing about Jericho here?"

I handed the menus back to Jericho, glancing up at him. "Can you please just pick for me?" I liked spontaneity, and giving up control meant a total surprise. The fact I could lean on Jericho to make simple decisions like what to have for breakfast, and he got off on his need for control, meant I could enjoy the surprise of what I got. It was a win-win.

He pulled the menu out of my hands and furrowed his brows as he scanned it, apparently taking his job very seriously. My dad was watching us with unhidden glee on his face, and I rolled my eyes. "C'mon, dad. Stop staring at us like a science experiment."

"Fine." He deflated a little but perked back up. "What do you do, Jericho? You look familiar."

I stifled a laugh. This should be good. Jericho shot me a glare out of the side of his eye before settling his attention back on my dad. "I'm in a band."

His eyes widened. "Wait." He studied Jericho closely, his eyebrows furrowing as he tried to piece it together. "Holy shit. Shadow Phoenix, right? I love you guys!"

Jericho let out a low rumble of a laugh. "Thanks, August."

"Don't mind me just freaking out a little bit over here." My dad took a sip of his water and choked on it. He had absolutely no chill. "Tell me how you two met," he managed to get out between hacking coughs.

I laughed, and Jericho chuckled quietly next to me as he handed the menus to the waitress who'd just come to take our order. He ordered for both of us, and my dad gave his order, and then she left us alone. "Jericho was in my mommy and me class."

My dad cracked up. "What? Why?"

Jericho leaned further into me and moved his hand under the table to rest on my thigh. I was hyper-aware of his fingers drawing a tiny circle around and around on my thigh. I squirmed, trying to get him to move higher, but infuriatingly he stayed in the same place, driving me crazy.

"My friend Kennedy dragged me along," Jericho supplied when my brain short-circuited.

My dad eyed Jericho skeptically. "You're not exactly a small guy. How'd she manage that?"

"Blackmail," Jericho shrugged, and my dad laughed.

"That'll do it."

"Moon came over to help me with my form, and the rest is history." Jericho winked at me, and my insides melted into a puddle. Our story wasn't quite that simple, but my dad didn't need all the details.

"Speaking of the studio, how's that going?" I knew my dad was asking about my part-time school and plans for what I wanted to do to expand. I hadn't talked about any of this with Jericho yet, and I didn't know how our lives would fit together. We hadn't exactly been together long enough to talk about the future, and with someone following me and everything going on with the band, we'd been taking things day by day.

Last year, when I told my dad I wanted to get my MBA and expand the studio to become an entire wellness center, he'd been supportive but also gently asked me if that was what I really wanted. I loved working for myself, and I loved yoga. But the day to day of running a business wasn't something I enjoyed all that much.

I was starting to realize I'd created a job for myself instead of a business that worked for me. And as far as jobs went, this one was pretty stressful at times. Would I be doing this job if it wasn't my business? Probably not. But now that I was already neck-deep in it, I didn't want to walk away from something I created.

"I had to fire Terra, so it's been pretty stressful because I haven't found a replacement yet. School's going fine, a bit boring, but I'm learning lots." The waitress dropped my stuffed french toast in front of me and my mouth watered. I smiled up at Jericho. "Good choice."

He chuckled and leaned down to whisper in my ear, "I know what makes you happy," and I shivered at the gravelly tone of his voice. His thumb was still drawing those circles that were driving me insane, except he'd slowly bunched my skirt up so his hand slipped under the fabric and was just on my bare skin.

My stomach growled, and I pushed down the insane urge to straddle Jericho right here in the restaurant with my dad sitting across from us. My panties were completely soaked, but I ignored my other hunger in favor of stuffing a huge bite of breakfast into my mouth. I groaned in a totally indecent way, and Jericho's fingers stilled on my leg before sliding up higher. I almost choked, and when I looked up at him through my lashes, his face was totally cool as if he wasn't affected at all by what was happening under the table.

"So you're going to keep pushing ahead with the wellness center then?" my dad asked, completely oblivious to the tension building and sparking between Jericho and me.

"That's the plan," I confirmed, and I was happy my voice didn't tremble. I took another bite of my food as Jericho's fingers inched higher with every circle he drew.

It took all of my concentration not to choke and to finish enough of my breakfast that my stomach was no longer pissed off at me. Once we'd all finished, my dad swiped his face with his napkin one last time and took a huge deep breath before tossing his napkin onto his empty plate.

"Have you talked to Jericho yet about your mom?" My stomach flipped, and my whole body stiffened like a bucket of ice water had just been dumped over my head. My mom's disappearance was a touchy subject with me. I refused to believe she'd walked out on her own, but unlike my dad, I'd come to terms with the fact that she was probably dead a long time ago. I'd mourned her and moved on, but that didn't mean I didn't miss her every single day.

But my dad? He'd never given up hope that she was still alive.

"Just a little," I admitted as Jericho looked at me with questions in his eyes. I had a feeling we'd be having a long discussion about my mom when we got back to my house.

My dad continued. "You know I hired a new PI a few months ago? He found a witness at a gas station about fifty miles from here that thinks he saw your mom that night. She was alone, Moon."

My heart battered my ribcage as I gasped. "No." I shook my head and squeezed my eyes closed. "She wouldn't have left us. She wouldn't have walked out on me." I refused to believe my mom left on her own.

Jericho lifted his hand off of my thigh and linked our fingers together in silent support. My dad shot him a grateful look. "We don't know what was going on with your mom, Moon Pie, but I know she would never have left you without a good reason. And that same PI has a lead that made him think she was still alive but in hiding."

Tears pricked the back of my eyes, but I wouldn't let them fall. Not for the woman who'd apparently walked out and let us think she was dead. "What does that mean?"

"It means your mom might be alive."

SIXTEEN

JERICHO

I clasped Moon's hand in mine tightly because, on our walk back from the diner, it felt like she might drift off from me and be lost to her thoughts. It was like she wasn't even present, letting me blindly lead her home. I liked her submissive to me, but this was something else.

For at least the moment, all the life seemed to have drained out of her, and she was a shell of herself. I wouldn't let that shit fucking stand. Not for a second. Before we left the diner, I exchanged contact info with August and asked him to email me everything his PI found. No matter how good the guy was, I knew Connor's team was better.

I'd do anything, pay anything to erase the lost look on Moon's face. As we stepped up onto her front porch, I tugged her against my chest and wrapped my arm around her back, using my other hand to tilt her chin up so I could look at her. "Okay, pretty girl. You've had enough time to sink inside yourself, but I'm going to need you to come back to me now so we can figure this out. Okay?"

My eyes darted between hers, watching the life slowly come back into her gaze as she blinked at me. Then she leaned forward and rested her cheek against my chest and wrapped her arms around me, clutching me tightly as if she thought I'd leave her too. My heart stuttered a little in my chest at how tightly she was clinging to me.

There wasn't a chance in hell I'd ever walk away from Moon Mayhem

Not when she brightened everything about my world and made me feel more than I ever had.

I'd never been in love before, so I didn't know what it felt like, but the way I'd heard it described, I was pretty sure I'd already fallen hard.

Finally, she nodded, and I breathed a huge-ass sigh of relief. She hadn't locked the door when we left because Indy was still standing guard. I swung the door open and guided Moon inside. She still looked shell-shocked as she glided across the small space and sat on the sofa. Indy raised his eyebrows and looked at me, but I shot him a glare. The last thing I needed was him asking questions right now.

I sat down next to Moon and pulled her against me, pulling the hair tie out of her hair and running my hands through it. I wasn't going to make her talk yet, but I would if she didn't start soon.

"One night when I was twelve, my mom tried to kiss me goodnight, and I wrinkled my nose at her and gave her all sorts of attitude about it, and then went to bed. When I woke up in the morning, the front door was open, and she was gone. I've never seen or heard from her since." She let out a shuddering breath, and I turned my head to lock eyes with Indy, hoping he picked up on my silent communication to come over and listen.

He flipped the deadbolt on the door and moved silently to lean against the living room wall behind us in a place Moon wouldn't see unless she turned her head away from me.

"When she was gone in the morning, her car was still here. Dad and I called the police and tried to file a missing person's report. Both of us were sure she wouldn't have walked out on her own, but the police told us we had to wait." She looked up at me with watery eyes, and I died a little inside at the pain in her expression.

"They said there was no sign of anyone breaking in or anything, so they thought she just went out and maybe didn't close the door all the way. Dad and I knew better. Mom wouldn't do that." Moon took another deep breath, and I glanced back at Indy, who was typing on his phone. "The police tried, but they found nothing and basically gave up on her case. They figured she just walked out. There was no body, no evidence of anything being out of the ordinary, other than that she was gone."

Moon let out a humorless laugh, and I pulled her tighter against me. She rested her head on my shoulder while I stroked her hair. "A couple of years into her being gone, I must've been about fourteen or fifteen at that point, I finally accepted she wasn't coming back. My dad and I got into a lot of fights back then because he spent all his free time and any extra money he had trying to track her down and got nowhere. He refused to give up on her, but I had to let her go so I could heal and move on. So I did. I mourned her, and the only one who supported me in that was Bexley."

"And now it looks like she might be alive and might've made the choice to walk out," I finished, making sure to keep my voice low and soothing.

She nodded. "How could she do that? *Why* would she do that? I'd never walk away from my husband, my *child*." Her voice was rising and a line formed between her eyebrows as she started to get angry.

"I don't know why she walked away, beautiful, but if she did, she must've had a good reason. You're allowed to feel pissed off. Hell, I'm pissed off at her for putting you through this. But we don't have all the facts."

She sniffled and looked up at me, her eyes wide and fucking adorable. My chest clenched with the force of my feelings for her. "I don't know where to start looking. I thought we'd looked everywhere."

"You don't need to worry about it. I've got this, okay?" Indy nodded at me before taking his post back up by the door. "Connor's going to handle it, and if she's out there, he'll find her."

She breathed out a sigh of relief or resignation; I wasn't sure which. Maybe both, who the fuck knew? But my phone had been vibrating in my pocket for the last five minutes, and I'd been ignoring it. Nothing was more important than being here for Moon when she needed me, but she seemed better now. Lighter.

More like her usual self, thank fuck for that.

I pulled out my phone and answered, holding it up to my ear. "What?" I barked out, not giving one single fuck about who was on the other end of the line.

"Jericho, mate. You're supposed to be here in an hour. None of the guys had heard from you, so I wanted to remind you," Harrison, our publicist's smooth, accented voice grated on my nerves.

"I'll be there." I hung up, not waiting for a response.

I leaned down to kiss Moon, pouring all the feelings into the kiss that I didn't have words for yet. I hated having to leave her now when she was sad and vulnerable, but I didn't have a choice. When I pulled away, she clung to me, and I fucking hated myself for not being able to stay. "I have to go do a stupid fucking interview downtown, but I'll be back in a couple of hours, and Indy will be here with you. I'll call Connor on my drive and get him on your mom's case, okay?"

She nodded and let me go, scooting back on the couch. The place she'd just been pressed against me went cold, and I clenched my jaw against the anger rolling through me. "If you need me, call, and I'll bail," I promised.

She gave me a small smile. "I'm not going to interrupt band business, Jericho. Don't worry about me; I'll be fine."

But I did worry about her, so fucking much. "Don't leave the house until I get back, please. I don't think I can handle worrying about you being out right now on top of everything else." I hated admitting it, but it was true. I was going to be useless in this interview, I already knew. My head was a fucking mess, and my body was tense as fuck.

"Jericho... You promised you wouldn't put limits on me," she gently reminded me.

I raked my hand through my hair. "Fuck, I know. Okay? I know. But just this once, do what I say and stay in the goddamn house. Please."

She studied me with her ocean-colored eyes before finally nodding. "Okay."

My shoulders relaxed a fraction. "Thank you."

"But you owe me," she added, tapping her kissable lips with the pad of her finger. "I think at least two orgasms when you get home should do it."

I let out a low chuckle and leaned over to capture her lips again before pulling back just a fraction and staring into her heavily-lidded eyes. "When I get home, you'll be lucky if I let you leave the bedroom until tomorrow."

My dick was already straining against my jeans, but I was out of time. I stood up and adjusted myself, but it didn't help. "That's a fucking promise."

She watched me walk to the front door, her gaze burning into my back, but I didn't look back because I wouldn't have been able to stop myself from carrying her off to the bedroom and ditching the meeting. The guys depended on me to be there, and I wouldn't screw them over.

I nodded at Indy as I walked outside, exhaling slowly into the late afternoon air. It only took me a few seconds to reach my Range Rover and climb inside, pushing the button to start it and waiting for the Bluetooth to connect my phone. When I pulled away from the curb, I hit the button to call Connor.

"Cole," he grunted my last name as a greeting.

"Jamison," I tossed back.

"What's up? Aren't you supposed to be at Harry's office?" I cracked a small smile at Harrison's nickname. We all used it behind his back because he hated it, and when he pissed us off, we used it to his face.

"I'm on my way. Did Indy text you earlier?" I drummed my fingers on the steering wheel.

"Yeah, something about Moon's mom. What do you need from me?"

"Her mom disappeared fifteen years ago, and it's suspicious as fuck. Her dad seems to think there's a possibility she's alive, a new lead. He's sending me whatever his PI found, and I'll forward it to Sebastian. But I was thinking that maybe her mom disappearing like that could have something to do with the fact she's being followed now. It's fucking weird that no one's picked up even a trace of her mom in all this time, yet a new lead pops up now at the exact same time someone's watching Moon?"

"Yeah, I'll admit that's an interesting coincidence," he admitted. "I'll keep Indy and Julian on rotation and have Sebastian start digging. If Moon's mom is out there, we'll find her."

"I know, that's why I called you. I trust you to handle this." The *or I'll kick your ass* was implied.

He chuckled. "Yeah, I've got it." And I knew he did. He wouldn't let me down, and more importantly, he wouldn't let Moon down.

"You going to be at this meeting?" I asked, not really caring but also not wanting to be a complete dick after I just asked him to do something for me.

"Nah, my newest addition's got guard duty for this one."

"Ryan?" I didn't know how Maddox managed to deal with the constant fear of something happening to the woman he loved, but somehow he dealt with it. He lived to make Ryan happy, just like Zen did with Kennedy and True did with Amara. I was starting to understand what they'd all been going through the past couple of years.

"Nope. My buddy Ronin finally decided to start making some real money and left his job with the SPD to join my crew. You'll meet him at the office."

"Great." My voice was flat. I hated meeting new people. I hated most people in general, and after meeting August this morning, I'd already reached my being pleasant to new people quota for the day.

Connor laughed. "Yeah, have fun. I'll call you when I find something on Moon's mom." He ended the call, and I drove the rest of the way with music blasting, trying to drown out my thoughts.

Harrison's glass-walled conference room was already full by the time I walked in, obviously the last one to arrive. That didn't mean that I walked any faster or gave a shit about them waiting on me. I intentionally slowed down my walk and sauntered in, dropping down in a chair next to Zen, who was sending a death glare at the hipster guy at the front of the table.

"Who's the asshole?" I asked him, not bothering to lower my voice.

"Blane Hoffman, douchebag extraordinaire." That name was vaguely familiar to me, but I couldn't place it.

"Should I know who he is?" I leaned back in my chair, joining my friend in his death glare just for fun.

"He's the tool who did the interview with Kennedy and me for *Pulse.*" I peeled my glare off of Blane while he finished prepping his shit for the interview and looked at True, who shrugged.

"The dude hit on Kennedy," True explained.

"In front of Zen," Maddox finished.

Griffin tried to cover up his snicker with a cough, and his brother elbowed him in the ribs.

"Not cool, Griff. You don't hit on another guy's girlfriend." Maddox glared at his brother, and I swung my glare at the newest member of our band, too.

"Yeah, Griff," I bit out. "That's a good way to get your ass kicked, or worse." I let the threat in my voice do most of the talking for me.

He smirked at me, and I clenched my fists to keep from launching myself across the table at him.

"He just likes fucking with you," Zen muttered. "If you ignore him, he'll knock his shit off."

Ignoring Griffin's poking at me went against everything that I was, every natural reaction I normally had. I wanted to destroy him so he could never take Moon away from me, not even a second of her attention. But he was in the band now, and that changed things. Slowly, I flattened my fingers against my thighs and exhaled.

Zen patted my shoulder. "You know Mad would never let him get away with laying a finger on Moon, right?"

I nodded, but my jaw was still tight. To distract myself, I scanned the room, and I noticed the guy Connor must've been talking about. Ronin. He was tall and built, with dark hair that flopped over his forehead and a shrewd glare that took in every detail of the room and the people in it. He leaned against the wall with his arms folded across his chest.

Blane clapped his hands together annoyingly loud, and we all turned toward him, a mixture of boredom and irritation on our faces. Or in Zen's case, pure burning hatred.

"Okay, let's get this shitshow over with, shall we?" He scooted his chair closer to the table and scanned the laptop screen in front of him. "Album number eight is underway, but there've been some massive changes in band structure. Rumor has it you guys weren't happy with Jericho here on drums anymore and kicked him to the curb in favor of the younger model. Care to comment?"

I gripped the side of my chair so hard, the leather creaked underneath my fingers. No one spoke, and I imagined everyone was just as shocked as I was that he just jumped right in. "I knew this was going to go off the fucking rails the second I saw *him* setting up," Zen noted, pushing out of his chair and leaving the room.

"Listen, you little-" Harrison started, but I cut him off with my hand held up. My muscles were coiled tight, ready to lash out with one wrong word. My eyes were cold and flat, and my lips curled up into a wicked smile.

"Wouldn't that make a great story? It might even give you some fucking credibility if you could bring a story like that forward, right?" I stood and prowled along the side of the table, dragging my hand across the back of the chairs separating Blane from me.

"It wouldn't matter to you that it wasn't true or that you'd be fucking with our careers, would it? No, I didn't think so." I stepped up beside Blane, whose face had gone ashen as I leaned down and rested my hands on the table beside him.

"So let me clear a few things up for you. I sure as fuck wasn't *kicked out* of my own band, you sorry piece of shit. And as for Griffin? He earned his spot here, just like everyone else. You can call it nepotism or whatever the fuck you want, but he's the best guy for the job. So how about you do your goddamn job and report the facts. Stop spewing inaccurate bullshit and trying to stir shit up."

I turned around to move back to my seat, completely over this shit already, when the jackass decided to speak up. "And I suppose you're going to tell me nothing happened with Richard Bennett?"

"Richard," Maddox coughed and grinned at me before he took over. "Dick didn't know what the fuck he was doing, so Jericho took over. There's nothing more to it than that."

Blane's lips curled into a predatory smirk. "Oh, really? That's not what he said."

"Jericho-" True tried, but I wasn't having it.

Spinning back around, I gritted my teeth as I tried not to lose my temper completely. I was vaguely aware of all the eyes in the room on me, and I also knew somewhere in the back of my mind that whatever I said or did in this room could, and probably *would*, end up in Blane's article.

And yet, not one single fuck was given. I probably should have stopped to think, but my anger was boiling over. I didn't want to be here, I didn't want to be doing this, and I sure as fuck didn't want to leave Moon alone after the morning she'd had.

"Dick was the shittiest producer we've ever had. Is that what you want to hear? He didn't know how to put the basic elements of a song together, for fuck sake. His music was complete fucking garbage, and we couldn't stomach putting our names on it. I would rather quit and walk away from music altogether than put my name on something he produced. So yes, we fired him against the label's wishes, and I stepped in because I know what the fuck I'm doing. But if I were Dick, I'd be looking for a new career because no one who wants to make music professionally should ever work with someone so amateur."

"Shit," Griffin muttered, a shit-eating grin spreading across his face. "Okay, that was officially badass."

Harrison seemed to shake off his shock at my outburst and step across the room to Blane. "That's going to be the end of the interview, mate. Time to go." He grabbed Blane's bag and started shoving his shit in it haphazardly. Blane stood up and started protesting, but Harrison shoved his shit against his chest, and Ronin took over, removing him from the building.

True laughed and stood up, clasping his hand on my shoulder. "Dude, the one time you decide to finally open your mouth in an interview, and you burn Dick's career to the ground." He didn't look upset about it, though. In fact, all the guys looked totally relaxed, and as always, I knew they'd have my back no matter what consequences came of this.

"At least the cat's outta the bag now, and I bet people are going to be hyped to hear the new album knowing you produced it," Maddox added, coming to stand beside us.

"And thanks for having my back. Sorry about Moon," Griffin tacked on, joining our little circle. Zen and Harrison both came back into the room, and the cloud of pissed off energy hanging around Zen had disappeared only to be replaced with a smug smirk. "Thanks for exploding at that fucker and saving me the trouble."

I chuckled, feeling my heart rate start to slow. Whatever had come out of my mouth in this interview would have consequences. The label was already pissed off, and when Marcus Hughes got word that I'd thrown his little boyfriend under the bus, I had a feeling he was going to come for us harder than ever. It was a good thing we'd always been prepared for a war because I had a feeling that was what was coming.

SEVENTEEN
MOON

"I owe you so huge for this." I moved over to the tiny table and plopped down, gripping my hot to-go cup between my fingers and blowing across the steaming surface of my tea. I took a tentative sip and winced when it scalded my tongue.

· Bexley took the seat across from me and set down her scone, brushing the crumbs off her fingers. "It's just one day, babe. Don't even worry about it."

"Well, it's a big deal to me. I still haven't had time to find a replacement for Terra, and if I miss another day of classes this quarter, I'm going to fall too far behind to make up."

"I may not be as flexible as you, but I can hold my own through a few yoga poses this morning. Don't worry; I've got you."

I blinked back stinging tears and took another sip of my tea, forgetting how hot it was and cursing as I burned my tongue again. It was just that kind of morning. Jericho got home super late and fell into bed with me and then woke up and left before the sun was anywhere close to coming up. I was still raw and worried about everything with my mom, and I was jumpy as hell because I knew now I was being watched.

My eyes flicked up to Indy, who took a table a couple of spots away from us, but his eyes swept the room constantly. I turned my attention back to my best friend and reached across the table to squeeze her hand. She gave me a small smile. "What's that for?"

"I'm just really grateful to have you as my friend. When we were five, and you kicked Archie Samson in the shin for pushing me down into the dirt, I knew we'd be friends forever. And with everything changing and going on right now, I'm just glad to have you in my corner." The corner of my eyes pricked with tears, and I dabbed at them with my napkin. I hadn't gotten much sleep last night, and I was always such a wreck emotionally when I was tired.

Plus, living life always looking over your shoulder was mentally exhausting.

"I'm not going anywhere. Now tell me about breakfast with your dad yesterday. I'm assuming the Hulk over there tagged along?" She tossed her head not-so-subtly in Indy's direction, and I laughed.

"No, actually, Jericho came."

Her eyebrows shot up. "Oh, shit. How'd August take meeting his future son-in-law?" She smiled at me sweetly and popped a piece of scone in her mouth, propping her chin on her knuckles and waiting for me to answer.

I rolled my eyes. "First of all, that's skipping a few steps, don't you think?"

Bex shrugged. "Not really. You two are practically living together already, and you're probably not being honest with yourself yet, but you totally love him."

I tossed my hands up, exasperated. "It's only been a few weeks, and he's just staying with me because of the creeper hanging around and watching me."

Bexley finished off her scone and balled up her napkin. "Sure, keep telling yourself that. No comment about the love bit, though, huh?"

I scowled at her, really not ready to go there yet, even if it felt like my chest was caving in last night when Jericho came home, obviously upset about something. "*Anyway*," I dragged the word out. "My dad was definitely fangirling hard over Jericho. Turns out, he's been a Shadow Phoenix fan forever, so he had a little bit of a freak-out."

Bexley snorted, almost shooting coffee out her nose. She grabbed a napkin and mopped up the bit dribbling out of her nostril. "Oh, my god, I can't believe that just happened." She coughed a couple of times. "I'd have paid good money to watch August go all fanatic on your new boyfriend."

"As entertaining as it was, that wasn't the most interesting thing that happened at breakfast," I murmured, leaning across the table to close the distance between us. Since I was being followed, I wanted to make sure this next part stayed between us.

She leaned in so our heads were huddled together over the small table. "What happened?"

I lowered my voice to a whisper. "My dad hired a PI to track my mom."

Bexley sat back and rolled her eyes. "That's not interesting. He's been doing that forever."

"I know, shh!" I urged her to lean back forward, and she did. "What's new is that the guy actually found evidence she left on her own *and* that she might still be alive."

Bexley sucked in a sharp breath. "No, shit?"

"No, shit. Jericho exchanged contact info with my dad and promised to help, so as far as I know, he sicced that guy's boss on my mom's case." I gestured to Indy, who was watching the front door intently.

"Cara might be alive? That's crazy." Her voice was quiet, and then she shook herself, and her focus landed back on me. "Are you okay?"

"Honestly? I don't really know how to feel. I'm sort of numb. I don't want to get my hopes up. It's been so long since she disappeared. And if she did leave on her own, how am I supposed to deal with that? It means she chose to walk away from us." I pressed my lips together but then let out a sigh. "I guess I just hope that she's alive, and then we can go from there figuring out the rest."

Bexley nodded in understanding and gripped my hand in hers. "That's a good place to start, babe."

I gave her a watery smile before checking my phone. "Shit, I'm going to be late if I don't go. Are you sure you're okay to open up the studio?"

She waved me off, pulling the keys to my business out of her pocket and sliding them down her index finger before twirling them around. "I think I can handle a morning in a super chill yoga studio. Go to class; I've got this."

We stood and tossed our trash, and Indy followed. She pulled me into a hug, crushing me against her, but that wasn't unusual. Bex always gave super tight hugs. Sometimes, she even made it hard to breathe.

She pulled back, and her gaze darted between me and Indy, who stood about a foot behind us. "Do me a favor and be extra careful today, okay? I woke up with a really bad feeling, and I'm worried about you."

A cold chill of unease settled down my spine. Bexley's intuition was almost never wrong, but hopefully, her bad feeling was about someone or something else and not me. "I'll be careful," I promised, meaning it.

She released me and stepped back with a nod. "Text me when you're done with school and let me know how it went."

I agreed and followed Indy out of the shop and to my car. I still had to hide my snort of laughter every time he folded himself behind the wheel. When we were both inside, I turned to him. "Why don't you bring your car or a bigger company car or something? This is ridiculous."

He shrugged. "I figured you'd be more comfortable in your own car."

That was unexpectedly sweet of him. "Thanks, but I'm really okay if you want to bring something bigger. I don't mind."

His nod was all I got, and he turned on the music. Turning it down, though, I faced him again. "I don't know if you know this about Bex, but she has this crazy intuition."

"I don't know what that means." Indy rolled to a stop and flicked the blinker on while we waited.

"It means sometimes she knows things before they happen, or sometimes she just gets a feeling about something—good or bad—and it almost always happens the way she thinks."

"So… she's a psychic," he scoffed and shot me a disbelieving look that I might be offended by if I hadn't felt the same way myself at first.

Shaking my head, I flicked my eyes to the ceiling. "Not exactly. Look, all I'm saying is she told me to be extra careful today because she had a bad feeling. I'm just passing along the message."

His lips turned up in a smirk. "Message received."

Indy pulled into the parking lot of UCLA and found a spot to park. We both climbed out, and I grabbed my backpack from the back seat, checking that I had everything. We started walking side by side onto the campus. "I have two classes today, Economics and Marketing. Are you going to sit in with me or wait in the hall?"

He gave me a look like I should know better. "I'm not taking my eyes off of you. There would be a line to murder me if something happened to you with Jericho at the front and Connor right behind him. I'd like to stay alive, thanks."

We found my first lecture hall and settled in. Honestly, I hated these classes. They bored me to tears, and I felt like I wasn't learning anything I could really use. But topping off my generic business undergrad degree with a fancy MBA felt like something I *should* do, even if it wasn't something I was all that excited about.

The professor droned on for over an hour, and I diligently took notes, even if half the time I spaced out on what he was actually saying. Somehow the connection between my ears and my fingers stayed true, even if everything went in one ear and out the other. At the end of class, Indy stood up from where he'd stayed beside me and stretched with a groan. "Jesus. We have to sit through another one of these things?"

I nodded, shoving my laptop back into my bag. "I know. But we only get a fifteen-minute break to walk across campus before the next one starts, so we better go."

We left the lecture hall and made good time across campus. We found a couple of seats together near the back of the room, and I pulled out everything I'd need. I found marketing a tiny bit more exciting than economics, but I didn't have high hopes for my poor attention span in this class, either.

Just as the last students trickled into the hall and found seats, the professor breezed into the room and jumped right into her lecture. There were over a hundred people in this class, if I had to guess, and there was a constant chorus of ruffled papers, shifting clothes, and soft murmurs of conversation. The door opened and closed at random as people came and went, but when Indy stiffened beside me, I looked up from my laptop screen in concern.

"What's wrong?" I whispered.

His eyes were locked on something, or someone, behind us in the dark near the furthest set of doors. He narrowed his stare before the doors opened and whoever he'd been watching left. He leaned closer and whispered, "Someone was trailing behind us on our way to this class. The same guy just came inside and had his phone up like he was taking pictures of us."

A full-body shiver worked through me, and my heart took up a punishing rhythm. "Are you going to go after him?"

He shook his head. "I can't. If I go after him, I leave you vulnerable. But we may have to start guarding in teams." He pulled out his phone and typed out a message, I'd assume to Connor, but I had no idea how their dynamics worked.

My concentration was shot, and the rest of the class went right over my head. With shaking hands, I packed up my bag and slung it over my back. "Can we please get out of here?" I hated how my voice trembled. I was terrified of what might be waiting for me outside of those doors, and while I trusted Indy, I'd never seen him in action. I had no idea what he was capable of, and he was only one person.

He nodded once, and we left the classroom in the middle of all the other students, my guess was to blend into the crowd. Indy grasped my hand so we wouldn't get lost in the sea of people, and he walked quickly, keeping his head on a swivel. I kept my eyes down and had to almost run to keep up with him as he dragged me across campus.

He came to an abrupt stop near the parking lot, and I almost ran into his back. My head whipped up, and with frantic eyes, I searched for danger around me, but I didn't see anything. "Why'd you stop?" I hissed.

"Because the guy who was following you and taking pictures of you was just looking into your car windows." Shit, shit, shit.

"What?" I squeaked.

"Fuck," he muttered, pulling me over to the small brick administration building nearby. He pushed me inside the small waiting room, and the receptionist looked up with a smile.

"She's just waiting for her Uber," Indy lied smoothly, forcing me down into a chair and leaning over me. "Call Jericho, ask him to pick you up. I'm going to follow the guy and see if I can figure out what the hell he wants."

He stood up, and I grabbed his sleeve. "By yourself?"

Indy smirked and reached behind him, pulling a handgun out of the waistband of his jeans. "Trust me, Moon. I can handle myself. Call Jericho."

And then he was gone out the door. The receptionist looked at me with wide eyes as I pulled my phone out of my back pocket and unlocked it with trembling fingers. "W-was that a gun?"

"Paintball gun," I lied, and she visibly relaxed. I pulled up Jericho's number, and it only rang once before he picked up.

"Hey, pretty girl. How was class?" he drawled as music blared around his voice. He was at the studio.

"Jericho…"

The music abruptly cut off. "Tell me."

I shuddered. "There was a guy following me. Indy took off after him, and I'm sitting in an admin building by the parking lot. He told me to call you and have you pick me up, but I know you're busy. I can just order a Lyft."

"Fuck, he left you there?" His voice was low and dangerous, and while I knew he was angry, it also turned me on. What was wrong with me?

"He didn't have much of a choice since he was by himself."

"The fuck he didn't. He could've gotten you home and figured something else out. Fuck!" he yelled as something slammed on his end of the line. "Don't move, Moon. I mean it. If anything happens to you, I'll…" his voice broke on the end before hardening. "I'll be there in fifteen minutes."

"Aren't you downtown?" It was at least a half an hour away.

"Fifteen minutes," he growled and ended the call.

EIGHTEEN
JERICHO

I was pretty fucking sure Moon's terrified voice was going to haunt me until the day I died. I grabbed Maddox to come with me. I needed someone to call Connor on the way to pick up my girl and find out what the fuck was going on.

I also needed someone who could hold me back from murdering Indy for leaving Moon completely vulnerable when someone was trailing her. We tore out of the studio and sprinted to my Range Rover. I tossed Maddox the keys because he drove like a fucking Formula One driver, and that was what I needed right now.

"Get us there as fast as you can," I ordered, and he shot me a grin.

"My absolute fucking pleasure." He was backing out before I even got my door shut, and I yanked the seatbelt across my body.

"Without rolling my fucking car," I added through clenched teeth as I gripped the handle above my door.

He laughed and turned up the music as he pushed down further on the gas pedal. Exactly twelve minutes later, we pulled into the parking lot, and I spotted a small brick building. I jumped out of the car before Maddox fully stopped and sprinted for the building. I almost ripped the door off its hinges as I flung it open, hurrying inside and dropping to my knees in front of where Moon sat against a wall with her arms wrapped around her knees.

"Oh, thank fuck," I murmured, pulling her out of the chair and onto my lap and wrapping my arms around her. She was trembling and, fuck, I might've been trembling, too.

Moon threw her arms around me and gripped me tightly, like she thought I might leave her, too. But I wasn't going any-fucking-where. "You're okay; I won't let anyone fucking touch you," I vowed to both of us, needing to say it aloud.

After a few minutes, both of our breathing slowed, and I could tell we were both calmer. I loosened my grip and leaned back to look at her. My legs were falling asleep underneath me, but I ignored the pins and needles feeling and focused on Moon. "You ready to go home?"

She looked around. "Where's Indy?"

Anger surged up inside me, but I shoved it down. Now wasn't the time. "I don't know. Maddox drove me, and maybe he found him. I could only think about getting to you."

Moon slowly disentangled herself from me and stood up, holding out her hand to pull me up with her. I shook out my legs as the feeling slowly came back. I held out my hand, and Moon took it immediately, and warmth burst in my chest. "I'm taking you home."

"What if-"

"To my house," I clarified. Whoever was watching her knew exactly where she lived and what her schedule was. It was time to shake things up and bring her back to my house. I'd been staying at hers because it was closer to her studio, and I didn't want to disrupt her life, but now that I knew the threat to her was real, I wanted her with me where the security was better, and all the guys were closer to us.

We moved out of the building and found Maddox and Indy talking next to my car. I shot Indy an icy glare. "We're going to my house. Grab Moon's car and meet us there." I left no room for argument as I helped Moon into the passenger seat of my car. I held out my hand for the keys as Maddox reluctantly handed them over and climbed in the back seat, grumbling about not being able to drive.

I scoffed. "Like I'd ever let Moon get in a car with you behind the wheel."

"I'm a good driver," he argued as I slid behind the wheel and started the car. "We didn't die on the way home," he pointed out, and I rolled my eyes. Moon and I had a whole lot of shit to talk about and figure out with Indy, but we could do it when she was safely in my house. Considering Indy had been alone when Maddox found him, I had to assume he hadn't caught the guy who'd been following them, which did nothing at all to improve my mood.

As I pushed the button to start the car, I glanced at Moon, but she was staring out the window with a glassy look in her eye. I reached across and pulled her hand into mine, weaving our fingers together and giving her a reassuring squeeze. She turned and gave me a soft smile before staring back out the window. Fuck, the normal vibrancy she walked through life with had completely drained out of her and what was left was just a shell of the woman she'd been this morning.

I sure as fuck wasn't about to stand by and let someone steal her radiance from her when I could do something about it. It was one of the things I loved most about her.

And yes, I said loved.

I was desperately and recklessly in love with Moon Mayhem.

But she didn't need my confessions today. Right now, she needed me to protect her and distract her, and I planned on doing both.

Maddox texted on his phone the whole way home, so I let the radio play quietly. As soon as we pulled through the security gate at the front of my house and into the garage, Maddox hopped out and announced Ryan would be here to pick him up, and he wasn't going to stay. He shot me a look, knowing full well I didn't want him here right now. Indy and probably Julian, at the very least, were going to be here soon, and I wanted to try and bring Moon back to herself before they showed up.

She slowly climbed out of the car but didn't really look around. She'd never been to my house, and suddenly I wasn't sure she'd like it—and I really wanted her to like it. I'd always loved my house, the modern architecture, the concrete floors and gray tones. But now, looking at it through Moon's eyes, I realized it was cold as fuck.

A lot like my life before I met her.

Having stayed with her the past couple of weeks, I missed the soft carpet under my toes, the bright green plants on every surface, and the colorful decor. Her house was filled with life, and mine was just… empty.

"Hey, pretty girl," I murmured, wrapping her in my arms as we stood in the garage. She rested her cheek against my chest, and I breathed her in. "Ready to go inside?"

Moon took a deep breath before letting it out. She peered up at me through long, dark lashes and a smile tugged at the corner of her mouth. "Sure, let's see where the magic happens."

A low chuckle rumbled through my chest as I reluctantly pulled away from her. "So, right to my bedroom, then?"

Her small smile widened as she ran her finger down my chest, sending my normal craving for her skyrocketing. "I was thinking more like the kitchen. I'm starving."

She was such a fucking tease, knowing exactly what she was doing, and I pulled her back against me so she could feel how hard she made me with her little game. "I could think of a few things to eat."

Moon laughed again, patting me on the chest this time and pushing away, dancing around me and moving through the garage door into my house, kicking off her shoes as she went. "You'll have to catch me first," she tossed over her shoulder as she took off running. It was a fucking relief to see some of her playfulness coming back, even if it was at the expense of my dick.

I tore after her, my blood pounding in my ears as the animal in me wanted nothing more than to catch her and make her submit, to push her to her limits and brand her with my touch. Stopping to listen, her footsteps echoed toward the back of the house where my gaming room was.

There were two entrances to that room, but one was out of the way, and I doubt she'd noticed it, so I snuck around, keeping my footsteps light and silent. I pressed my back against the wall right outside and listened, keeping my breath shallow and slow even as my heart ricocheted around in my chest. Right now, I was the most dangerous hunter walking the earth, and Moon was my prey.

I peeked around the corner, holding my breath as I quickly scanned the room for her. It didn't take me long to spot her, and when I did, my pulse jumped. She'd tucked herself behind the heavy curtains that hung around the floor-length windows, but I could see her sparkly painted toes sticking out from under the fabric.

Moving like a ghost, I held my breath as I skated along the wall, careful not to make a single sound before ripping back the fabric and capturing her in my arms. She squealed and batted at me but then dissolved in a fit of giggles, and I couldn't help but laugh along with her. "Now that you've got me, what are you going to do with me?" Her voice was breathless and throaty, and my dick perked back up at the sound.

I tightened my grip around her and picked her up off of her feet, carrying her over to the plush sectional I kept in this room. It was the most comfortable piece of furniture I had and the one I used the most, sitting here for hours gaming. "Well, I thought for starters…" I let my voice trail off as I dropped her onto the cushions and crawled over her, hovering my body on top of hers but not letting my bodyweight drop. "I could make you come a few times before I feed you."

She shivered underneath me, and her pupils blew out, the ocean blue fading into nearly black. Her tongue darted out and licked her lip, and I chased it with my own, nipping her bottom lip before kissing her like my life depended on it.

The hunter claiming my prize.

Pulling back slightly, I grabbed the hem of her shirt and yanked it up over her head, tossing it. Her lacy bra was like a beacon, drawing my attention to the fact it needed to disappear immediately. She reached up and grasped for me, trying to pull me back down to her mouth, but I leaned back further, slipping easily into my well-controlled facade. Inside, I was burning with the need to consume her. But on the outside?

I was calm as fuck.

"No touching unless I say so, pretty girl." I ran my knuckle along her sternum as she arched into me, but she obeyed my command with her eyes trained on me, practically begging me to let her touch. But I knew what she really needed. The same depravity inside of me was mirrored in her, a more innocent version, but it was there nonetheless.

Moon whimpered as I leaned over her body, reaching to the end table that stood next to the couch and grabbing my gaming headphones. I was weird as fuck and still liked to use corded headphones when I gamed, and this was an unexpected benefit. "Clasp your hands together," I rasped, barely recognizing how low my voice had gotten.

She bit her lip as she carried out my demand, and my dick pushed painfully against my jeans. For now, I ignored it. The time to sink into Moon would come soon enough, but right now, I wanted to play with her, to enjoy the spoils of victory.

I wrapped the cord around her wrists tight enough so she couldn't break free, but not so tight that it would hurt her or damage her perfectly unblemished skin. My eyes met hers once she was restrained, a silent question passing between us, and she nodded, letting me know she was okay with what we were doing. I pressed my lips to her wrist, feeling her pulse quicken under my touch.

"Keep your hands above your head." I pushed her hands up, and she moved them the rest of the way while I sat back and took her in, drinking in every inch of exposed skin on her torso and hating the denim still covering way too fucking much of her insane body. I unhooked her bra and immediately realized I fucked up tying her hands before I took it off, so I moved away from her and strode into the kitchen, letting her whimpers of protest fuel the fire burning through my veins.

The knife blade glinted as I pulled it out of the drawer, and I stalked back to the couch, moving back over Moon. "Hold still, beautiful." I laid the blade against her skin and slid it underneath the lace of her bra, slicing through the delicate fabric and watching as it fell away. The knife clattered to the floor as it dropped from my hand, and I lowered my face to her tits, pulling one hardened nipple between my lips and rolling the other between my fingers.

A gasp tore from Moon's lips, and she bucked her hips against me. Her wrists flexed against her bindings, and I switched up my approach, swapping my mouth to her other nipple and swiping my tongue lazily across it. I looked up at her face where she watched me closely, her swollen lips parted, and I'd never seen anything more fucking sexy in my entire life. I wanted those lips wrapped around my cock, moaning my name, turned up in a satisfied smile.

Slowly, so fucking slowly, I dragged my tongue down her torso, across the soft skin of her stomach, and swirled it around her belly button before continuing lower. I flicked the button on her jeans open and lowered the zipper while pressing kisses to her stomach.

Moon lifted her hips to help me pull her jeans and panties off of her, and once they were gone, I sat back and took in the bare perfection of her laid out before me. Hunger flooded my veins, pushing me to lean down and swipe my tongue across her smooth opening and pulling her clit into my mouth. She bucked against me, but I didn't speed up, didn't let go, and instead took my fucking time savoring her.

My tongue drew lazy circles around her core, lapping her up, teasing her until her thighs tightened around my head, and I backed off, instead pressing kisses to the inside of her thighs. When she relaxed, I did it again, bringing her right to the edge but never letting her fall off the cliff.

Again and again, I teased her until she cried out in frustration, bringing her hands down and trying to grip my hair to bring me back to where she wanted me. But I backed off further, enjoying watching her flush and squirm, knowing that I was the only one who could relieve the tension built up inside her body.

Knowing I was the one who'd put it there in the first place.

My dick was like fucking granite, and I stood up, enjoying the wild look in Moon's eyes and dragging my gaze down her flushed and writhing body as I pulled my jeans off and lowered myself back between her legs. I gripped the base of my cock, and ran it across her opening, coating myself in her arousal and loving every fucking second.

I'd never been harder, and every cell in my body was screaming at me to push inside her, to give us what we both wanted so fucking desperately. But I wouldn't give in. My body didn't control me, *I* controlled *it.* Stroking myself slowly, I watched her watching me. "Do you want to come, pretty girl?"

Her eyes widened, and she nodded. "Plea-"

I slammed inside her in one thrust, bottoming out, and we both groaned at the feeling of coming together. She screamed and her eyes rolled back in her head, and from the way her walls clenched around my cock in waves, I knew she just came. "Did I tell you you could come?" I growled, gritting my teeth and slowly pulling out after she finished. I tried to act detached like the cold, emotionless guy I used to be, but I found control wasn't as important anymore.

Still, it was like muscle memory going back to that place, but I wasn't sure I liked it. She shook her head and I moved back inside her as my control frayed again. My heart thrashed in my chest as old fears tried to creep in and my hips faltered in their movement.

"Look at me, Jericho." Moon's soft demand brought me back, and I met her eyes, inhaling sharply at the mixture of lust and wonder shining back at me. In her eyes, I'd never hurt her. She wanted me, but more than that, she fucking *trusted* me. I focused my attention back on her, telling the voice in my head to go fuck itself and getting lost in the feel of being inside Moon.

I fucked her like my life depended on it, like every thrust of my hips chased my demons further and further away, and she took it all, crying out my name and convulsing around me so many times I lost count. Our bodies were both slick with sweat from the effort, but it only added to the riot of sensations, and as I pushed her to the brink, her words no longer coherent, her cries echoing off the cold walls of my empty house. I fell over the edge, detonating like a fucking bomb inside her until I was spent and collapsed on top of Moon, only catching myself at the last second to hold my full weight off of her.

The only sound in the room was our harsh breathing as we both came down, and I brushed the sticky strands of her hair off of her face, kissing her gently in complete opposition of what I'd just done to her body.

I reached over and untied her hands, inspecting her wrists and pressing a kiss to the inside of each one. Moon wrapped her arms around me loosely, like she didn't have the strength to grip me as tight as she wanted. Her stomach betrayed her, though, and growled loudly. I couldn't help the chuckle that rumbled through my chest, and I reluctantly moved off of her. "How about you start the shower, and I'll order food?" I offered, holding my hand out to help her up off the couch.

She took it and stood, and I again let my gaze rake over her hot as fuck body. She was just the right amount of curvy, but she wasn't soft. She had muscles underneath her smooth skin earned from years of contorting herself into all sorts of different positions. My dick perked up at the thought of all the ways I could bend her to my will in the bedroom, but now I needed to take care of my girl.

"That sounds incredible. Lead the way to the bathroom." I grabbed her hand, and we walked naked through my house, the concrete floor cold under my bare feet, but I never noticed it before. I wondered what Moon thought about it.

We stepped into my bedroom, and I took in the dark wood accent wall behind my low-slung platform bed and again found myself wondering what Moon thought about all the darkness in here. "This house is very you," she pointed out, and I had no fucking clue what she meant by that. "Dark, a little bit mysterious, but also alluring and charming in its own way." She laughed softly. "A lot different than my house, but not in a bad way."

She looked up at me then, and the faint light from the fixture overhead made her eyes glitter, and I pressed my lips to hers, running my hand through her hair. I nipped at her lip, and suddenly my dick was at full attention again, recognizing how close Moon was to my bed. I wanted to lay her down, push her legs over her head...

"I know what you're thinking, but I *really* need food," she laughed, and I let her go, running my hand down my face.

"Fuck. Okay. Bathroom's in there." I pointed to the room off to my right. "You get started, I'll order food and then no promises on keeping my dick to myself before we eat."

She laughed again as she ran her palm down my chest and across my abs as her eyes darkened hungrily. "Better hurry then."

And I did fucking hurry. As soon as the water turned on, I stalked to the kitchen, grabbing the nearest takeout menu I could find and barking an order into the phone. I wasn't even sure what the hell I chose or how much, just listed off a bunch of the shit on there and called it good. We could figure it out when it got here. For now, I had more important shit to do, like seeing how deep down Moon's throat my cock could go.

Takeout containers were spread in a half-circle around us as we lounged on the couch in my gaming room. Moon wore one of my t-shirts, and my eyes kept drifting to the exposed stretch of thigh where the cotton kept inching up with her movements.

We'd stuffed ourselves, and now both of us had controllers in our hands, fully immersed in the game we usually played together online. It was so much fucking better in person where I could walk my fingers up her inner thigh and brush them across her bare pussy before the next mission started.

She made me laugh when the game started, and our other team members signed on to play, but I had no interest in anything but playing with Moon, and she swatted me away. A little crease formed between her eyebrows, and she bit her lip in concentration and attacked the video game like she did everything else, throwing herself fully into it headfirst.

I was entranced by her, in awe of how beautiful she was with damp hair, no makeup, and in nothing but my shirt. I fucking tanked our team because I couldn't pay attention long enough to do any damage, but I couldn't care less.

During a break, I tossed my controller, and Moon hopped up, walking to my kitchen with a graceful gait. When she walked, it almost looked like she was dancing, and I had to wonder when the fuck watching someone walk had become so goddamn fascinating to me.

But it wasn't just watching anyone, it was watching *Moon*, and that made all the difference.

"Do you want a beer?" Moon called from the kitchen.

"Sure, thanks."

I still wore my headset, and DeathMinion was bitching at me for my shit performance on the last mission, so I almost missed it when the sound of shattering glass carried from the kitchen.

"What the fuck?" I yelled, ripping off the headset. "Moon?" I was already running across the house, and when I stepped in the kitchen, she was staring out the window, and her face was white as fuck. An unnatural, unsettling color that made all the food I'd just eaten turn over in my stomach. I jumped over the spilled beer and broken glass to pull her into my arms and check her over, making sure she was okay.

"What happened?" I asked her a little more forcefully than I meant to, but fuck, my heart was pounding, and I was on high alert.

"There was someone out there, looking in the window at me. They had a camera." A full-body tremor ran through her, and I pulled her closer, reaching in my pocket for my phone. I'd been so wrapped up in Moon all night I forgot all about the fact Indy was supposed to be here. So, where the fuck was he? And who was outside my house?

I found his number in my phone and pressed the call button. He picked up after two rings, and I clenched my teeth to rein in my anger. Moon didn't need me lashing out right now. "I'm on my way," Indy started before I even said anything.

"Where the fuck have you been?" My voice was low, and I tried to keep the anger out of it, but I failed miserably.

"I went to Moon's to get her some clothes and then to meet up with Connor and debrief about today. I'm almost to your house now." Fuck, I wanted to be pissed off at him for that, for leaving Moon here unguarded, but I couldn't. She wasn't unguarded, she was with me, and some piece of shit had managed to get past gate security and onto my property to scare my girl.

I knew from experience gate security was a joke, but I should've been smarter. "Get here, and we need to talk." I hung up, fully intending to beat myself up about what a shitty job I'd done as Moon's protector, but she clung to me like I was her safe place, and that chipped away at my self-loathing.

One thing was for fucking certain, though—there'd be no more mistakes made where Moon's safety was concerned, or I would lose my fucking mind.

NINETEEN

JERICHO

"We need to figure out what the fuck is going on," I fumed after stepping out of my bedroom and meeting up with Indy, Julian, and Connor in the living room. It'd taken me an hour to get Moon to fall asleep, and in that time, Indy called Julian and Connor over because this problem wasn't going away.

Just watching wasn't working anymore. Whoever was watching Moon wasn't going away, and they were getting ballsier by the day. A fear like I'd never known tore through me twice today—earlier when Moon was followed at school, and tonight when a pane of glass had separated her from someone who I figured meant her harm. Why else would they be following her?

I dropped down on my couch, glaring at anyone who dared meet my gaze. I was a tempest—destructive and ready to rage and tear everything apart if I had to. I was barely controlling myself, and my whole body shook with the effort.

Connor leaned forward and rested his forearms on his thighs. He was calm, and it was pissing me the fuck off. "Here's what we know. It's two people following Moon, both men. One is taller than the other, which is how we know it's not the same guy. They always use a different car, and the plates Ryan got at the restaurant were stolen, so that was a dead end."

My fingers clenched and unclenched over and over in a rhythm that was keeping me just on this side of violent as he continued. "We've been digging into

Moon's background to see if we can figure out why anyone would want to follow her, but that's been a dead-end, too. We've moved onto her parents, and August is clean. Her mom, though…"

I looked up at him. "What about her mom?"

He met my glare with his steady gaze. "Cara Mayhem doesn't exist."

"What? What does that mean?"

"When Sebastian dug into her, it was like every trace of her had been deleted out of the system. There's no birth certificate, no marriage license or driver's license. No health insurance or bank accounts. Nothing. Not one single thing."

"That's fucking weird, right?" I looked around at the other two guys sitting quietly beside Connor, hoping someone might have some answers. So far, all I had was more questions.

"It's weird," Julian confirmed.

"So, here's what we're going to do," Connor stood, starting to pace the room. "I'm going to have Sebastian set up surveillance around your house. I'm going to have a team of two with Moon at all times, and Julian is going to talk to August and see if he can figure out what the hell is going on with her mom. But if I had to guess? I'd say whoever's following Moon now is related to Cara's disappearance. What that means, I have no fucking clue." He stopped in front of me and lowered down so he was crouching in front of me, looking me in the eye.

"But I promise you we *will* figure it out and put a stop to this shit."

I nodded at him, trusting he'd do what he said but hating that there wasn't more to be done right now. I wanted Moon to feel safe. I wanted her to *be* safe.

Connor stood back up to his full height and moved over to sit back down. The corner of his lip twitched. "Have you talked to Maddox tonight?"

I shook my head. "Not since this afternoon, but there was shit going on, so we didn't really talk."

"Well, you might want to call him. He's planning something for tomorrow, and I'd bet everything I own he's going to demand you be there."

Julian and Indy passed a look of amusement between them. "What's he planning?"

"I'll let him explain, but you should pack a bag for a couple of days in Vegas." My eyes rolled up toward the ceiling. Fucking Maddox. Vegas was the last place I wanted to be right now with all this shit going on, and Indy must've picked up on my mood.

"It might be a good thing, getting out of here for a couple of days. Connor, Julian, and I will all be there, but whoever's watching won't expect her to go out of town. Sebastian can set up without stepping on your toes, too," Indy added.

Rubbing my eyes, I sighed. I was suddenly fucking tired all the way down to my bones, and I wanted everyone to get the fuck out of my house so I could go curl my body around the girl asleep in my bed and reassure myself that she was okay. It looked like I wouldn't get my wish because now I'd always have at least two of these assholes lingering around at all hours of the day.

Right on cue, my phone vibrated, and I looked down at the group text.

Maddox: Pack your shit, we're going to Vegas.

Zen: WTF, I have a kid. You can't just spring Vegas trips on us anymore.

True: What he said ^

My fingers flew across the keyboard. At least I wasn't the only one less than thrilled with Maddox about this.

Jericho: Why?

Maddox: I can't wait anymore

True: ...I don't know what that means

Maddox: To marry Ryan, dumbass. I want to surprise her in Vegas

Zen: You're not even engaged

Maddox: You weren't engaged before the day you married Kennedy

Zen: Touche

Jericho: When?

Maddox: Tomorrow. Pack yo shit!

True: I'll call my mom

Fuck, it looked like this was actually happening. No matter what was going on my life, if one of the guys asked me to be there, I was fucking there. The same was true for them. The three guys who'd been sitting on my couch had moved off deeper into the house, but I didn't worry about what they were doing. They'd keep watch over Moon so we could sleep, and with that thought, the anger drained out of my body, and I stood up, trudging down the hall and crawling into bed with the girl who'd stolen my heart.

Thanks to Maddox's spur of the moment planning, the next morning was hectic as fuck. Moon had her phone glued to her ear, trying to figure out how to cover her studio for the next couple of days while I tossed clothes in a bag for us. Indy had packed her a bag, but if she was missing anything, I'd just buy her whatever she needed in Vegas.

As a group, we were used to last-minute changes and going with the flow, though it wasn't as easy now that Zen and True had families, but even still, by noon, we were pulling into the hanger and climbing onto the jet.

Moon's eyes got so wide when she saw the band's plane that it was almost comical, and I had to laugh. Kennedy shot me a smug as fuck smile, and I flipped her off.

We settled into our seats, and I looked around at everyone who'd come with us. Outside of security and Griffin, everyone was paired up, and for the first time, I was happy not to be alone. Moon laced her fingers with mine, squeezing my hand gently as Ryan and Maddox sat across from us. Ryan's eyes were bright as she greeted Moon like an old friend.

"Do you like flying?" she asked Moon, and my girl nodded her head.

"I love it, especially takeoff. When the engines rev and that feeling in your stomach when the wheels leave the ground. There's nothing else like it," Moon gushed, practically bouncing in her seat. Ryan had the exact same energy, and I glanced at Maddox, raising my eyebrow. He shrugged and settled into his seat, asking Hilda for a drink before dropping his hand possessively on Ryan's thigh.

I watched him watching her and wondered if I looked like that when I stared at Moon. Maddox had an expression on his face of complete devotion like Ryan was the only thing in the world he could see. He looked like I felt when I was in Moon's orbit, and it hit me hard that I didn't want to spend even a second without her.

Then insecurity crept its way into my thoughts, and I wondered if she felt the same way or if I was just a new experience for her. But then she looked at me, and my worries evaporated at the look in her eye. It was like she let me look into her soul, and what I saw there drew me in and wrapped me up in warmth and love. You couldn't fake the reverence in her eyes as she looked up at me and my heart felt like it was exploding with warmth.

As the plane taxied down the runway, Ryan and Moon chatted excitedly about the weekend in Vegas. I shot Maddox another look, and this time he grinned at me. None of us told the women in our lives what this weekend was really about, and Maddox made up some weak-ass excuse about a live band he wanted to go see.

The flight was short, and before I could even pass out for a nap, the wheels were touching down in Sin City. I glanced at Maddox, and he wore an uncharacteristically unsure expression on his face, but when Ryan looked at him, he buried that shit down inside and shot her a lopsided grin.

We made our way off the plane and piled into the limo Maddox had waiting for us. Moon had never been to Vegas before, so she jumped up through the open sunroof in the limo, and Kennedy, Amara, and Ryan all squeezed out with her. Maddox got our attention while the girls weren't looking at shook his phone. I pulled mine out of my pocket and took it off airplane mode, ignoring all the messages except for the group text.

Maddox: Meet me at the bar in the lobby after you put your bags away

The limo pulled up in front of Encore, and I looked up at the sleek hotel. Moon gasped as she stepped out, and I wrapped my hand around her waist, pulling her back against my chest as she shielded her eyes and looked up. "Wow," she breathed, and I was reminded that places like this weren't something she was used to.

"Wait until you see our room," I murmured against her neck, hating Maddox more than a little bit for robbing me of the opportunity to get Moon naked as soon as we stepped foot in the hotel.

We checked in, and the elevator ride was long and torturous. Zen and

True were glaring at Maddox, too, and I chuckled. We'd rented out the entire floor. None of us wanted to risk someone invading our privacy, and Connor and the guys he brought with him broke off from us when we stepped off the elevator.

Moon and I had the closest room to the elevators, so I pushed the door open and let her move past me, breathing in her sweet strawberry scent as she stepped inside. When it clicked behind me, I didn't even bother looking at the decor. I'd been in so many hotel rooms at this point they all basically looked the same. Instead, I hauled Moon into my arms, kissing the shit out of her while she melted into me.

Unfortunately for me and my dick, Maddox needed us downstairs, so I handed Moon my credit card and told her to find the girls and buy something nice to wear tonight. I knew she hadn't brought anything like what she would need for hanging out with us in Vegas. There'd be paparazzi at some point.

With one last kiss, I left her in the room, promising to meet back up in a couple of hours. I pushed the button for the elevator, and while I waited, both Zen and True came out of their rooms and met up with me.

"Fuck Maddox. He couldn't let us have half an hour?" Zen grumbled. I felt the same way.

"This is the first night Amara and I have had without Phoenix in a month," True complained.

"If all you needed was half an hour, maybe you have bigger problems than Maddox," I joked, but neither of them appreciated my attempt at humor. They sent me twin glares, and I laughed.

"Wait until you have kids, man. You learn all sorts of new tricks out of necessity," True said before stepping onto the elevator, and we followed him in. "Not that I'm complaining."

Griffin shoved his hand between the doors just as they were closing and stumbled into the elevator, breathing heavily. "Couldn't have held the door?"

"I thought you'd be downstairs with your brother already." I shrugged.

Zen elbowed me and grinned. "Is this giving you any ideas?"

My eyebrows furrowed. "What are you talking about?"

True laughed and exchanged a look with Griffin. "Dude, you're already serious about Moon. We can tell. You've never been like this with anyone."

I folded my arms across my chest. "And what exactly am I like?"

Griffin rolled his eyes. "Possessive as fuck for one thing."

"And whenever you're in the same room as Moon, you don't stop watching her. You look like you're obsessed," Zen pointed out and then held up his hands when I glared at him. "Fuck, I'm not judging. I fully admit to my obsession with my wife."

True nodded. "Same. I own my addiction to my wife, too. This isn't us giving you crap. We just want to know where you're at."

The elevator dinged softly before the door slid open, and I exhaled a long breath. The guys weren't wrong. I *was* obsessed with Moon. When I wasn't with her, I was thinking about her. She'd managed to burrow into even the darkest corners of my mind, and there was no escaping it. I didn't *want* to escape my feelings for her. I wanted her to dig in deeper until we were so entwined, we could never be torn apart.

"She's… everything," I said simply, shoving my hands in my pockets. The words were true. Love didn't feel strong enough for what I felt for her.

They dropped the inquisition as we stepped into the lounge in the hotel lobby. Maddox sat at the bar with a crystal glass in front of him, and we stepped up behind him. Griffin patted him on the back, and he spun around with a huge smile on his face. "About time you assholes showed up."

"You're lucky we got down here so fast, and you owe me for leaving my wife in that hotel room alone while I deal with your shit," Zen grumbled, scowling at Maddox, who just laughed.

"Fair enough. So, I'll cut to the chase. I told Ryan to round up the girls and take them shopping for dresses and shit because we'd take them out to dinner, so we have a couple of hours while they prep for that and do whatever it is girls do." He sipped his drink before continuing. "In the meantime, I already made reservations for us at Paris Las Vegas."

"You're proposing up in the Eiffel Tower?" True shifted to the bar without waiting for an answer to his stupid question, ordering a beer.

"No, I thought I'd do it at the Bunny Ranch," Maddox quipped, rolling his eyes. "Between now and then, I need to ring shop and pick a chapel. You all brought suits, right?"

We all nodded, and he relaxed. "I think the best thing to do is divide and conquer. The two of you," Maddox pointed at Griffin and me, "are shopping for rings with me. And you two," he gestured to Zen and True, "find the venue and make an appointment. We've got," he glanced at his phone, "two and a half hours until I'm supposed to meet Ryan."

Maddox turned his head back toward Zen and True. "Oh, and you might want to make dinner reservations for the rest of you. Paris is something I want to do just Ryan and me."

"Yeah, because you don't want us to witness your humiliation when she turns you down," Griffin teased his older brother, and Maddox glared back.

"Fuck off with that bad energy." Just to slam his point home, he flipped Griffin off, too, and I chuckled.

"Got something to say, Jericho?" Maddox turned his glare on me.

"Not a damn thing."

"Good. Time to go buy my future wife a ring." He slid off the barstool, and Griffin and I fell into step behind him, stepping out into the burning desert heat. As he ordered a car, my mind swirled with the one thought I couldn't get out of my mind now that the guys had brought it up—Moon walking down the aisle, her bright smile shining only for me, every step bringing her closer to being officially, legally, and completely *mine.*

Maybe Moon's spontaneity was rubbing off on me. It was way too soon to admit that shit out loud, though... right?

Row after row of sparkly gems shone up at me through the glass display case. "How the fuck are you supposed to know which one to get?"

Maddox shrugged, his eyes a little too wide in his face and just a little panicked. Griffin helped himself to the complimentary champagne and lounged on one of the long, tufted benches spread throughout the high-end store. "I figured I'd know it when I see it."

Griffin snorted. "Solid plan, bro."

Mad glared at his brother. "What are you, twelve? You've never even had a girlfriend, so what could you possibly know about picking out an engagement ring?"

Griffin pulled himself up off the bench and swaggered over to his brother, leaning against the case and peering down inside like he was looking for something. "That one." He pointed, and Maddox narrowed his eyes as he looked at the ring his brother found.

"Okay, how the fuck did you do that? It's perfect." Maddox sounded bewildered, and I bit back my laugh. He was freaking out a little bit, and I didn't want to make him feel worse. My own heart was pounding in my chest as my earlier thoughts hadn't stopped taunting me.

The salesman helped Maddox figure out the wedding band, and after Mad paid a shitton of money, he promised he'd have the rings sized and ready to pick up in an hour. My stomach flipped over, and a cold sweat broke out across my whole body. Fuck, was I doing this?

As the brothers started to move toward the front door, the word escaped my lips before I could stop it. "Wait."

TWENTY
JERICHO

I patted my suit pocket for the thousandth time in the past twenty minutes and let out a deep exhale when I felt the little velvet box inside. I felt a little crazy for taking this step with Moon so soon, but we'd been getting to know each other for months over our video game.

And I swore when she looked at me, I saw the same devotion and possession I felt for her in her eyes, too.

The guys and I decided to skip dinner with our wives and girlfriends, or in Griffin's case, himself, and just meet up at the chapel. I was too nervous to eat, and Kennedy texted Zen that the girls weren't going to be ready until we were supposed to meet at the chapel. They still had no idea what was going on since Maddox didn't trust them not to tell Ryan, so she'd left the rest of the girls to go meet up with him at Paris.

Zen, True, Griffin, Connor, Indy, Julian, and I all hung around outside the chapel, waiting for Maddox's text letting us know if this was actually happening.

"Looks like you've got a second career in the making," Zen broke the tense silence between us by messing with Connor, who just grunted.

"What do you mean?" Griffin asked.

"Connor married Kennedy and Zen and me and Amara. If all goes well, he's going to be doing the same for Maddox and Ryan," True explained, leaning back against the stucco wall of the Little Vegas Chapel.

Griffin shot me a look but didn't say anything, and I swallowed hard. I didn't know why it was important to me to keep my plans for Moon a secret, but I just didn't want to share them with anyone until I talked to her. I wanted to keep her to myself in our own little bubble. It was bad enough that Maddox and Griffin knew already, and it was a relief that Griffin kept his damn mouth shut.

"It's basically Shadow Phoenix tradition at this point. I think it'd be bad luck now if you or Jericho got married and Connor didn't do it," Zen added, checking his phone and grinning down at hit as his thumbs flew across the screen. That smile was reserved for one person only—his wife.

Everyone's phone vibrated simultaneously, and I looked down at the group text where Maddox had sent a picture of Ryan beaming at the camera wearing the ring he'd picked out on her left hand. "Guess that means she said yes."

"How long until they get here?" True wondered. "I want to call my parents and check on Phoenix."

I squinted up at the Eiffel Tower replica looking in the distance. "Fifteen minutes, maybe?" I guessed.

"Perfect." He pressed his phone to his ear and walked away from our group. Sometimes it was hard to reconcile the guys we used to be with who we were becoming now. Zen and True were completely devoted to their families, Maddox was like a different person since he got Ryan back, and even though I didn't think I'd changed that much, Moon had already made a huge impact in my life.

I was lighter. I smiled more, laughed more, and generally felt more alive and free than I ever had.

A black SUV pulled up outside the chapel, and Kennedy and Amara climbed out first, making their way to their husbands. I watched, holding my breath as Moon climbed out of the car. She was hypnotically beautiful with her multi-colored hair styled in messy waves and her curve-hugging dress that hit at mid-thigh and had some sort of holographic sequins all over it that changed color with every small movement she made.

Her gaze met mine across the parking lot, and the rest of the world fell away as I watched her walk toward me. Black spots crept into my vision as I realized I'd forgotten to breathe. As she stepped into my arms and I pulled her against me, I finally inhaled, and the scent of her filled my lungs.

"You look incredible," I murmured against her neck before dropping a kiss to her velvety skin. She shivered under my touch like she always did, and her responsiveness had my dick already at half-mast.

She stepped back a little as her eyes raked over my body. "Yeah, well, I've never seen anyone as sexy as you in that black suit. It looks like it was made for you."

I chuckled. "That's because it was."

"Well, as much as I like you in this," she ran her hand along my chest and down my abs, which I had come to realize was one of her favorite ways to touch me, "I like what's underneath even more." Her hand slid back up my stomach to rest above my heart.

Maddox and Ryan showing up stole her attention from me, and I hated them for it just a little bit. I always wanted Moon's focus, lapping up every drop of her interest in me. All three girls rushed over to do that squealing thing around Ryan that made my ears feel like they were fucking bleeding.

When the girls were done, we all headed inside the chapel. All of us found places to sit in the chairs behind the archway up front. I clasped Moon's hand as she took the seat next to me, and I watched the sparkle in her eyes as her whole face lit up.

Maddox took his place at the front with Connor officiating, and I barely heard a word as he and Ryan exchanged vows and rings. I couldn't tear my eyes away from Moon, memorizing every expression, and wiping away her tears when they kissed. My heart was full and warm and also beating out of my fucking chest at what I was about to do.

The ceremony had gone by in a flash. It felt like I'd barely fucking blinked and it was over, and I hoped no one noticed I wasn't paying attention. Everyone filed out of the room, but Griffin hung back, talking to Connor and shooting me a look. He'd done that on purpose, running interference for me, and I'd have to remember to thank him for that later.

I shot off a text to our group chat, letting them know we'd meet them at the restaurant and then pulled Moon up out of her seat as my heart thundered in my chest. "Wait here for a second, beautiful."

She looked at me curiously but did what I said, and I walked up to Connor. "How do you feel about performing another one of those?" I asked quietly, and his eyebrows shot up.

"Now?"

I nodded. "If she's up for it." I turned to Griffin. "And you're staying as our witness." I didn't leave room for debate. It was a statement, a command, and for once, he didn't argue, tilting his head toward me in agreement instead.

I walked back over to where I'd left Moon and took her hand in mine. A tiny crease formed between her eyebrows, and I smiled as I smoothed it out. "I know how much you love life and how spontaneous you can be, and that's not usually me," I started, and she squeezed my hand. "But there's something about you that sets me free. You make me want to take every leap with you, and when I see life through your eyes? It's beyond words. I know it's fast, and maybe it's fucking crazy." I shook my head and chuckled nervously.

"But I love you, Moon Mayhem. I fucking *love* you, and I want to do every wild adventure you've got planned by your side. I want to do it as your husband, and as much as that should fucking terrify me, it doesn't. I've never wanted anything more in my entire life than to spend every single day looking at the possibilities in the world and wondering which ones we're going to conquer together. So," I finished, swiping the tear that broke free and was running down her cheek before pulling the little blue box out of my pocket and dropping to my knee. "What do you say? Will you marry me?"

"Now?" she whispered, her eyes darting to Connor and then to Griffin, who was snapping pictures of us with his phone. I scowled at him, but he just flipped me off and kept clicking away.

"Now."

She bit her lip, and then a wide smile stretched across her face before she dropped to her knees in front of me, so she was looking me in the eye. "I love you, too, Jericho, and yes!" She yelled that last part, throwing her head back and her arms straight up in the air like she was cheering.

My whole body vibrated as I slid the ring down her finger, and she didn't even look at it before throwing her arms around me. I stood, picking her up with me and pressing my lips to hers. She opened to me immediately, and I wanted to drown in her and never stop, but we had to get to the restaurant, and I wasn't ready to give up our little secret just yet.

I reluctantly pulled away and nodded to the man hovering behind us. We handed over all of our information, and in just a couple of minutes, we had an official marriage license. "Do you want to walk down the aisle?" I asked her. I hadn't really planned out what would happen beyond asking her to be my wife.

She shook her head. "No, we're already up here. Let's let Connor do his thing." She grinned up at him, and he laughed.

Griffin moved around us, snapping pictures, and I glared at him. He better not have shared that shit with any of the guys before Moon and I were ready.

I brushed a colorful strand of hair off of her forehead. "I'll give you the wedding of your dreams when we get home where your dad can be there and walk you down the aisle. I promise." I worried she wouldn't want to do this because she was close to August and would want him to be here, but fuck if I wasn't selfish and didn't want to wait another day to marry her once I got the idea in my head.

She slid her palm up my cheek, and her fingers brushed through the short hair on the side of my head. "I don't want another wedding. I just want this one, and it'll be perfect because it's you—it's *us*. My dad will understand, and Griff's going to take video. Right?"

My glare bored into the side of his face, daring him to deny her anything she wanted, and he shot her a thumbs up.

"Ready?" Connor asked. He didn't even have a tablet or phone or paper or anything, and I had to admit I was impressed.

We both nodded as I pulled our wedding bands out of my pocket and handed them to Connor before clasping both of Moon's hands in mine.

"Since we don't have an audience for me to speak to, I figure we'll just move right into the vows part since that's the most important. Is that okay with you two?" Connor started.

I looked at Moon, and she looked thoughtful. "Yes, but we're saying our own vows."

"Okay, then. Moon, do you take Jericho, grumpy bastard that he is, to be your husband?" I glowered at him, and he just smirked back at me.

She laughed softly and laced her fingers with mine. "I do."

"And Jericho, do you take Moon, who's way too good for you, to be your wife?"

"Why did we want him to do this again?" I asked Moon, and she giggled, which made my whole chest burn with warmth. "And yes, I do."

"Moon, go ahead and do your vows," Connor prompted, and she took a deep breath before staring up into my eyes.

"There's something so refreshing about relinquishing control and letting someone else help shoulder the burden of life. I never understood that until I let you in, first over our game, and then when I met you in real life. I've never found someone who made me feel like you do. It's like you're magic, brought into my life to make all my dreams come true. With every breath I take, I love you more, and nothing in life or death will ever change that." My eyes burned as she spoke, and I was fucking ruined by her words.

"I promise you a life that will never be boring, that will be full of taking chances and sometimes falling on our asses. But, no one will ever love you more than me. No one will ever fight for you more than me, and no one will ever want you more than me." Her pupils dilated as she looked up at me, and a flush crept across her cheeks. I swept my fingers down the side of her face, and she leaned into my touch, closing her eyes for a second, and I did the same, trying to collect myself before it was my turn.

"You're up, Jericho." Connor's voice startled me out of my thoughts. I almost forgot he was here, I was so entranced with the magnetic girl standing in front of me.

There were so many things I wanted to say, so many promises I wanted to make that I wasn't sure where to even start. "I love you," I whispered, bringing the back of her hand to my lips. Now that I'd said the three words out loud, I wanted to say them all the fucking time.

"I love you, too," she whispered back with a smile.

I took a deep breath. "I've fucked a lot of stuff up in my life, and because of that, I decided a long time ago I was done letting people in. Then you came along and blasted right through every single blockade I'd built around myself. I don't even know when it happened, but you've tunneled so deep into my heart and soul at this point that you'd have to kill me to ever get you out."

I wiped away the tears running down her face and kissed her on the nose. "Just like you, life with me will never be boring. I can't promise I won't be an asshole from time to time or get possessive or jealous, because I'm pretty fucking obsessed with you." She laughed through the tears streaming down her face.

"But I can promise to love you more than I love myself, to protect you with my life, and to do everything I possibly can to make you happy," I promised.

"Holy shit, Jericho's actually human. I can't believe no one else gets to see this," Connor commented, and Griffin snickered. I was too fucking happy to do anything more than flip him off, so I let them get away with it just this once.

"Just do the rings, asshole," I ground out, and Connor chuckled, dropping Moon's ring into my hand and mine into hers.

"Moon, repeat after me: This ring is a symbol of my never-ending commitment, love, and devotion to you."

She looked in my eyes and slid the ring down my finger, repeating his words.

"Your turn, Jericho."

"This ring is a symbol of my never-ending commitment, love, and devotion to you," I vowed, pushing the ring onto her finger and pressing a kiss to her palm.

"Now that all the sentimental stuff is out of the way, I get to pronounce you husband and wife. Jericho, time to kiss your wife," Connor announced, and Griffin whooped behind me, recording the whole thing as I pressed my hand into Moon's lower back and tugged her into my body, bending her back as I captured her mouth in a claiming kiss. My hand tangled in her hair as my tongue found hers, and hunger burst through my veins.

My phone vibrated in my pocket, but I ignored it, kissing the shit out of my wife and not wanting to come up for air. But then Griffin broke the spell. "Okay, newlyweds. Everyone's at the restaurant and wondering where the fuck we are. Time to go."

I set a dazed and flushed Moon back on her feet, swiping my thumb under her lip to fix her lip gloss. "Did we really just do that?" her awed voice barely carried up to my ears.

"Yep," a wicked grin stretched across my face. "And now you're mine."

TWENTY ONE
MOON

"I don't want to steal Ryan and Maddox's spotlight." I held out my hand as we drove to the restaurant, inspecting the brand new sparkly accessory Jericho had just used to pledge his everlasting love. I was still overheated from the promise in the kiss that sealed our vows and pressed my thighs together to try and get some relief.

My phone vibrated, and I glanced down at it.

Bex: What'd you do? I know you did something.

I grinned at my best friend's uncanny intuition and slipped it back into my clutch, turning back to Jericho.

"So, what do you want to do?" Jericho sat next to me in the back seat of the SUV while Connor drove, and Griffin tapped at his phone from the passenger seat. My new husband's fingers were teasing the skin of my upper thigh, which sent sparks of heat shooting straight to my core with every stroke.

"Let's keep the wedding just between us until we get home. It's only one more day," I suggested, realizing he knew that but also that Jericho was possessive and me wanting to hide the fact he was my husband might hurt him.

"I'm good with that," he surprised me by saying.

"Really?"

"Really. Besides," he nuzzled his nose into my hair and ran it along the curve of my neck. "I like having a secret just between us."

I glanced up at Griffin and Connor in the front seat. "Not quite just between us."

He scoffed. "Neither one of them would dare breathe a word of what happened tonight, or they'll see how unforgiving I can be." The threat in his tone made me shiver, but not in fear. For some reason, I didn't want to examine too closely, I was attracted to the dangerous and dark part of Jericho. It was hot as hell, and holding myself back from climbing into his lap here in the back seat was getting harder and harder.

"Can't we stop at the hotel for like fifteen minutes?" I realized I sounded whiny, but I couldn't help it. At this point, my clit was practically throbbing, and I needed relief.

Jericho's dark chuckle rumbled across my skin as his fingers slipped underneath the soaked fabric of my lace panties and brushed my entrance. "Fifteen minutes wouldn't even come close to enough time for everything I want to do to you tonight."

One of his fingers slid inside me, and I bit my cheek to keep from crying out as my core clenched around him. He cursed, sweeping his thumb across my clit, and I whimpered. "Shh, beautiful girl. I don't want them to hear my wife when she comes all over my fingers," he whispered against my ear.

His rhythm picked up as he added another finger, and I pushed against him, needing more but climbing higher at the same time. Fire licked through my veins as an inferno built with every drive of his fingers, every swirl of his thumb against my clit. His hand came up to cover my mouth, stifling my moan as my entire body tensed up and then detonated. I broke apart in his arms, and then his soft words and caresses put me back together.

"Fuck, I almost came in my pants," he growled low right next to my ear. "That was the hottest thing I've ever fucking seen in my life." We were both breathing hard, and I watched in the dark, lit up only by the lights of the Strip as he brought his glistening fingers up to his mouth and licked them clean. It was dirty as hell but also so hot, which perfectly summed Jericho up.

I hadn't even fully caught my breath yet before we were pulling up to the restaurant, and I stepped out in a daze, straightening my dress. Jericho still sported an impressive bulge behind his zipper, and he stepped away from me, taking a couple of deep breaths. "I can't look at you, or I'll be hard all night."

Laughing, I slipped my rings off and dropped them into my purse, holding out my hand for Jericho to do the same. He reluctantly set his heavy band in my palm, and I added it to my bag. "After tomorrow, I'm never taking that off again," he promised and I agreed. I didn't want to take mine off, either. But as much as tonight was ours, it also wasn't.

Maddox and Ryan had been waiting more than a decade for this, and I wasn't going to take it away from them. I was glad Jericho had agreed easily. His relationship with his bandmates was one of the things I loved most about him, the way he cared about them. It showed how big his heart really was.

We finally showed up inside, and dinner was loud and celebratory. We all had a little too much to drink, a couple of fans interrupted for autographs, selfies, or just to shake the guy's hands, and when dinner was winding down, I decided I wanted to test the old *what happens in Vegas* slogan by doing something wild.

As everyone stood up from the table and started making their way out, I grabbed all the girls in a makeshift huddle near the table. The guys eyed us but kept walking, giving us our space. "Okay, who's up for doing something a little out there?" I asked.

Kennedy's smile got wider, Amara bit her lip, and Ryan was already nodding her head. "What do you have in mind?"

I tucked my phone back into my purse, having called ahead and made arrangements for us. "Turn here," I ordered Connor, who sat behind the wheel of one of the two SUVs we were spread out in. Indy was behind the wheel of the other car behind us, and we pulled up to *Sin & Seduction*, the club I'd found online.

The guys piled out of the car behind us, and all wore looks of shock and confusion. "What the hell are we doing here?" Maddox finally asked, and a devilish smile broke out across my face.

"Give us five minutes, then follow us inside, boys," I ordered instead of answering, and the girls and I flounced off inside.

We met Raul, the club manager and the guy I'd talked to on the phone, just inside. Indy followed us and looked decidedly uncomfortable, but he could deal with it. I wouldn't let his mood ruin our fun.

He glared at a couple of the bouncers who were looking at us salaciously, but I figured he'd handle it and followed Raul and the rest of the girls backstage. When I told Kennedy, Amara, and Ryan about this idea, they thought the best way to pull it off was to pretend to be other people so no one got the tie in to Shadow Phoenix, and so backstage, Raul showed us to a room with tons of skimpy costumes and wigs for us to change into.

I eyed a pair of sparkly platform stilettos that had to be at least six inches tall, debating whether or not I'd be able to walk in them, let alone dance. "Girl, you're braver than I am if you attempt those," Kennedy commented with a laugh. "I'd break both damn ankles."

The rough glitter rubbed against my palm as I grabbed them off the shelf. I grinned at her. "I have excellent balance, so wish me luck."

"Luck," the three women huddled around me said at the same time.

We dug through the tiny outfits and colorful wigs, and finally, everyone had found something to wear. I stepped into a tiny scrap of fabric trying to pass as a dress, and pulled it up so it clung to my curves. I adjusted the short fiery red wig I'd pulled on to disguise myself and turned to Amara. "What do you think?"

"I think Jericho's going to murder every guy in this place for looking at you in that outfit," she stated before a mischievous smile crept onto her lips. "Help me find something that will make True do the same thing."

I laughed and helped, and when we were all dressed in skimpy clothes, wigs, and way too high shoes, we practiced walking a few times before Raul asked us for the songs we wanted to dance to. None of us planned on getting fully naked up on stage, so we'd strategically glued pasties on and then handed over our song choices. I wondered how Jericho would feel about mine.

"Okay, this was your idea, so you're going first," Kennedy declared, shaking out her hands and hopping up and down as much as she could on her ridiculous heels. "Remind me how you managed to talk me into this again?"

"You all wanted to do something crazy you'd never normally do, so here's our chance. When will you ever be able to say you took over a strip club and shook your ass on stage for your man again?"

"It's not my man I'm worried about shaking my ass for; it's everyone else. What if someone has a camera?" Amara bit her lip nervously. Of all of us, she was the most conservative.

"That's what the wigs and makeup are for," I reassured her, tugging a little on the scarlet bangs covering my forehead.

"You're up, hot stuff," Raul stepped backstage and announced, and a whole flock of flamingos took flight in my stomach. This was definitely pushing my boundaries, but I loved the feeling of adrenaline surging through my veins. It made me feel alive. My senses heightened, my heart pounded, and my eyes opened wide, and the sultry beat of *Rope Burn* by Janet Jackson began to pulse over the speakers.

I threw back the curtain and tilted my chin up high, pushing my shoulders back and my barely-covered breasts out. I strutted across the stage, swinging my hips as I went. My eyes locked with Jericho's as he sat front and center. They were dark and possessive and flashed with anger. I pushed back the smirk that wanted to play on my lips, the promise of punishment in his gaze fueling me forward.

Tearing my eyes off my husband, I looked around the club as I grabbed the pole in the middle of the stage and swung myself around, tossing my hair over my shoulder and rolling my hips. The club was empty except for the security guys who were pointedly looking away and Jericho, Zen, True, Maddox, and Griffin.

I closed my eyes and got lost in the beat pulsing. My fingers circled the cool metal of the pole and gripped tightly as I swung my body around it. I shook my hips, and my eyes snapped open as hands gripped me from behind. They spun me, and I found myself looking up into my husband's black eyes, glittering with dark promises. "That's enough," Jericho's clipped words dripped with violence, and a shiver ran through my body.

He was shielding me from the view of his friends sitting around the stage, and I peeked around him. All of them had scowls on their faces or clenched jaws and tense body language, except for Griffin, who was leaning back with a devious grin on his face.

I pouted a little, not ready to be done with my fun. "Can we at least stay and dance together?"

Jericho's muscles were bunched tight, and he looked like a snake coiled and ready to attack. Not me, but like the girls had commented, anyone who had gotten a glimpse of me dancing my ass off on that stage. "Fuck, Moon. If anyone looks at you the wrong way, I'm going to want to rip their eyes out."

I ran my hand down his body and pressed closer, feeling every hard ridge of his body against mine, and his arms came up around me. "Just for a little while?"

Menace radiated off his body. "One song."

"Three."

His jaw ticked. "Two."

"Deal." I grinned up at him and pressed a kiss to his lips. I grabbed his hand and dragged him off the front of the stage with me, teetering in the ridiculous heels I had on. He scooped me up in his arms. "But, you're taking those fucking shoes off before you hurt yourself."

Instead of fighting him, I melted into his body, enjoying how easily he carried me and resting my cheek against his chest. When he pushed backstage, Kennedy shot me a knowing look. Jericho ignored all the girls and sat down with me on his lap, ripping at the straps on the shoes and pulling them off my feet with surprisingly gentle hands considering the amount of anger he was suppressing.

His calloused fingers rubbed over my skin where the shoes had been digging into my feet. "Where are your normal shoes and clothes?" he asked so quietly I almost couldn't hear him, but there was unmistakable fury laced in his tone.

I pointed at the little cubby Raul had given us to store our stuff, and Jericho tilted his head at Kennedy, not moving an inch. She rolled her eyes but got up and grabbed my stuff, handing it over. I took it and thanked her while Jericho stood up and carried me to a changing room. "I can walk, you know."

He just glared down at me as he pulled the curtain shut behind us. Jericho finally loosened his hold on me while he sat down, and I stood up, tugging the wig off of my head and tossing it at him before shaking my hair out. I giggled as it smacked him in the face; he hadn't been expecting me to throw it.

His eyes narrowed on me, burning with so much intensity he stole the breath from my lungs and heated my core. A need to feel his hands on me tore through my body, and I reached up and slid the thin strap off one shoulder and then the other. I never took my eyes off Jericho, and he moved forward like he couldn't help but get closer, resting his elbows on his knees and swiping his lower lip with his thumb as he watched me with dark eyes.

Pure carnal energy came off him in waves, spinning us in our own little web of desire and setting my body on fire as heat pooled in my core. I stripped the dress off and kicked it away, stepping between Jericho's legs in nothing but my thong and some glittery nipple pasties.

"What the fuck are these?" He asked, leaning back and brushing his thumb across the sparkling shield.

"What I wore so no one out there would see my nipples." At the reminder of what almost happened on that stage, he wrapped his arms around me and sunk his teeth into the sensitive skin of my hip, making me yelp before he swiped his tongue across the mark he'd just left above my drumstick tattoo, turning the sting into pleasure.

"No one gets to see you like this," he growled, tugging me down so I laid across his lap with my ass in the air and my whole body clenched in anticipation. Jericho's need to control—to punish—intrigued me, and I had a feeling I was about to get a front-row seat to the show.

He slid his palm across my skin before his fingers worked their way under my panties. He tugged them away from me and brushed the tips of his digits across my soaking wet slit. A low moan rushed up my throat when he did it again.

"You like pushing every single one of my fucking buttons," Jericho murmured while his fingers stroked against my sensitive flesh, but he never pushed them inside me, never touched my clit, never gave me what I so desperately craved.

"Please," I whimpered, knowing it was pointless. Knowing it would make him want to punish me more, and maybe that was what I wanted, too.

His hardness poked into my stomach as I laid sprawled out across his lap, evidence of how much he enjoyed this game, too. He shifted his hips and pressed up against me, and we both groaned. "You tortured me, made me watch as you danced for my friends. Did you want this to happen? Did you want to make me jealous as fuck? Did you want to make me prove to you I'm dead fucking serious about you being mine and only mine?"

My mouth had gone dry, and I bit my lip to keep from begging him again. All I could do was nod as I squirmed in his lap, desperate for him to slide his fingers inside of me or give me some relief. Instead, he withdrew, rubbing his slick fingers across my ass in an almost soothing rhythm before pulling his hand back and smacking it across my skin, leaving a sting that he rubbed his hand across gently before repeating the process again.

The stinging tingle left in the wake of his palm made my core throb, and Jericho's control must've reached its end because he pulled me up and rushed to unbutton his jeans, yanking them down over his hips and freeing his cock. I licked my lips, wanting to taste him, but he held me off, gripping my hips and pulling me down to straddle his lap instead. "If you put your mouth on me, I'm going to fucking lose it," he gritted out, and my heart pounded in my chest.

"What do you want me to do?" I whispered, brushing my lips across his neck and feeling his frantic pulse.

"I want you to fuck me," he said bluntly, completely owning his desires, and I held onto his broad shoulders and lifted myself, waiting for him to positioning himself at my entrance before sinking down slowly. My eyes fluttered closed, and I tossed my head back, reveling in the feeling of him filling me, stretching me, making me feel whole again.

My thighs shook as I bounced up and down his length, but Jericho was impatient and dug his fingers deeper into my hips, pounding into me from below. My eyes opened and locked on his, and as good as he was making my body feel, the vulnerability in his eyes was what overwhelmed me.

I cried out as a storm tore through me, his fingers pinching my nipple as my hips rocked against his, chasing the high only Jericho could give me. I cried out as I shattered around him, and he covered my mouth with his hand, but we weren't quiet, and the only thing that separated us from everyone else was a thin curtain. But as he followed me over the edge, pumping into me a few more times before finding his own release, I didn't care who might've heard us or what they thought.

I loved this man, my protector, my husband, with everything in me. We were both breathing heavily as my head fell forward onto his shoulder, and he stroked my hair, neither of us in a hurry to break apart and go back to the club. He pressed a kiss to my temple. "Think that'll hold you over until we get back to the hotel?"

All I could do was let out a contented sigh as he wrapped his arms around me and pulled me closer into his body. His phone vibrated in the pocket of his jeans that were still halfway down his thighs so it tickled my leg, but he ignored it.

When it stopped, it started up again right away. "You should probably get that," I mumbled. In my post-orgasm haze, I was seriously contemplating whether I could fall asleep like this.

He moved his hand off my back and dug around in his pocket before pulling out his phone and answering the call. "What?"

His whole body stiffened underneath me, and his grip on me tightened as he listened to whoever was talking on the other end of the line. A few minutes later, when he hung up, he wrapped his arm back around me. "We have to go home."

His words were like a bucket of ice water tossed on me, ripping me out of the comfortable cocoon I'd just been in. "What? Why?"

"That was Sebastian. Someone trashed your studio."

TWENTY TWO
MOON

I'd been in a daze the entire flight home. Jericho took care of everything, and I hadn't even noticed what he said to our friends or how I got onto the flight home. He shot me a worried glance from where he sat behind the wheel of his Range Rover as he pulled up in front of my store.

Indy slipped out of the backseat as soon as we stopped, and I watched in a detached sort of way as he crossed the parking lot and pulled open what was left of the destroyed door to my studio. Halfway inside, he stopped and glanced down at the sidewalk, pulling out his phone and seemingly snapping some pictures.

"It's going to be okay," Jericho's quiet words filled the silence in the car, and I leaned into them, wanting to believe he was right.

All I could do was nod woodenly as he let go of my hand and got out of the car, stepping around the front and opening my door. He reached across my body and unhooked my seatbelt, weaving our fingers together and tugging me out of the seat. "I've got you," he promised, wrapping his arm around me and holding me upright against his body as we walked toward the remains of what had once been my dream.

And as I blinked at the destruction, taking in all the ruined walls, destroyed floors, and broken glass everywhere, I realized I wasn't upset about my studio being attacked. It was so much more than that. If I didn't have my studio, what would I do with myself? I didn't have a backup plan, and the loss of the one steady thing in my life was depressing.

On top of that, who would do this? And why? I had so many questions and no answers as I picked through the rubble. There was nothing to be saved, though, and it didn't take long for me to swallow the uncertainty and desolation and push back outside.

It was only then I noticed the graffiti on the sidewalk, and I leaned against Jericho, who hadn't left my side once. He wrapped his arms around my stomach as we both stared down at it. "What is that?"

His chin rested on top of my head. "A crown, I think?"

Indy stepped up beside us. "A broken crown."

"Should that mean something to me?" I asked, looking over at him.

He shrugged. "Have you ever heard of Reign of Chaos?"

"What the fuck is that?" Jericho glanced over at Indy but got distracted when red and blue flashing lights swept over the parking lot, and the police showed up.

"Reign of Chaos is a motorcycle club. That," he pointed at the broken-looking crown painted onto the sidewalk outside my front door, "Is their logo, for lack of a better word."

My brows knitted together. "A motorcycle club? Like *Sons of Anarchy* or something?"

Indy nodded. "Or something. They're a lot worse than the club on that show."

"But how could they possibly even know who I am? I don't ride a motorcycle, and I've never met anyone in a motorcycle club before, let alone this specific one." I wracked my brain, trying to think about any connection I might have, but I came up blank.

"We'll deal with that later. Right now, we need to deal with the police." Jericho's voice rumbled against my back, and suddenly I was tired down to my bones, and my knees started to give out with exhaustion. Jericho caught me and carried me to the car, sliding me inside.

"Let me and Indy handle the cops. Julian just showed up, and I'm going to have him sit with you, okay?" His dark eyes scanned my face and darkened with concern.

I didn't want to let go of where I'd grabbed his hand. I didn't want Julian. I wanted my damn husband, but I also knew one of us had to deal with this mess, and I could barely keep my eyes open. My eyes drifted closed as a heaviness settled around me, and Jericho gave my hand a final squeeze and stepped away.

The sounds around me all blended together as I moved in and out of consciousness until Jericho's raised voice had my eyes snapping open, and Julian stared out the window beside me, observing where Jericho and Indy were talking to a couple of police officers. "She's my fucking wife, that's what authority I have to talk to you, so do your goddamn job," I heard him say, and my heart clenched at hearing him call me his wife. It still didn't feel real.

Julian raised his eyebrows at me. "Wife?"

"We had an eventful trip," I admitted, a smile tugging at the corner of my lips for the first time since last night at the strip club.

My phone buzzed in my pocket, and I pulled it out as Bexley's name flashed across the screen. "Hey, Bex."

"Moon? Are you okay? Your dad texted me that someone broke into the studio." Her voice sounded a little frantic.

"How'd dad find out?"

"He said Jericho texted him." I looked out the window where he was glowering at the cops and smiled.

"You need to talk to your dad, Moon. He sounded weird when he heard about the break-in. I have a feeling."

I yawned. "You and your feelings." Jericho opened the driver's door and gestured for Julian to get out before he slid behind the wheel. *Bexley,* I mouthed at him as he started the car. I put the call on speaker so we could all talk.

"Hey, Bex," Jericho said as Julian climbed into the back seat, and we pulled away from the curb.

"Hi, Jericho. I hope you're taking good care of our girl." He looked at me and flashed me a tired half-smile before resting his hand possessively on my thigh.

"Always," he promised.

"We're going home to get some sleep, but I'll call my dad in the morning. Well," I looked outside at the rapidly brightening sky. "Later this morning," I corrected.

"Fine, but don't forget."

"She won't," Jericho answered for me, and I said my goodbyes, hanging up with Bex and resting my head on Jericho's shoulder. I must've passed out because when I opened my eyes again, I was lying in Jericho's bed with his body curled around me as he slept. The sun was bright, and it looked like early afternoon.

I carefully slid out from underneath the arm he had wrapped across my body and sat up, closing my eyes against a sudden rush of dizziness. The last forty-eight hours had been madness, and I hadn't gotten nearly enough sleep, but my bladder was protesting, and Bexley's warning was playing on repeat in my mind.

I tiptoed across the room and into the bathroom, and when I opened the door back up, I almost jumped out of my skin. Jericho was leaning against the doorframe in nothing but a pair of black boxer briefs, and my eyes automatically dropped to his tattooed chest and stomach before snapping back up to the cocky smirk on his face.

"What are you doing?" I meant to snap, but instead, I just sounded a little breathless.

He pushed off the wall. "You weren't in bed, and I wanted to make sure you were okay after last night." He gripped my shoulders and studied my face. I sighed and let my head fall against his chest.

"I'm okay. Not sure what the attack means or what I'm going to do next, but I'm okay. I had insurance, but until I know what's going on and who attacked the studio, I'm not going to rebuild." Jericho's arms tightened around me. "I don't even know if I want to rebuild," I admitted my innermost thoughts out loud, the ones I usually pushed deep down inside, not wanting to admit them even to myself.

"Well, guess what? You can do whatever the fuck you want because you're strong and smart and capable as fuck. Plus, you married me, which means you have great taste."

I laughed and punched him in the shoulder. "Conceited much?"

He tilted my chin up and raised his eyebrow. "Am I wrong?"

I bit my lip and shook my head. His eyes darkened as his thumb pulled my lip out from between my teeth, and he pressed his lips to mine in its place. The kiss was slow and languid as if we had all the time in the world, and I fell into him willingly, wanting his embrace to wash away all the stress and uncertainty.

Unfortunately for me, one of our phones buzzed across the room, and Jericho pulled back, stalking across the room and looking at his phone before crawling across the bed and grabbing mine. He swiped to answer. "Hey, August."

I climbed onto the bed beside him as he talked to my dad. "Sure, give us an hour." He hung up and moved off of the bed, walking into his closet and pulling on a pair of joggers that hung so low on his hips they should be criminal. My mouth watered at the way his abs tapered into his pants and how little they left to the imagination.

"What'd my dad want?" I was finding it hard to concentrate on anything but the sight in front of me.

Jericho didn't answer and instead walked to the door, yanking it open and calling for Indy. "We're leaving in half an hour."

Indy's answered, but I couldn't make out the words through the half-open door which Jericho swung closed. "Time to get ready to go, pretty girl. Your dad wants to talk to you. He sounded upset."

My brows furrowed. "Upset? About my shop?"

He shook his head. "Maybe, but I think there's a whole fuck of a lot more going on than just what happened last night, and August knows more than he's letting on. So get your sexy ass in the shower so we can get going."

I perked up. "Are you going to come in there with me?"

He chuckled darkly. "No. We both know that if I get in that shower with you, we won't leave his bedroom for the rest of the day. Now go," he ordered, slapping me on the ass as I walked by him, sticking my bottom lip out as I pouted.

"Fine, but you owe me a donut. And coffee." I still left the door open in case he changed his mind.

The warm paper cup cradled between my hands gave off the heavenly scent of coffee and sugar as I held it up and inhaled, closing my eyes and enjoying how just the aroma was waking me up. Jericho drove us toward my dad's house, and when I got into the car, he had a steamy cup of coffee and not one but two donuts waiting.

He was the best. He eyed me as I sank my teeth into an apple fritter, moaning as the cinnamon-sugar dough melted on my tongue. A smirk played at his lips, but he didn't say anything. The grip he had on my thigh tightened a little, so I knew he wasn't as unaffected by the sounds I was making as he wanted to pretend.

When he pulled into my dad's driveway, the house I'd grown up in, the coffee and donut I'd eaten on the way over suddenly seemed like a horrible idea as they sloshed around in my turning stomach. My dad was acting cagey and weird, and I had no idea what he could possibly want to talk to me about. If he was so worried about what happened last night, he could've come by Jericho's to make sure I was okay.

I had a suspicion there was a whole lot more to the story, and I wasn't sure I wanted all the details. Sometimes it was better to keep your head in the sand.

"Hey," Jericho's rich, gravelly voice broke me out of my spiraling, and I turned toward him. "No matter what he tells us, no one is getting through me to get to you. That's a fucking promise, Moon."

I gave him a wobbly smile. As protective as Jericho was, that didn't make me feel better. I didn't know what was going on, but I didn't want him to get hurt either. Having him in my corner made me feel stronger and freer than I ever had, but now I had an extra person to worry about.

I couldn't really win.

He pulled my hand between his, sandwiching them together as Indy subtly slid out of the back seat and stood next to the car in the driveway. "I promise it's going to be fine, okay?"

"Okay."

"We need to find out what he knows." His voice was soothing but firm, commanding. "I won't let you go the entire time."

He must've been able to sense my nerves because his watchful eyes never left me and he kept me firmly pressed up against him the entire walk up the driveway and into my childhood home.

My dad greeted us and gave me a tight hug before shaking Jericho's hand. He offered us drinks and then led us to the living room. "Sit, sit."

He shuffled around and sat in the armchair across from the couch Jericho and I sat down on. Indy stood by the entryway into the kitchen, leaning against the wall. "Dad, before you start, you should know Jericho and I got married when we were in Vegas."

My dad's eyes widened as Jericho's hand tightened around mine, but other than that tiny reaction outwardly, he was completely calm, his face impassive and shut off of all emotion. I'd noticed that was a defense mechanism he seemed to use when assessing how someone would react. I wasn't worried about my dad's reaction, though. I liked to jump in with both feet when I made a decision, and I owned my shit. "Really? Wow. I didn't expect that so soon."

"When you know, you know," Jericho said, wrapping his arm around me and hugging me into his side.

"We can get into the details later, but what was so important we had to rush over here?" I knew I sounded a little bratty, but I was tired and nervous about what my dad seemed to be hiding.

He seemed to shrink in on himself as I exchanged a glance with Jericho, who then narrowed his eyes at my dad. He was fidgeting nervously, which just made me more anxious.

"Spit it out, August," Jericho barked, quickly losing patience with this whole situation.

"It was the Reign of Chaos that attacked your store last night, right?" he started with a shaky voice, and Indy piped up from his position by the door.

"Right."

Dad nodded to himself, taking a deep breath and blowing it out. "Okay, okay. Everything's starting to make sense."

"Are you kidding, Dad? Nothing makes sense!" I threw my hands up, frustrated with everything that had been happening, and more than a little tired of feeling like I was being watched.

"Just listen, Moon Pie. Your mom... she had a history with the Reign of Chaos."

Jericho's muscles tensed as he sat forward, and my eyebrows furrowed in confusion. "What? How?" I thought back to my mom, the one who used to bake cookies for my friends and me after school and who threw on rainboots and took me outside to stomp in puddles when it rained. I couldn't picture her having anything to do with a dangerous motorcycle gang.

My dad's bright blue eyes locked on mine, his filled with sorrow and regret. "I never told you about this because I honestly thought it was in the past, until last night. When Jericho told me about your studio, I knew it was connected somehow, and maybe that means everything is connected; your mom's disappearance, everything."

Movement drew my attention to Indy, who pulled out his phone and started typing. I turned back to my dad. "What does Reign of Chaos have to do with mom?"

"That's just it. It has everything to do with your mom. When your mom was a little girl, her dad joined up with the gang. I don't know if she ever told you, but she was born and grew up in Nevada."

I shook my head. "She never told me." Jericho's thumb rubbed across my knuckles.

"Right, well, her dad was a lower level guy, but he was clever and resourceful and willing to do anything they asked, so he worked up the ranks quickly. At first, your mom loved getting to go to the clubhouse for barbecues, and the other members' kids became her friends. But as she got older, she started noticing some of the messed up stuff the club was into. She'd see her dad washing blood off his hands or out of his clothes, or some of the other guys passing guns around."

He took another deep breath, and his eyes darted to Jericho, who sat still as a statue next to me with his mouth pressed into a flat line and his eyes so dark and filled with malice, I worried about what he might do to whoever was responsible for everything that was happening.

"Your grandfather, he was cunning, and while he never hurt your mom or your grandma physically, he did something so much worse to your mom." My dad was practically trembling as he told the story of my mom's history, the one she'd never told me herself, and I wanted to comfort him, but I held myself back, needing to know the rest.

"What'd he do?" I asked quietly.

"He wanted to work his way up in the club, and he had. But he'd climbed as high as he was going to, which was only about fifth in line to the top. So, he used the one bargaining chip he had—your mom. See, the guy in charge, he had a son, and in this club, they treat the leader like a king. His son? He's royalty, and he can't be with just anyone. Your grandfather made a deal—he'd get to be second in command and in exchange he'd marry off your mom to the king's son, to the prince."

Jumping up, I started pacing because I wasn't able to sit still anymore. "Moon-" Jericho started, but I talked over him.

"Are these people insane? Who *does* that anymore? Arranged marriages? And their illegal little club isn't even close to the same thing as a monarchy!" I stopped and flopped back down on the couch. "This is America. They couldn't just force mom to marry the guy, and obviously, it didn't work because she married you and had me."

My dad nodded. "Your grandfather planned to marry her off when she was seventeen, so he'd still have control over her. He threatened her future, told her she wouldn't be able to leave the compound unless she agreed, and she did, but only to bide her time." He smiled wistfully. "Your mom was just as cunning as her father, and she started digging into places she shouldn't. She never told me what she had, but she found something on the club and then ran. She changed her name and started over. You know the rest from there."

"I do," I agreed. "But what I don't understand is why they're coming after me now."

My dad smiled sadly. "Remember when I told you I hired that PI, and he found evidence your mom might be alive?" I nodded. "If I found the evidence, I'm sure the club did, too. I never thought they'd still be looking for her after all this time, but if they figure out who she really was, they know who you are, too. And if what your mom told me about them is true, you're the best leverage they have to get her to come forward and hand over whatever she's got."

Jericho stood and walked out of the room without a word, his jaw clenched tight and anger radiating off of him. Indy caught me as I tried to follow. "Let him have a minute," he murmured, holding me back with an arm around my waist.

Of all the things I thought my dad would tell me when we showed up here today, nothing could have prepared me for this. Suddenly, I found myself thrust into the middle of a world of violence and blackmail with no clue how to get myself out of it.

When Jericho came back, his knuckles were bloody, but his energy was calmer. He turned to Indy. "You got all that?" Indy nodded once. "Good. Tell Connor we need to meet now."

He finally turned to me and what I saw in his eyes made me crumple. He was pissed off, storm clouds gathering behind his blackened gaze, but more than that, he was *terrified.* Jericho wrapped me in his arms, and I clung to him, breathing in his familiar clean scent and trying to find strength in his embrace.

I just hoped we'd be prepared for whatever was coming next.

TWENTY THREE
JERICHO

Someone wanted to use my wife as leverage to get to her mother. My fucking *wife*. They'd have to get through me first, and there was no goddamn way that would ever happen. I'd use every dollar I'd ever made to keep her safe if I had to.

I'd do whatever it took, including taking anyone out who threatened her.

My body rippled with tension as I stalked around the room, unable to hold still or sit down. Connor, Indy, Sebastian, and the new guy Ronin were all crowded around the coffee table in my gaming room. Moon had passed out in what was now our bed, exhausted as soon as we got home from her dad's house.

"I have an entire history on the Reign of Chaos for the past thirty years. It's a lot of shit—newspaper articles, financial records, police reports—and all of it really messed up. If you've got a USB drive, I'll transfer it so you can look at it when you've got time," Sebastian offered.

I raked my hand through my hair. "Yeah. I've got one down in my studio." Taking off, I jogged down the stairs at the back of the room toward the recording studio I had downstairs, but when I flicked on the light, my anger sparked all over again.

All my shit had been tossed, ransacked for who the fuck knew what purpose. My equipment was thrown on the floor and smashed to pieces; the glass in the room had been shattered. My sheet music was crumpled, ripped, and tossed everywhere. I gritted my teeth and yanked my phone out of my pocket, stabbing at the screen until I finally found Connor's number. "Come down to the studio," I hissed as my phone creaked ominously in my hand because I was clenching it so hard. I didn't wait for him to respond, just hung up and dialed Zen.

"Do you have the backups I sent home with you of our last session?" I demanded.

"Yeah, why?" He sounded distracted. Nico was crying in the background.

"Someone fucked up my studio, and my laptop is gone."

"Shit." It sounded like he was moving away from Nico. "Any idea who did it? And how they got in?"

"Fuck if I know. We went to Moon's dad's house for a little while today, and nobody was here. Connor's here now. Thank fuck Sebastian installed surveillance equipment last week."

"Yeah." He blew out a breath. "Let me know if you need me; I'll come over."

My body still burned with rage but knowing I had so many people on my side helped take it down a notch. "Thanks, will do."

I ended the call as footsteps pounded down the stairs, and Connor burst into the room with Ronin on his heels. "What the fuck?"

"Yeah, you tell me." I folded my arms over my chest and surveyed the damage all over again. This time, I noticed a torn sheet of paper stuck into the wall with a knife. I moved over to it and yanked it off the wall.

When you start a fire, you're bound to get burned.

Well, what the hell did that mean? I handed the note off to Connor, rolling my eyes. "Look at the note. It's not a mystery who was behind this."

"Dick," he confirmed, crumpling the paper in his hand and shoving it in his pocket. "What's his endgame here? He can't possibly think this is going to get you to hire him back."

I pushed down the anger boiling under the surface. "He's not smart. Maybe, like the dumbass he is, he thought he'd scare me into quitting. It's obvious as fuck he doesn't know me even a little but if he thinks this is enough to do anything other than piss me off." I swept my hand vaguely around the room.

"I'll deal with this mess later. Right now, I'm more worried about the clan of motorcycle-riding douchebags out to get my wife."

Ronin's hand clamped down on Connor's shoulder. "Okay, then. Let's go back upstairs and figure out where we go from here."

He looked like the kind of guy who'd fuck you up if you came across him in a dark alley, but he had this calm about him that I bet made him a good cop. We trudged up the stairs and back to the living room where Sebastian had his face buried in his laptop.

I flopped down on the couch, and Ronin and Connor sat, too. My fingers ripped at tangles in my hair as I raked them across my scalp again. "ROC isn't our only problem. My studio's trashed, my laptop with everything we've recorded is gone," I announced to the room because Sebastian and Indy hadn't been downstairs with us to see the mess.

Sebastian's brows were furrowed above his thick-rimmed glasses. "Shit," he bit out, his fingers moving impossibly fast across the keyboard. He finally stopped, spinning his laptop on his lap so we could all see the dark screen. "Whoever broke in came in through the back, but they took out the cameras before they did. I've got nothing."

"I already know it was that fuckwad, Dick." Still, evidence would have been nice.

"How?" Sebastian wondered, turning his computer back around.

"If the studio had only been trashed, I might've been convinced it had something to do with ROC. But my laptop was gone, the recordings are missing. That's taking it to a whole other level, and it feels personal as fuck. The only person who'd want to take our new music is Dick." I exhaled, leaning back against the couch. All this shit piling up was exhausting. I wished more than anything I could be up in bed wrapped around Moon, far away from our real-life nightmare.

"We can deal with Dick later. Zen has copies of everything, and I backed up to the Cloud. He had to know I wouldn't just keep one copy on my computer, so this was a message to get in line. Unfortunately for him and the label, I don't give a fuck about their contracts or expectations. All I care about is making good music. So, for now, we ignore his petty temper tantrum and move on to making sure Moon doesn't get hurt by the Reign of Chaos."

"You can start by looking over the files I sent you. I don't think you should dismiss the attack on your studio so quickly. There's something you're going to want to see in the ROC inf-"

He was interrupted by a loud bang on my front door, and Indy jerked away from the wall he'd been leaning against and stalked across the house, ripping the door open. His soft curse floated through the house, and we all stood up on edge.

He stormed into the room carrying a box tied with a bow before setting it down on the coffee table in the center of us all.

"What the fuck is that?" Ronin asked, leaning closer and reaching out to touch it, but Connor slapped his hand away.

"Don't touch. We don't know what's in it."

I rolled my eyes. "For fuck sake," I grunted and then tore off the bow and the lid. Inside were the smashed remains of my laptop.

Sebastian snorted. "You think Dick's serious about you hiring him back?"

"The *Pulse* interview hit last week, and word spread like wildfire around the industry that he's the shittiest producer the label has and that they've been forcing him on musicians for years. He just got what he had coming." I shrugged. "If he's waiting for me to admit I was wrong and come crawling back to have him produce, he's going to be waiting for eternity because it will *never* happen."

The box felt surprisingly light in my arms as I picked it up and walked to the garage door, pushing it open and tossing the box out. I didn't need a reminder of how much Dick was starting to fuck with my career.

Sebastian was whispering to the guys when I came back into the room and stopped when I moved into hearing distance. "Out with it," I demanded.

Sebastian looked to Connor, who nodded once. "In all the digging I did on Reign of Chaos, there was nothing that tied any of this together or made sense to me. Why would they be after Moon now? Why are they watching her? What do they gain by attacking her business? So many questions... and their financials painted an interesting picture." He clicked around a few times before passing me his computer. I stared at the screen, unsure of what I was looking at.

"What is this?"

He pointed at the screen. "That's their bank account info. Obviously, I can't track everything because bad guys don't exactly keep all their money in a normal bank. But, I was able to hack into a couple of offshore accounts. They're into a lot of heavy stuff, stuff that would make your stomach turn. Human trafficking. Drugs, weapons, standard stuff for gangs like theirs. And also kidnapping and murder for hire stuff, too. If you can think of a crime, they've got their fingers in it."

"What does any of that have to do with Moon?" Ronin asked, and I filled them in on what August told us this morning about her mom's history with the gang.

Sebastian had taken back his laptop and was typing frantically. I looked away from him and back at the other guys in the room as Ronin started talking. "If I had to guess, I'd say when August hired that PI to track Cara, when he started digging some sort of alert was tripped or something and ROC got the notification at the same time. No one knows where Cara is at this point, but they could easily find Moon. Maybe they want to use her to draw her mom out."

A shiver ran down my spine before my resolve hardened. "They won't touch her."

"No, they won't," Connor agreed. "But in the meantime, we keep watching and digging. Indy and Julian will stay on guard rotations, and Sebastian will fix the camera issue."

"I'll see if I can figure out what Cara had on ROC that they would care about fifteen years later," Ronin added.

"And what about Dick?" Connor's sharp stare held me from across the room.

"What about him?" I growled, losing patience with all of this and feeling the weight of the fucking world heavy on my shoulders.

"He's clearly not going away. What do you want to do about him?"

"Ignore him. We've got bigger problems. Montana's digging into our legal options with the label, and eventually, he'll see that his little games mean nothing to me, and he'll give up and move on. Marcus will fuck over some other poor musician's career by forcing Dick on them, but it won't be our problem anymore."

Connor appraised me with flinty eyes and a tight jaw. "If that's how you want to play it, but what he did tonight was a blatant slap in the face. He's showing you he's not done with you yet."

"If he does anything else, we'll talk about fucking him up. Until then, drop it," I growled, frustration pouring off of me in waves. "Make sure my wife is protected at all times no matter the cost," I added, standing up and ignoring the questioning stares burning into my back as I walked back toward my bedroom.

A tiny smile tilted the corner of my lips up as I stepped into the room and peeled off my clothes. Now everyone would know what Moon and I were to each other. Our secret was out.

TWENTY FOUR
MOON

My skin was sticky with sweat as my eyes fluttered open. My tangled hair covered my face, and I reached up and brushed the damp strands off of my forehead. Heat was all I felt. It surrounded me and coated my flesh, and I kicked off the blankets to get some relief.

Jericho's body was wrapped around mine protectively, his arms tucked around me tightly, holding me firmly against his hard body while he slept like he couldn't bear to let me move even an inch away from him.

I kicked off the blanket, and cool air brushed over my skin, and I sighed in relief. I tossed and turned all night, plagued by strange dreams that made no sense. I didn't know if my subconscious was trying to tell me something or just cope with all the crap I'd learned about my parents over the past forty-eight hours.

Either way, it didn't matter. I was done lingering in the past, feeling sorry for myself for what could have been and wondering why my mom chose to leave like she did. If what my dad said was true, she was in danger, and she'd put us in danger by having us in her life.

If she left to protect me, how could I be angry about that?

My stomach let out a growl as I shifted under the weight of Jericho's arms. I hadn't eaten dinner last night, and now I was starving, my limbs shaky from low blood sugar. Jericho groaned as he stirred behind me. "Morning, baby," he rasped into my ear, his voice still hoarse from sleep. There's was nothing sexier than Jericho's voice first thing in the morning. The already rich, smoky bass he always spoke with dropped even lower and got even raspier when he was just waking up.

A shiver ran down my spine as the words rolled off his tongue, and I arched my back, pressing myself against his morning wood. His eyes snapped fully open, and his palm slowly crept up my torso until he grabbed a handful of my boob.

All the thoughts of breakfast evaporated from my mind as he massaged the pillowy flesh and plucked at my nipple with his rough fingers. He leaned over me and sealed our lips together, kissing me with a force and hunger as he rolled me onto my back and moved on top of me.

Long gone was our sluggish wakeup and in its place were frenzied movements as we clawed at each other, ripping off what little clothes we wore. I'd never experienced this side of Jericho—the one that wasn't in complete control. He seemed reckless this morning, his kisses wild and primal, and I loved every second of it.

He slammed inside me in one thrust, and I tore my mouth away from his, crying out at the sudden fullness. We moved together, though, never stopping to adjust. This was a purging of demons, a releasing of pent-up fears and tension, and all I could do was hold on for the ride.

His pace was desperate and frantic, and he grasped at me like this was the last time we'd ever be together, like he thought I'd disappear. Like commanding my body wasn't enough, he wanted dominion over my soul, too, and at this moment, I'd gladly give him anything and everything he demanded.

Jericho owned my body as his skin slapped against mine, his fingers trembling as they rubbed my clit, building an intense wave inside of me and forcing it out. I exploded around him, every muscle in my body clenching before releasing in a relaxed sort of blissed-out state that made me feel like I was floating. As I came down, he pulsed inside of me, yelling my name, and I listened as it echoed around the concrete fixtures in the room.

We caught our breath, clinging to each other in our own little bubble of safety and happiness, neither of us wanting to speak to shatter the illusion we created. But my stomach took the decision out of my hands, growling loudly between where our bodies were still connected. Jericho's rumbling laugh vibrated against my skin, and his breath brushed across my neck, where his face was buried between me and the pillow.

"Let me feed you, beautiful." I nodded as he sat up, pulling us apart, and holding out his hand to help me out of bed. I swayed a little on my feet, the long night and vigorous morning activities catching up to me, and he stood beside me, brows furrowed in concern as he watched me wait out my crappy equilibrium.

"Are you okay?" Concern marred his voice, but I grinned up at him, reaching up to smooth the crease between his brows with my index finger.

"Fine, just starving. I'd kill for a bagel and some OJ." He let go of my hand and pulled on his boxers while I tossed his discarded t-shirt over my head.

"Done." He crossed the room and kissed me on the temple before pulling me out of the room. A girl could get used to a wakeup like that.

Over breakfast, Jericho filled me in on what went down last night with his studio, the package, and the info Sebastian found on the ROC. He told me about Ronin's theory about why they were after me, too. I wasn't sure how I felt about any of it. It still felt surreal to know that my mom was possibly alive and tangled up in really bad gang shit.

On top of that, to know that they were after me for some unknown reason was unsettling. I wasn't sure if it was better before I knew who was actually watching me or if knowing made it worse. From what Jericho told me, this club was as bad as it got, and somehow I'd managed to get on their radar.

Goosebumps ran down my spine as I watched my husband pull a pair of dark denim jeans over his muscular legs as he got ready to go meet up with the band. "Are you sure you have to go?" I pouted, fully aware that he did, in fact, have to go and that I was being a little bit of a baby.

It didn't stop me from wanting him to stay with me today.

His lips quirked up in a half-smile. "Yes, and please don't beg me to say because I sure as fuck can't say no to you, but with Dick out to sabotage our album and Marcus breathing down our necks about shitty focus groups, I can't afford to slack off."

I stepped into his outstretched arms and buried my face in his chest, inhaling his clean scent. "Make something amazing today, okay?"

He kissed the top of my head, and his mouth moved in my hair with his words, "I will."

I watched as he drove off in his black Range Rover before Indy snapped at me to get away from the window. Now that Jericho was gone, I figured it would be a good time to start making calls about my studio and figuring out what to do next.

After a couple of infuriating hours spent mostly on hold and getting tossed around from clueless person to clueless person, I'd had enough. "Ugh!" I yelled before pushing back away from the counter, where I had papers scattered across the surface.

I walked over to the fridge and yanked the door open, looking for something to eat even though I wasn't very hungry. My discarded phone buzzed across the counter, and I slammed the door closed, grabbing it and answering the call. "Hello?"

"Is this Moon Mayhem?" the uncertain female voice on the other end asked.

I went still as my heart started pounding. "That's me. Who's this?"

"I'm Lynn Breccan, a nurse at Creekside Hospital. I'm calling because you're the emergency contact of a patient we admitted last night."

My blood ran cold as I leaned against the counter, my heart pounding a hectic beat against my ribs. "Who?" I whispered as Indy came into the room and met my eyes before moving quickly to stand beside me. His hand reached out and wrapped around my arm, steadying me as I closed my eyes.

"An August Mayhem. He was dropped off in front of the emergency room last night with life-threatening injuries. We've just now stabilized him."

My stomach flipped, and I lost the battle to stay on my feet as I sank to the floor, the room spinning as I tried to remember how to breathe. I barely registered Indy plucking the phone out of my fingers and taking over the conversation. His words sounded far away like they were down a long tunnel, and I couldn't quite make them out.

Tears sprang up in my eyes as I thought about my dad, the calmest and most loving person I knew, helpless and broken lying in a hospital bed all alone and fighting for his life. Streaks of tears spilled down my cheeks as Indy crouched down in front of me. His lips moved, but I couldn't hear what he was saying.

He stood, picking me up off of the floor. Finally, his voice broke through the haze. "We're going to the hospital." He pulled out his keys and tucked my phone into my pocket, and I leaned against him as I stumbled my way to Jericho's garage. Indy slid behind the wheel of a black sports car and started the engine, and I got in the passenger seat, staring blankly out the windshield while my mind raced.

The door behind me opened, and Julian climbed in the tiny back seat, closing the door, and Indy took off. "I called Connor, and he's sending Ronin over," Julian explained to Indy, who grunted in response.

My whole body trembled as I pulled out my phone and called Jericho, but I got his voicemail. I left him a quick message just asking him to call me before typing out a text.

Moon: Indy's taking me to the hospital. Please call me as soon as you get this.

I stared at the little checkmark showing the message had been delivered and desperately hoping for the three bouncing dots to start, showing he was typing back to me, but after a few minutes of nothing, the screen faded to black. Fresh tears welled in my eyes, and I tried to blink them away. Even though Indy and Julian were here with me, they weren't exactly friends. I didn't want to face this alone.

Silent tears ran down my face, and as we pulled up to the hospital, I wiped them away. I had to be strong for my dad. I didn't know what condition I'd find him in, but it wouldn't help anything if I was falling apart when he was the one who'd gone through something terrible.

I walked into the hospital flanked by Indy and Julian, feeling tiny between them despite my five-ten height. "You sit, I'll go find out what room he's in," Indy ordered, and Julian guided me over to the waiting room. I checked my phone again, but Jericho still hadn't responded to my message. Instead, I typed out a text to Bexley.

Moon: Dad's in the hospital. I'm not sure what happened yet. I can't reach Jericho, and I don't want to be alone.

Bexley: OMG. Which hospital?

Moon: Creekside.

Bexley: Be there in 30.

I let out a sigh of relief. Bexley was my person and would sit with me as long as I needed her to. Ever since we were kids, it'd been that way. We'd always been there for each other no matter what was going on. She'd been the person I leaned on most when my mom disappeared, and she'd been the one to encourage me to never give up on her during the days when the search felt hopeless.

"He's in the ICU, fifth floor," Indy reported, stepping back and waiting for me to stand up and follow him to the bank of elevators off to the right.

The ride up was silent, but I could see the two of them silently communicating through glances over the top of my head. I was in too much shock to care.

We stepped off the elevator and into a tiny waiting room that smelled like stale coffee and sadness. It had half a dozen chairs and an old TV playing an infomercial in the corner. I turned to my bodyguards. "I'm going to the nurses' station to ask about my dad. You two wait here."

Indy grabbed my arm as I turned to leave. "That's not how this works, Moon. Where you go, I go."

I huffed but didn't argue as Indy followed me out of the room and down the hall. We stopped in front of the corner desk. A couple of people in scrubs sat behind it, including a man with gorgeous mocha skin who looked up at us. "Can I help you?"

"We're here to see August Mayhem." My voice sounded stronger than I felt, and I was glad I'd been able to hold myself together. Inside I was freaking out.

His eyes softened. "And who are you, honey?"

"I'm his daughter, Moon. This guy's with me." I tilted my head over at Indy. I didn't want to explain who Indy was and deal with the questions that would come with that. I wanted to see my dad.

"I'll take you back, but patients up here only get short visitation windows of fifteen minutes at a time," he explained. "I'm Tre Jackson, by the way." He held out his hand, and I took it, relaxing into his calming energy. I was happy he was one of the people caring for my dad.

"What happened to my dad, Tre?" I asked, not wanting to wait any longer.

"I'll let the doctor explain everything to you when he does his rounds next, which is in," he glanced down at his watch. "About half an hour." Tre stopped outside of a room, his hand moving onto the handle.

"I'm going to warn you, Moon. Your dad… he doesn't look good. Brace yourself for that, because it might be a shock." He gave me a minute, and while he stood watching me with concern, my heart raced, and a cold sweat broke out over my whole body. Every instinct in me was screaming at me to turn around and go back to the waiting room. I knew that the second I laid eyes on my broken father in that bed, the image would be seared into my memory forever.

But I was all he had, and I wouldn't abandon him like that when he needed me. I wouldn't leave him alone. With one last deep breath, I pulled my phone out of my pocket, checking for a message from Jericho, but there was nothing. Choking back my disappointment, I shoved my phone back into my jeans and steeled myself for what was to come. Indy clasped his hand on my shoulder, letting me know he was there with me, and I reached up and grabbed his hand, needing to hold onto someone.

"Ready?" Tre asked, and I nodded. He swung the door open and stepped out of the way. Even though I knew it would be bad, that didn't stop the choked sound that left me as I took in the sight of my father in that hospital bed. Tears spilled over my eyes and down my cheeks as my whole body shook. My knees went weak, and I felt myself starting to sink to the ground, but Indy hauled me back up and plastered me to his side.

"Be strong for him, Moon," he reminded me, and his words broke through my anguish. I swallowed and wiped my tears on the sleeve of my shirt. My dad's face was so discolored and swollen, I couldn't even tell it was him. His eyes were swollen shut, his lips were split, and tubes ran out of his nose and mouth. There were bandages around his head, and it looked like machines were breathing for him. There was a beeping announcing his steady pulse to the room.

On shaky legs, I gently pushed away from Indy and moved toward my dad, standing beside the bed. I took his hand into mine, being careful of the IV line running into the back of his hand. His fingers were cold to the touch, and he didn't return my squeeze. "What happened to you, daddy?" I cried, sinking onto the edge of his hospital bed. "Please come back to me."

I sat and begged him to wake up, crying and pleading, and silently bargaining with any entity that might help. But when our fifteen minutes were up, Tre gently reminded me that it was time to go. The only place on my dad I felt safe touching was the palm of his hand, so I traced a heart there and whispered an *I love you* before leaving the room behind Tre and trailed by Indy.

None of us spoke until we were back in the waiting room. I felt a weird combination of agony and numbness as he explained the doctor would be by in a few minutes to explain everything. Indy offered to get coffee, and I nodded woodenly, not really wanting the caffeine but unsure what else to do.

I stared at the wall until Bexley's voice shook me out of my stupor. She rushed into the room and yanked me into her arms, crushing me to her body, and I absolutely crumbled. I clung to her and cried and screamed and wailed until my throat was sore, and my eyes were swollen, but a little of the sorrow had faded.

I was utterly spent, exhausted from the emotional outpouring as we sat down, Bexley beside me, holding onto each other. Indy came back with our coffee, and I glanced at Julian, who was staring pointedly at the wall and ignoring everything that just happened between my best friend and me. Indy's brows furrowed at he looked Bex up and down as if making sure she was okay, but he didn't say anything, and she rolled her eyes at him.

The doctor walked in and broke up the weird tension in the room. "Miss…" he trailed off as he squinted his eyes down at the file in front of him, and I sighed heavily, gathering myself and standing. "Mayhem?" he called out in a disbelieving tone.

"That's me," I confirmed, inwardly cursing my parents *yet again* for their creative naming skills, but with my dad looking like death and in the hospital, I figured I'd let my usual irritation slide.

My mom used to tell me that with a name like Moon Mayhem, I was destined for an exciting life. Maybe she was right. I craved freedom and adventure, and the minute someone told me what to do, I danced away from them with my middle finger held high. Maybe it was the Mayhem in me, but nothing ever felt right unless it was a little bit reckless too.

But the danger I was experiencing now wasn't something I enjoyed or wanted to continue. I quickly realized safety and security weren't as guaranteed as I once thought.

"And actually…" I glanced at Bex, biting my lip nervously because she was definitely going to kill me. "It's Moon Cole now."

Bexley's jaw dropped, but I had bigger issues to worry about right now than explaining my spur of the moment nuptials.

"Right. Mrs. Cole, your father underwent an assault that fractured four of his ribs, punctured a lung, lacerated his kidney, and fractured his orbital bone. He also had this carved into his chest." He pulled a picture out of his file, and acid shot up my throat. I covered my mouth with my hand and looked away, but the jagged bloody crown engraved on my dad's chest would haunt me for the rest of my life.

Indy stepped forward and took the picture from the doctor, snapping a picture of it on his phone before handing it back.

I sucked in a breath, trying to process everything, but the doctor wasn't finished yet. "Those aren't even the worst injuries. He sustained trauma to his head that caused his brain to swell. Right now, he's in an induced coma to allow the swelling to resolve, but at this point, we're not sure when," he gave me a sympathetic look, "or if he'll regain consciousness."

My legs wobbled underneath me, and Bexley shot up, reaching out and grabbing onto me. She asked the questions I couldn't vocalize as my world was imploding before me. "When will you know if he's going to get better?"

The doctor shook his head sadly. "The first twenty-four hours are critical, and we're about to take him down for a scan. We should know more in a couple of hours." He reached out and awkwardly patted my hand. "He's young and in good health. We're hopeful that he'll come out of this just fine, but he needs time."

I nodded. "Is…" I cleared my throat. "Is there anything I can do?"

"Talk to him during the windows you're allowed to visit. Studies have shown that coma patients respond well to familiar stimuli. I'll be back when I have the scan results to update you." Julian and Indy both got up and followed the doctor out, asking follow up questions that my brain couldn't handle.

"He's going to be okay, Moon," Bexley comforted me, and I trusted her. Her gut was never wrong.

"You really think so?" I needed to cling to any reassurance she was willing to give right now to keep from coming apart at the seams.

"Yes, but in the meantime, I think you and I are due for a long conversation about a certain tall, dark, and hot drummer that's apparently now your husband." She scowled at me, and my lips twitched in the closest thing to a smile I could get right now. I appreciated her for trying to give me a little bit of normalcy in the chaos of this moment.

My chest ached when I thought about how much I needed Jericho right now. *Why wasn't he answering my text?* I couldn't afford to dwell on it right now. I didn't have the energy. Instead, I turned back to my best friend. "You know what they say. What happens in Vegas…"

TWENTY FIVE
JERICHO

"I want to change shit up for this song. Something doesn't feel right about it," I announced, stalking into the booth and leaning against the soft eggshell coating on the wall that dampened the sound.

"What's wrong with it?" Maddox wondered, strumming the strings of his bass.

"I think we need a shakeup. Zen and True are gonna switch places for this one," I decided, and once I said it aloud, I realized it was exactly what we needed. A perfect fit for this particular song. True's voice was just as good as Zen's, and Zen was just as good as True on guitar, but we'd all settled into our roles and gotten fucking complacent.

We had the opportunity to do something completely different. Fuck the label and their expectations. True had a good enough voice to sell millions of his solo record and win a Grammy. He should have no problem fronting the band for this tune.

And to their credit, the guys didn't say one goddamn word in protest. They had complete trust in me and my vision, and they carried it out perfectly. True set down his guitar and stepped up to the microphone while Zen moved to the back of the room and grabbed his own guitar out of the case. I gave them a minute to warm up and for Zen to tune his guitar. I was itching to pick up my phone and check in with Moon, but I needed complete focus when I was in the studio, so I brushed the thought aside.

"You guys ready?" I asked. Griffin nodded and tapped his stick on the symbol with a grin. Maddox rolled his eyes at his brother, and Zen and True looked at each other before looking back at me. "We're ready," True confirmed.

I stepped out of the room, letting the glass door close behind me. I was assaulted again by the feeling that I should check my phone, make sure Moon was okay. It wasn't just a thought but a prickle of unease rolling down my spine. But I chalked it up to my overprotectiveness and let it go. Once we got a good recording of this song, I'd call her and reassure myself she was fine.

It took another hour before I had a recording I was satisfied with, but I'd been right to make the guys switch up their places. I was starting to realize that we didn't have to be confined by the roles we'd locked ourselves into over the years. This was a chance to completely reinvent ourselves without giving a single fuck about what anyone thought about it.

We could be anything we wanted to be.

Begrudgingly, I had to admit Griffin was badass on drums. He filled my spot with ease and perfection, and there was no one else I would've ever let step in to fill my shoes but him. When the guys finally finished and filed out of the booth for a break, I let myself check my phone. My blood ran cold as I stared at the message on the screen.

Moon: Indy's taking me to the hospital. Please call me as soon as you get this.

"Fuck," I bit out, frantically searching for my keys and dialing Moon's number. It went straight to voicemail. I hung up and called Bexley, but she didn't pick up either. My heart was racing. What hospital was she at?

"What's wrong?" Zen asked, concern lacing his features.

"Moon. She texted me that Indy took her to the hospital a couple of hours ago, but I don't know which one. I should've checked my phone. Fuck!" I yelled, kicking the chair I'd been sitting on, so it flew across the room. True dodged out of the way.

Instead of shying away, the guys rallied around me. "I'll call Kennedy and see if she heard from her," Zen offered.

"I'll check with Connor." Maddox pulled out his phone and started tapping at the screen. I tried calling Moon again while Griffin walked over and plucked my keys out of my hand.

"You're not driving like this," he stated calmly, and I wanted to smash his face in, but I took a deep breath instead as True packed up my laptop and walked across the room, holding open the front door. "Let's go."

I didn't even question him as I moved forward on autopilot, holding my phone up to my ear, listening to pointless ringing as Moon's voicemail picked up again. I wanted to throw my phone against the wall as my frustration erupted and boiled over, but a tiny logical part of my brain was still in control and knew if I did that and she called me, she wouldn't be able to get through.

Griffin slid behind the wheel while Zen and Maddox followed True out, and he locked up behind us. I jumped in the passenger side of my Range Rover, and Maddox, Zen, and True climbed in the back.

"Kennedy hasn't heard anything, man. Sorry," Zen apologized, sitting back against his seat.

Maddox talked quietly into his phone but ended his call, leaning forward into the space between Griffin and me. "They're at Creekside."

Griffin didn't hesitate, slamming on the gas and propelling us forward. I gripped the door handle and glared at the newest member of Shadow Phoenix, who drove like he had a fucking death wish, just like his older brother. I didn't dare tell him to slow down. Fuck that. I needed to get to my wife.

"What happened?" I demanded, tightening my grip on the handle as we flew around a corner. "Christ," I bit out as it felt like we went up on two wheels.

"Connor didn't have any details. Indy texted him that he and Julian were taking Moon to Creekside, and he needed backup to guard the house since both of them were going."

My mind filled in the blanks with all sorts of fucked up scenarios, and with every mile we drove, my imagination got more and more disturbing until I'd convinced myself I was going to walk in and find her dead. I was already planning out my vengeance before we even stepped foot inside the hospital.

I jumped out of the car before it even stopped, sprinting into the building and up to the first nurse I found. "I need to know where my wife is," I demanded, breathing hard. I probably looked insane, but they saw that shit all the time.

"Who's your wife, sir?" the nurse asked while leading me over to a desk and stepping behind it to type into her computer.

"Moon Mayhem… or Cole," I added on, not sure what name Moon would have given.

"I don't have a Moon registered anywhere in my system. I'm sorry." My heart was beating wildly as a frantic need to find her gnawed at my insides. I opened my mouth to snap at the nurse, to push her to look again when I spotted Julian out of the corner of my eye. I stalked across the busy emergency room and grabbed his shoulder as he walked away from me. I didn't think he'd seen me come in, and he definitely hadn't noticed the rest of the guys coming in through the doors now.

He spun around, tense and braced for a fight, and his eyes narrowed when he saw me. "About time you showed up."

Resisting the temptation to shake him until his head detached from his neck, I growled out, "Where. Is. My. Wife?"

Someone choked behind me, but they wisely kept their shit to themselves. I didn't have time to answer their questions about Moon and me getting married. That shit could wait. I had to make sure she was okay first.

Julian shrugged my hand off of him and folded his arms across his chest. "Fifth floor. ICU." Then he turned and stalked away.

I shoved my hand through my hair. The ICU? "Fuck."

True moved forward and mashed the button for the elevator. I was suddenly terrified to move forward, afraid of what I might walk into. If Moon was hurt, I didn't know what I'd do or how I'd deal with it. Violence pushed into my veins as I bunched my muscles, needing an outlet for all of the emotions battering my mind and body.

Gentle hands pushed me forward into the waiting elevator and out of my destructive thoughts. Maddox patted me on the back after his shove. "We've got your back. She's going to be okay."

I straightened my spine and clenched my jaw, balling my fists in preparation for whatever awaited me when the metal doors slid open. No matter what it was, I could face it with my brothers at my back. I'd go through anything I had to to get to Moon.

When the doors slid open, I stepped out onto a bland tiled floor that my boots squeaked on with every step. I'd only managed a couple of steps before a nurse greeted our group, his eyebrows practically in his hair they were up so high. "You guys… You're Shadow Phoenix."

My fingers flexed, but Zen stepped in front of me, sliding a smile onto his face. "That's us. Can you help us find someone? We were told she was up here."

The guy nodded like a bobblehead, too fucking excited for the setting. "Yeah, anything you need."

Zen shoved his shoulder into mine almost playfully, and I knew he was trying to project casual confidence I didn't feel right now. "Is there a Moon Mayhem," he side-eyed me before turning back to the nurse, "Or Cole here?"

I watched as the guy shut down, his face becoming completely impassive. "I can't share patient information with you, no matter how famous you are."

I stepped around Zen and leaned into the guy's personal space. "Tell me where the fuck my wife is."

His eyes widened. "Your wife? So *you're* Moon's husband? Huh." His stare drifted off, so he was looking at nothing at all, and I gripped the front of his blue scrubs in my fist until his gaze snapped back to me.

"Where is she?"

He lifted his arm and pointed at a room down the hall. I released my hold on him, and he stumbled a little. Out of the corner of my eye, I saw True reach out and steady him, probably apologizing for my shitty behavior, but I had a singular focus and remembering to be marginally pleasant to people ranked so far down the list, it wasn't even funny.

I stormed into the tiny waiting room, and my eyes swept over the empty chairs until they landed on Moon's wild, colorful hair. Her and Bexley were huddled together, and my shoulders slumped in relief. It washed over me like rain, cleansing away all the anxiety and anger and helplessness since I'd gotten her text.

Her eyes lifted to meet mine, and then we were crashing together as she threw herself into my arms, clinging to me like I was her lifeline, and if she let go, she'd be lost. Her sobs shook her whole body as tears soaked my shirt, and I just held her. She wrapped her legs around my waist, and I sank onto the hard, plastic chair, breathing her in and enjoying the tidal wave of relief that she seemed to be okay.

My hands ran down her body, checking for any injuries she might have. When I came up empty, I pulled back a little from her and looked into her clouded eyes, and I brushed the hair away from her face. "Why are we here, baby?"

Her eyes filled with tears again as she took a deep, shuddering breath. "M-my dad," she choked out before her head dropped back to my chest and sobs wracked her body again. I rubbed her back. What the fuck was going on? What did August have to do with anything?

Bexley waved at me and caught my attention as the rest of the guys strolled into the room, taking the empty chairs and leaning against the wall wherever they could find space. With the five of us, the two security guys, and the girls, this place was beyond cramped.

I raised my eyebrow, and she mouthed *ROC*. I gripped Moon tighter, relieved as fuck that she hadn't been the one attacked, but it pissed me off that someone hurt her like this anyway. August was a good guy, and, like Moon, he wasn't involved in anything shady as far as I could tell. His only crime was loving his wife and daughter, and I sure as fuck wasn't going to stand by and let someone hurt my new extended family.

I adjusted my grip on my girl and turned toward Maddox, locking eyes with him. We held an entire conversation in just that look. We'd done this shit so many times before. As a group, we always took care of our own. It was instinct at this point. We knew what each other needed, and when one of us couldn't do what needed to be done, the others stepped up. It'd been a long fucking time since I needed my brothers, but I had a feeling to get through this shit with the ROC, I was going to need all of them, even the new one.

Maddox stood and walked out into the hall, looking for the nurse who'd greeted us when we first got here. I needed answers, and he was going to get them. What happened to August to land him in the ICU? What was wrong with him? And as Moon tightened her grip on me, digging her fingers into my skin so hard I briefly wondered if it'd bruise, I wondered if August would be okay.

Just as my ass was starting to go numb from the chair, Maddox sauntered back into the room. I pressed a kiss to the top of Moon's head, smoothing her unruly waves down and sliding my hand down her back. "I've gotta go talk to Mad for a minute." She whimpered in protest and only dug her fingers in harder until Bex moved up on one side of me, and Indy came up on my other side.

"Leave her with us, she'll be fine," Bexley kept her voice soothing as she sat in the chair beside me, and Indy sat on my other side. I stood up and let Moon's body slide down my own, trying and failing to ignore the press of her soft curves against me. I wanted to literally sweep her off her feet, carry her out of here to a place where only we existed, and spend the rest of my life buried as deep inside of her body and soul as I could go.

Unfortunately, that wasn't realistic, so I handed my wife off to her best friend, who wrapped her up in a fierce hug. Moon's eyes followed me as if she thought I'd disappear if she blinked. I followed Maddox out of the room, and True, Zen, and Griffin followed us. I stopped short of being out of Moon's sight. I wanted her to feel safe, and for some unfathomable reason, she felt safe with me.

I still didn't think I deserved her. I was twisted inside, and I didn't want to drag her down into my dark depravity, and yet I was a selfish motherfucker, and I couldn't stay away. Instead, I'd do everything I could to be worthy of her love, including making sure she always knew she was safe with me and how much I loved her.

"What's going on?" Zen asked.

Maddox ran his hand across the stubble on his jaw. "August was attacked last night, and someone dumped him outside the ER. They have him in a coma right now while they give his brain a chance to heal from the damage, but they don't know if he'll wake up."

My chest tightened as I glanced up at Moon again. No wonder she was so upset. Besides Bexley and now me, her dad was the only family she had left.

"Do they know who attacked him?" True wondered, fidgeting with his phone.

"The Reign of Chaos," a deep voice answered from behind us as Connor moved into our makeshift circle.

"How do you know that?" Griffin finally spoke up. He'd been quiet since we walked into the hospital.

"Sebastian. He hacked into the security feed at August's job. They took him last night when he finished his shift. They're brazen fuckers, I'll give them that. They didn't even try to hide who they were. Leather cuts, motorcycles, and all." Connor tilted his head in greeting at Indy and Julian.

"Dude, I don't know how to say this, but…" Maddox hesitated, nervously watching me as if he was deciding how to tell me something that would piss me the fuck off.

"Just tell me," I ground out through clenched teeth.

"They carved a crown into August's chest. There was never any doubt who did this."

The helplessness and anger boiled over, and I pulled my hand back and threw my first into the wall, barely feeling the sting of split skin and bruised knuckles. I pulled back to do it again, to add to the crater in the drywall I'd created, but someone grabbed my arm and stopped me. I looked back with a glare. Griffin.

"This isn't going to help your girl feel better, seeing you lose control like this. You want to help her? Keep your shit together. You can take it out on me later."

My shoulders sagged as I slipped down the wall, sinking to the floor and burying my face in my hands. With all the adrenaline and anger pouring out of me, weariness and exhaustion took its place. I couldn't let it take over, though. Not when Moon needed me.

I took a deep breath and then stood up, squaring my shoulders. "It looks like we're going to be here a while. True and Griffin, you grab food. Maddox is on coffee duty, and Zen see if you can find some blankets and pillows we can use to make this shithole of a room more comfortable while we wait." I fell easily into taking control of the situation.

Control.

What a concept. Something I'd spent my entire life grasping onto like it was the most important thing, but it was all an illusion. We never really had control, and the ROC taught me another important lesson in what it meant to be truly powerless.

It was a feeling I hated, and I vowed to myself right then I'd never allow someone to make me feel powerless again. It was time to go on the offensive, to make them see they had fucked with the wrong person.

TWENTY SIX

JERICHO

"Moon," I whispered, not wanting to wake up anyone else as I gently shook her awake. "Wake up, pretty girl."

She groaned softly from where she slept on the hard ground of the hospital waiting room. We'd managed to find a couple of blankets and a pillow, but it was still hard as fuck. She'd refused to go home, though, so here we were. Zen and True had gone home hours ago. Both of them had kids and wives to worry about.

Ryan came by to relieve Julian sometime in the middle of the night, and Maddox had been hovering around her protectively since she showed up. I couldn't blame him; if Moon was responsible for guarding someone from a scary as fuck motorcycle gang, I'd lose my fucking mind. I didn't know how he was keeping himself from doing exactly that, but if the dark circles under his eyes, wrinkled clothes, and beard he was starting to sport were any indication, he wasn't handling it well.

I lowered myself to the ground next to Moon and pulled her into my lap, and she immediately curled into me. My grip tightened, and I pressed a kiss to her forehead, whispering against her skin, "Baby, your dad's awake. He wants to see you."

Her eyes snapped open at my words. "What?" She scrambled up off of me and stumbled, still half asleep. She rubbed her eyes, and I grabbed her hand, standing up beside her.

Griffin thrust a cup of coffee into her hands, and I gave him a grateful nod. He looked like shit like we all did. We looked like we'd slept in a hospital waiting room, so that checked out.

Her hand shook as she lifted the cup to her lips. The nurse, Tre, walked into the room looking well-rested and freshly showered, and I glared at him. I was still pissed about how he held out on me yesterday. "Ready to go see your dad?" he asked my wife, smiling at her like she made his whole day better, and I bristled. He was a little too familiar with Moon, and I didn't like it. That look in his eye, the one that said he wanted what was mine, pissed me the fuck off.

Maddox shot me a look then glared at the nurse. I couldn't be a possessive asshole now because Moon needed me to be better than that, but Maddox had my back. With that one look, he told me as much.

Moon blinked at the nurse and then nodded slowly. "I know you said only one person could go in at a time, but I need Jericho there with me." My chest swelled at her words. She *needed* me. Yesterday was still haunting me, and I'd deal with the self-loathing and guilt over not being there for her when she called, but right now, I pushed it aside. I'd be whatever she needed me to be for now.

The nurse eyed me with disapproval, but he finally relented. It didn't matter what he said, whether he gave his approval or not, I wasn't letting my girl out of my sight, and he couldn't do shit about it. "Fine. He's waiting." He spun on his heel, expecting us to follow.

Moon gripped my hand in hers as we strode down the hall and followed into August's small room. The man looked so pale and small in the hospital bed, surrounded by wires and tubes, it was unsettling.

"Mr. Mayhem? Your daughter's here," the nurse announced, stepping up beside August and checking the printout of a machine next to him.

Moon shuffled up beside his bed, and I moved with her, never letting her go. August's eyes rolled around behind his eyelids before cracking open and searching the room before landing on Moon. He exhaled in relief, and his voice cracked when he spoke. "Moon Pie."

She gripped his hand but fell back against my chest as if I was the only thing keeping her standing, and I wrapped my arm around her waist. "Hi, dad."

His eyes shifted up to me and widened a little bit in surprise. "Jericho."

"You look like shit, August." I tried to lighten the mood, and a smile played at his lips.

"That's what happens when you go a few rounds with a group of mean bikers." He tried to sit up but winced and gave up as the nurse shot him a disapproving look. August looked like he was on the brink of falling asleep again, just this short interaction sapping his energy, but as his eyelids got heavier, he seemed to realize he was fading and jolted awake, tightening his hold on Moon's hand.

"The men that attacked me—they had a message." His voice was scratchy and faint. I had to strain my ears to hear him over all the goddamn beeping of the machines in the room.

"What message?" Moon asked.

"They want whatever your mom has on them, and if she doesn't come forward and hand it over, they're going to come after you. They're going to use you as bait to lure her out, sweetheart." August's fear-filled eyes shot up to meet mine, and I saw what he couldn't say out loud in front of Moon. He was terrified for his daughter. Rather than stand up to these men before, her mom ran. Did she care enough to come forward now that her daughter was in danger?

And even if she did, how the fuck were we supposed to let her know that was what the ROC wanted?

I bit my cheek, the metallic taste of blood flooding my mouth as I forced myself not to lose my shit. Breaking apart this hospital room, yelling at August for not knowing where his wife was, none of it would help this situation. It might make me feel better in the moment, but it'd hurt Moon, and that was something I'd never do.

Tears streamed down Moon's face, and I turned her around, hugging her against me and taking deep breaths to calm my riotous heart.

August started to slip into unconsciousness again, and I tugged on Moon's hand, urging her to let him go so I could get closer. I patted him on the cheek, and his eyes snapped open, but they were unfocused, and sweat beaded along his forehead. He was in pain and exhausted, but I couldn't let him sleep yet. "You really have no idea what it is Cara has on them or where she is?"

His eyes shot to Moon and back to me. He knew something. I fucking *knew* it. "Tell me what you know," I growled, but he pressed his lips into a flat line. Whatever it was, he wasn't about to betray his wife to save his daughter, and that pissed me the fuck off. My fingers coiled into a fist, but I held back. This man was still my wife's father, even if he was a goddamn coward.

I leaned closer so I was practically whispering in his ear. "The next time you wake up, I'm sending my head of security in here, and you're going to tell him everything you know. You may be willing to hide shit to protect your wife, but I'm willing to do any-fucking-thing to protect mine. Understand?"

His eyes widened, but he nodded. Maybe it would make him feel better to talk to Connor, but Connor would report everything back to me, so what did I care if he talked to him instead of me. As long as we figured out where the fuck Cara had been hiding, that was what mattered.

I straightened, and August closed his eyes. Moon's face was streaked with tears, and I reached up and dried them. "He's going to be okay, beautiful, and we're going to find your mom." She sunk into me as we left the room, but the weight of this situation was intense. What the fuck had I gotten myself tangled up in?

And more importantly, how the fuck was I going to get us out of it?

"Here he is," Zen announced as we walked back into the waiting room. The guys were standing in a circle, and he had his phone held up in the middle. He and True must've come back while we were in with August, and they looked freshly showered and well-rested, the bastards.

Moon leaned up and pressed a kiss to my cheek before she let me go and moved over to update Bexley. I tore my eyes off her and joined my bandmates. "Yeah, here the fuck I am. What?" I snapped, not in the mood to deal with any more shit.

"Aldrich called me this morning." Montana sounded on edge, which made the hairs on the back of my neck stand up.

"Yeah? Is it unusual for our lawyer to call you considering we're in a fucking legal standoff with the label?" I asked, rubbing my eyes. It felt like they were filled with sand. I couldn't remember the last time I slept.

"No, but you're not going to like what he had to say."

Maddox sighed next to me. He looked as fucked up as I felt and kept sneaking glances at his wife, who stood right outside the door on watch with Indy. "Just tell us," I demanded, too tired to play games.

"Marcus Hughes and Pacific Records are suing you for breach of contract. They're demanding you either get back in the studio with Richard Bennett producing or pay them damages for breaking the contract."

"How much?" True was twisting his nose ring as he asked.

"Twenty-five million dollars."

We were silent at her words, and rage percolated under my skin. Who the fuck did these assholes think they were?

"What are our options?" Zen questioned, shifting on his feet. We had the money. We'd been smart over the years, and we could take the hit, but this was a matter of fucking principal. We shouldn't have to. Montana hired Aldrich Thompson to dig through our contract and figure out how to get us out of it. We all agreed we'd rather take the hit financially if we had to than stick our names on the piece of shit record Dick would produce.

"Aldrich is still digging. He seemed to think there was a clause that if you gave up the rights to all of your past albums, they could release you from the current contract. But you wouldn't get royalties from any of that music moving forward, and the label could do whatever they wanted with it. You'd have no say or control."

Fuck. That was *not* ideal.

We all looked at each other, but I was too fucking tired to think about making this decision now. "Let us know what Aldrich finds. For now, we'll keep making the new album as if the label hadn't threatened us. Fuck them if they think they can intimidate us into doing their bidding. Dick will *never* get his talentless hands on our music again," I growled before moving away from them and back over to Moon.

I couldn't handle having her out of my sight or away from me for any period of time. When I sat down beside her, she stood up and then sat down on my lap, resting her head on my shoulder. I needed to talk to Connor about August, but it could wait.

Her fingers played in the short hairs at the back of my head, and I closed my eyes, leaning into her touch. "I heard what Montana said," Moon confessed quietly, her voice almost a whisper.

I chuckled. "The room isn't exactly small, beautiful. It's not surprising you heard."

"I'm sorry."

Blowing out a breath, I stroked her hair. I needed her closeness right now. She made me feel settled, calmer, and in control. "It's fine. We'll figure it out. Right now, the most important thing is keeping you safe. Do you want to go home soon? Take a nap and a shower, grab some food before we come back?"

She nodded, her hair tickling my chin. "Yeah, I think dad will be asleep for a little while. Since he regained consciousness, I can relax a little bit."

I almost smiled at that. Almost. Moon felt safe with me, and I was glad she felt like she could relax, but I was on high fucking alert. Someone was trying to hurt my wife, and I wouldn't rest until they were fucking handled.

"I'm going to go talk to Connor about going home, then we'll get the fuck out of here. Hospitals give me the fucking creeps," I admitted, wrinkling my nose. Moon laughed softly and slid off my lap. I missed having her pressed against me, but I had shit to do.

Weaving through the bodies scattered around the room, I stepped outside and found Connor down the hall a little bit, talking quietly on his phone. This whole place felt like death, and it was one of those situations where you didn't want to speak too loud. If you did, you might wake the dead.

He saw me coming and ended his call, turning his full attention on me. "What's going on?"

"August woke up, and he knows some shit, but he wouldn't tell me with Moon in the room. I let him know I'd be sending you in the next time he was up for visitors. Find out what he knows about the ROC and what Cara has on them."

Connor nodded. "What else?"

I started pacing, unable to hold still. "I want to take Moon home. We need a fucking break, but with that goddamn gang after her, I need you to have someone check the house before we go, and at least one of your guys needs to come home with us."

He brought his phone up to his ear. "Get to Cole's house. Search it top to bottom, let me know when it's clear." He barked orders into the device. "Stay there until we get there."

He hung up and crossed his arms, flashing the ink he hid underneath his long sleeve shirt. "I'm sending Ronin over, and I'll go with you when we get the all-clear."

Blowing out a breath, I leaned against the wall to wait. If I went back into the waiting room and sat down, I'd fall asleep. Even my bones were tired, and I wasn't quite sure how I was still standing. Pure fucking will and adrenaline, I guessed.

I closed my eyes, blocking out the fluorescent lights while we waited for the call, and Connor didn't talk to me. I wasn't much of a talker, and the people I surrounded myself knew not to fill up the space with pointless small talk. That was a quick way to piss me off.

"Yeah," Connor's gruff voice startled me out of the light sleep I must've drifted into. Fuck. I scrubbed my hands over my face, fully alert now. I'd been so fucking tired at points in my life that I couldn't think straight, but never once had I fallen asleep standing up. That was an unwelcome new experience.

"Fuck. Don't call the fucking cops. Hold them until we get there. We're on our way," he commanded, hanging up and slipping his phone into his pocket.

"Ronin caught a couple of guys inside your house planting surveillance equipment. He took them down and restrained them, but I thought you might want to question them yourself." I didn't miss the knowing glint in his eye. I had no problems getting my hands dirty if the occasion called for it, and this right here?

This was what the monster inside of me was fucking made for.

"Give me two minutes," I grunted and moved into the waiting room and over to Moon.

I crouched down in front of her, taking her chin between my fingers.

"Beautiful, I need you to stay here a little longer. I'll have Maddox and Ryan bring you home in just a little while, okay? Please just trust me."

I wanted her as far away from the house as I could get her right now, and I knew she'd be safe with them. Maddox would never let anything hurt Moon, and his wife was one of the best people on Connor's team. I'd seen her take down grown men without breaking a sweat. Maddox nodded at me from his spot across the room. He'd handle keeping Moon safe.

"Okay," she agreed, her eyes soft as she looked at me. "I love you," she murmured against my lips before kissing me. Despite my exhaustion, her kiss drew me in, sending sparks to every nerve ending in my body and waking me right the fuck up. She was better than caffeine.

She didn't ask me any questions, just trusted that I'd take care of her. It was a heady fucking feeling, knowing someone trusted me that much, and I sure as fuck wasn't about to betray her faith in me.

TWENTY SEVEN

JERICHO

"Where are they?" I snarled as I slammed the door to my house open. Who the fuck would dare come into my home? These guys obviously bought into the image I portrayed in the media of the shy, quiet rock star who kept to himself.

They had no fucking idea of the beast I could unleash given the right motivation. No idea at all.

Connor slowly followed behind me, content to hang back and let me deal with this my way. There was a reason he wasn't a cop. The law was too restrictive, and it didn't always get results. But here, there were no limits. I would get fucking answers, and there would be blood.

"Down in your basement. I had Ronin put them in the gym." Smart. The gym had black floors, and that would be easy to clean blood off of.

Stomping down the stairs, my hands flexed, itching to smash into something. Ronin stood rigidly outside the room that housed my gym, looking uncomfortable with how lawless this situation was. Considering where he'd come from, I wasn't surprised, but there was no fucking room for that bullshit here. "If you can't handle this, get the fuck out," I ordered, not waiting to see what he decided.

Cool air greeted me as I stepped into the dark space, and two figures sat on the floor, back to back and bound at the wrists. I walked up to the one on the left and kicked him—hard. "Wake up, fucker."

He groaned and looked up at me with a defiant sneer. "Fuck. You."

I laughed. So far, this was going exactly how I expected it to. His arms were tattooed completely like mine, but the ink had long faded, the lines no longer sharp. His grey goatee hung down to his chest, and deep wrinkles were etched into his face. They both wore leather vests signaling their allegiance to the Reign of Chaos. I wanted to rip them off their bodies and make them watch as I burned them, but that could come later.

Now I needed information.

Rolling my neck, I loosened the muscles. Staying calm was a necessity. If I took it too far and killed one of these guys, that would create a whole other mess with the club that I didn't need to deal with. The weight of my knife in my pocket drew my attention, and I reached inside, pulling it out and flipping the blade open.

I crouched down in front of the man with the goatee. Out of the corner of my eye, I saw Connor take Ronin's place. "Why are you following my wife?" I didn't want to waste time playing games with these guys. I wasn't going to pretend I didn't know who they were.

"Thought I might show her what it's like to be with a real man," he taunted, his lips curling into an ugly grin that showed off his tobacco-stained teeth.

Pulling my fist back, I slammed it into his face and hardly felt the sting in my knuckles as I watched blood pour from his nose. "Next time you disrespect her, I won't be so nice." I wiped my hand on my black t-shirt, moving my knife between my hands. "Now let's try this again. Why are you following my wife?"

"Eat me." He glared at me defiantly. His loyalty to the Reign of Chaos would never let him answer my questions without the right kind of encouragement, but I didn't mind. I stood up and turned back to Connor. "Bring me a chair," I ordered, and he spun on his heel and left.

Turning back to the men on the floor, I ignored the smaller man and refocused on the man with the goatee I'd already been talking to. I only needed one of them to break and give me the information I needed, but it was good to have a spare. "Last chance to answer my questions the easy way," I offered, glancing down at the nametag on his leather vest. "Bomber."

Bomber glared at me as Connor carried a metal chair into the room. We both grabbed underneath Bomber's arms and hauled him up into the chair. He struggled, and Connor punched him in the face so fast, I didn't think Bomber saw it coming. "Hold still." Connor reached into his pocket and pulled out some zip ties, but Bomber wasn't going to make this easy. He bucked his big body, kicking out with his feet, so I stepped in front of him and threw my fist in his face again and again until he stopped fighting.

My knuckles ached, but I barely registered the pain. The adrenaline was zipping through my veins, and Connor and I made quick work of cutting the ties behind his back and using the new zip ties to secure each one to an arm of the chair. Yanking his boots off, I did the same with his feet.

In a way, I was glad these assholes had broken into my house because now I'd have the chance to figure out what the fuck they wanted. The other started spouting all kinds of bullshit about how he was going to hurt Moon or kill me, so I sent Connor upstairs for tape, and he came back and shoved it over the guy's—Vandal, according to his vest—mouth. "Time to shut the fuck up before I knock your ass out like I did your friend," I warned.

I patted him on the chest condescendingly as he lunged at me, or at least as much as he could while tied up on the hard ground. His muffled words made no sense, so I ignored him, standing up and walking back over to Bomber. I slapped his cheek a few times. "Time to wake up."

Both of his eyes were already swelling, and he was bleeding from his nose and lip. He had a cut over one cheek, and his head drooped down to rest on his chest. He groaned as he came to, blinking his eyes a few times. "I'm going to kill you," he promised, and I laughed.

"Yeah, I've heard that before. Now, how about you answer my questions, and we can both move on with our lives?"

"Fuck you," he repeated, spitting in my face.

Disgusting.

"You're going to wish you hadn't done that." My voice was low and deadly as I caught the towel Connor tossed me from the cupboard down here and wiped my face with it. I sauntered back over to Bomber, twirling my knife between my fingers. "You didn't want to answer my other question, so how about you answer this one? Why were you in my house?"

"I'm not telling you shit." He was breathing hard, and I eyed him, wondering how much stress his old, out of shape body could take before it gave out on him. He didn't exactly look like the picture of health. This was probably the most time he'd spent inside a gym in at least twenty years.

"We'll see," I murmured, holding my knife to his index finger as he stiffened. "I bet being in a gang of criminals, you probably need your trigger finger, huh?" I pushed a little harder on the blade, breaking the skin and watching blood start to pool under the knife.

I looked up at his face, and his skin had turned an unhealthy shade of red, but he kept quiet. "Nothing to say?" I questioned, digging the knife in further, slicing into his skin.

"Fuck," he bit out but said nothing, so I pressed my weight down and finished what I started, slicing his finger off and holding it up for him to see as he screamed.

"I wonder how many of these you can lose before you finally answer my questions?" I mused, tucking his finger into the pocket of his vest. His blood coated the blade of my knife as I pressed it to his middle finger on the same hand. "Now. Why the fuck were you in my house?"

Bomber was panting through the pain. "You were supposed to be some diva rockstar," he muttered, and I chuckled.

"I'm a lot of things, Bomber, but a diva isn't one of them. As you can see, I've got no problem dealing with the more unpleasant shit if I need to. Now answer my goddamn question." Danger dripped from my voice, daring him to defy me. I may have started by taking a finger, but I sure as fuck wouldn't end there if he didn't give me answers.

His whole body sunk in on itself as my knife dug into his middle finger, making him bleed. My fingers were sticky, coated with his blood. "Fine. Fuck. Fine! I'll tell you." His partner on the ground writhed, and his muffled voice carried over to us, but I got up and walked over to him, giving him a solid kick to the ribs or three.

"Shut the fuck up." I kicked him again just because I could before going back to Bomber. "Tell me."

"We were here to install cameras and microphones and shit."

I pressed the knife back down into his skin. "I'm not fucking stupid," I snapped. "I knew what you were doing. My question was why."

"Because we need the footage!" he yelled as I dug the knife in.

"What footage?"

"The footage Cara stole. She has a video, and we want it back." I glanced back at Connor, who was watching us intently. I raised my eyebrow at him, and he stepped forward out of the shadows.

"What's on it?" he questioned, moving closer.

Bomber shrugged, wincing as the movement made his finger push against my blade. "Not my job to ask."

"What makes you think it would be in my house?" I pushed, adjusting my hold on the knife.

"That girl that's been staying here with you, she's Cara's daughter-"

"There you go treating me like I'm stupid again, Bomber," I chastised, hitting the bone in his finger with my blade, and he cried out.

"Fuck! Okay, okay!" he yelled as bloody spit flew out of his mouth. "Cara popped back up on our radar a couple of months ago. We figured she'd reach out to her daughter, so we've been following her so we could grab Cara," he explained, his chest heaving with the effort to deal with the pain.

"And what if Cara never came for her daughter? What then?" I asked, my voice dark and cold.

Bomber's eyes flashed with fear. He took one look at me and must've realized no matter how he answered this question, I was going to be fucking pissed. "And don't fucking think about lying to me."

He answered, but it was too quiet for me to hear. "What was that?"

"We would have taken her and used her as bait!" he screamed as I stepped on his toes, grinding my boot into the digits, breaking a few.

"That's what I thought." I lifted my foot off of his mangled toes. "Last question."

He moaned, and his head lolled on his chest as he panted. "How exactly did Cara pop back up on your radar, as you put it?"

"Over the years, we'd been able to track her, but we'd always been a step behind. We had a list of her aliases and an old one she hadn't used in years checked into a hotel using a credit card."

I turned and looked at Connor, who raised an eyebrow. We were no doubt thinking the same thing. For someone who managed to stay hidden for fifteen years, that seemed sloppy as fuck. Did Cara *want* us to find her?

"What was the alias?" I probed, turning back to Bomber. Sweat was pouring down his face, and he looked like a fucking disaster.

"Lucy. L-Lucy Mills," he let out a shuddering breath.

I stood, taking my knife with me. Grabbing a fresh towel out of the cabinet, I washed my hands and rinsed the blood off my blade while Connor stepped up beside me.

"You want a turn?" I asked, watching as the pink water swirled around the drain.

"I think that's all he knows." He glanced over at the two men on the other side of the room, his expression bored. "What do you want to do with them? The ROC's gonna be pissed you took his finger."

I smirked at him. "That's why I've got you." I glanced over at Bomber. "Plus, I gave him his finger back. If he hurries, he can probably get it reattached." I laughed. "Maybe."

"You're enjoying this too much," he noted with a smirk of his own. "You sure you don't want to join up with my team now that you're getting a taste for working behind the scenes?"

"Fuck, no. It'd be dangerous to let the demons out to play if it wasn't absolutely necessary." A shiver ran through my body, and my mind drifted to Moon. She was waiting on me so she could come home, so I needed to wrap this shit up.

Moving back in front of Bomber, I leaned down. "If you get that evidence back, will your club back the fuck off of my wife and her family?"

"That's not my call to make, but it's possible."

"Here's what's going to happen, Bomber. My friend here is going to take you and your buddy to the hospital and drop you off, and you're going to tell your boss or whatever to back the fuck off."

"I can't-"

"I didn't ask you to speak, so do yourself a favor and shut the fuck up," I snapped. "If your club comes after my wife again, you're going to start a war, and when I find my mother-in-law, and I will, I'm going to use that evidence and every connection I have to take you the fuck down instead of giving it back. Understand?"

He nodded, and I backed up, walking back over to Connor. "Take them to the hospital and drop them off like they dropped August. I'm going to go pick up Moon."

Connor glared at them with his arms folded over his chest. "Do you want to do anything to them for what they did to August?"

I'd thought about it, but right now, my top priority was protecting Moon. Starting a war with a notorious biker gang wasn't going to help me achieve that. I shook my head. "Not right now. They're going to be mad enough about this," I waved toward Bomber and Vandal.

Connor chuckled. "You're right about that." He shifted, leaning his hip against the counter. "Ronin will drive you back, and I'll have Indy stay here and sweep the house for whatever bullshit they managed to plant before we caught them."

I didn't even bother washing the rest of the blood off of my arms or changing clothes before I found myself sprinting upstairs to grab Ronin and get back to Moon. I'd already been gone too long. I wondered if she'd still look at me like I was her whole world if she knew I'd tortured a man today, made him bleed and hurt, and enjoyed it.

I didn't know if I could bear her seeing the darkness I buried deep inside, and maybe it'd been unfair to marry her without her knowing that side of me.

Dread filled me as I climbed in the car, Ronin beside me, and sped off to face what I'd done, hoping I didn't ruin my marriage by trying to protect Moon.

TWENTY EIGHT
MOON

Jericho walking into the waiting room was the second best thing I'd ever seen, right behind my dad waking up from his coma. There weren't words for how exhausted I was. I'd slumped over against Bexley earlier and nearly passed out.

The dizziness I'd been waking up with the past week was back in full force, too, making the room spin and me feel nauseated. I was glad I hadn't eaten anything as my stomach lurched again, but I really needed a shower and sleep.

With the little bit of energy I had left, I jumped up out of the seat and flung myself into Jericho's waiting arms. He wrapped me up, and I collapsed against him, inhaling his clean scent. Every muscle in my body relaxed with him here. "I missed you," he murmured against my hair, holding me tighter.

"I missed you, too," I sighed, not wanting to move or let go.

"I'm going to take you home, and you're going to shower and sleep, then I'm going to feed you, and we're going to talk." I warmed at his words, wanting to let him take care of me. I loved his demanding nature, his possessiveness, and how he always put my needs first.

The usual twitchiness I'd be getting by now in a relationship was nowhere to be found, which just proved I'd made the right decision in following my heart to Jericho. I had no desire to flee, no doubts about him or how he made me feel. My relationship with him was pretty fucking great.

"We're going home," he announced to the room, and I felt his words rumble through his chest, tickling my cheek. He pulled away, taking my hand instead, as we walked out of the room, but I turned back at the last minute.

"Thank you guys for being here with me. It really means a lot," I addressed everyone who'd sat here with me over the past couple of days before turning back and letting Jericho lead me down to the car with the new security guy trailing behind us.

As we climbed in the car, the security guy—Ronin, I think—got into the back seat, and Jericho drove us home, never letting go of my hand the entire way. His inked skin was streaked and speckled with rust-colored spots that I hadn't noticed in the crappy hospital lightning. "What is this?" I asked, stroking my hand over his skin, and he tensed.

"Blood."

My eyes widened, and I checked him over, but he chuckled. "It's not my blood, pretty girl."

"Oh." I didn't know what to say about that. "Who's blood is it?"

Jericho took his eyes off the road to glance over at me. "We'll talk about it when we get home." His tone left no room for argument, and I didn't have the energy to press him, so instead, I leaned across the console as another wave of dizziness hit me and I closed my eyes, resting my head on his shoulder.

Strong arms wrapped around me, lifting me, and I nuzzled into the comforting embrace. Jericho's deep chuckle made my lips curve up into a sleepy smile as he carried me into the house. I didn't open my eyes, too tired to worry about how heavy I was or any of the other crap I would normally think about if I had the energy. Instead, I relaxed and let myself drift until my feet touched cool tile, and I snapped my eyes open.

My arms were draped around Jericho's neck as he tugged my shirt up, pulling it off of me and tossing it aside. I moved to grip the counter as he unbuttoned my jeans and dragged them down my legs, and when he was done, he pulled off my underwear, so I stood naked in front of him. "Shower first, then sleep," he commanded, his voice husky as his heated eyes ran over my body. He reached inside the shower and turned it on, undressing while the water heated up.

He stripped off his clothes, and I couldn't take my eyes off his broad shoulders, the ridges of his abs, the ink splashed across so much of his skin, and his already semi-hard cock that made me want to drop to my knees and show him what he did to me just by existing.

He reached for me, and the speckles and streaks of blood shone red-brown under the lights as we stepped into the shower, and I watched the spray erase it from his skin. My body heated, surprising me by how turned on I was that he wore someone else's blood on his skin. "Who's blood is this?" I asked again, brushing my hand along his skin and holding it up to watch the red droplets wash away.

Jericho's big body pressed up against me, and he lowered his forehead so it rested on mine. "A biker from the Reign of Chaos," he admitted, running his fingers down my arm and making me shiver with his touch.

"And how did you get his blood on you?" I sounded breathless as my whole body tuned in to the man standing in front of me, hoping he'd answer my questions and then satisfy the craving he was building up in me.

He leaned back, locking eyes with me and searching mine for something. Finally, he blew out a breath, looking resigned, and he looked away. "He broke into the house, and Ronin found him. He tied him up, and I took him to the basement and hurt him until he told me what I wanted to know." He lifted his eyes back up, but they were hard now, cold and guarded. "Now you know how much of a monster you married."

His jaw was locked tight, and I reached up, stroking my hand along his cheek. "Thank you for doing that for me," I whispered, leaning up to kiss him. It should've felt wrong for his words to turn me on, but it didn't. He'd tortured someone for me, to protect me.

Jericho looked at me incredulously. "You're not upset? Maybe regretting your life choices? Because I've got to tell you, if you are, I don't think I can let you walk away from me. I'll follow you to the ends of the earth if I have to."

I reached up and tangled my hands in his hair, bringing his face down so our lips were almost touching, and I watched as water droplets gathered on his lashes. "I will never regret you. You're everything I never knew I needed, and this part of you? The part that's dangerously protective of me? It doesn't make me want to run; it makes me want to love you harder, to let you fuck me until we unravel each other, to unleash the demons inside of you, and play with them. There is nothing you could do that would make me turn away from you."

He groaned and crashed his lips to mine, slamming me into the wall while I wrapped my legs around his waist, my fatigue forgotten. The cold tile at my back did nothing to cool the fire burning through my body at Jericho's touch. His kisses were burning me alive, but I welcomed the inferno. The steam around us made the air hazy, and it was like we were the only two people in the world.

His lips moved to my neck, nipping, kissing, and sucking his way down to my breast, where he pulled my nipple into his mouth, gently biting my sensitive peak. I cried out his name, shifting my hips to grind against his erection, wanting to feel him fill me up, and he slid his hard-on along my slick entrance, up and down, up and down, brushing my clit with every pass.

My whole body trembled, and my limbs were tingly as I clawed at his back, pressing myself as close to him as I could get but still he teased me. I whimpered in frustration. "Please, Jericho."

"You never have to beg me for what's yours, Moon. You want to feel my cock inside your sweet little pussy?" He rubbed me again, his length making me see stars as it brushed along my heated flesh.

I nodded, and in one thrust, he was inside me. We both groaned at the fullness, the feeling of our bodies connecting. It was like a sigh of relief to be so close, and when he started to move, I was lost to the sensation. Every punishing thrust, stroke of his fingers, or flick to my clit pushed me closer to the edge, building me higher and higher.

Jericho's strokes were erratic as he thrust wildly like he was trying to use my body to purge himself of his sins. "Fuck, baby. You're wrapped so tight around my dick I can't think straight," he growled, and I lost it as he swelled inside of me, clenching around him and falling over the edge, screaming his name. I came so hard I thought I blacked out for a minute, and when I came to, Jericho was pressed up against me breathing hard.

The water turned cold, so I dropped my feet shakily to the ground as he stepped back, severing the connection between us, and I knew I was exhausted and being emotional, but I wanted to cry at the loss. He must've seen my trembling lower lip and eyes welling up with tears because he wordlessly pulled me against his body, holding me with one arm while grabbing the shampoo with the other. He never let me go while he washed me from head to toe quickly, washing himself too before turning off the water and wrapping me up in a fluffy grey towel.

He wrapped one around his waist, and then bent down and lifted me into his arms, carrying me to bed. Once I was tucked under the covers with my wet hair in a tangled mess around me, I couldn't keep my eyes open anymore. He crawled under the blanket beside me and pulled me against his chest, kissing my cheeks and my forehead. "Sleep, beautiful. I'll tell you everything in the morning."

As if his words were the command my body needed, I gave in and surrendered to my exhaustion, letting my dreams pull me under.

A loud banging noise woke me the next morning, followed by my stomach spasming. "Ugh," I moaned, rubbing at my abdomen. When was the last time I'd eaten anything?

I reached out, but the bed beside me was cold. Another loud clang came from outside the bedroom, so I pushed back the blankets, bracing for the dizziness, but it didn't come. I stood up, going into the closet to grab one of Jericho's t-shirts, and I quickly brushed my teeth. When I looked in the mirror, my hair was an absolute nest of tangles, so I threw it up in a messy bun and called it good.

My bare feet slapped against the cold concrete floor as I made my way to the kitchen. Jericho stood shirtless with his back to me, sweatpants hung criminally low on his hips, and his back muscles tensed and flexed as he moved, pulling pots and pans out. The counter was a mess of ingredients and dishes, and when he turned around and noticed me, he had a scowl on his face.

A giggle escaped me before I clamped my hand over my mouth and his eyes narrowed at me as he stalked around the kitchen island toward me. "What's so funny?" I stepped back, but he advanced like he was stalking his prey.

I liked being hunted if he was the hunter.

"Nothing," I squeaked, turning and going into a full-on sprint, but I only made it about five steps before he caught me around the waist, lifting me up and against his muscular body.

"Caught you," he murmured, licking my ear and making me shiver, but he let me down and walked back into the kitchen.

"Seriously, though… what are you doing?" I pulled out a chair at the bar side of the island and slid onto it.

"I was trying to make you breakfast, but I don't know shit about cooking. True tried to talk me through it on video chat, but I think he just made it worse." He gestured to where his phone was propped up next to the stove, and True was grinning at us.

"Hey, Moon," he greeted, and I waved at him.

"Hi. Thanks for trying to help, but at this point, I think we need to call in a professional." I jumped off the chair and went in search of my purse. Jericho had left it by the front door, so I dug around until I found my phone.

"What kind of professional?" Jericho called from the kitchen, and I bit my lip to keep from laughing as I walked back into the room.

"It's this really fancy thing called food delivery. I want pancakes and hashbrowns," I announced, before picking my order and sliding my phone over to him. "Put in what you want, and I'll order it."

He scowled at me but finally picked up the phone. True laughed. "A girl after my own heart. If you order extra hashbrowns, I can be there in ten minutes."

"We're not doing that, make your own hashbrowns," Jericho snapped before ending the video chat. He tapped my phone a few times before handing it back, and I placed the order.

"While we wait for that, you can explain to me why you had some biker's blood all over you last night." I stood and walked into the gaming room. It was the most comfortable room in the house, and I could tell he spent the most time here, outside of his studio.

The comfy cushion enveloped my body as I sunk into it, and Jericho sat right beside me, pulling my legs into his lap so he could run his hands across my skin. "Guys like the ones in the Reign of Chaos, they only respond to violence. They wouldn't tell me a goddamn thing if I didn't make it painful," he started, brushing his fingertips across my skin.

Fingertips that were capable of so much pain, but that also made me feel loved and cherished and *alive*. Fingers that brought me an insane amount of pleasure.

"Okay, so you hurt at least one of them. What'd they tell you?" I didn't need him to rehash all the bloody details.

"What your mom has is a video, and they want it back. They've been following you because they planned to use you as bait. They wanted to take you, Moon," his eyes grew dark and stormy, turning almost black as he got lost in his thoughts, but I touched his hand, bringing him back.

"They have a list of aliases she's used since she disappeared. From what they said, they believe she's definitely alive." He watched me intently, trying to gauge how I'd react to that bit of information, but I didn't know how to feel about my mom's disappearance. Had she done it to protect my dad and me? Right now, it seemed like it was doing nothing but hurting us, and combined with the pain of losing her and never knowing if she was okay for all of those years, the whole thing seemed stupid.

So much pain, and for what?

I swallowed back the hurt and focused on Jericho instead. "They've been tracking her for years?"

He nodded, moving his hand up to my thigh absently, and I squirmed as his touch made my skin tingle in its wake. "They've always been a step behind her, but she either messed up and used an old alias on her list, or she did it on purpose because she wants us to find her. Either way, she triggered whatever alert they had on her."

"She wants me to find her," I whispered, knowing deep down it was true. "But why now?"

Jericho shrugged. "Maybe she's been keeping tabs on you and knows how close the ROC's getting, but if she comes to you, she knows they'll capture her."

"That makes sense, I guess." I chewed on my lip as I thought it over. "What happens if we find her, and she does have the evidence they want?"

"We have two choices. We can either make a deal with the Reign of

Chaos to hand it over in exchange for them leaving us the fuck alone, or we can give it to the police and let them get taken down."

"Isn't the right thing to do to hand it over to the cops?" I wondered, lacing my fingers in his and sitting up so I could lean my head against his shoulder.

He reached up and pulled the elastic out of my hair, running his fingers through the tangled mess. I smiled despite the heavy conversation. Jericho loved playing with my hair. "There's a reason your mom hasn't come forward with the evidence for fifteen years, Moon. I don't think it's that easy. A club as powerful as the ROC? I bet they have all sorts of law enforcement in their pocket."

I hadn't even thought about that. "Shit."

"I think we need to find your mom and find out what she has, what she knows, and why she never went to the police with it. Then we can decide what to do."

I nodded, closing my eyes and enjoying the feel of his fingers against my scalp and running through my hair. "Okay."

We fell into a comfortable silence, both of us lost to our thoughts when the doorbell rang, and Jericho's phone buzzed at the same time. I laughed. "I'll get the door, and you answer that."

After grabbing our breakfast from the delivery guy, I moved into the kitchen and grabbed silverware. I wanted to eat and get dressed and then go back to the hospital to check on my dad.

I carried the food back to the gaming room where Jericho's phone was pressed to his ear, and his expression was thunderous. "I'm not working on it this week. Period. We can pick back up next week, but with shit up in the air with the label and everything going on with the ROC, my creativity is at exactly zero. Anything we put together now is going to be garbage."

He sat listening to whoever was on the other end of the line before making an agreement to get together next week and hanging up. He tossed his phone onto the coffee table and leaned back against the couch, closing his eyes and letting his head fall back.

I watched him but tore into the takeout, too hungry to wait. Bacon-y goodness melted on my tongue as I dug into my breakfast. "Who was that?" I asked around a mouthful of greasy hashbrowns.

He turned his head in my direction and opened one eye. "Zen. He wanted to get back in the studio today, but it's not going to happen. I'm not up to it. We'll go back when I say, and I told him to give me a week."

I handed him his omelet. "Is that going to hurt your album release schedule?"

He laughed humorlessly. "At this point, who the fuck knows? The label are assholes; we're essentially giving them the middle finger right now. We might not have a release schedule at all, or we might get to set it for ourselves. With everything going on, it's really the least of my worries right now."

Nodding, I bit into my pancake, moaning at the sweet taste, and Jericho's eyes darkened, but he didn't say anything. He started eating while he watched me, and it was hot as hell. "Where do you want to start with finding my mom?"

He got up to go grab us drinks and yelled from the kitchen, "I got the alias she used, and I'm going to give it to Sebastian today. If she really wants you to find her, she'll use it again."

He sounded so sure and confident, I found myself hoping he was right. No matter how angry I was that she left me, Cara was still my mom, and I wanted the chance to see her again, even if it was just to ask her why she left in the first place.

TWENTY NINE
JERICHO

An ache in my shoulders woke me up from the deepest sleep I'd ever had. What the fuck happened last night?

I tried to roll over but couldn't, burning pain in my wrists making my eyes fly open, but I groaned and immediately slammed them shut. The bright sunlight hurt, and worse than that, I couldn't seem to get them to focus.

When I tried to sit up, my head swam, and I fell back down to the pillow, finally noticing that my wrists were tied to the headboard. "Moon," I called, my voice sounding like I'd swallowed a fuck ton of sandpaper. It was gravelly and hurt to speak.

Only silence greeted me, and my heart started to race as I tried to clear the mental fog and think back to yesterday. We called in Sebastian and gave him everything we knew. He left last night promising to update us when he had something on Cara. Then Moon had passed out on the couch, and I'd carried her to bed. She hadn't been awake for hours when I finally fell asleep.

So how the fuck did my hands end up tied to the bed, and why was my head pounding?

"Fuck." I twisted my wrists, and the rope that'd been used to tie me down cut into my skin, but I didn't stop, yanking and turning until finally, the rope gave way. "Moon!" I called again, wincing as my throat burned, but she didn't answer.

Adrenaline spiked and flooded my system as I jumped out of bed, stumbling on shaky legs. "Indy!" I couldn't remember if he was the one on guard duty last night, but one of them had to be here.

I rounded the corner of my bedroom into the hall, catching myself on the wall before I fell. My body was shaky as hell, and my stomach lurched. It felt like I had the worst hangover in the world except I knew I hadn't had a fucking drop of alcohol.

Skidding to a stop before I crashed into him, I fell to my knees by the front door where Indy was slumped over against the wall, and the door was splintered open. "Fuck!" I yelled, gripping his shoulders and shaking him.

"Wake the fuck up." I slapped him a couple of times to try and get him to wake up, and he groaned.

"What?" he hissed before he even opened his eyes. His voice was groggy, and I looked him over, finding a small bruise on his neck.

"They took Moon." The words tasted like poison leaving my lips. Saying them out loud was like admitting defeat. If I didn't speak them into existence, the problem wasn't real, right?

Except she was fucking gone. She vanished during the night, and there was no goddamn way she'd left without telling me, or at the very least one of the security guys. Moon was religious about following security protocols. She said they made her feel safe.

I left Indy to shake off the cobwebs and ran back to my room, frantically searching for my phone. It wasn't on the nightstand where I left it, and when I dug through the blankets, I found Moon's phone tangled in the sheet. "Shit," I muttered, scrolling through the contacts and finding Bexley.

It took her three rings to answer, and I was practically tearing my hair out while I waited for her to pick up. "Moon? What's going on? Why are you calling me so early?" her voice was still thick with sleep. I hadn't bothered checking the time, but a glance at the clock told me it was six in the morning.

"Bexley, it's Jericho. Moon's missing." I tried to keep my voice calm, but I was freaking the fuck out.

"What?" she screeched. "Since when?"

"I don't know, I woke up groggy as hell and tied to my bed. Indy was down, too, and there's a puncture wound on his neck so I think we were drugged.

The front door's busted in, and her phone's still here. Please tell me you're hiding her or you've heard from her."

"She's not here. I haven't heard from her since yesterday." I heard rustling on her end of the line. "I'm getting dressed, and I'll be there in ten." She hung up without another word, and I tossed Moon's phone, still searching for mine. I found it under the bed with a cracked screen, but it still worked.

"You better have a good fucking reason for calling me this early," Zen's pissed off voice made me want to snap.

"How about my wife being kidnapped by a gang of violent criminals?" I retorted, on the edge of exploding with how out of control and helpless this situation made me.

"What? Jesus, fuck. I'll get the guys, and we'll be there in a few." He hesitated. "Did you call Connor yet?"

"No, he's next."

"He's here. I'll fill him in and bring him along." He ended the call, and I shoved my phone into the pocket of my sweats. Since the ROC had been stirring shit up, Connor had been posting people from his team with all of us twenty-four-seven.

Fuck of a lot of good it did.

Stalking back out to the kitchen, I didn't know what to do with myself. My stomach was in fucking knots, and I couldn't think straight. I sure as fuck didn't want to eat anything. The only thing on my mind was getting Moon back. If she wasn't okay, I didn't know how I'd survive it.

I hadn't realized I'd been staring off into space until a hand fell onto my shoulder. I spun around and punched without looking, reacting to whoever dared to touch me. I was like a wild animal uncaged, torn apart from my mate, and willing to destroy anything that got in the way of getting her back.

Indy flew back into the wall as blood poured from his nose. My chest heaved as I dragged oxygen into my lungs. "Fuck," he grunted. "I deserved that."

Stalking forward, I gripped his shirt in my fist. "You sure as fuck did. How the hell did this happen?"

He eyed me warily, guilt flashing in his eyes as he looked away with his jaw clenched. He lowered his hands and let the blood drip freely from his nose. "After you went to sleep last night, I was checking the locks, making sure all the windows were sealed and shit. I looked down for a second to check that the camera feeds were working on my phone, and the door crashed in. Before I could react, four of them were on me, and they stuck me with something. The next thing I knew, you were waking me up."

He met my eyes. "I'm sor-"

I held up my hand. "Don't. You can apologize when we get her back. Now I need you to find my fucking wife before they hurt her." I wanted him dead. I wanted him to pay for letting this happen. It was his fucking job to make sure Moon stayed safe, and he failed. I didn't want to hear his apology; I wanted to make him bleed.

But that wouldn't help find Moon faster, so I clenched my fist and walked away, heading down to the gym to hit something until everyone showed up, and we could form a plan.

𝄞

Sweat covered me from head to toe, my muscles ached, my knuckles were a bloody mess, but my mind was clear when I went upstairs half an hour later. My game room had been taken over by Connor and his team and my bandmates plus Bexley. They were having a hushed conversation but went silent when I walked in the room.

"Tell me what you've figured out," I demanded, stalking across the room and ripping open the fridge to grab out a bottle of water. I went back to the couch and sat on the edge while I drank, not wanting to relax or be comfortable. I was poised and ready to jump up and into action in less than a second.

"The cameras did their job," Connor started, nodding at Sebastian, who turned his laptop screen toward me and hit play. I watched as a big-ass black SUV pulled into my driveway, and six men poured out. They kicked in my door, and the inside cameras showed four of them overwhelming Indy and him going down easily. I looked over at where he sat, and his jaw ticked while he looked away. He looked almost as pissed as I felt. It's why Connor's team was so good;

they took their failures personally.

Two of the bastards walked down the hall toward my bedroom like they knew exactly where they were going, but there were no cameras inside, so it was quiet for a few minutes before they carried my unconscious wife out the front fucking door. The rage I'd worked so hard to burn out in the gym reignited, and I threw my water bottle against the wall.

"Where'd they take her?" I stood up, unable to sit still.

"Dumbasses didn't bother blacking out their license plates," Sebastian muttered, turning his laptop back and typing for a few seconds. "I've got them on traffic cams heading into the desert. Looks like they took her back to their home base in Nevada."

"We've done some recon. That place is a fucking fortress. We aren't getting in unless they let us in," Julian explained, digging through a pile of pictures stacked on the table until he found the overhead satellite shot of their compound.

"So, if we can't get in there, how the hell are we getting Moon out?" I clenched my teeth, reigning in the overwhelming need to destroy something.

"We find Cara and get the evidence. Then we trade it for Moon," Connor laid out, leaning forward and resting his elbows on his knees.

I scoffed. "As if it's that simple. August has been searching for Cara for more than a fucking decade! And you expect us to find her in, what? A day?"

"We don't have a choice if you want Moon back," Connor asserted.

"She left us a hint, a trail, Jericho," Indy pointed out, and I glared at him. He was the last person I wanted to hear from right now.

"I've already started searching," Sebastian added, pressing a couple of keys. "The hotel that we flagged her at never actually saw her. I went through all their security footage and ran it through facial recognition with a picture I snagged off of Moon's hard drive." I wasn't even going to touch the fact he'd hacked into my wife's computer. It was such a Sebastian thing to do and ranked so low on my list of concerns right now, I let it slide.

"She was never there, which means she did it on purpose. Maybe she left a clue there for Moon to find, but since Moon isn't going to be able to search, we need to go look." All of our phones buzzed at the same time, and Sebastian continued. "I just sent you the information on the hotel and a picture of Cara. I'm certain she won't be there, but maybe the hotel staff will know something. I'm going to follow up on the alerts I put on her alias, and you all should go to the hotel."

"It's a place to start." Julian stood, and we all followed.

"Give me ten minutes." I needed a fast shower and to throw on some clothes.

"What about us?" Maddox asked. "I know this is shitty timing, but Aldrich called last night. He found a way out of the contract. He wants to meet this afternoon to go over our options."

"I can't think about any of that shit while those assholes have Moon. I need the four of you to deal with it and let me know when a decision needs to be made about what we do." My career was important to me, but there was no contest on where my attention was going to go between it and my wife.

"We'll handle it, Jericho. Text us when you find something, and we'll let you know how the meeting goes," Zen added, standing up and the rest of the guys followed him giving me sympathetic smiles. They'd all be losing their fucking minds right now if any of their wives went missing, so I knew they could relate to how I felt.

"You're going to find her, man," True dropped a comforting hand on my shoulder, but I shrugged it off. I didn't want to be comforted. I wanted to feel pain, to feel the anger at myself manifested on my skin.

Zen, True, and Maddox walked out, but Griffin hung back. I hated to admit it, but I was starting to like the kid. I'd never fucking tell him, though.

"You want me to hang back and come to the hotel with you? All that contract shit doesn't really involve me." He ran his hand through his messy, dark hair.

I surprised myself by nodding. "Yeah, an extra set of eyes won't hurt, but no fucking around. You come along, you help or I'll leave your ass at the hotel."

"Deal."

I got ready in record time, and when I came back into the game room, Sebastian had made himself at home, spreading out his equipment around him. Connor, Indy, and Julian stood, and Julian stepped out to bring the car around.

We piled in, and the drive to the hotel was mostly done in tense silence. As we pulled up to the front, Julian waved off the valet. "What's our plan?"

"I'm going to talk to the front desk staff and show Cara's picture, see if they've seen her. You and Griff search the lounge in the lobby and depending on what the front desk staff says, we'll move our search grid as needed. Julian stays with the car in case we need a quick exit," Connor detailed his plan.

We hopped out of the car and made our way inside, splitting up once we stepped through the doors. Griffin and I talked to the bartender who hadn't seen Cara, and we searched under the bar, around all the stools, and under and around all the booths lining the walls.

Frustrated, we met up with Indy and Connor, who had better luck than we did. "She checked into room 1127. I got the key, and we'll go search there."

"That's Moon's birthday," I told them, feeling like we were onto something. We rode the elevator up to the eleventh floor, and my heart raced. She *had* to have left something behind. If she didn't, what would that mean for our search?

Connor used the keycard to open the door, and we stepped inside, immediately starting our search. Indy stepped into the bathroom and started pulling toiletries off the shelf under the sink, Connor went to the desk in the room, Griffin moved to the lounge area, and I started in the bedroom.

I checked the easy places first—the nightstand drawers, under the pillows—but there was nothing. I got down on my hands and knees and looked under the bed but only found empty floor. As a last-ditch attempt to find something—*anything*—I ran my hand around the underside of the box spring. At the end of the bed, my fingers ran across a tiny slit in the thin fabric covering the wood slats. I dropped onto my back and slid my head underneath, finding a tiny slip of paper shoved into the tear.

337701

1181937

4098587555

The three numbers were written in a scrolling print, and I clutched them in my fist while pushing out from under the bed. "I found something," I announced, standing up and walking back into the main room. "But I think we're going to need Sebastian to figure out what the hell it means."

I held out the piece of paper, and Connor took it first, narrowing his eyes at the numbers before passing it to Julian and then Griffin.

"Holy shit, she actually left a message," Griffin breathed, and I was too afraid to let myself hope we'd be able to find her this easily.

"They're coordinates." Sebastian took one look at the paper and figured it out. "And a phone number."

"She left her location and phone number in that hotel room?" I asked, not really believing after all her years of staying hidden, she'd made it that simple. But then, had it been simple? We had to flag her, search the area, and know what the numbers meant.

"Where are the coordinates for?" Connor asked, studying the tiny piece of paper like it had secrets it had yet to reveal.

Sebastian chuckled, something I wasn't sure I'd ever heard him do before. "Clever lady, hiding right under our noses. Long Beach."

"Shit," I hissed. That'd make it a lot easier to get the evidence from her. "Fuck it. I'm calling that number."

I pulled out my broken phone and entered the digits. She picked up on the first ring. "Moon?"

"No, afraid not. She's been kidnapped by a ruthless gang of bikers. Wouldn't know anything about that, would you?" I snapped, feeling nothing but pissed off at this woman for putting my love in this situation.

"Who are you?" she sounded tired and resigned.

"My name's Jericho, and I'm your daughter's husband. I'm going to be your worst nightmare until I get her back, so can we cut the shit and meet somewhere so you can hand over whatever you've got, and I can save my wife?" I had exactly zero patience for doing a whole getting-to-know-you chat with my mother-in-law.

"Right. We have a lot to talk about. Meet me at the Queen Mary in an hour," she said before she ended the call.

"It was her. Get the car; we're going to Long Beach."

THIRTY
MOON

I couldn't catch my breath, and my lungs ached from the effort to suck in air. My heart was beating crazy hard, and my need to escape was strong. In short, I was panicking. I woke up disoriented in a pitch-black room, and I couldn't see anything. It was as if my eyes were closed even though they weren't, but because of that, my other senses were heightened.

The room smelled musty and of old cigarette smoke, which made me want to gag, and somewhere a leaky faucet dripped. I had no idea where I was, but my wrists were bound behind my back, and I was sitting on a hard floor propped up against a wall. "This is fine, you're fine," I whispered, but I felt a little like that meme where the dog's sitting in the room on fire trying to convince himself everything's okay.

I clamped my lips shut as muffled voices carried into the room. I couldn't make out what they were saying yet, but it sounded like they were moving closer.

My whole body tensed as I braced myself for whoever was out there to come inside. One thing was for sure—I wasn't at home anymore. The pounding in my head and lingering queasiness made me think I'd been drugged—that, and the huge hole in my memory between when I'd been asleep in bed beside Jericho last night and where I found myself now.

Shit.

Jericho.

My man was probably on the brink of murder, trying to figure out where I went. I smiled at the thought. He'd come for me; I had no doubt. But how long would I have to wait? And could I survive this situation long enough to give him time to get to me?

I didn't have a choice. I had to.

It wasn't hard to figure out who took me. It wasn't like I went through life leaving a trail of enemies in my wake. No, this was the work of the Reign of Chaos. The question was what they wanted from me and where we were.

A sharp pain shot through my arms as I worked my wrists against my bindings, but they didn't budge. I needed to search the room for something to cut the rope with. Luckily, my legs were untied. They shook when I stood, using the wall to support myself as I got to my feet, but I was able to take a few steps along the wall. I could see nothing, so I slid along the wall taking quiet, careful steps.

The floor squeaked under my foot, and I froze, holding my breath and waiting for the voices outside to come bursting through the door, but they didn't. I exhaled slowly, trying to be quiet as I crept along the wall, finally finding what felt like a doorknob.

The voices were louder now, and I could hear them clearly. There were at least two, and they were both men.

"The Prez'll be down to question her soon," one man said, a clicking noise accompanying his words. It sounded like he was flicking a lighter lid open and closed over and over.

"Why's he wasting our time on this bitch? That bastard husband of hers took my fucking finger," the other guy complained. These must've been the guys Jericho caught breaking into our house.

"You got it reattached, man. Stop whining."

"It doesn't work the same," he grumbled.

"Shut the fuck up. Cara has no choice but to come forward now that we've got her daughter. You know why we can't let this shit go. If that tape were to come out, it'd expose us, and we wouldn't be able to sweep it under the rug anymore. You know our influence was shaken with last year's elections."

I still had no idea what was on that tape or what this club was into. Everything these guys said just made me have more questions.

"We could just deny that shit. We have enough legit businesses to throw any investigation off our trail. The video's almost twenty years old. It's not current."

The first guy moved closer to the door, but I didn't want to move away yet. They had legal businesses, too? That was news to me. I stayed where I was even as sweat trickled down my back. My heart raced so fast, I was starting to feel faint.

"Statute of limitations, dumbass. There's no limit on how long they could come after us for the shit that's on that video. That's why we need it back."

"Besides," I could hear the smile in guy number two's voice. "If she doesn't show up for her daughter, we've got other options, right?"

"Right," the first guy confirmed. "We'll force Marcus to make the drummer's life even harder than he's already been doing."

What the hell? Did he mean Marcus Hughes, the head of Pacific Records that I met at Fury Fest? The information didn't make sense in any other context.

The second guy scoffed. "So far, they've ignored all of Marcus's threats."

"We've been holding Marcus back. What he's done so far is child's play. Who would've thought that the label we got to clean our cash would work as a way to protect the club?" guy one mused, flicking his lighter again. "When we let Marcus do whatever he wants to that band, they'll turn their resources on doing whatever we want. And what we want is that fucking tape."

Guy number two laughed humorlessly. "Yeah, this bitch's husband already showed he'd do whatever he had to do to keep her safe. He's probably losing his fucking mind right now."

"Probably," guy number one agreed, but they started to move off, and I couldn't hear them very well anymore. I still had no idea where I was, but I was sure about who'd taken me.

I was more confused now than ever. What was on that tape? And the Reign of Chaos owned the label Shadow Phoenix was signed to?

Nothing made sense, but I took a deep breath and pressed on, slinking along the wall inch by inch and trying to find something sharp to cut my restraints with. I didn't know what they'd do to me if I waited here to be questioned. I'd seen *Sons of Anarchy*. I had an idea what that kind of interrogation looked like, and I had zero interest in getting tortured today.

Smooth wall ran along under my fingers until finally, I ran into a wall that, upon further investigation, turned out to be a bar. I made my way around the back, hoping to find a bottle of liquor I could break or a knife they'd left behind.

My eyes had adjusted to the light, but I still couldn't see anything other than big shapes around the room. There looked to be stacks of something in the corner—chairs, maybe? And this bar. I slid along the front and finally around the corner behind it. I couldn't reach up high, so any alcohol on shelves behind the bar wasn't something I could count on using. But I bumped into a stack of glasses on the bar top, and that worked just as well. I knocked my shoulder into the counter a few times, pushing to get the glasses to fall.

When one finally toppled off the counter and shattered at my feet, I ducked down and held my breath, waiting for the door to burst open and someone to come in and catch me, but it never happened. I finally breathed, sitting on the ground and using my fingers behind me to, as carefully as I could, search for a big chunk of glass that I could grab and use to saw the rope.

Shards of glass nicked my fingers, making me wince as they drew blood and made me sting, but it might've been my only chance to escape. If my mom didn't cooperate, and I had no delusions that she would, considering that she'd been missing for years and never let me know she was alive, I had no idea what they'd do to me to get what they wanted.

I finally found a chunk big enough and gripped it the best I could between my bloody, slippery fingers. I found a decent angle and sawed the rope along the jagged edge over and over until it finally broke free. I almost cried out in relief but held back at the last second, swallowing it down. I didn't want to be caught.

My shoulders ached as I brought my hands in front of my body and rubbed my sore wrists, ignoring the blood I was smearing all over myself. They weren't big cuts, there were just a lot of them, and they looked worse than they felt. Maybe it was the adrenaline, but I'd deal with it later.

Right now, I had bigger problems like how to escape.

I wiped my hands on my shirt as I crept back to the door, feeling more in control now that I had back the use of my hands. I found the door and slowly turned the handle, squinting, and blinking at the bright light that almost blinded me when I cracked the door open. I listened but heard nothing but silence.

Widening the gap in the door, I peeked out, but the hallway outside was empty. The walls were plain white and scuffed all over the place like a thousand fights had broken out here, men being thrown around, punches being thrown. At least that was what I imagined based on the random dents that lined the hall.

I stepped out with one foot, slowly shifting my weight forward. The floor underneath me didn't squeak, so I crept forward until I was fully outside the room. The door closed behind me with a resounding click, and I found myself holding my breath again and waiting to see what might happen. When no one stormed the hall, I took off in a light jog, keeping my weight on my tiptoes so my footsteps wouldn't be heavy.

I had no idea where I was going, and the hallway I'd escaped from turned into another hall when I rounded the corner. There were no windows, and this place was starting to feel like a fortress. Around another corner was another hallway, but this one looked different. Doors were lining one side of this hall, and I started trying knobs, hoping I could get into one that might have a window I could climb out of.

It was risky, I might run into some of the club members, but it was a chance I had to take if I wanted to escape. It was only a matter of time before Jericho and Connor, and everyone came for me, but I didn't know what the Reign of Chaos would do to me. From what I'd seen and heard, they didn't have limits on the violence they were willing to undertake in order to get what they wanted.

Somehow they were convinced I knew more than I did, or that my mom would come for me.

I knew the only person coming for me was Jericho.

After trying a ton of handles, one finally turned, and I stepped inside, closing the door behind me as softly as I could. It looked like a messy bedroom with beer cans and clothes scattered everywhere, and I tried not to look too closely as I tiptoed through the mess toward the window. I pressed my palm against the warm glass and lifted it up.

It slid open easier than I hoped, and hot, dry air hit my skin. I could see all the way to the horizon with only a few cacti blocking the view. There was brown sand as far as the eye could see until it met the bright blue sky. I was in the desert.

Shit.

It sort of reminded me of where we'd been for Fury Fest, or when we came to Vegas. And with that much wide open space how would I ever get away without them seeing me?

Still, I had to try.

I threw one leg over the windowsill and folded in on myself, slipping out and pulling my other leg with me. When my feet hit the ground, I slid the window closed and turned to press myself against the wall. I looked around, trying to find something I could use to escape, maybe a car or truck or something.

I snuck to the edge of the building and peeked around the corner, spotting a row of bikes lined up neatly. Not only were they so far away that someone would likely spot me before I got to them, but I had no idea how to even start a motorcycle, let alone ride one.

Frustration welled up and my eyes stung. I wanted to cry, to sink down against the wall and give up because it looked so hopeless, but I couldn't. It wasn't in me to admit defeat.

There were no other vehicles, and at that point, it started to sink in that I was going to have to run for it. I ducked back around the corner and took a few deep breaths to calm my racing heart before pushing off the building and taking off at a sprint.

I didn't dare look back as I tore across the dirt and sand, but it didn't take long before the sun was beating down on me, sweat making my clothes stick to my overheated skin. I pumped my legs harder as my lungs burned from the effort of pushing my body so hard, but I couldn't stop. Tiny rocks tore into my bare feet, but still, I kept running. There was nowhere to hide out here, but I had to keep going. I had to get free.

I pushed my body harder, ignoring the protest of my legs and my heart pounding a punishing rhythm against my ribs, but footsteps suddenly sounded behind me, and I knew I'd been caught. I was already slowing down, pushed to my absolute limit when a body slammed into me from behind, making me tumble to the ground.

My limbs tangled and scraped against the dry desert floor as I rolled, scrambling to get back up and keep going. But the leather-clad man that caught me had no intention of letting me go. "Stop fucking fighting," he ordered, jabbing a needle into my neck.

I reached up and scratched at his face, etching deep, red grooves down his cheek that welled with blood, and my lips curved up into a satisfied smile as darkness overtook me. These bastards weren't getting anything from me without a fight.

THIRTY ONE
JERICHO

"They say this ship is haunted," Griffin noted from where he sat in the passenger seat, scrolling through his phone. We pulled into the nearly-empty parking lot and took a spot near the museum.

"You believe in that shit?" I wondered, watching as Connor's SUV pulled in beside us. Connor and Indy hopped out of the front, and Julian got out of the back. Griffin and I got out and met them.

"You gotta admit, it'd be fucking awesome if ghosts were real. I'd come back and haunt Gal Gadot." I scowled at him, not wanting to talk about anything other than getting my wife back.

"Do we have any idea where we're supposed to meet her or what we're looking for?" Connor asked, scanning the parking lot. We all looked around, and I broke off from the group, moving toward the massive black and white ship docked right in front of us.

I felt her before I saw her, but I didn't move to look at her or flinch when she moved beside me. "Well, my daughter has good taste," she chuckled, and I turned to look at Cara Mayhem.

Her and Moon didn't look all that alike, except Moon had her mom's eyes—that ocean blue color that had me wanting to dive right into my wife's soul looked back at me now, and all it did was piss me off.

"Yeah, and I'd really like to get her back, so how about you hand over whatever it is you've got on the ROC, and we can do the whole meet-the-family bit later?" I snapped, completely out of patience.

"If that's how you want this to go," she agreed, slipping a thumb drive into my palm. I looked down at it, turning it over.

"All this trouble over this," I mused, slipping into my pocket. "What's on it?"

She sighed and turned around, leaning her back against the railing in front of me. "The Reign of Chaos was supposed to be my life. I'm sure you heard from August by now about my father and what he did, how he signed away my life without giving me a choice," she explained, her tone angry, but I couldn't blame her. I'd be pissed off, too.

"Yeah, he told Moon and me a little about that," I confirmed, folding my arms across my chest. I could feel the weight of six pairs of eyes watching us, but I ignored them.

"Growing up, I idolized the club. I thought the big bikers were so cool. They'd take me for rides on the back of their bikes and make me mocktails at the bar. They treated me like their little mascot. But as I got older, I started noticing the drugs, the girls with bruises on them hanging around the club, the guns. Always so many guns." Her eyes were far off and distant like she was looking into the past.

"When I was around sixteen, I snuck out of the house. I had a stupid crush on one of the prospects, a guy who was eighteen and the quintessential bad boy. I was supposed to meet him at the club, only I stumbled on them moving in a group of girls who were tied up and looked bruised and dirty. I hid because I knew whatever that was wasn't good. When they'd packed them into one of the bike trailers and pulled out of the lot, I snuck inside and got into the security room. I stole the tapes, and then I ran. I changed my name, my look, and I started working at a diner. That's where I met August."

I turned and faced the same direction she was, watching the guys as they looked at us. "Why didn't you turn this over before now? Why not give it to the cops and let them handle it while you stayed with Moon?"

I couldn't imagine ever walking away from my wife or future children. I would burn down the world before I let them think I didn't want them or that

I was dead. "I had to. The Reign of Chaos knew I had the tape. They've been bribing the local and federal law enforcement for years. Who was I supposed to give it to?" She folded her arms over her chest. "I'd been able to hide, and marrying August was just another layer in masking my identity. I didn't think they'd ever find me, and I got sloppy covering my tracks. I just wanted to live life, you know? Enjoy my family."

If Cara was looking for sympathy, she wouldn't get it from me. "I can't imagine ever voluntarily leaving Moon."

She laughed, but it was humorless. "You say that now but you have no idea what it's like to be threatened by these guys."

I scoffed. "They've been threatening Moon and me for weeks. I found a couple of them in my house, Cara, and through it all, I never left Moon. You don't know what you're talking about."

"Well, maybe you're braver than I am. I'm glad she has you, you know," she admitted, turning to look up at me. "You're going to take good care of my girl, right?"

"You don't have the right to ask that of me, but I'll always take care of Moon." I tucked my hands into my pockets, wrapping my fingers around the plastic thumb drive. "But I hope now that you've handed this over and we're handling it, that you'll talk to your daughter when I get her back. She deserves better than to wonder for fifteen years if her mom's alive or not and whether she didn't want her anymore." I bit out that last bit, getting more and more pissed off as I thought about how unwanted Cara made Moon feel.

I glared down at the woman next to me. "She thinks you threw her away like a piece of trash and doesn't understand why."

Cara sucked in a breath, her eyes shining with tears. "I never wanted her to think that. I wanted to be with her more than anything, but I couldn't turn over the video. The ROC's reach is further and deeper than you could possibly imagine. Cops, judges, senators. They have their illegal business, but they've worked hard to funnel their blood money into legal pathways. I've learned a little bit about hacking and spent the last ten years tracking them. If I handed that video over, I would've exposed myself, and they wouldn't stop at just hurting me. They'd have come after August and Moon, too."

I pushed off the railing and started to walk away, but I stopped and turned back. "If I were you, I'd go to Creekside Hospital and pay August a visit. I'm sure he'd like to hear all about why you thought abandoning him was a good idea. I'm going to go save my wife."

I didn't wait for a response from her. I had her phone number now, she was out in the open with no reason to hide, and I did hope, for Moon's sake, that Cara wanted to be in her life and make amends. But for now, I couldn't worry about that shit. I pulled the drive out of my pocket and tossed it to Connor. "Reach out to the ROC and make a deal. I want to swap that for Moon," I ordered, and he nodded.

"Let's go back to your place and give this to Sebastian. I'll make the call on the way," he decided, climbing into the passenger seat of his SUV. I climbed into the passenger seat of mine, tossing Griffin the keys. I had too much shit on my mind and didn't want to have to focus on the road, too.

It took us almost an hour to get home, but every mile we drove, my muscles bunched tighter and tighter. I was tired of waiting. They could be hurting Moon right now. I needed to fucking *act,* and this waiting around bullshit wasn't going to work for me anymore. Connor needed to have made a plan.

When we got to my house, I jumped out and slammed the door, stalking in through the garage and into the game room where Sebastian still sat with his face buried in his laptop. I moved a couple of his papers to sit down, and he glared at me out of the corner of his eye but didn't say anything, which was good because then I would've had to punch his face in.

My phone buzzed in my pocket, and I pulled it out, answering without checking who was calling. "What?" I snapped.

"Dude, dial it back," Maddox growled, and I heaved out a sigh.

"You know you'd be just as on edge as I am if someone kidnapped Ryan, so fuck off. What do you want?" It was the best I could do. My focus was completely on Moon, but I knew the band had our own shit going on, too, and I couldn't ignore that.

"I know, and I wouldn't call if it weren't important, but we finished our meeting with Aldrich and Montana, and I thought you'd want to know what's up."

I ran my hand through my hair and watched as Connor, Indy, Julian, and Griffin walked inside. They moved in a group to the kitchen instead of coming into the room, so I turned my attention back to Maddox. "Yeah, how'd it go?"

"He found a loophole that'll let us out, but it's gonna be expensive. We don't have to pay the label anything, but we have to hand over all our old music rights. But if we do, we'll be free of Marcus and Pacific."

Griffin came in and sat beside me, and I put Maddox on speaker. "Your brother's here with me. Repeat what you just told me," I demanded, and Maddox filled Griffin in.

He blew out a breath. "I wasn't a part of the older music, so this part doesn't matter to me what y'all decide, but I'd rather we have complete control of our music going forward if my vote counts for anything."

I nodded. "I don't want anyone having control over us, even if it costs us our body of work. That's okay. Taylor Swift made it work, and we will, too. But those fuckers aren't getting one more cent from us." We were all quiet for a minute. "What do you guys think about forming our own label?" I questioned. It was something I'd been tossing around for a while. I craved control and gaining complete oversight over not only our music but the idea of finding other musicians and guiding them through their career was appealing as fuck.

"I hadn't thought about it, but it makes sense. Would you run it? I don't mind investing, but I have no interest in running it," Maddox explained.

"Yeah. I think I'd actually really fucking like it. Talk to the guys; we'll figure it out after I find Moon. But in the meantime, you've got our vote on getting us out of that contract. When you decide, let Aldrich know."

"Good, and I expect a fucking text the second you have Moon back," Maddox added before hanging up. I looked over to Griffin. "You're on text duty."

He shot me a crooked smile. "Does that mean I get to come along to find Moon?"

I glared at him. "Don't get cocky, but I want you there," I mumbled, looking away. Griffin had stayed by my side this entire ordeal, and I had to begrudgingly admit that he wormed his way into my good graces.

Connor came back into the room, followed by his guys, and they took their spots around the couch, pushing Sebastian's papers out of the way. He glared at us as he scooped them up into piles but he could just fucking deal with it. "I made contact with them. They want us to meet at a mile marker just over the border in Nevada in three hours. If we hand over the video, they'll give us Moon. I told them if she's been harmed, we'll release the video to the media. I also promised we wouldn't keep any copies, but I planned on going back on that promise. Turns out, after talking to Sebastian, they'll be able to trace it, so I'm not taking the risk."

"I don't care what we do with the video as long as it doesn't put Moon at risk," I announced, standing up. "But I'm packing Moon a bag, and then we're leaving, so be ready in ten minutes. We will not be late," I narrowed my eyes, staring them each down individually.

"We'll be ready," Connor agreed, and I left to go get ready.

When I walked back into the room a few minutes later, they were crowded around the laptop. "Fuck," Connor grunted, slamming the laptop lid closed and ripping the stick out of the side. "Those are some sick motherfuckers."

He turned to me and handed the stick over. "I may have to hand this back right now, but I'll never forget what's on that video, and I'm not letting it go. I'm not ready to make a move against them now, but I sure as fuck am not going to let them get away with what they're doing. Imagine all the people they've hurt over the years since that tape." He jumped up and stomped from the room. Connor was a protector at heart like me. Cara told me what was on that tape, so I didn't need to see it to know it was fucking bad.

He wouldn't be able to move on from what he'd seen, but that was a problem or another day. Right now, the only thing that mattered was rescuing Moon. We could deal with the fucked up crimes of a murderous biker gang later.

I walked into the garage and climbed into my Range Rover, Griffin sliding into the passenger seat beside me. Connor looked pissed when he got into the other car, but gave me a tight nod as Indy and Julian climbed into the car with him.

I pressed the gas pedal, not wanting to wait any longer to go. I was impatient, my muscles twitching, and both my mind and heart raced. I wanted Moon back, and I wasn't leaving this meeting without her. As we merged onto the highway, I turned to Griffin. "Did you bring any weapons with you?"

He shook his head, and I pressed my lips together. "Do you know how to shoot?" I finally asked, and he rolled his eyes. "Dude, I'm from Texas. Learning to shoot is basically mandatory."

I nodded toward the glove box. "Open that."

He did and pulled out the handgun I kept in there, raising his eyebrow at me.

"Don't look at me like that. Shit gets crazy sometimes, and you never know when you might have to handle something unpleasant."

He snorted. "Unpleasant, right."

"Just shut the fuck up and hold onto it. I'm not going to have Maddox trying to kick my ass because his little brother got killed by some motorcycle-riding thugs."

He ignored me and turned back to his phone but tucked the gun into the back of his waistband first.

The drive felt like it took for-fucking-ever, and by the time I spotted the small crowd of bikes and people in the middle of nowhere on the side of the road, I was practically crawling out of my fucking skin. "They better not have hurt her," I growled, slowing down and finally stopping a little ways back from them. Connor pulled in right behind me.

Griffin and I looked at each other before wordlessly climbing out of the car, and I glanced back, waiting for Connor and the guys. The little plastic stick weighed heavy in my pocket as we walked toward the bikers, taking our time. I didn't want them to see how rattled I was.

A tall clean-shaven guy with salt and pepper hair, but surprisingly, no tattoos or facial hair leaned against his bike in a way that showed he was the leader. He lifted himself up and strode toward us with a swagger that said he knew he was in control here. "Got my video?"

He got straight to the point, and I could appreciate that. "I want to see my wife first," I countered.

He looked back at a couple of younger guys who were standing by a car and nodded. The door was opened, and he disappeared for a second, before standing back up. I saw her bright hair first, and my knees went weak. My gaze roamed her entire body as she stood up and stepped away from the car. Our eyes locked across the distance and the air electrified between us.

"Are you okay?" I mouthed at her, and she gave me a small smile and nodded. Relieved breath left my body in a rush. They grabbed her arm and pulled her forward, and I saw red at their hands on her. I wanted to destroy them, but there were more of them, and no doubt, they were heavily armed.

I wouldn't do anything stupid in the name of vengeance if it risked Moon coming home safely with me. Connor shifted until he was standing next to me. "Give me the stick; I'll go make the exchange."

He had at least three guns on him from what I could see and didn't look the least bit intimidated. I knew it killed him to hand this over and let them go, but the fight against the Reign of Chaos would have to happen another day.

I dug in my pocket and pulled it out, dropping it in his hand. He wrapped his fist around it and moved forward. "Let her go," he ordered, walking right up to the leader. He looked Connor up and down and then nodded.

The two young guys holding Moon took their hands off her, and she walked quickly toward me. Griffin stood next to me, his shoulder almost touching mine, and he stiffened as she started walking. My eyes were locked on my wife, but I trusted him to watch the guys who were still too close to her. He finally relaxed as she passed by Connor, and he leaned against me. "He just handed over the stick, and it looks like he's talking a lot of shit."

I didn't take another breath until Moon collapsed into my arms. I closed my eyes and breathed her in, relishing in her sweet strawberry scent as I held her close to my body. "Don't ever get yourself fucking kidnapped again," I scolded, but we both knew it was halfhearted at best. Going forward, I'd have to fight my instinct to never let her out of my sight again.

She laughed before kissing me softly. "Can we go home?"

"Go get in the car," I ordered, watching until she'd climbed inside before I turned back. Connor came to stand beside me.

"If you touch my family again, I'll hunt every last one of you until there's no one left," I promised, and the leader—Devil, according to his vest—threw his head back and laughed.

"I'd like to see you try." His face was serious now, thunderous and looking every bit the gang leader he was. I didn't give a fuck, and I wasn't scared of him.

"Don't tempt me. Now, leave us the fuck alone." I turned around, giving him my back and daring him to give me a reason to take him down, but he didn't. Connor followed right behind me, and Griffin went and climbed in the back of my car.

"You know I can't let that shit go, right?" Connor lowered his voice as he stood beside me just before I opened the door.

"I know," I confirmed. "But don't drag Moon into whatever you decide to do."

"I won't," he promised. "It's going to get ugly. I'm going to need a plan."

My lip quirked up into an almost-smile. "Let me know if you need me."

He chuckled and then left me to take my wife home. I'd never been more relieved in my entire life than at this moment, with Moon sitting beside me healthy and on our way home. I'd never let anything hurt her again, and maybe someday I'd get payback for what they took from me when they took the person I loved most in the world.

"Hey, there's something I overheard while I was in the compound that seems important," Moon's soft voice pulled me out of my relief and had my nerves standing on edge all over again. Out of the corner of my eye, I noticed Griffin leaning forward to listen in, too.

"Do you want to do this now? We can wait until tomorrow," I hedged, not wanting to push her.

She shook her head, her tangled hair falling into her face. "The ROC owns Pacific Records. I think that Richard guy was acting on their orders, maybe even Marcus, too."

My heart was pounding, and I glanced at Griffin in the rearview mirror. His jaw was clenched, and he was already tapping away on his phone. "You telling Connor?" I wondered, gripping the steering wheel so tight my fingers hurt. How the hell did all of this connect together?

Griffin glanced up at me and nodded. "Yeah, he says he's adding it to his list of shit he needs to deal with when it comes to the ROC."

I decided to let it go for now. I had my girl back and she was safe, my band had cut ties with our suddenly toxic label, and it was all in Connor's hands. My job was to make music, and Connor could handle whatever else the ROC decided to throw his way. I'd stay out of it unless he needed my help.

For today, Moon's safety was enough.

THIRTY TWO
MOON

My whole body hurt as I jolted awake. I groaned and looked around, quickly realizing I was in my own bedroom with Jericho's arm across my waist. He pulled me closer, and I laid back, snuggling back into him. My heart was still racing, but I took a few deep breaths and felt better.

I was so tired, absolutely exhausted from the whole ordeal I'd just been through. I couldn't believe a gang of bikers had kidnapped me. How had this become my life?

I must've drifted back off because a door banging open somewhere in the house made me jump. "Wake up, assholes!" Kennedy shrieked before jumping on our bed. Jericho sat up and scowled at her, but all I could do was laugh.

"How could you not call us after the daring rescue?" Kennedy demanded, punching Jericho in the shoulder.

"Hey!" he scowled, looking down to make sure the blanket had me covered, and I smiled sweetly up at him. He sighed and turned back to her. "It was Griffin's job to let you guys know. Take up your issues with him."

Kennedy glared at him before breaking into a face-splitting grin. "You can make it up to me by giving me Moon this morning for brunch."

"I was going to go see my dad this morning," I protested, but she shook her head.

"Nope. He's getting discharged this afternoon, and your mom's taking him home."

I bolted upright and gaped at her. "What? Did you say my mom?" Last night after we got home, Jericho and I practically fell into bed. We were both exhausted, and it was late when we got in, so we hadn't talked about how he found me or any of the details.

"Yeah, I met your mom," Jericho filled in, looking at me almost shyly except I knew he wasn't shy at all.

My hand flew up to my mouth. I didn't know how to feel. Was I happy she was back? Relieved? Angry? I felt a little bit of all three if I was being honest, and I needed a little space to unpack everything. "Shit," I finally breathed, kicking my feet out of the blankets and wiggling out of Jericho's grasp. Kennedy watched us with an amused look on her face. "I'll be waiting by the front door. You've got five minutes to get dressed before I come back in and get you. Bexley and Amara are waiting in the car."

It took me three minutes to change, pee, and brush my teeth. I threw my hair up in a messy bun, kissed Jericho, and bolted for the front door. I was starving and excited to see my friends after everything I'd been through. I figured they could excuse my less than put-together appearance because, you know, *kidnapping.*

Sliding huge sunglasses on my face, I let Kennedy lead me to Amara's car, and I got in the back. After I closed the door, Indy pulled it open and gestured for me to move over as he slid in next to me. I rolled my eyes but did what he said. "No one's after me now. You can stay."

He lifted his eyes to the front seat where Bexley was sitting but quickly shifted them away. I bit my lip to keep from grinning. I'd have to ask her about that later. He shut the door, and we chatted on our way to the restaurant.

After we piled out of the car at the upscale little restaurant, Bex dug around in her purse. She gave up with a huff and sidled up to me. "Hey, so you wouldn't happen to have any tampons in that giant purse of yours, would you? I forgot to restock after last month."

I reached inside and found one, passing it over before realizing I couldn't remember the last time I had my period. Shit.

Bexley must have seen the look that crossed my face because she told everyone to go in without us. "What's that look of panic about?"

Biting my lip, I admitted, "I don't remember when my last period was."

Her eyes lit up. "Really?"

"Why are you so excited about this? It's probably just stress." I wasn't convinced anything was off yet. Maybe I hadn't even missed my period.

"One way to find out," she said, giving me a sly grin and glancing down the street. "Look! A drugstore. Perfect." She spun and looked around. "Indy!"

He'd been standing off to the side, giving us our space. "What's up?" He looked between us.

"We're going to the drugstore real quick. I figured your head would blow up if I didn't let you know." She flipped her purple hair and dragged me down the sidewalk. I glanced back at Indy to see his jaw clenched and eyes narrowed in our direction, but he followed.

The drugstore was only a couple of blocks down, and I pulled out my phone and shot Kennedy a text letting her know we'd be back in a few minutes. Indy trailed behind us as Bexley dragged me through the aisles until we stood before a huge display of condoms and pregnancy tests. "I feel fine, I don't think this is necessary," I complained.

"Shh, let me have this. I've always wanted to be an aunt!" she squealed, scooping a bunch of different tests into her arms and moving with purpose to buy them. I followed behind her, my heart pounding.

As the bored cashier scanned the boxes, Bexley turned to face me. "Can you imagine how cute your babies would be?"

I hadn't really had a chance to think about it, but I let my mind wander until Indy coughed somewhere behind me. I spun and noticed his wide eyes as he looked away, pretending he hadn't seen anything. "Not a word," I ordered.

"Yes, ma'am." He tried to hide his grin, and I glared at him, but Bexley grabbed my arm and pulled me back to the back of the store.

I dug my heels in. "No way. I'm not doing this here."

"Oh, yes, you are. We need answers before we go drink copious amounts of mimosas at brunch." She pushed through the bathroom door, and we both went into the single toilet room, locking the door behind us. She opened the bag and ripped open the box, scanning the instructions.

"Here, pee on this," she demanded, thrusting her arm out at me with a little white stick in her hand. I rolled my eyes and grabbed it, pulling down my jeans.

"At least turn around," I muttered, squatting over the toilet. I had a thing about public bathrooms and would never sit on a public toilet. I hovered, thank you very much.

I peed quickly, and mid-stream, she turned and passed me another test. I finished up and set the tests on the sink, washing my hands. "How long do we have to wait?" I asked, ignoring how my hands were shaking and my stomach was in knots.

I hadn't felt sick or anything, so I wasn't convinced anything was going on.

"Three more minutes," she said, watching the timer on her phone without blinking. It gave me time to think, and somewhere in the back of my mind, I always knew this was a possibility. It wasn't like we'd been careful or tried to prevent it. Honestly, the thought of a mini Jericho running around made me feel a whole bunch of warm fuzzies.

I didn't want to hope and then be let down. I always knew someday I wanted to be a mom, but I figured it'd be a long way off. In fact, with Jericho, everything came out of nowhere. I hadn't planned to get married for years and years, and yet when he swept into my life, everything fell into place. He fit in my life like he was made to be there, and if the test was positive, I'd be beyond happy.

"Time!" Bexley announced, and our eyes locked. "You want to check, or you want me to?"

My heart leaped into my throat. "You check." I closed my eyes and took a deep breath, hearing Bexley's clothes rustle as she moved to the sink.

She sucked in a breath. "Moon…" My eyes snapped open, and when I looked at her, she had a wide smile. "You're knocked up, girl!"

My knees went weak as I started to fall to the ground, and Bexley rushed over and caught me around the waist. I was pregnant? I couldn't believe it.

"You can't tell the girls at lunch," I finally managed, taking a few deep breaths and pulling away from Bexley. I walked over and picked up the tests, tossing them in my purse and then splashing water on my face.

"Why not?" she wondered, folding her arms and eyeing me.

"Don't look at me like that. It's not what you think. If I don't tell Jericho first, he'll be furious. You know what'll happen. The girls will go home and tell their husbands, who will get to him before I do. It's bad enough that Indy knows."

She waved her hand dismissively as she went to open the door. "He doesn't know anything for sure."

"You're not drinking at brunch," I decided. "It was so important for us to know now, and if I don't drink by myself, it'll be suspicious. If we both don't, it'll be a trend."

"You're lucky I love you," she grumbled, and we left the store with Indy trailing us. I just hoped I could keep it together over the next hour.

"How are you going to tell him?" Bexley wondered as we walked along the sidewalk back toward the restaurant.

"I have an idea," I said, and my lips curled into a smile.

"Jericho?" I called out when I walked in the front door. Brunch had been fun. After spending time with the girls, I was rejuvenated, but I had a secret weighing on me that I couldn't wait to unload. I didn't know if Jericho ever wanted kids—we hadn't talked about it yet. Everything was still so new. But, I'd seen him with Nico and Phoenix in that first class, and he was a natural.

"Back here!" he yelled from what sounded like the gaming room, so I went that way, finding him with his headset on mid-game. I ignored what he was doing and plopped down in his lap, and he smirked, tossing his controller.

"We have a date." I grabbed his face between my palms and kissed him deeply before pulling away and hopping up. I reached my hand down for his and pulled him up.

"What are we doing?"

"You'll see. Go change into workout clothes," I said, smacking his ass as he walked away and laughing as he glared at me.

"You're lucky I love you," he grouched as he left the room. He wasn't wrong, I *was* lucky he loved me, and I'd never forget it.

When he was done, I rushed into the room and threw on my yoga clothes, too, before joining him by the front door. "Indy's going to drive us."

I opened the door, and he followed me out, climbing into the back seat of his Range Rover with me. Indy took off, trying and failing to hide his smile. I shot him a death glare in the rearview mirror. He better not ruin this for me, or I'd find some way to torture him for it.

We pulled up to a yoga studio a few miles from mine. I'd made friends with the owner at a small business event a few years ago, and we got together every couple of months. She agreed to hold a special class for me this morning.

That spot between Jericho's eyebrows furrowed. "You were held by kidnappers yesterday, and you want to do *yoga* today? I figured we'd be laying on the couch relaxing all day."

I shrugged. "Yoga relaxes me."

He sighed, resigned. "Okay." I bit back a laugh.

We moved inside, and Indy took up a place by the studio door, and as Jericho carried our mats into the studio and found us a place, I leaned close to the bodyguard. "Don't say anything."

He mimed zipping his lip and then laughed, surreptitiously pulling out his phone and hitting record. I rolled my eyes but went over to Jericho. There were a few other women in the class, and he narrowed his eyes at me. "Is this mommy and me yoga?"

I didn't answer, dropping down onto the mat and pulling him down with me. Once we were sitting cross-legged on the ground facing each other, I grinned at him. "Yes, it's mommy and me yoga. Don't you remember how we met?"

He chuckled. "How could I forget?"

"Well…" I reached behind me and pulled the stick out of where it was hidden in the band of my yoga pants. His eyes dropped to it and narrowed. He looked confused for a second before it must've clicked, and his head snapped up.

"Are you fucking pregnant?" he asked a little too loud, and some of the women looked scandalized. I giggled at my big, dark, tattooed husband leaving a trail of offended mommies in his wake.

All I could do was nod, and he jumped up, picking me up and spinning me around. I held on tight and wrapped my legs around him feeling tears prick my eyes. "Are you serious right now? Don't tease me," he warned, his voice sounded a little shaky and warmth spread through my whole body. He was as excited as I was.

He stopped spinning, and my feet touched the ground. I pulled back a little so that I could see him better. "I'm not kidding. I found out at brunch."

"What the fuck kind of brunch were you having?" He glanced over at where Indy wore a shit-eating grin over by the door. "And did that asshole know before me?"

Oops.

He started to move toward Indy, and I gripped his arm, holding him back. "He only knew because he stood outside the door while I took the test. No need to murder the guy."

He settled his cold, dark scowl on the man by the door who just laughed. I sighed. "We're not going to get to do yoga, are we?"

"No, baby, we're not. We're going home, and then we have a dinner date at your dad's house." He picked me up and growled at Indy to grab our mats as he stalked back out to the car, gently putting me inside and climbing in after me.

"Why are we going home?" I asked innocently, batting my eyelashes at him.

"I need to be inside you. I was trying to be patient and let you recover, but it's been too fucking long." His voice was calm and absolutely controlled, but it made me shiver. I liked the dark, cold side of him just as much as the hot passionate one. Maybe even more.

I'd been surprised when he didn't try to touch me last night, and I was too tired to think much about it, but now I was burning up. I slid closer to him as his hand fell onto my thigh, and his fingers danced higher and higher.

Indy climbed in the driver's seat, and Jericho barked at him to get us home before turning his attention back to me. My heart raced as we flew down the road, and I smiled as I let my imagination run wild about what was to come.

After a long afternoon in bed, we sat in the car, and my nerves exploded. My palms were sweaty, and my heart raced. I glanced at the house, not quite believing my mom was inside. Jericho moved to get out, and I grabbed his arm. "Wait."

He moved back and looked at me with concern. "We don't have to go in there if you don't want to. You know I'm still fucking pissed at Cara for doing what she did."

I reached up and smoothed the skin between his eyebrows from his scowl. "I know. It's not that. I've been thinking about what I want to do with my studio. When you were telling me about the label on the way home yesterday, I want in. I want to help and work with you. With the baby, I want to make it as easy as possible to spend time together. And I love going to see bands. I've actually been to see a local band a few times that I think has serious potential. I know I'm not a professional like you, but I know what I like. So, I want to invest the insurance money in the label, so we're partners."

He grinned and kissed the back of my hand. "Are you sure? You know I wouldn't take you away from your passions."

I shook my head. "I know, but teaching yoga and running my studio was never my passion. I enjoy doing yoga, but I love it as a hobby. I didn't realize it stopped relaxing me a long time ago until I didn't have to drag myself into work to do it every day."

"How did I get so goddamn lucky?" Jericho asked, looking at me with so much wonder I started to blush.

"I ask myself the same thing all the time." I turned to face him fully. "But you should know that even though I'm settling down, that doesn't mean you've tamed me. I don't think I'll ever be one of those moms from the yoga class who are content just to be home and raise a bunch of kids."

"But you want a bunch of kids, right?" he pressed.

My eyebrows felt like they raised up to my hairline. "You want more than one?"

He shrugged. "I don't know how many I want, but I don't like limits."

I laughed. "*You* don't like limits? The guy who needs control in every area of his life doesn't want to plan this out?" I teased.

His lips quirked up in a grin. "Maybe my wife's rubbing off on me."

Blowing out a breath, I turned back to look at the house. "Guess I can't stall anymore. Hold my hand the whole time?"

"I won't let go for a second," he promised, and I opened the door.

THIRTY THREE
MOON

When the front door opened, it felt like I was in someone else's body living someone else's life. How could my mom be here? How could this be real? I'd tried to hold onto hope that she was alive, but as the years passed, that hope dwindled until I'd taken up talking to her spirit as a way to try and stay close to her.

Yet here she was, in the flesh, looking healthy and happy, and for some reason that irritated me. She stood back to let us pass, and when she closed the door, she turned to look me over. "Moon... You grew up so beautifully."

"No thanks to you," I snapped, and she sighed, her shoulders slumping. Jericho stepped slightly in front of me as if he wanted to shield me from this unpleasantness with his body, but I patted his arm, gently pushing him back. I had to face this on my own. Well, gripping his hand tightly, but still.

"I'm sorry, so sorry for everything. I hope in time you can give me a chance to explain." I watched as she twisted her hands together, and something inside of me just melted. What was I doing? I'd spent years wishing for this moment, willing to give up anything and everything for just another few minutes with this woman.

So why was I pushing her away when I finally got the chance?

I let go of Jericho and moved forward, wrapping my arms around my mom. She jumped in surprise before hugging me tightly to her. Her body shook as she cried, and I couldn't hold back the tears streaming down my face. She smelled the same, like comfort and sugar cookies.

"Are you all planning on staying in the foyer all day?" my dad called from somewhere deeper in the house, and I pulled back from my mom, laughing through my tears.

Jericho stood nearby, watching me with concern. "You okay?"

I nodded. "I'm good, promise." He relaxed at my words, and the three of us walked into the living room where my dad was laying on the couch. He looked a lot better than when I'd last seen him, and his recovery had been just short of miraculous according to what Jericho told me.

"Hey, Dad," I greeted, leaning down to kiss his cheek and squeezing his hand. "How are you feeling?"

"Like I got hit by a truck, but all things considered, pretty good," he chuckled, and his eyes sparkled like I hadn't seen in years. He looked over at my mom, and I could see the love was still there. All those years and he'd never given up on her. One glance at my mom and I saw the same look in her eyes.

I moved out of the way, opting to sit on Jericho's lap in the chair across from the couch instead. My mom moved to sit on the edge of the cushion by my dad with her hand clasped in his. "I know we have a lot to talk about, but I think it can wait," I decided. "Today's a day for happy news. Dad's home and on the mend, mom's back and not going anywhere..." I paused, waiting for her to confirm before I continued.

"Never again," she promised, looking between dad and me.

We hadn't talked about when to tell people before coming over here, but I looked at Jericho, and he gave me a small nod, snaking his arm around my waist possessively and splaying his palm across my stomach. I melted into him, loving being back in his arms. I never wanted to experience being forcefully separated from the people I loved again.

"And you guys are going to be grandparents," I announced, biting my lip to hide my grin. Had we planned it this way? No, not necessarily. But we also hadn't *not* planned it. This child, our baby, was meant to be here. I firmly believed that, and there was nothing but happiness inside me knowing I was going to be a mother.

It was made even sweeter knowing my mother was going to be here for me, be involved in helping me figure out how to navigate all the uncertainty coming my way. It was a gift I never thought I'd get the chance to have, and I wouldn't take a second of it for granted.

My mom shot up off the couch, and her hand flew up to her mouth. Her eyes immediately filled with tears, and I felt my own stinging in response. "Are you sure?" she croaked, trying to fight back the emotion.

"Pretty damn sure," Jericho chuckled, squeezing me a little tighter as I leaned against him.

My mom moved across the room and threw her arms around me, sobbing into my hair as she held me. I let some of my tears fall, too, mourning all the years we'd lost but letting it go with each drop that fell. I wasn't the kind of person who held grudges or held onto anger.

It was toxic, and I didn't want to live my life with regrets. Even though my mom was back, that didn't mean I'd change how I lived. I still wanted to experience everything life had to offer. It'd become my mission when I thought I lost her, and now it was so ingrained in me that I didn't think I could stop pushing boundaries and finding new things to try even if I wanted to.

I'd feel like I wasn't being true to myself.

She finally pulled back, and I leaned back into Jericho. "We just found out, I haven't even gone to the doctor yet, but I couldn't hold it in," I admitted, a wide smile on my face. This whole scene was so surreal.

Mom went and sat back down by my dad. "We thought we'd just order takeout, so I did pizza because it's easy. I hope that's okay." She looked uncertain, and I reassured her it was.

"So, while we wait on dinner, Moon, your dad tells me you own a yoga studio, and it was vandalized?" my mom asked, reaching for the cup of water on the table and sticking a straw in before helping my dad take a sip.

I nodded. "The ROC trashed it. I've been debating on reopening, but truthfully, I don't think that's what I want to do anymore. I'm going to close it down and take the money to invest in a new project."

My dad looked at me in surprise. "What project?"

"The guys from the band and I are breaking with our label and starting our own. Moon wants to invest and come work on it with me," Jericho filled in as his fingers ran across my stomach, making my body heat up with every pass. I squirmed on his lap, and he gripped my hip with his other hand, holding me still.

"Oh, that's right. August mentioned you were in a band." My mom set the cup down and laced her fingers with my dad's, and I got all the warm fuzzies I used to when I was a kid and would see them together.

Dad groaned. "Not just *a* band, Cara. One of my favorite bands, Shadow Phoenix. I can't believe you've never heard of them."

Mom laughed. "I didn't have a lot of time to discover new music or go to shows when I was in hiding."

"I'm not technically in the band anymore," Jericho added, not sounding at all upset about it. Sometimes I wondered if he'd miss touring or being in the studio with the guys, but in his own way, he was still making music. He never gave me any indication he was unhappy with his decision, so I went with it.

"What are you planning on doing with the label, Moon?" my mom asked as the doorbell rang.

I hopped up to get it, bringing the pizzas back to the living room. "We haven't talked about the details yet, but I've always loved going to local shows and seeing bands who have, like, twenty fans. Some of them are terrible, but I've definitely seen some gems over the last year. I want to do more of that, bring them to Jericho and see what he thinks. Plus, I know a lot about running a business. I don't think any of the guys from the band have actually run their own businesses before."

"We haven't," Jericho assured me, rubbing my back as I took a bite of the veggie pizza my mom ordered.

I reached forward and grabbed another slice, holding it up for him to take a bite and then leaning over to lick off the tiny bit of sauce that got on the corner of his lip. His eyes darkened, and his grip on my hip tightened. My breath caught at the look of pure fiery desire burning in his eyes, and I could feel him hardening underneath me.

Our eyes were locked, and I swallowed my bite, but suddenly my appetite wasn't for food anymore. Jericho took the piece of pizza in my hand without breaking eye contact and finished it off before licking my fingers clean.

I shuddered at his touch, and he broke our stare down. "Moon's tired, and we're going to go."

"But you just got here," dad started to protest, but my mom laughed.

"August, they're newlyweds. You remember what we were like. Just let them go, we'll catch up later."

I reluctantly moved off of Jericho's lap, and he stood, holding me in front of him, and I giggled at how he tried to hide his hard-on from my parents. It was so insanely awkward; all I could do was laugh. "Thanks for dinner, I'll text you later," I tossed out as Jericho dragged me out of the room. He barely grunted a *goodbye* at my parents before we were slamming the door.

I looked up at the grey sky as we jogged to the car. He pressed me up against the door, grinding his hips into mine as I wrapped my leg around him. He hit just the right spot, and I moaned softly, gripping his shirt and trying to pull him closer. He nipped at my lip before sucking it into his mouth, and then he tore himself away.

"We need to get home," he growled, but his eyes were nearly black and so wild, I knew if I pushed him a little, I might be able to get him to snap his control and let the feral part of him out to play.

I took a few deep breaths to steady myself and then climbed inside. Jericho leaned over, letting his fingers brush my skin as he secured my seatbelt before closing me in and moving to the other side. My body felt overheated, the blood in my veins burning their trails under my skin and pooling in my center.

My panties were soaked, and my nipples were so tight, every breath I took had them brushing the fabric of my bra and shooting straight to my clit. I watched Jericho climb behind the wheel, his muscles bunching and shifting with both tension and grace under his skin, and I ached to feel his powerful form moving inside me.

The air was warm and felt charged as we pulled out of the driveway, and the rain was falling steadily. It had gotten progressively harder until it was raining so hard it was a challenge to see out the windshield, and the wipers couldn't keep up.

I leaned over, brushing my hand along his thigh, moving slowly and progressively higher and higher until I brushed the impressive bulge behind his zipper only to move back down and start the torturous journey all over again. He groaned every time, shifted in his seat, and clenched his jaw but said nothing.

The leather on the steering wheel creaked under his grip, where he held it to tightly, but he still managed to keep himself together. I didn't think it would take much more to push him over the edge, and I was right.

Traffic came to a standstill in front of us, and Jericho hit the wheel in frustration. "Fuck this," he fumed, turning and speeding off down a side street. It didn't take long before we left the city behind and climbed into the hills. He turned off on a forest service road and threw the SUV into park, ripping his seatbelt off and climbing out of the car.

I bit my lip as I watched him stalk toward me as the rain soaked his black t-shirt so it clung to his muscles. My heart sped up as I watched him pull my door open, the water running down his face. He tugged me out of the seat, and the rain soaked through my clothes almost immediately, but I barely felt it. I couldn't look away from how wild his eyes were as he pulled me to the front of the car and lifted me up onto the hood.

The skirt I wore clung to my thighs, and he pulled them apart, stepping between my legs. The warm metal of the hood was underneath me, and the contrast between the cool rain and the heated car had my whole body in sensory overload.

His kiss was manic as he pulled me closer, gripping my thighs while his tongue explored my mouth. He tasted like pizza and mint, and I wanted him to devour me. I wrapped my arms around him, pulling him closer, wanting more of everything he was doing. Jericho's hand trailed up my thigh, finally finding my panties and tugging them to the side.

He wasn't being gentle or taking things slow. As he tore his lips off of mine and bit my neck, he shoved two fingers inside me, and I cried out at the fullness but also the relief.

"Oh, god," I moaned, wrapping my legs around his waist.

"I'll only fuck you after you come on my fingers, so be a good girl and come," Jericho growled in that hot as hell commanding voice he used when he was taking control.

My whole body was trembling as the rain drenched my skin, and Jericho's thumb found my clit and rubbed just the way I liked. It only took a few strokes before I was falling apart under his touch, screaming and writhing on the hood of his car while the rain fell around us.

When I opened my eyes, I looked around and noticed we were surrounded by woods. Jericho wore a self-satisfied smirk as he brought his fingers to his mouth and sucked them clean before keeping his eyes locked on mine as he flicked the button on his jeans open. He leaned forward, making me slide back toward the windshield, and he climbed up after me like a predator who had his prey in his sights.

"We can't do this here," I protested, but it sounded weak even to my own ears. My voice was husky, and we both knew I wanted this just as much as he did.

Jericho shoved my dress up and ripped my panties off of my body as he dropped his head and pulled my nipple into his mouth, sucking hard as I let out a whimper. Every stroke of his tongue shot straight through my body to my core like a bolt of lightning. He covered my body with his, ripping his jeans down his hips until his cock sprang free, and he pushed inside me without warning.

I reached for him, but he caught my hands and tightened his grip as he moved inside me, pushing my hands above my head and pinning me to the warm metal as he drove into my body frantically, playing my body like his instrument and daring me to surrender as I gasped for breath.

Finally, I couldn't hold out any longer. My back arched and my toes curled as he pounded into me even harder. My walls clenched around him as I hit my crescendo, convulsing around him as he followed me into his own release, growling out my name as he spilled inside me.

He let go of my hands and hovered over me, looking into my eyes as water dripped off his hair and fell on my forehead. I giggled, and he gave me one of the biggest smiles I'd ever seen on his face.

"Feel better?" I asked, wiping the water off of his cheek.

"Much," he agreed, dropping a kiss to my lips before climbing off the car and fixing his jeans before holding out his hand to help me down. "Now that I've had an appetizer, I can patiently wait for the entree at home."

I adjusted my skirt and climbed into the car, feeling completely satisfied and a little sleepy. "Can't wait," I mumbled, letting my eyes drift closed. Everything in my life was falling into place, and I'd never been happier.

EPILOGUE
JERICHO

Six months later…

"Whoa!" Moon exclaimed as her arms flew out to her sides to keep her balance as if I'd ever let her fall.

I chuckled, stepping closer behind her and wrapping my arm around her round stomach. I rubbed my palm across her belly as my little boy kicked at my hand. Leaning close to her ear, my lips brushed across the shell as I whispered, "I'd never let you fall." She shivered, but I pulled back slightly, still keeping an arm locked around her.

The blindfold across her eyes shifted as she moved, but it didn't slip off. I stopped her and pulled her back against me, loving how her body fit perfectly with mine. Moon sniffed at the air, and I laughed. "You're cheating."

Her lips curved up into a smile. "Hey, I can't help it if I have a super sniffer now with this little guy." She rubbed her stomach, and my chest tightened. "Are we at the beach?"

I shook my head, not even trying to wipe the stupid smile from my face. I reached up and untied the knot on the back of the fabric tied around her head and let it fall away. Her eyes widened before her forehead winkled. "What am I looking at?"

Laughing, I moved to stand in front of her, throwing my arm out like a gameshow host. "Our new house."

I watched her face for her reaction, and her eyes lit up. "Really?"

Nodding, I stepped back toward her and grabbed her hand, weaving our fingers together. Her head craned back as we walked to the front door. There was a four-car garage, and the stucco was at least half covered by vines and roses climbing up the house. It looked like a cozy cottage on the California coast only huge.

When I left Zen's a couple of weeks ago and saw it for sale, I knew I had to buy it. It reminded me of Moon, a little wild, colorful as fuck, and looked like home. "Look at the vines, they're gorgeous," she observed, a little breathless as she walked up to the side of the house and ran her hand through the tangles of greenery.

Moving into this neighborhood seemed to be a rite of passage for every single one of the guys of Shadow Phoenix, and I was no exception. I wanted to be close to my friends so our kids could grow up together. Even a fucking year ago, I never would've imagined my life would be here.

"Want to see the inside?" I kissed the back of her hand while I watched her reaction to what I'd done, soaking in every crinkle of her nose, smile on her face, or sparkle in her eyes.

She nodded enthusiastically, and I laughed again, something I spent more and more time doing over the last six months. I unlocked the door, and we stepped inside. "Wow," she breathed, spinning around to take in the high ceilings, stark white walls, and Mediterranean tile.

She walked across the open-plan room as if drawn to the living room where one entire wall was windows looking out at the deep blue water of the Pacific. She spun and wrapped her arms around my waist, bending forward when her stomach pressed against me. "We really get to live here?"

"If you want. If you hate it, we can find a different house." I tried to sound casual and non-committal, but it was hard to find a place in this neighborhood, and I already had to pay over market value to get this one.

"No, I love it," she sighed happily, and I held her tighter, resting my chin on the top of her head and staring out at the sea. Having her here made it feel like home even with no furniture.

"Let's finish the tour, and then we've gotta go. That show you wanted to see starts in about an hour," I reminded her, pulling away and leading her through the house. I watched as she pointed out all the things she wanted to change and how she couldn't wait to splash colors all over the plain white walls.

When we were done, I locked up the door behind us, pocketing the keys. I nodded to Indy, who waited by the car. He stayed with us pretty much all the time now. The ROC had left us alone for the past six months, but now that Moon was pregnant, I sure as fuck wasn't taking any chances.

He held open the back door to my Range Rover, and Moon maneuvered her body inside. I chuckled as I watched her finally settle in, trying to catch her breath. "Baby, you should've let me help you," I gently scolded, trying to hide my grin. She scowled at me, but it was so fucking cute.

Indy climbed into the driver's seat and met my eyes. I noticed him trying not to laugh, and I almost lost it. We understood each other now, and I trusted him with the most important people in my life. He'd earned back my trust over letting Moon get taken. Now that I had her back, I could see there wasn't anything he could do to stop what happened with the ROC.

He started the car and took off, driving us to the little hole in the wall bar where the band Moon insisted I see was playing tonight.

"You shouldn't be going out to see bands without me," I insisted, stretching my arm around Moon and pulling her close, but she scoffed and rolled her eyes.

"I take Indy with me, and I'm pregnant, not helpless," she argued, leaning her head against my shoulder. Moon took every opportunity she could to nap, and it looked like this would be one of them. I loved it when she passed out on me, snoring softly. I'd hold her close, touch her skin, watch as her mouth fell slightly open, and her muscles relaxed. I was obsessed with my wife and could watch her sleep all night if I let myself.

It was a bonus if my son was doing gymnastics in her stomach and I got to feel him.

Indy and I stayed quiet and let Moon sleep the entire trip, and when he parked in the bar's packed lot, I gently woke Moon up. "Wake up, pretty girl. Time to go inside."

"Mmm, or we could go home and have some quiet time," she mumbled as she slowly walked her fingers up my abs and across my chest. I grabbed her wandering fingers and kissed them before setting it back in her lap.

"After the show. You promised the band you'd come see them, didn't you?" I probed, wanting her to get moving. I may have relaxed a lot of my control issues and tight grip I held on life, but I still fucking hated being late.

She whimpered a little bit, and I laughed. "Come on," I climbed out of the car and held out my hand to help her out. When her feet hit the ground, I ran my fingers through her hair, trying to tame the wild, colorful waves and laughing when I failed.

I led the way inside, and Indy followed behind Moon. We kept her between us as she moved up toward the stage. The band was just starting their set, and I pulled out a chair for her at one of the many empty tables near the stage, and she sat down. I didn't think it was a good sign that not many people were here to see the band, but I promised Moon I'd reserve judgment and I was a man of my word.

I leaned down and brushed my wife's hair behind her ear. "Want something to drink?"

She bit her lip. "Cranberry juice and onion rings." I hadn't offered food, but I knew better than to tell her that. If onion rings would make her happy, she'd get as many onion rings as she could eat.

I ordered and carried our drinks back, passing Indy a beer. He didn't ever drink more than one beer when he was out with us, but he took it with a tilt of his head and went back to scanning the room. I sat across from Moon, and the band started playing.

Their sound was a mix of pop and rock, with heavy guitar and drums, but the girl fronting the band had a haunting voice that hit every note with tonal perfection. I was riveted and couldn't take my eyes off them. The singer was a tiny girl whose voice didn't fit her body, but she looked like she'd been born to be on stage, with a presence that was fucking magnetic, and the three guys behind her on stage were no slouches either.

The guitarist ran through his chord progressions and stayed on tempo, the drummer commanded the song, and the keyboardist's hands flew across the keys with practiced ease.

I didn't impress easily, and I had to admit I was fucking impressed.

When the song ended, and I was able to tear my eyes away, I looked over at Moon, who was watching me with a goddamn smug smile on her face.

When the next song started, I pulled my phone out and recorded a video, shooting it off to Zen, Maddox, True, and Griffin.

"What's the band's name?" I yelled over the music to Moon, and she pulled a pen out of her purse and scribbled on the cocktail napkin she'd pulled from under her drink.

Tuesday Told a Secret.

I tucked the napkin into my pocket and turned back to watch the show, hardly blinking the entire time. Their songs were all original, the lyrics meaningful, but at the same time, they were catchy like the pop songs you heard on the radio. Despite the lack of crowd, there was something here.

Moon had good instincts, and she was right about this group. As the band wrapped up their set, I flashed her a look that promised I'd do wicked things to her later tonight as a thank you for finding this little gem, and her cheeks flushed as she bit her lip.

I adjusted myself under the table, pulling my cold control over myself. I wouldn't give in to my desire to fuck Moon right now, but later all bets would be off. I stood up as the band started packing away their instruments, and I held my hands out for Moon, helping her up. I pushed my body up against hers and leaned down. "Are you wet for me, beautiful girl?"

As she looked up at me, I watched her pupils dilate and knew I had my answer. A cocky grin found its way onto my face, and I ran my fingers down her arm, watching goosebumps rise in the wake of my touch. "Give me an hour, and I'll have you screaming my name," I promised before turning back to the stage. "Introduce me?"

Moon made a choking sound before stepping up to the stage beside me. "I can barely remember my own name," she murmured before clearing her throat. "Bellamy?" she called out to the petite girl with the memorable voice.

She spun and noticed Moon, hurrying to the edge of the stage. "Moon! You came!"

My wife laughed. "I did, and I brought this guy with me." She patted my chest with her palm and shot me an adoring look. "This is my husband, Jericho," she introduced, and I stuck out my hand.

Bellamy's eyes widened, and the three guys behind her finally noticed our interaction and moved up beside her. "Jericho Cole. Holy fuck. I can't believe you just listened to our music."

I chuckled, totally used to people being starstruck around me. "You guys sounded awesome. Do you have a YouTube channel or...?"

All their heads nodded simultaneously, and I bit back another smile. I had a reputation to uphold. "Can you DM me the link? I'm interested in seeing what else you guys can do."

"Absolutely," Bellamy answered for the group, pulling out her phone, and mine vibrated a few seconds later. I checked, and she'd sent me the link.

"Thanks. Can I see your phone?" She handed it over with a shaky hand, and I dialed my number before ending the call and entering her contact info into mine. I passed her back her phone. "Once I check out your channel, I'll be in touch. I have some ideas for your music. Are you guys currently signed with a label?"

"No, you're the first one who's even come to see us," the keyboardist admitted, and the guy on bass elbowed him.

"You're not supposed to tell him that," he hissed, and this time I couldn't hold back my laugh.

"Look, guys. I'm new at this whole scouting new bands thing, but I know my fucking music, and you have talent. The guys from Shadow Phoenix and I are starting our own label, and we're looking for our first band to sign. You just impressed me with your set, and I'm almost impossible to impress, so your odds are good that I'm going to check out your channel and be calling you tomorrow. But if I do, you need to be ready to jump in the studio and take this shit seriously. You'll have to live your music, be willing to give up everything else until you make it. If you're not ready for that, I'm not interested."

"We're ready," Bellamy promised, and I lifted my eyebrow.

"We'll see. I'll be in touch." Moon said her goodbyes, and we turned to leave. I rested my hand on her lower back, and she leaned into me.

"I told you they were good." I could hear the smile in her voice as we walked out the door.

"You did," I agreed, helping her into the car.

"Are you going to sign them?"

"They're the best band I've heard since we started looking. I'd be a fucking idiot to take my time on this. We're lucky no one else has heard them yet." I closed the door and waited for Indy to start the drive home.

"They're gonna make it, aren't they? I've gotten kinda attached to Bellamy," she admitted, rubbing a hand over her stomach, and I put mine on top.

"Is he kicking?" I wondered, and she nodded, moving my hand lower and to the side where I felt my son pushing against her stomach.

After a few quiet minutes, I answered. "I'll do everything I can to make sure the world gets to hear *Tuesday Told a Secret*."

She smiled up at me, and it hit me—my life had never been better than at this moment, and it was only just beginning.

THE END

SIGN UP FOR A
HEATHER ASHLEY

NEWSLETTER

And get exclusive sneak peeks, previews, and behind the scenes info from author Heather Ashley that you won't find anywhere else! You'll even get a free bonus as a thank you!

heatherashleywrites.com/newsletter

JOIN MY READER GROUP AND
BECOME A MEMBER OF THE

WILD RIDE CREW

Want to talk about what you just read? Join us backstage in my reader group!

facebook.com/groups/thewildridecrew

NEXT IN THE SERIES:

TAINTED IDOL

As the newest, youngest, and self-proclaimed hottest member of Shadow Phoenix, I just started living my best rock star life.

Parties, groupies, and being up on stage? Nothing even came close to the constant racing heartbeat and adrenaline rush of being on top. Thanks to my borther Maddox, overnight all my dreams came true.

UNTIL MAGNOLIA STEPPED INTO MY LIFE WITH HER UPTIGHT SOUTHERN CHARM AND LITERALLY COCK-BLOCKED ME

She made it her mission to keep me from having any fun, breaking any rules, or causing any more chaos while we're on tour. She doesn't understand that I wasn't the kind of guy who'd ever bend to authority, and I sure as hell wasn't made to be domesticated.

RULES WERE MEANT TO BE BROKEN. AND I KNEW JUST HOW TO BREAK HERS.

www.amazon.com/dp/B08HLFL4V7

Printed in Great Britain
by Amazon

52745919R00178